This book is a puzzle.
Decipher, decode, and interpret.
Search and seek.
If you're worthy, you will find.

ENDGAME SERIES

Novels:
The Calling
Sky Key

Digital Novellas:
Endgame: The Training Diaries Volume 1: Origins
Endgame: The Training Diaries Volume 2: Descendant
Endgame: The Training Diaries Volume 3: Existence
Endgame: The Zero Line Chronicles Volume 1: Incite
Endgame: The Zero Line Chronicles Volume 2: Feed
Endgame: The Zero Line Chronicles Volume 3: Reap

Novella Collections:
Endgame: The Complete Training Diaries
Endgame: The Complete Zero Line Chronicles

SKY KEY

AN ENDGAME NOVEL

JAMES FREY

AND

NILS JOHNSON-SHELTON

HARPER

An Imprint of HarperCollinsPublishers

Sky Key: An Endgame Novel
Copyright © 2015 by Third Floor Fun, LLC.
Puzzle hunt experience by Futuruption LLC.
Additional character icon design by John Taylor Dismukes Assoc.,
a Division of Capstone Studios, Inc.
All rights reserved. Printed in the United States of America. No part of this book may be used or reproduced in any manner whatsoever without written permission except in the case of brief quotations embodied in critical articles and reviews.
For information address HarperCollins Children's Books, a division of HarperCollins Publishers, 195 Broadway, New York, NY 10007.
www.epicreads.com

Library of Congress Control Number: 2015943986
ISBN 978-0-06-233262-2

16 17 18 19 20   PC/RRDH   10 9 8 7 6 5 4 3 2 1
❖
First paperback edition, 2016

90 days.

LITTLE ALICE CHOPRA

Chopra Residence, Gangtok, Sikkim, India

"Tarki, Tarki, Tarki ..."

Clouds drift over the Himalayas, sun reflecting off their snowy slopes. Kanchenjunga, the world's 3rd highest peak, looms over Gangtok. The city's residents go about their day—working, shopping, eating, drinking, teaching, learning, laughing, smiling. One hundred thousand peaceful, unknowing souls.

Little Alice struts across her back lawn, blades of grass tickling her toes, the smell of a brushfire rising from the valley. Her fists are at her hips and her elbows jut behind her like wings. Her knees are bent, her head forward. She moves her elbows together, apart, together, apart, clacking and cawing like a peacock. She calls, "Tarki, Tarki, Tarki," which is what they call the old peacock that's lived with her family for the last 13 years. Tarki eyes the girl and does a half turn and ruffles his bright neck feathers and clacks back. His tail fans, and Little Alice dances with glee. She runs to Tarki. He takes off, Little Alice chasing.

The hard lines of Kanchenjunga are in the distance, hiding the Valley of Eternal Life below its frozen slopes.

Little Alice knows nothing of this valley, but Shari knows it intimately. Little Alice follows Tarki to a rhododendron bush. She is less than a meter from the brilliant bird when he bows his head and blinks his eyes and scratches at something under the bush. The bird pushes into the leaves. Little Alice leans closer.

"What is it, Tarki?"

The bird pecks the dirt.

"What is it?"

The bird freezes like a statue, its head low but cocked, stares at the ground with one wide eye. Little Alice cranes forward. Something is there. Something small and round and dark.

The bird makes a horrible sound—*Creeeeaaaaaak*—and bolts toward the house. Little Alice is startled but doesn't follow. She holds out her hands and pushes the waxy leaves aside and wriggles into the bush, puts her hands on the ground, finds.

A dark marble, half-buried. Perfectly round. Carved with strange markings. She touches it and it's as cold as the void of space. She digs around it with her fingers, makes a small pile of dirt, pries the sphere free. She picks it up, turns it around and around, frowns. It is painfully cold. The light from the sky filters, changes, is suddenly bright bright beyond bright. Within seconds everything is white and the ground is shaking and a giant crash explodes over the hillsides, rattling the cliffs and the mountains, shaking the trees, the grass, the pebbles in the streams. The sound fills everything.

Little Alice wants to run, but can't. It's as if the little marble has frozen her to the spot. Through the light and the sound and the fury, she sees a figure drifting toward her. A woman, maybe. Young. Petite.

The figure draws closer. Its flesh is pale green and its eyes sunken, its lips curled. An undead corpse. Little Alice drops the marble but nothing changes. The ghost gets close enough so that Little Alice can smell its breath, which is excrement, burning rubber and sulfur. The air grows hot and the creature reaches for Little Alice. She wants to scream for her mama who can save her, for help, for safety, for salvation, but no sound comes, no sound comes.

Her eyes shoot open, and she *is* screaming. Awake now. Drenched in sweat, a two-year-old girl, and her mama *is* there, holding her, rocking her, saying, "It's okay, *meri jaan*, it's okay. It was just the dream. It was just the dream again."

The dream that Little Alice has been having over and over every night since Earth Key was found.

2

Little Alice cries, and Shari wraps her in her arms and lifts her from her bedcovers.

"It's okay, sweetheart. No one is going to hurt you. I will never let anyone hurt you." And though she says it every time Little Alice has the dream, Shari doesn't know if it's actually true. "Nobody, sweet girl. Not now, not ever."

5

SARAH ALOPAY, JAGO TLALOC

Crowne Plaza Hotel, Suite 438, Kensington, London

"How did you get it?" Sarah asks, running her finger over Jago's jagged facial scar.

"Training," Jago says, staring at her, watching for signs that she's coming back to him.

It's been four days since Sarah retrieved Earth Key from Stonehenge. Four days since Chiyoko died. Four days since Sarah shot An Liu in the head. Four days since the thing underneath the ancient stone monument sprang to life and revealed itself.

Four days since she, Sarah, killed Christopher Vanderkamp. Pulled the trigger and put a bullet in his head.

She has not been able to say his name since. Won't even try. And no matter how many times she kisses Jago or wraps her legs around him, showers or cries or holds Earth Key in her hands, replays the message that kepler 22b broadcast over the television for the world to see, no matter how many times, Sarah can't stop thinking of Christopher's face. His blond hair, his beautiful green eyes, and the spark that was in them. The spark she took when she killed him.

Sarah has only spoken 27 words since Stonehenge, including these. Jago is worried about her. At the same time, he is encouraged by her.

"How exactly, Feo?" she asks, hoping that it's a long story. Hoping that it will hold her attention, that Jago's words will be as good a distraction as his body.

She needs to think of anything but *what happened*, anything but *the bullet she put through his skull*.

Jago obliges. "It was my third real knife fight. I was twelve, cocky. I'd won the other two easily. The first against a twenty-five-year-old ex-Player who'd lost a step, the second against one of Papi's up-and-coming bag carriers, a giant nineteen-year-old we called Ladrillo."

Sarah brushes her finger over the harsh rise of the scar where it dives under his jawline. "Ladrillo." She pronounces it slowly, enjoys saying it. "What's that mean?"

"'Brick,' which was exactly what he was. Heavy and hard and dumb. I feinted once and he moved. By the time he was ready to move again, the fight was over."

Sarah lets out a halfhearted chuckle. Her first laugh since Stonehenge, her first smile. Jago continues. "My third fight was against a kid a little older than me but smaller. I'd never met him before. He'd come up from Rio. Wasn't Peruvian. Wasn't Olmec either."

Jago knows that talking about himself is good for Sarah right now. Anything to get her mind away from what she did: killed her boyfriend, found Earth Key, and triggered the Event, sealing the deaths of billions. Playing, fighting, running, shooting—those would probably be better. Talking about them will have to do in the interim.

"He was a *favela* kid, skinny, muscles like cords wrapped around bones. Fast as an eyeblink. Didn't say anything other than 'Hi' and 'Better luck next time.' Smart, though. A prodigy. Of blades and angles of attack. He'd been taught, but most of what he knew he was born with."

"Sounds like you."

"He *was* like me." Jago smiles. "It was like fighting my reflection. I'd stab and he'd stab back. I'd swipe and he'd swipe back. That was how he parried, by counterattacking. He wasn't like anyone else I'd trained against—ex-Players, Papi, no one. It was a little like fighting an animal. Quick, impeccable instincts, not so much thinking. They just attack. You ever gone toe to toe with an animal?"

"Yeah. Wolves. Those were the worst."

"*A* wolf or—"

"Wolves. Plural."

"No guns?"

"No guns."

"I've done dogs, never wolves. A mountain lion once."

"I wish I could say I was impressed, Feo, but I'm not."

"I already got in your pants, Alopay." Jago tries some weak humor.

"Don't need to impress you."

She smiles again and punches him under the sheet. Another good sign that maybe she's coming around.

"Anyway, I couldn't hit him. The rule was first blood and the fight's over. See red and stop. Simple."

"But the scar—that cut was deep."

"*Sí.* I was stupid, stepped right into it. Honestly, I was lucky. If he hadn't got me on the face like this—it nearly took my eye, you know—he probably would have killed me."

Sarah nods. "So—blood, red, stop. He says 'Better luck next time' and leaves and that's it?"

"I had to get stitched up, but yeah. And of course, since I was training, there was no anesthesia."

"Ha. Anesthesia. What's that?"

Jago smiles big this time. "Exactly. Fucking Endgame."

"Fucking Endgame is right," Sarah says, her face betraying no emotion. She rolls onto her back and stares at the ceiling. "*Was* there a next time?"

Jago doesn't speak for a few seconds. "*Sí,*" he says slowly, drawing it out. "Less than a year later. Only two days before my birthday, right before I became eligible."

"And?"

"He was even faster. But I'd learned a lot, and I was faster too."

"So you drew first blood?"

"No. We had blades, but after a couple minutes I punched him in the throat and collapsed his windpipe. When he went down I stepped on his neck. Didn't spill a drop. And I can still see his eyes. Uncomprehending, confused, like when you shoot an animal. It doesn't understand what you've done. It was outside the rules of his nature, this *favela* boy, best knife fighter I have ever seen. He did not understand that his rules did not apply to me."

Sarah doesn't say anything. She rolls onto her side, her back to Jago. *I'm in bed with a murderer,* she thinks.

And immediately after, *But I'm a murderer too.*

"I'm sorry, Sarah. I didn't mean to—"

"I did it." She takes a deep breath. "His rules didn't apply to me either. I chose to do it. I killed him. Killed . . . Christopher."

There. She said it. Her body starts to shake, as if a switch has been thrown. She pulls her knees to her chest and shakes and sobs. Jago moves his hand over the skin of her bare back, but he knows it's a small comfort. If it's any comfort at all.

Jago never thought much of Christopher, but he knows that Sarah loved him. She loved him and she killed him. Jago isn't sure he could have done what Sarah did. Could he shoot his best friend from back home? Could he kill José, Tiempo, or Chango? Could he put a bullet in his father, or, even worse, his mother? He's not sure.

"You had to do it, Sarah." He's said this 17 times since they checked into the hotel, mostly unprompted, just to fill the air.

Every time it has rung hollow. Maybe this time more than ever.

"He told you to do it. He understood in that moment that Endgame would kill him, and he knew the only way to die was in the service of helping *you.* He *helped* you, Sarah, sacrificed himself for your line. You had his blessing. If you'd done what An wanted, Chiyoko would be the one with Earth Key, she would be the one on her way to winni—"

"GOOD!" Sarah screams. She isn't sure what's worse—having killed the boy she grew up loving or having caught Earth Key as it popped out of Stonehenge. "Chiyoko shouldn't have died," she whispers. "Not like that. She was too good a Player, too strong. And I . . . I shouldn't have shot him." She takes a deep breath. "Jago . . . everyone—*everyone*—is going to die because of me."

Sarah curls into a tighter ball. Jago bumps his fingers along her vertebrae.

"You didn't know that," Jago says. "None of us did. You were just doing what kepler 22b said. You were just Playing."

"Yeah, *Playing*," she says sarcastically. "I think Aisling might have known . . . Christ. Why couldn't she have been a better shot? Why couldn't she have shot us or taken out our plane when she had the chance?"

Jago has wondered the same about Aisling—not about taking down the Bush Hawk, but definitely about what she was trying to tell them. "If she had shot us down, then Christopher would still be dead," Jago points out. "And you and I would be too."

"Yeah, well . . ." Sarah says, as if that would be preferable to everything that's happened since Italy.

"You were just Playing," he says again.

No words for several minutes. Sarah resumes crying, Jago continues to caress her back. It's one in the morning, drizzling outside, the sounds of cars and trucks on the wet street below. An airplane now and then, Heathrow-bound. A far-off whistle, like a boat's. A police siren. The faint sound of a woman laughing drunkenly.

"Fuck kepler 22b and fuck Endgame and fuck Playing," Sarah says into the silence.

She stops crying. Jago lets his hand fall into the sheets. Sarah's breathing deepens and slows, and after several minutes she's asleep. Jago slides out of bed. He gets in the shower, lets the water run over him. He thinks about the knife fighter's eyes, about how they looked as life abandoned him. About how Jago felt, watching, knowing he'd taken that life. He gets out and towels off, dresses silently, eases out of the hotel room, the door closing silently behind him. Sarah doesn't stir.

"*Hola*, Sheila," Jago says to the clerk when he reaches the lobby.

Jago has memorized the names of everyone who works at the hotel and in the restaurant. Aside from Sheila there are Pradeet, Irina, Paul, Dmitri, Carol, Charles, Dimple, and 17 others.

They're all doomed.

Because of Sarah. Because of him. Because of Chiyoko and An and all the Players.

Because of Endgame.

He exits onto Cromwell Road and pulls his hood over his head. *Cromwell,* Jago thinks. The hated puritanical lord protector of the English Commonwealth, the terror of the interregnum. A man so loathed and reviled that King Charles II had his body exhumed so it could be killed all over again. The body was beheaded and the head placed on a pole outside Westminster Hall, where it stayed for years, getting picked at and spat on and cursed until there was nothing but a skull. That head rotted away not more than a couple kilometers from where Jago walks on this night. On this road named after the usurper.

This is what they're fighting for. To keep devils like Cromwell and libertine kings like Charles II and hate and power and politics alive and well on Earth.

He's begun to wonder if it's even worth it.

But he can't wonder. Not allowed to. *"Jugadores no se preguntan,"* Papi would say if he could hear Jago's thoughts. *"Jugadores juegan."*

Sí.

Jugadores juegan.

Jago sticks his hands in his pockets and walks toward Gloucester Road. A man 15 centimeters taller and 20 kilograms heavier than him wheels around the corner and slams into Jago's shoulder. Jago does a half spin, keeps his hands in his pockets, barely looks up.

"Oi, watch it!" the man says. He smells like beer and anger. He's having a bad night and looking for a fight.

"Sorry, mate," Jago replies, imitating the South London accent, moving on.

"You havin' a laugh?" the man asks. "Tryna be hard?"

Without warning, the man swings a fist the size of a toaster at Jago's face. Jago leans backward, the fist breezes past his nose. The man swings again, but Jago sidesteps.

"A right fast little twat," the man blurts. "Take your hands out your pockets, *mate*. Stop fuckin' about."

Jago smiles, flashes his diamond-studded teeth instead. "Don't need to."

The man steps forward and Jago dances toward him, slamming his heel onto one of the man's feet. The man cries out and tries to grab him, but Jago kicks the man's stomach. The man doubles over. Jago's hands are still in his pockets. He turns to walk away, toward the all-night Burger King down the street, to get a couple of bacon cheeseburgers. Players need to eat. Even if one of them claims to be done with Playing. Jago hears the man quickly pull something out of his pocket. Without turning to look Jago says, "You should put that knife away."

The man freezes. "How'd ya know I got a knife?"

"Heard it. Smelled it."

"Bollocks," the man whispers, surging forward.

Jago still doesn't bother to take his hands out of his pockets. The silver metal flashes in the lamplight. Jago lifts a leg and kicks straight back, hitting the man in the ribs. The knife misses Jago as he folds forward and lifts his foot and cracks the man in the chin. Then Jago brings his foot down on the man's knife hand. His wrist slams into the ground, the instep of Jago's shoe on top of it. The knife comes free. Jago flicks it away with the toe of his shoe. It falls over the edge of the curb and clatters down a drain. The man moans. This skinny shit beat him without even taking his hands out of his pockets.

Jago smiles, spins, crosses the street.

Burger King.

Sí.

Jugadores juegan.

But they also need to eat.

Odem Pit'dah Bareket
Nofekh Sapir Yahalom
Leshem Shevo Ahlamah
Tarshish Shoham Yashfeh

HILAL IBN ISA AL-SALT, EBEN IBN MOHAMMED AL-JUKAN

Church of the Covenant, Kingdom of Aksum, Northern Ethiopia

Hilal moans while he sleeps. Whimpers and shakes. His head, face, right shoulder, and arm are burned from the incendiary grenade the Nabataean lobbed at him as he retreated underground.

Eben pulled him to safety. Threw blankets on him, snuffed out the flames, tried to calm him, injected him with morphine.

Hilal stopped screaming.

The power was out when the attack came, despite the backup systems. Eben called Nabril in Addis on a hand-crank radio, and Nabril said the power failure was the result of a solar flare. A huge one. One like he'd never seen before. The strange thing was that it was concentrated there, on Aksum, just at the moment that Hilal was writing his message to the other Players. Just as the Donghu and the Nabataean knocked on the hut's door. All of which was impossible. Solar flares disrupt wide areas, entire continents. They don't have pinpoint accuracy. They aren't aimed.

Impossible.

Impossible, except for the Makers.

Eben considered this in the immediate aftermath of the ambush as he attended Hilal by lamplight. Eben had two Nethinim assistants, both mutes. They placed Hilal on a stretcher, hooked him up to an IV, took him seven levels beneath the surface of the ancient church. Eben and the Nethinim bathed Hilal in goat's milk. The white liquid turned pink. Charred flecks of skin floated to the surface.

They prayed silently as they worked. As they tended. As they saved. Bubbling skin. The crisp, sulfuric smell of disintegrated hair. The creamy waft of the milk-and-blood mixture underneath.

Eben cried quietly. Hilal had been the most beautiful of any Aksumite Player in 1,000 years, since the legendary female Player Elin Bakhara-al-Poru. Hilal had the blue eyes, the perfect, smooth complexion, the straight white teeth, the high cheekbones, the flat nose and perfectly round nostrils, the square chin, and the tightly curled hair that framed his smooth boyish face. He looked like a god. All gone now. Burned away. Hilal ibn Isa al-Salt would never be beautiful again.

Eben sent for a surgeon from Cairo to perform three skin grafts. An eye doctor came from Tunis to try to save Hilal's right eye. The grafts were successful from a medical standpoint, but Hilal will always be gruesome. A patchwork of the formerly beautiful boy. The right eye was saved, but his vision will surely be affected. And it is no longer blue. Now it is red. All of it save the pupil, which is milky white.

"It will never go back," the eye doctor said.

He was so beautiful. A king for angels. But now. Now he appears to be half a devil.

Eben thinks: *But he is our devil.*

It's been nearly a week since the attack. Eben kneels next to Hilal in a plain stone bedchamber. A small wooden cross over the bed frame. A white porcelain sink against one wall. Some pegs for robes. A small chest containing fresh sheets and bandages. A hook on the headboard for the IV. There is a small cart with a heart rate monitor, wire leads, and electrodes. The Nethinim—both of them tall and strong, one a man, one a woman—stand attendant, silent, armed, just outside the door.

Hilal has slept the entire time. He occasionally moans, whimpers, shakes. He is still on morphine, but Eben is already weaning him. Hilal has learned to live with pain, and while this pain will be more intense and permanent than what has come before, if Hilal is to continue with Endgame, then he is going to have to acclimate.

To more pain. To disfigurement. To his new body.

If he is *not* going to continue, then Eben needs to know. And for that, Hilal needs his mind to be clear.

So he is being weaned.

While Hilal has slept, Eben has prayed. Meditated. Remembered Hilal's words: *I could be wrong,* Hilal said before the morphine took him. *The Event could be inevitable.*

Eben knows this is not the case. Not after what the being said on the television. Not after the solar flare that pinpointed Aksum. The Makers *are* intervening. The only other possibility is that the Corrupted One somehow did it. The being that the Aksumites have been searching for all these centuries. Searching for in vain. The one called Ea.

But even the Corrupted One does not have the power to control the sun.

So Eben knows: it *was* the Makers.

And Eben knows that this is savagery. They brought humans to life and they are supposed to oversee our near extinction, to reset the Earth life-clock and let the planet recover from the damage done, but They are not supposed to interfere with the Playing of Endgame. They made these rules, and now They break them.

Which means that perhaps it is time.

Time to see what's inside the legendary, but very real, container.

It's been waiting since Uncle Moses faked its destruction and secreted it away and told the sons of Aaron to protect it at all costs. And never to look upon it or open it. And he commanded: *Only break the seal on the Day of Judgment.*

That day is near.

This is the end of an age.

Soon the mighty Aksumites will take their charge and see what power rests between the gilded wings of the cherubim of glory. Soon Eben ibn Mohammed al-Julan will risk destruction for the sake of Endgame. Once Hilal returns to consciousness and clarity Eben will break the covenant with the Makers and see if the line of Aksum can give them a taste of their own medicine.

FRONTIERS OF SCIENCE, MAY 1981

In March 1967, an intercept technician with the USAF Security Service intercepted a communication between the pilot of a Russian-made Cuban MIG-21 and his command concerning a UFO encounter. The technician has since stated that when the pilot attempted to fire at the object, the MIG and its pilot were destroyed by the UFO. Furthermore, the technician alleges that all reports, tapes, log entries, and notes on the incident were forwarded to the National Security Agency at its request. Not surprisingly, several months later the agency drafted a report entitled UFO Hypothesis and Survival Question. Released in October 1979 under the US Freedom of Information Act, the report states that "the leisurely scientific approach has too often taken precedence in dealing with the UFO question." The agency concluded that no matter what UFO hypothesis is considered, "all of them have serious survival implications."

ALICE ULAPALA

Knuckey Lagoon, Northern Territory, Australia

There is Alice and there is Shari and there is a little girl wedged between them, frightened and whimpering. Shari and Alice stand back to back, crouched in fighting stances, Alice with her knife and a boomerang, Shari with a long metal rod tipped with a tangle of nails. Circling them are the others, also armed, cooing clucking snarling threatening. Beyond them is a pack of dogs with red eyes and men dressed in black and armed with rifles and scythes and billy clubs. Above them is a scrim of stars and the keplers' faces and their seven-fingered hands reaching, their razor-thin bodies still, their mocking laughter ringing. In their midst there is a distortion in space like a hole in the stars. And before Alice can consider all this, the others move at once and the little girl screams and Alice throws her boomerang and pushes her knife into the chest of the short tanned boy, who spits in her face as he bleeds, and the little girl screams and screams and screams and screams.

Alice shoots up in her hammock, her fists gripping the edge so she doesn't tumble out, her hair a wild dark explosion, moonlight reflecting off its curls in white turns.

She takes a breath, slaps her face, checks her boomerangs. Checks her knife. Still there, embedded in the wooden column above the eyelet holding up one end of her hammock.

She is on the porch of her little shack near the lagoon. Alone. Beyond the lagoon is the Timor Sea. Behind her, on the other side of the shack, is the scrub and bush of the vast Northern Territory. Alice's backyard. She has been at home meditating, listening to the dreamtime and tracing the songlines with her memory. Thinking of the ancestors, the sea and sky and earth. She has been there since the kepler broadcast his "Play on" message and since she received another clue in her sleep. This one not a puzzle, but explicit and direct, if not exactly fixed.

She wonders if other Players got new clues. If one of the others has already figured out where she is. If one of them is drawing a bead on her right now with a sniper rifle, in the distance, silent and deadly.

"Bugger you!" she yells into the darkness, her voice spreading over the dry land. She flips out of the hammock and stomps to the edge of the porch, wiggles her toes, lets her arms out wide. "Here I am, you hoons—take me!"

But no shot comes.

Alice snickers and spits. She scratches her ass. She watches the bright light of her clue, a mental beacon in her mind's eye. She knows exactly what it is: the location of Baitsakhan, the Donghu, the terrifying toddler, the person who wants to kill Shari and maybe this girl Alice has seen in her dreams over and over. Alice guesses that this girl is Shari's Little Alice, but why the Donghu, or anyone, would want her killed isn't clear. Why Little Alice is important—*if* she's important— remains shrouded.

Regardless, Big Alice is going to find Baitsakhan and kill him. That is how she will Play. If this leads her closer to one of the three keys of Endgame, so be it. If it doesn't, so be it.

"What'll be'll be," she huffs.

A shooting star cruises the firmament and fades in the western sky. She spins, walks inside her shack, snatches her knife from the wooden post. She picks up the receiver of an old push-button phone, curly cord and all. She punches in a number, puts the receiver to her ear.

"Oi, Tim. Yeah, it's Alice. Look, I'm on a freighter tomorrow predawn, and I need you to use your unmatched skills to locate a certain someone for me, yeah? Might've mentioned her. The Harappan. Yeah, that's the one. Chopra. Indian. Yeah, yeah, I know there must be a hundred million Chopras in that country, but listen. She's between seventeen and twenty, probably on the older end of that spectrum. And she has a kid. Maybe two or three years old. Here's the kicker, though. The girl's name's Alice. That oughta narrow it a little. Yeah, you call me on this number when you get it. I'll be checking the messages. All right, Tim. Good on ya."

She hangs up and stares at the backpack on her bed. The black canvas roll covered with weapons.

She has to get ready.

And she told her Students, her Acolytes:

You can feel it.
Everything that is good is a facade.
Nothing worthwhile lasts.
If you are hungry, you eat, and you are full, but that fullness just reminds
you that you will be hungry again in the future. If you are cold, you make
a fire, but that fire will die, and then the coldness creeps back in. If you
are lonely, you find someone, but then they get tired of you or you get tired
of them and, eventually, there you are—alone again.
Happiness, satisfaction, contentment, all of these create a veil spread
thinly but convincingly over suffering. The pain awaits, always,
underneath.
Everything the children perceive themselves to be and all that they
devote themselves to—food, sex, entertainment, drink, money, adventure,
games—exist to insulate them from fear.

Fear is the only constant, which is precisely why we should listen to it.
Embrace it. Keep it. Love it.

Greatness comes from fear, Students. Using it is how we will fight.
Using it is how we will win.

—S

AN LIU

On board HMS Dauntless, *Type 45 Destroyer, English Channel, 50.324, -0.873*

Beep.

SHIVER.

Beep-beep.

SHIVER.

Beep-beep.

SHIVERBLINKSHIVERBLINK.

"CHIYOKO!"

An Liu tries to sit, but he is restrained. At the wrists and the ankles and across *SHIVERblinkblink* the chest. He glances left and right and left and right. His head is killing him.

Killing.

The pain radiates over his right eye and around his temple and to the back of his skull and down his neck. He can't remember how he got here. He's on a gurney. Sees an IV stand, a rolling cart with a heart and respiratory monitor. *BLINKshiverblink.* White walls. Low gray ceiling. A bright fluorescent light overhead. A framed picture of Queen Elizabeth. An oval door with an iron wheel in the middle. A black four stenciled above it.

He can feel the room shift and hear it *blinkblink* hear it creak.

A wheel on the door.

The room shifts and creaks in the other direction.

He's on a boat.

"Ch-Ch-Ch-Chiyoko . . ." he stammers quietly.

"That's her name, eh? The one who got flattened?"

A man's voice. *SHIVERblinkSHIVERblinkblinkblink.* It comes from

23

above his head, out of eyeshot. An lifts his chin, strains at the straps. Rolls his eyes up until the pain in his head becomes almost unbearable. He still can't *SHIVER* he still can't see the man.

"Chiyoko. I was wondering." He hears the scratch of a pen on paper. "Thanks for finally telling me. Poor girl just got flattened like a pancake."

Flattened? What's *SHIVERSHIVER* what's he *blinkblinkblink* what's he talking about?

"D-d-d-don't say—"

"S'matter? Something in your mouth?"

"D-d-d-don't say her n-n-n-name!"

The man sighs, steps forward a little. An can just make out the top of his head. He is a white man with tan skin and a mop of brown hair, straight thin eyebrows, and deep lines in his forehead. The lines are not from old age but from frowning. From yelling. From squinting. From being British and way too serious.

An already *shiverBLINK* already knows: British Special Forces.

"W-w-w-where—"*SHIVERSHIVERSHIVERblinkSHIVER*. It hasn't *SHIVER* hasn't been this bad *SHIVERSHIVERSHIVER* . . .

The tremors haven't been this bad since Chiyoko left him in bed that night. His head whips back and forth and his legs shake and shake. *SHIVERblinkSHIVERblink*. He needs to *blinkblinkblinkblinkblink* to see her. That will calm him down.

"Twitchy lad," the man says, stepping around to the side of the gurney. "You wanna know where your girlfriend is, that it?"

"Y-y-y-y-y—"

An is stuck on the sound. He keeps saying it, his mind and mouth on a loop.

"Y-y-y-y-y-y—"

The man places a hand on An's arm. The hand is warm. The man is skinnier than An expected. His hands are too big for his body.

"I have questions too. But we can't talk until you've gotten ahold of yourself." The man turns away. He picks up a syringe from a nearby tray. An catches a glimpse of the label: serum #591566. "Try to breathe easy, lad." The man pulls up An's sleeve on his left arm. "It's just a pinch."

No!

SHIVERblinkblinkblinkSHIVERSHIVER.

No!

"Breathe easy now."

An convulses. He feels whatever he's being injected with move through his arm, into his heart, his neck, his head. The pain disappears. Cool darkness washes into An's brain, like the waves outside, gently rocking the ship back and forth, back and forth. An feels the drug pull him beneath the surface, down into the dark ocean. He's suspended. Weightless. He doesn't *shiver*. His eyes don't *BLINK*. All is quiet and all is dark. Calm. Easy.

"Can you speak?" The man's voice echoes as if it is in An's mind.

"Y-yes," An says without much effort.

"Good. You can call me Charlie. What's your name, lad?"

An opens his eyes. His sight is fuzzy around the edges, but his senses are strangely acute. He can feel every centimeter of his body. "My name is An Liang," he says.

"No, it's not. What's your name?"

An tries to turn his head but can't. He's been restrained further. A strap across his forehead? Or is this the drug?

"Chang Liu," he tries again.

"No, it's not. One more lie and I won't tell you anything about Chiyoko. That's a promise."

An begins to speak but the man claps one of his big hands over An's mouth. "I mean it. Lie to me one more time and we're done. No more Chiyoko, no more you. Do you understand?"

Since An can't move his head at all, can't nod, he widens his eyes. Yes, he understands.

"Good lad. Now, what's your name?"

"An Liu."

"Better. How old are you?"

"Seventeen."

"Where are you from?"

"China."

"No shit. Where in China?"

"Many places. Xi'an was last home."

"Why were you at Stonehenge?"

An feels a tickle in his ear. A scratching noise close by.

"To help Chiyoko," he says.

"Tell me about Chiyoko. What was her last name?"

"Takeda. She was the Mu."

A pause. "The Mu?"

"Yes."

"What is a Mu?"

"Not sure. Old people. Older than old."

An hears the *scritch-scratch* noise again. He places the sound. A polygraph. "He's not lying," the man says. "Don't know what he's talking about, but he's not lying."

An hears a tinny voice over an earpiece. Someone else is watching and listening. Giving Charlie with the big hands and wrinkled forehead instructions.

"What you inject in me?" An asks.

"Top-secret serum, lad. I tell you more than that and I have to kill you. It's not your turn to ask questions yet. I'll let you ask yours after you answer a few more of mine, deal?"

"Yes."

"What were you helping Chiyoko with at Stonehenge?"

"Get Earth Key."

"What's Earth Key?"

"Piece of puzzle."

"What kind of puzzle?"

"Endgame puzzle."

"What's Endgame?"

"A game for end of time."

"And you're playing it?"

"Yes."

"Chiyoko was too?"

"Yes."

"She was Mu?"

"Yes."

"What are you?"

"Shang."

"What is Shang?"

"Shang was father of my people. Shang are my people. Shang is me. I am Shang. I hate Shang."

Charlie pauses, writes something on a pad that An can't see. "What does Earth Key do?"

"Not sure. Maybe nothing."

"Are there other keys?"

"Yes. It is one of three."

"Earth Key was at Stonehenge?"

"I think yes. Not sure."

"Where are the other two keys?"

"Don't know. That is part of the game."

"Endgame."

"Yes."

"Who runs it?"

He cannot resist saying the words. "Them. The Makers. The Gods. They have many names. One called kepler 22b told us of Endgame." The serum they put in him tickles the synapses in his frontal cortex. It is a good drug, whatever it is.

Charlie holds a picture over An's face. It's of the man from the announcement that was made on every screen in the world—TV, mobile phone, tablet, computer—after Stonehenge changed, after that beam of light shot to the heavens. "Have you seen this person before?"

"No. Wait. Maybe."

"Maybe?"

"Yes . . . yes I see it before. That is disguise. Could be kepler 22b. Could not be him—her—it. Not a person."

Charlie takes the picture away. Replaces it with a picture of Stonehenge. Not as it was, quaint and ancient and mysterious, but as it is now. Revealed and altered. An unearthly tower of stone and glass and metal rising 100 feet in the air, the age-old stones that marked it jumbled around the tower's base like a child's discarded blocks.

"Tell me about this."

An's eyes widen. His memory of Stonehenge stops before anything like that appeared. "I do not know about that. Can I ask question?"

"You just did, but yes."

"That is Stonehenge?"

"Yes. How did this happen?"

"Not sure. Can't remember."

Charlie leans back. "I guess you wouldn't. You were shot, you remember that?"

"No."

"In the head. You concussed pretty badly. Lucky for you, you've got a metal plate in there. A metal plate coated in Kevlar. Some bloody foresight, that."

"Yes. Lucky. Another question?"

"Sure."

"Can you tell me what happened?"

Charlie pauses, listens to the little voice in his earpiece.

"We don't really know. You were shot, we know that. With a special kind of bullet that only a handful of people have ever seen. You were clutching the end of a rope that led to the body of a young man. Or what was left of his body. He was blown up above the chest. Only his lower torso and legs were left."

An remembers. There was the boy he put the bomb leash around.

There was the Olmec. There was the Cahokian.

"Your girlfriend, Chiyoko—"

"Not say her name. Her name is my name now."

Charlie gives An a hard stare. His eyes are blue, then green, then red. It's the drugs, An tells himself. The good drugs.

"Chiyoko," Charlie says, emphasizing the name, savoring it in a way that stings An. "She was right next to you. One of the stones toppled onto her when this thing under Stonehenge came up. Crushed the lower two-thirds of her body. Killed her instantly. We had to scrape her up."

"She next to me, though?" An asks. His eyelids flutter. "After I shot?"

"Yes. Was she the one who shot you?"

"No."

"Who did?"

"Not sure. There were two others."

"These two, they had the ceramic and polymer bullets?"

"Not sure. The guns were white, so maybe."

"What are their names?"

"Sarah Alopay and Jago Tlaloc," An says, struggling to pronounce these foreign names.

"They're playing this game too?"

"Yes."

"For who?"

An's eyes flutter again. "F-f-f-or their l-l-l-lines. She is Cahokian. He is Olmec." An's head jerks. Fresh pain sizzles across his medulla oblongata. The good drugs are wearing off.

Charlie holds another sheet of paper over An's face. Two security images. "These two?"

An squints. "Y-y-yes."

SHIVER.

"Good."

Charlie whispers something incomprehensible into a microphone.

Beep. Beep-beep. Beep. Beep-beep.

The heart-rate monitor. Other details in the room are coming back to An. The edges of his vision aren't fuzzy anymore. He is resurfacing from the dark waters. The *SHIVERS* are back.

"Where is Ch-Chi-Chiyoko?"

"Can't say, mate."

"On this boat?"

"Can't say."

"C-c-c-can I see her?"

"No. You've only got me from now on. No one else. Just you and me."

"Oh."

An's head jerks. His fingers dance.

"Are-are-are . . ." He trails off, gives up, whispers. "The game, you understand . . ."

"Understand what?"

"You all die." An says it so quietly that Charlie can barely hear.

"What?" Charlie asks, turning an ear toward him.

"You all die," An breathes, quieter still.

Charlie leans over. Their faces are less than half a meter apart. Charlie squints, his forehead wrinkles. An's eyes are closed. His mouth is agape. Charlie says, "'You all die'? Is that what you sai—"

An bites down hard. A plastic cracking noise comes from inside An's mouth. This Charlie can hear very clearly. And then An exhales, blows out with a hiss like a punctured balloon, and an orange cloud of gas shoots from behind his teeth and right into Charlie's face. Charlie's eyes go wide and fill with tears and he can't breathe. His face burns, his skin is on fire everywhere, his eyes feel like they're melting, his lungs are shrinking. He falls forward onto An's chest. It only takes 4.56 seconds, and after that An opens his eyes again.

"Yes," An says. "Y-y-y-you all die."

An spits the fake tooth from his mouth, the poison inside one that he spent years gaining an immunity to. The tooth clicks across the metal floor. The little voice in Charlie's earpiece is screaming. Two seconds later an alarm sounds, reverberating through the metal hull of the boat. The lights go out. A red emergency light flips on.

The room shifts and creaks. Shifts and creaks.

I'm on a boat.

I'm on a boat and I have to get off.

The future is a game.
Time, one of the rules.

MACCABEE ADLAI, BAITSAKHAN

Tizeze Hotel, Addis Ababa, Ethiopia

"It is I," Maccabee Adlai, Player of the 8th line, says into an inconspicuous wireless microphone. He speaks a language only 10 people in the entire world understand. *"Kalla bhajat niboot scree."* These words have no translation. They are older than old, but the woman on the other end of the call understands.

"Kalla bhajat niboot scree," she says in return. They have proven their identities to each other. "Is your phone secure?" the woman asks.

"I think. But who cares. The end is so close."

"The others could find you."

"Screw the others. Besides," Maccabee says, wrapping his fingers around the glass orb in his pocket, "I would see them coming. Listen, Ekaterina." Maccabee has always called his mother by her first name, even when he was a boy. "I need something."

"Anything, my Player."

"I need a hand. Mechanical. Titanium. Don't care if it's skinned."

"Neurologically fused?"

"If you can do it quickly."

"Depends on the wound. I'll know when I see it."

"Where? How soon?"

Ekaterina thinks. "Berlin. Two days. I'll text an address tomorrow."

"Good. Listen. The hand isn't for me."

"Okay."

"It's not for me, and I need you to put something in it. Something hidden."

"Okay."

"I'll send you specs and code over encrypted botnet M-N-V-eight-nine."

"Okay."

"Repeat it," Maccabee says to his mother.

"M-N-V-eight-nine."

"It'll arrive twenty seconds after this call ends. The name of the file is *dogwood jeer.*"

"Understood."

"I'll see you in Berlin."

"Yes, my son, my Player. *Kalla bhajat niboot scree.*"

"Kalla bhajat niboot scree."

Maccabee hangs up. He logs into a ghost app on his phone, launches it, and hits send. *Dogwood jeer* is off. He turns the phone over, removes the battery, and throws it into the waste bin next to the hotel's front desk. He takes the phone in both hands and, as he crosses to the gift shop, cracks it down the middle. He goes to a refrigerator full of sodas and opens the door. The cold hits him in the face. He pulls the air into his lungs. It feels good.

He reaches into the back of the case for two Cokes, drops the phone. It clatters behind the racks.

He pays for the Cokes and heads back to the hotel room.

Baitsakhan is on the couch in the junior suite. He sits on the edge of the cushion, his back straight, his eyes closed. The gauze on his wrist stump is blotted by spots of dark blood. His remaining hand—his right hand—is in a fist.

Maccabee closes the door. "I got you a Coke."

"I don't like Coke."

"Of course you don't."

"Jalair liked Coke."

I wish I were Playing with him instead, Maccabee thinks. He twists open his soda, it makes a little hiss, he takes a sip. It tickles his tongue and throat. It's delicious. "We're going to Berlin, Baits."

Baitsakhan opens his deep brown eyes and gazes at Maccabee. "The wind doesn't blow me there, brother."

"Yes, it does."

"No. We have to kill the Aksumite."

"No, we don't."

"Yes, we do."

Maccabee pulls the orb out of his pocket. "There's no point. Hilal is nearly dead. He isn't going anywhere. Besides, his line would be guarding him. It would be suicide to go back there now. Better to wait it out. Maybe he dies anyway and spares us a trip."

"Who then? The Harappan? To avenge Bat and Bold?"

Maccabee approaches Baitsakhan and lightly slaps his stump. Maccabee knows this hurts, but Baitsakhan only sucks his teeth.

"She's too far away. Others are much closer—others who *have* Earth Key. Others who are Playing by the rules. You remember what the orb showed us, don't you?"

"Yes. That stone monument. That girl called Sarah getting the first Key. Yes . . . You're right."

Maccabee thinks, *That's the closest thing to an apology I've ever heard from him.*

Baitsakhan nods. "We need to go for them."

"I'm glad you agree. First things first. You need to get your arm fixed."

"I don't want it fixed. I don't *need* it fixed."

Maccabee shakes his head. "Don't you want to shoot your bow again? Rein a horse and swing a sword at the same time? Wring the life from the Harappan with two hands instead of one?"

Baitsakhan tilts his head. "These things aren't possible."

"You ever heard of neurofusing? Intelligent prosthetics?"

Baitsakhan wrinkles his brow.

"I swear," Maccabee says, "you and your line are from a different century. What I'm saying is that we're going to lend you a hand, so to speak. A *better* hand than the one you had before."

Baitsakhan holds up his stump. "Where does such magic happen?"

Maccabee snickers. "Berlin. In two days."

"Fine. And then?"

"And then we use this," Maccabee says, holding up the orb that Baitsakhan can't touch, "to find the Cahokian and the Olmec and take Earth Key for ourselves."

Baitsakhan closes his eyes again and takes a deep breath. "We hunt."

"Yes, brother. We hunt."

"Speculation remains rampant about what's going on at Stonehenge in the south of England. It's been nearly a week since locals reported seeing a predawn beam of light surge to the heavens, preceded by massive booming sounds that rang out only seconds before. Given the ancient monument's mysterious history, people are saying that anything from aliens to secret government agencies to Morlocks, which are a kind of underground-dwelling troglodyte—yes, you heard correctly—are responsible for whatever is going on there. We go now to Fox News correspondent Mills Power, who's been in nearby Amesbury since the reports started pouring in. Mills?"

"Hello, Stephanie."

"Can you tell us anything about what's going on?"

"It's been very chaotic. This quaint village is overrun with people. Government trucks travel constantly to and from the site, and the air is thick with helicopters. I've even been told by an anonymous source that three high-altitude CIA or MI6 Predator drones are in the skies twenty-four hours a day keeping watch. The whole area's been declared off-limits, and a mix of British, French, German, and American authorities have even covered the site with what is essentially a massive white circus tent."

"So no one can actually see what caused this alleged beam of light?"

"That's right, Stephanie. But the light isn't alleged. Fox News has obtained four separate smartphone videos of the beam, as you can see in this footage."

"Wow . . . this is the first time I'm seeing—"

"Yes. It's shocking. You can see the beam shooting up in this one—apparently from an area of Stonehenge called the Heel Stone. But the really strange thing, Stephanie, is that all four phones stopped recording at the same moment, even though the people operating them tried to keep shooting."

"Stonehenge is—was—a tourist attraction of sorts, Mills. Has anyone—besides the people who took those videos—has anyone come forward from the site itself? Any eyewitnesses?"

"As I said, things are very much under wraps here—literally. There are rumors of people being held by the authorities, and that some may be on HMS *Dauntless*, a Royal Navy destroyer currently in the English Channel. Of course, a military spokeswoman wouldn't confirm or deny these rumors, based on the fact that this is an ongoing investigation. When pressed on exactly what they're investigating, the standard response seems to be—quote—'unexpected developments in and around Stonehenge.' That's it. All we know for certain is that, whatever has happened, they don't want people to know what it is."

"Yes, that is . . . that is obvious. Mills, thank you very much. Please keep us abreast of any new developments as they become available."

"Will do, Stephanie."

"Uh, next on Fox News, the ongoing crisis in Syria, plus a heartwarming story from the meteor impact site in Al Ain, United Arab Emirates. . . ."

AISLING KOPP

John F. Kennedy International Airport, Terminal 1 Immigration Hall,
Queens, New York, United States

Aisling Kopp saw the impact site on the way in through one of the
plane's small oval windows. That black bowl-shaped scar in the
city, 10 times more devastating than any of the pictures from 2001's
man-made terror attack.

But something about it had changed.

It wasn't that it had been fixed up or cleaned away—that would take
decades. What had changed was at the crater's center, the very point
of impact. Now, instead of ash and rubble, there was a clean white dot.
A tent. Just like the one that covered whatever had happened at
Stonehenge. Whatever the Cahokian and the Olmec had done to the
ancient Celtic ruin.

One of *her* line's places. An ancient La Tène power center.

Used. Taken away. And covered up.

The white tents are like signals to Aisling. Governments are scared,
ignorant, groping. If they can't fix what's happened—the meteors,
Stonehenge—then they'll shroud the damage until they figure it out.
They won't figure it out, though.

A few minutes after the plane arced over Queens, she saw something
else. Something she *wanted* to see. There, in Broad Channel, on the
stretch of land bridging the Rockaway Peninsula to the Queens
mainland. Pop's house. The teal bungalow on West 10th Road, still
standing after the meteor that hit several miles to the north, killing
4,416 souls and injuring twice as many more. It would've been so
much worse if the meteor hadn't landed in a cemetery. The already
dead bore the brunt of its impact.

Aisling is still alive. And her house still stands.

For how much longer, Aisling doesn't know. How much longer will JFK stand? Or the government's white tents? Or anything at all?

The Event is coming. Aisling knows when but not where. If it's centered on the Philippines or Siberia or Antarctica or Madagascar, then Pop's wooden house will survive. New York will survive. JFK will survive.

But if the Event hits anywhere in the North Atlantic, towering waves will crash down on the coast, washing away miles and miles of houses. If the Event hits on land, if it hits the city, then her home will go up in flames in a matter of seconds.

She's convinced that wherever the Event is concentrated, it will be an asteroid. It has to be. That's what she saw in the ancient paintings above Lago Beluiso. Fire from above. Death from above, just like life and consciousness from above. A massive hunk of iron and nickel as old as the Milky Way that will crash into Earth and alter life here for millennia. A cosmic interloper of massive scale. A killer.

That's what the keplers are. Killers.

That's what I am too. In theory.

She moves forward in the long, slow immigration line.

Why didn't she shoot the Cahokian and the Olmec when she had the chance? Maybe she could have stopped everything. Maybe, for that brief moment, she held the key to stopping Endgame.

Maybe.

She should have shot first and asked questions later.

She was weak.

You have to be strong in Endgame, Pop used to tell her. Even before she was eligible. *Strong in every way.*

I'll have to be stronger to stop it, she thinks. *I won't be weak again.*

"Next at thirty-one," says an Indian woman in a maroon sport jacket, interrupting Aisling's apocalyptic train of thought. The woman has smiling eyes and dark lips and jet-black hair.

"Thanks," Aisling says. She smiles at the woman, looks at all the people in this vast room, people from every corner of the world, of every shape and size and color, rich and not-so-rich. She's always loved JFK immigration for this reason. In most other countries you see a predominance of one type of person, but not here. It almost makes her sick, thinking that it will all be gone. That all these people from so many different walks of life will no longer smile, laugh, wait, breathe, or live.

When will they find out? she wonders. *As it happens? In that split second before the end? Hours before? Weeks? Months? Tomorrow? Today?*

Today. That would be interesting. Very *interesting.*

The government would need a lot more white tents.

Aisling arrives at desk 31. There is one person in line before her. An athletic African-American woman in a royal-blue jumpsuit with fashionable bug-eyed sunglasses.

"Next," the immigration officer says. The woman crosses the red line to the desk. It takes her 78 seconds to clear.

"Next," the officer repeats. Aisling approaches, her passport ready. The officer is in his 60s with square eyeglasses and a bald spot. He's probably counting the days to his retirement. Aisling hands over her passport. It's worn and has been stamped dozens of times, but as far as Aisling is concerned it's brand-new. She picked it up at a dead drop in Milan on Via Fabriano only hours before going to Malpensa airport. Pop had sent it via courier 53 hours earlier. The name on it is Deandra Belafonte Cooper, a new alias. Deandra was born in Cleveland. She's been to Turkey, Bermuda, Italy, France, Poland, the UK, Israel, Greece, and Lebanon. Pretty good for a young woman of 20 years.

Yes, 20 years. If the meteors had landed just a few weeks later, she would have aged out. But Aisling celebrated her birthday while she was holed up in that cave. Although "celebrated" is a pretty generous word for eating spit-roasted squirrel and drinking cold mountain spring water. She did enjoy a few sugar cubes after her meal, along with two small pulls off a flask of Kentucky bourbon. But it was no party.

"You've been around," the agent says, leafing through the passport.

"Yeah, took a year off before college. Which turned into two," Aisling says, shifting her weight from one leg to the other.

"Headed home?"

"Yep. Breezy Point."

"Ah, local girl."

"Yep."

He slides the passport through the scanner. He puts down the little blue book. He types. He looks bored but happy—that retirement is looming—but then his hands pause for a split second over the keys. He squints very slightly and adjusts his posture.

He keeps typing.

She's been standing there for 99 seconds when he says, "Miss Cooper, I'm going to have to ask you to step aside and see some of my colleagues over there."

Aisling feigns concern. "Is there something wrong with my passport?"

"No, it's not that."

"Can I have it then?"

"No, I'm afraid you can't. Now please"—he holds up one hand and places the other on the butt of his holstered pistol—"over there."

Aisling already sees them from the corner of her eye. Two men, both in fatigues and armed with M4s and Colt service pistols, one with a very large Alsatian panting happily on a leash.

"Am I being arrested?"

The officer snaps the strap off his pistol but doesn't draw. Aisling wonders if this moment is the most exciting of his 20-odd years as an immigration officer. "Miss, I am not going to ask again. Please see my colleagues."

Aisling holds up her hands and widens her eyes, makes them watery, like how Deandra Belafonte Cooper, the non-Player world traveler, would look in the situation. Scared and fragile.

She turns from the officer and walks haltingly toward the men. They don't buy it. In fact, they take half a step back. The dog stands, as his handler whispers a command. His ears perk, his tail straightens, the hairs on his neck bristle. The man without the dog moves his rifle into the ready position and says, "That way. You first. No need for a scene, but we need to see your hands."

Aisling dispenses with the act. She turns, puts her hands behind her back, just under her knapsack, and hooks her thumbs. "That all right?"

"Yes. Walk straight ahead. There's a door at the end of the room marked E-one-one-seven. It will open when you get to it."

"Can I ask a question?"

"No, miss, you cannot. Now walk."

She walks.

And as she does, Aisling wonders if they are going to put her under a white tent too.

"Tango Whiskey X-ray, this is Hotel Lima, over?"

"Tango Whiskey X-ray, we read you."

"Hotel Lima confirms idents of Nighthawks One and Two. Good night. Repeat, good night. Over."

"Roger, Hotel Lima. Good night. Protocol?"

"Protocol is Ghost Takedown. Over."

"Roger Ghost Takedown. Teams One, Two, and Three are in position. We have eyes?"

"Eyes are online. Op on oh-four-five-five Zulu."

"Op on oh-four-five-five Zulu, copy. See you on the other side."

"Roger that, Tango Whiskey X-ray. Hotel Lima out."

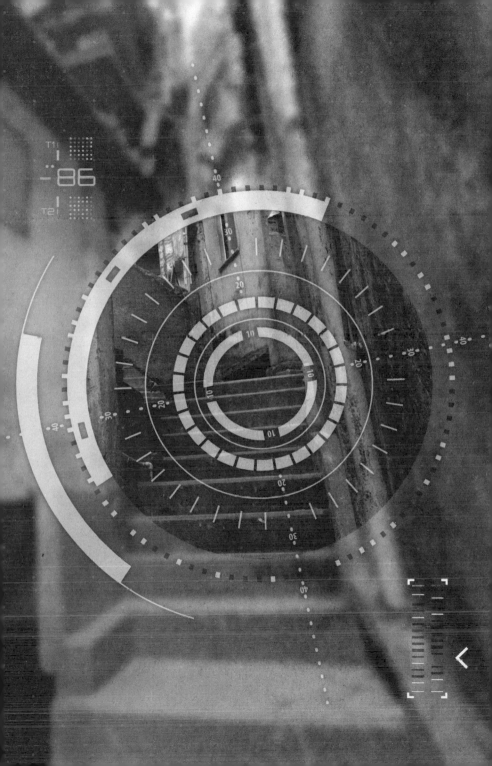

JAGO TLALOC, SARAH ALOPAY

Crowne Plaza Hotel, Suite 438, Kensington, London

The news is on all day in the background while Jago talks with Renzo to finalize their transportation. Sarah packs. Not that they have much to pack. When he's done with Renzo, Jago goes over their emergency escape plan, should they need it. The one that winds through the nearby Tube tunnels and sewers. Sarah listens, but Jago sees that she's not paying attention. They eat more Burger King—breakfast this time—savoring every greasy, salty bite. The Event is coming. The days are numbered for this kind of fast-food deliciousness.

Sarah meditates in the bathtub, tries not to cry about Christopher or triggering the end of the world, and miraculously succeeds. Jago exercises in the living room. Rips off three sets of 100 push-ups, three sets of 250 sit-ups, three sets of 500 jumping jacks. After her meditation, Sarah cleans their plastic-and-ceramic guns. She has no idea who made them, but each is identical to a Sig Pro 2022 in every way save material, color, weight, and magazine capacity. When she's finished, she puts one by her bedside and one by Jago's. His and hers. Nearly jokes that they should be mongrammed but doesn't feel like joking. Each pistol has 16 rounds plus an extra 17-round magazine. Sarah fired one bullet at Stonehenge, killing Christopher and hitting An, probably killing him too. Jago fired one that grazed Chiyoko's head. Other than their bodies, these are the only weapons they have.

Unless Earth Key counts as a weapon, which it very well might. It sits in the middle of the round coffee table. Small and seemingly innocent. The trigger for the end of the world.

The news on the TV is BBC. All day it's the same. The meteors, the mystery at Stonehenge, the meteors, the mystery at Stonehenge, the meteors, the mystery at Stonehenge. Sprinkled here and there with some stuff from Syria and Congo and Latvia and Myanmar, plus the tanking world economy, reeling from a new kind of financial panic that, Sarah and Jago know, is the result of Endgame. The suits on Wall Street don't know that, though. Not yet, anyway.

The meteors, and the mystery at Stonehenge. Wars, crashing markets. The news.

"None of this will matter once it happens," Sarah says in the early evening.

"You're right. *Nada.*"

A commercial. A local ad for a car dealership. "I guess some of it I won't miss," Sarah says. Maybe she does feel like a joke.

Jago should be happy about this. But he just stares at the TV. "I don't know. I think I'll miss it all."

Sarah glares at Earth Key. She was the one who unlocked . . . no. She has decided to stop blaming herself. She was only Playing. She didn't make the rules. Sarah sits on the edge of the bed, her hands planted firmly on the mattress, her elbows locked. "What do you think it'll be, Jago?"

"I don't know. You remember what kepler 22b showed us. That image of Earth . . ."

"Burned. Dark. Gray and brown and red."

"*Sí.*"

"Ugly . . ."

"Maybe it'll be alien tech? One of kepler's amigos pushes a button from their home planet and—*poof!*—Earth is screwed."

"No. It's got to be more terrifying than that. More . . . more of a *show.*" Jago flicks the remote, the TV shuts off. "Whatever happens, I don't want to think about it right now."

She looks at him. Holds out a hand. Jago takes it and sits on the bed next to her and pushes his shoulder into hers.

"I don't want to be alone, Jago."

"You won't be, Alopay."

"Not after what happened at Stonehenge."

"You won't be."

They flop onto their backs. "We'll leave tomorrow, like we planned. We're going to find Sky Key. We're going to keep Playing."

"Yeah," she says unconvincingly. "Okay."

Jago takes her head and turns it gently. He kisses her. "We can do this, Sarah. We can do it together."

"Shut up." She kisses him back. She feels the diamonds in his teeth, licks them, nibbles at his lower lip, smells his breath.

Anything to forget.

They fool around, and Sarah doesn't say "Play" or "Earth Key" or "Sky Key" or "Endgame" or "Christopher" for the rest of the evening. She just holds Jago and smiles, touches him and smiles, feels him and smiles.

She falls asleep at 11:37 p.m.

Jago doesn't sleep.

He is sitting in bed at 4:58 a.m. Stock-still. No lights. Two windows looking over a slender courtyard to the left of the bed. The blinds are open, ambient light suffuses the glass. Jago can see well enough. He's already dressed. Sarah is too. He watches her sleep. Her breathing slow and steady.

The Cahokian.

He tries to remember a story his great-grandfather, Xehalór Tlaloc, told him about a legendary battle between humans and the Sky Gods that took place hundreds of years ago. A battle that the humans, who according to Xelahór didn't even have guns at their disposal, somehow managed to win.

4:59.

If he and Sarah both want to survive, they will need to beat the Sky Gods a 2nd time. But how did the humans do it? How could humans with spears and bows and swords and knives defeat an army of Makers? How?

5:00.

How?

The air changes. The hair on Jago's neck stands up. He whips his head to the door. The crack of light from the hall is unbroken. He stares at it for several seconds, and then it goes out.

He grabs his pistol from the side table. Pokes Sarah with a bony elbow. Her eyes pop open as Jago clasps a hand over her mouth. His eyes say, *Someone's coming.*

Sarah slides to the floor. She grabs her pistol and quietly charges a round. She rolls under the bed. Jago slips to the floor and rolls under too.

"Player?" Sarah whispers.

"Don't know."

Then Jago remembers. He points his chin to the center of the room. Earth Key is still on the coffee table!

"Shit," Sarah says.

Before Jago can stop her, Sarah slides out and gets to her knees, but then she freezes. Jago peers past her legs. There, just outside the windows, are two black tactical ropes, dancing back and forth.

"La joda!" Jago whispers.

And then the door bursts open. Four men in staggered single file push into the adjacent living room. All black, helmets, night vision, toting futuristic-looking FN F2000 assault rifles. At the same moment there's a thud from outside, and the windows crack in every direction. Two men immediately rappel down the ropes and kick the glass. It shatters inward, shards raining onto the floor. The men swing in and land right in front of Sarah. She's in a deep crouch, her gun leveled on the face of the lead soldier. She hesitates to shoot, and she hates herself for it.

But her senses are sharp, and she notices that the rifles have a strange attachment where the grenade launcher would normally be.

"Don't move," the lead soldier says with a British accent. "Except to lower your gun."

"Where's the other one?" asks the lead who came through the door. One of the men behind him says, "Going thermal. There—"

Pop-pop!

Jago fires and rolls to his right, away from Sarah. Both shots hit the legs of the man who switched his goggles. This man's shins are armored, but Jago guessed as much, and the bullets tear through the flesh and bone just above his feet. He falls to the floor, crying out. None of the other men move to help. Instead they begin firing.

But not bullets.

Sarah springs straight up from her crouch, pulls her knees to her chest, her head nearly touching the ceiling. Two darts sail beneath her. *Thup-thup.* They hit the wall.

Thup-thup-thup-thup-thup. Jago's on his feet too. He yanks a metal lamp from the bedside table and dances forward, twirling and ducking and spinning. Four darts zip through his shirt, a 5th grazes his hair, but none hit flesh. A 6th clangs off the metal of the lamp.

"Net!" says the lead soldier that came through the window. The man behind him fires a weapon that looks like a small RPG.

A dark blob expands through the air, heading for Sarah. She fires twice, hitting two of the metal balls that give the net its weight and propel it forward, but it's no use. The net is coming for her.

Jago underhands the lamp toward Sarah. The net hits the lamp and the mesh wraps around it like a closing fist. Sarah drops to the floor, deflecting the snarled lamp to the side. Both Players then surge forward, firing simultaneously, twisting their bodies as they move, making themselves harder to hit with the darts.

Impossible to hit.

Jago fires across the room at Sarah's assailants, using the angle to blast the night-vision goggles off both their faces without actually killing them. Sarah fires across the room at the men facing Jago. She hits two of the dart-gun attachments mounted to the rifles, hits one of the men square in the middle of his bulletproof vest, and with her 5th shot shoots the TV on the far side of the room. It explodes in a shower of sparks, blue and orange and green. The men stand their ground. "Go lethal!" one shouts.

Jago drops to his knees as the first soldier live-fires. Half a dozen 5.56 x 45 millimeter rounds scream over Jago's head as he brings the top of his pistol hard into the man's groin. Jago fires twice at the men just behind the lead soldier, hitting one on the hand and the other on the shoulder. Jago then reaches up and pulls a grenade off the man's vest. Just by the shape and weight he can tell that it's a flashbang.

At the same time, Sarah moves toward her two men. One lets off a volley, which she evades by leaping out the broken window.

She grabs a rope and slides down the outside of the building six feet. She pops the pistol into her waistband with her other hand. While she's sliding, she loops the free end of the rope over her foot. She reaches out and grabs the other rope and loops it around her other foot. Then she lets go with her hands and swings backward. She tucks her chin to her chest and pushes all the air out of her lungs as her back slams into the side of the building. She can feel the pistol come free. She is upside down, like a high-wire circus performer, the ropes and her flexed feet keeping her from falling headfirst down three stories. She hears her gun clatter to the ground in the courtyard below as she reaches behind her ankles and grabs each rope and pulls herself up so that her feet are only inches below the edge of the window.

Jago sees Sarah launch out the window, doesn't worry about the lightning-quick Cahokian, closes his eyes, throws the flashbang against the far wall.

The room lights up, and a loud noise echoes over everything and out into the London night, bouncing off buildings and into the street and sky. Jago stands and pistol-whips the back of the lead officer's neck. He goes down in a heap. Jago sees that the man he shot, still lying on the floor, is taking aim with his rifle. Jago pirouettes around the next stunned soldier, grabbing him by the shoulders, just as the prone soldier fires. Two quick bursts. But every slug sails into the Kevlar vest of the man between them. Jago jumps sideways, throwing the man forward onto the metal coffee table. He's already unconscious from the impact of the slugs.

Earth Key rolls across the table and stops, teetering on the edge, as if it doesn't want to fall.

Jago's about to spin and help Sarah when a knife flashes out of the cloud of smoke. It slices Jago near his right hand, the one with the gun, and cuts deep across the wrist. The gun falls to the floor, bouncing off Jago's foot. The knife slices upward, nearly catching Jago. He folds back to avoid it and bends so far that he has to plant his hands behind him to keep from tumbling over. One lands on the cold surface of the coffee table, the other on the muscly leg of the soldier who took a dozen point-blank slugs to the back. Jago feels a tactical knife strapped to this thigh. He draws it and wheels and gets his feet back under him. The soldier with the knife steps out of the smoke, ready to fight.

Jago sets his feet and covers his throat with his free hand. The man lunges from the smoke. Jago sidesteps, and the blade catches him fast along the left forearm, slicing his shirt open but not his skin.

The angle of attack allows Jago to push the man farther to the side. He drops his blade, steps forward, plants his left hand on the man's arm just above his elbow, and grabs his wrist with his other hand. He pushes hard into the arm and yanks the wrist in the other direction, and the man's arm snaps clean at the elbow. The man screams, and Jago feels the tendons release the knife. It falls, the heavy handle causing it to flip over. Jago kicks up his heel and hits the knife on the butt. It reverses course, sailing upward. Jago releases the man's wrist and snatches the blade out of the air.

Just as he catches it, the man head-butts Jago across the forehead, which hurts, especially since he's still wearing a helmet.

If pain mattered to Jago, this would have been a good move.

But pain doesn't matter to Jago.

The Olmec cups his left hand over the back of the soldier's neck and brings the blade up fast into his throat. Warm blood shoots over Jago's hand. He steps away as the man gets busy dying.

While Jago fights, the two tasked with capturing Sarah recover from the flashbang. They look at each other and then out the window. They ready their rifles and step to the edge. The guns swing into the air, the men clear left and right and don't see her. Then one clears up while the other clears down.

Sarah waits. Still hanging upside down, she crunches up and grabs the unsuspecting man by the cuff of his shirt. She pulls hard and falls back, and the man comes with her, arcing out of the window. He falls to the ground, yelling the whole way until there's a sickening sound and silence. Sarah looks up, knowing the other soldier is still there. Their eyes meet. He pulls the trigger and fires wild.

Thk-thk-thk-thk-thk! A volley rings out, but because Sarah is still swinging, he misses, the bullets making high-pitched firecracker noises on the concrete and metal in the courtyard below. He aims again, and has her sighted this time. Sarah keeps her eyes open. Christopher had his eyes open. She will too.

But then the man slowly pitches forward and falls out of the building, a knife planted to the hilt in the back of his neck.

"You all right?" Jago calls from inside the room, his body still frozen in the throwing position.

"Yes!"

"There's one more."

Jago spins to the wounded man on the floor. The man says, "Rooster call! Repeat, rooster call!"

Jago drops instinctively as something zips into the room from outside and, unfortunately for the soldier, hits him dead in the face. His head explodes.

"Sniper!" Sarah yells from outside.

"Coming!" Jago shouts.

Sarah's a sitting duck. She points her feet and drops, the rope running over her ankles and under her heels. Just before hitting the ground, she flexes her feet and extends her hands over her head. She slows.

Her hands meet the ground. She kicks the ropes free of her ankles and folds out of a perfect handstand.

She's safe from the sniper. In the room above, Jago sets off two more flashbangs. They're loud, and he can't hear a thing as he vaults forward, sliding over the coffee table, grabbing Earth Key. Three rounds explode in the floor just behind him. He scurries forward, only a few meters to go. The coffee table takes the next three sniper rounds. A meter. A round sings by, only centimeters from his head.

Screw this.

Jago stands, yells "Catch!" and throws Earth Key out the window. He dives out after it and snatches one of the ropes with both hands. Sniper rounds, coming from the north-northeast, ping off the building. His hands burn. His hands bleed. He twists, gets his feet on the exterior wall, comes to a stop. The sniper lost his angle and isn't firing anymore. Jago loops the rope under his butt and rappels the last six meters to the ground.

"Catch yourself," Sarah snips. Jago spins just in time to grab an F2000 that Sarah throws at him. It claps into Jago's bleeding hands. He doesn't care about the pain. He likes it.

He's Playing.

Sarah bends to pick up the other rifle and the pistol that fell from her waistband. Jago pulls the knife out of the man's neck. Sarah takes two flashbangs from one of the men. Jago pulls a spray canister off the hip of the same man, along with a satchel not much bigger than a baseball.

"What's that?" Sarah asks, squinting at the canister.

"Aerated C4," he says almost giddily.

"Whoa. Never messed with that. You?"

"Naturally."

"That bag the blasting caps?"

He looks. *"Sí."*

"Great. Now let's get out of here."

Jago nods. "You got Earth Key?"

Sarah pats a small lump in a zippered pocket. "Good throw."

Without another word they take off at a dead sprint.

A few seconds later Jago points, and Sarah sees it. An exposed section of Tube tracks for London's District and Circle lines. They make it in 15.8 seconds from the side of the hotel, and 7.3 seconds after that they are in the dark secluded safety of the tunnels. As they scramble into the shadows, the image of Christopher infiltrates Sarah's mind, his head exploding, followed by his body. She tries to beat the image back, and she does. Moving, fighting, Playing are all at least good for one thing: forgetting.

iii

ALICE ULAPALA

CMA CGM Jules Verne, *Passenger Cabin, En Route from Darwin to Kuala Lumpur*

Alice doesn't like beds as much as she does hammocks, especially on ships, so she's slung her hammock across her small cabin. She lolls around, letting the motion of the sea swing her back and forth.

She tosses a knife end over end and catches it. Tosses and catches. Tosses and catches. One slipup and it could land in her eye, skewer her brain.

Alice doesn't slip up.

She's not thinking of much. Just the knife and of slaughtering Baitsakhan when she finds him.

And of the fear on Little Alice's face. She has seen it in her dreams so many times that it's burned into her consciousness.

Little Alice.

Screaming.

What is it about this girl she's never met? Why does Alice care about her? Dream about her?

Shari's a good nut, that's why. I am too. The rest are bastards, so fuck 'em.

Her satellite phone rings. She picks it up, presses talk.

"Oi, that Tim? Yeah, yeah. Right. Good! And you spoke to Cousin Willey in KL, yeah? Great. Uh-huh. Uh-huh. Naw, none of that. Just my blades. No, Tim, I mean it! I don't need any guns, I'm telling ya. You know me. Purist and all. Oh, all right, fine. You make a good point. Every one of these Player bastards is probably armed to the teeth, true and true. Just keep 'em small, and only hollow tips. Yeah. Yeah. Listen, any news on the rock? Anyone figure out where it's gonna hit? 'Cause when it does, your Alice doesn't want to be nowhere near. You neither? 'Magine that."

She flicks the knife into the air above her head. It turns nine times. She catches it between her index finger and her thumb. Tosses again.

"Any luck with Shari? Oh, really? When were you gonna tell me, ya wanker? I oughta come back there and carve your freckle out, Tim. Well, what is it, then?"

She catches the knife by the handle and leans so far out of the hammock that she thinks she's going to flip out, but she doesn't. She sticks a leg out the other side and is perfectly balanced. She scratches a number on the wall. 91-8166449301.

"Thanks, Tim. Don't die until you get to see it all go down. Gonna be a sight. Yeah, later, mate."

She presses talk again, settles into her hammock, calls Shari's number. Rings 12 times, no one answers.

She calls again.

Rings 12 times, no one answers.

She calls again.

Rings 12 times, no one answers.

She calls again and again and again and again, and she will keep calling until someone does answer.

Because she has something very important to tell the Harappan. Something very important indeed.

SHARI CHOPRA AND THE LEADERS OF THE HARAPPAN LINE

Best Good Fortune Banquet Hall, Gangtok, Sikkim, India

They are all here.

Shari and Jamal, Paru and Ana, Char and Chalgundi, Sera and
Pim, Pravheet and Una, Samuel and Yali, Peetee and Julu, Varj and
Huma, Himat and Hail, Chipper and Ghala, Boort and Helena,
Jovinderpihainu, Ghar, Viralla, Gup, Brundini, Chem, and even Quali,
toting a three-week-old Jessica, who is wrapped in soft linen cloths of
alizarin and turquoise.

The other children are here too, more than 50, too many to name,
from two to 17, including Little Alice. They're playing and caring for
one another in the adjoining room and in the herb-and-rock garden
beyond, leaving the grown-ups alone, as they have been instructed.
Seventeen servants are there, all of whom double as guards, and
there are 23 more who are only guards, armed discreetly, stationed all
around the hall.

They have been meeting, eating, and drinking juice and chai and
coffee and lassis—never alcohol for the Harappan—for over three
hours. The smells of curry and coriander, lentils and bread, turmeric
and cream and hot oil, lemon and garlic and onions, fill the air, along
with the rich and heady odor of bodies and sweat and cinnamon and
rosewater dabbed behind ears and along necklines.

All of them talking at once.

For three hours they were polite and respectful, catching up with one
another, kindnesses exchanged, the familiarity of close relations.
But 16 minutes ago the arguing started.

"The Harappan cannot sit on the sidelines," Peetee says. He is 44 and the tallest of their clan, a former trainer in cryptography. He has dark, deep-set eyes that tell of sadness, and henna-dyed hair that speaks to his vanity.

Gup, a 53-year-old ex-Player and bachelor who lives in Colombo and who fought against the Tamils just for the diversionary nature of violence, nods with him. "Especially now that Endgame is under way. What is the point of our Player retreating like this? We are teetering on the precipice of, of, of—well, if not our destruction then certainly a sea change for humanity. The Event will see to that."

"The Player has her reasons," says Julu, one of Shari's aunts. She speaks without taking her eyes from her hands, which are habitually fingering a strand of crimson prayer beads.

"Reasons?" several of them blurt at once. *"Reasons?"*

"What reason could there possibly be?" a booming female voice asks from the far end of the table. "I demand to know. It looks to me as if she fled at the drawing of first blood." The voice belongs to Helena, 66, a former Player, the 2nd-most esteemed of the last 208 years. She is squat and round and strong and still swift. "A *finger*? I would have given an eye and a lung and a leg before I came hopping home. I would have given an arm and my hearing and my tongue! No, I would have given *all*! I would *not* have come home for any reason but death!"

Boort, her husband of 46 years—they were married at the stroke of midnight on the day she lapsed—reaches out and pats her forearm. "Now, Helena."

"Aand mat kha!" she exclaims, shucking off Boort's hand so she can point at Shari. "That—that—that *girl* gave up! She gave up. She never even made a kill in all of her training! Takes some effort to wiggle out of that time-honored obligation. More effort than what she put into Playing. I had thirty kills before I lapsed. But her? No! She is too *good* for death. Imagine that! A Player of Endgame. A Player of Endgame who also happens to be a *mother*. Can you believe it? That is what we have pinned our hopes to. A spineless quitter."

Now the room is quiet; Helena's words are like a volley of gunshots, everyone taking cover, not yet ready to poke their heads back out. Shari, for her part, does not flinch at any of it. She sits straight-backed and listens. Her eyes have moved to each speaker, and so now she stares at Helena. Her stare is calm and confident. She loves Helena like family, in spite of her ire. Loves all of these people.

Helena bristles at Shari's look, which she mistakes for insolence. "Do not glare at me like that, Player."

Shari tilts her head to the side as if to apologize, but remains silent. Her eyes drift past Helena to the children's room, where she picks out a flash of Little Alice's bright-pink trousers among the wheeling limbs of children. Jamal squeezes her knee under the table, just as he would if they were alone in their yard, watching a sunset.

"Helena, you may be right, but it serves no purpose to compare Shari Chopra to you or any other Player." This is Jovinderpihainu, a former Player and the elder of the Harappan line. He is 94, as sharp as he was when he was 44, even 24. He is small and shrunken in his orange robes, skin as wrinkled and creased as the fabric. "She chooses a different path. She always has. We mustn't question it."

"But *I am* questioning it, Jov!" Helena persists. This is what everyone calls him, except the children, who call him Happy. They love his smiles, practically toothless, his last shocks of silver hair always sticking out every which way. He doesn't smile much anymore, not since Endgame began. The children wonder why.

Jov raises a hand, a familiar and crystal-clear indication that he has heard enough. "I will repeat, but not again: this is not about you, Helena." Helena crosses her arms. Boort whispers some soothing words into her ear, but she gives every appearance of not listening to him.

"Perhaps we should ask Shari's father, hm?" Jov says. "Paru? What have you to say? Your daughter has taken a strange route in the game. Have you any insight?"

Paru clears his throat. "It is true that my daughter is not a natural killer. I am not sure that, had I been chosen in the past, I would have been much different. But while Shari may not be the bloodthirstiest among us"—he is interrupted by scattered snickers—"I can say one thing with confidence. Shari is the most compassionate soul of everyone in this room, yourself included, Jov. With respect."

Jov nods slowly.

Paru takes a deep breath, trying to meet every set of eyes upon him. "Compassion may not seem like much of a weapon for Endgame. It is not hard like a fist or sharp like a sword or fast like a bullet. It does not travel in straight lines delivering death. It is not final, but it can be fierce. This I know. If Shari can survive and somehow win, then we will be better for it. The new world of men will need compassion just as much as it will need resourcefulness and cunning. Maybe more, if this blessed Earth will be as broken as we believe it will be. Ask yourself, my family—if the Harappan are to inherit the aftermath, would you prefer our champion to be a ruthless killer, or one who has mastered her fear and found her heart? One who can teach her disciples the ways of compassion in lieu of the ways of the fist?"

"Thank you, Paru," Jov says. "You speak wisely. I wonder, though—"

"But how"—a soft but clear voice interrupts—"will she win if she is here, and not out there pursuing Sky Key?"

This is Pravheet, a youthful 59, perhaps the most respected member of the Harappan line, even more than Jov. He was the Player during a false start of Endgame, one of only three false starts in history. The infamous Chasm-game perpetrated by the Zero line in 1972. The one that he alone exposed, but not before felling four Players of other lines. It was Pravheet who single-handedly obliterated the Zero line—that delusional band of outsiders—in the aftermath of the Chasm-game. Most importantly, Pravheet is the one who, after lapsing, swore never to kill again. He became an ascetic for 23 years before taking Una as his wife and making a family of his own. During his seclusion he studied the ways of the ancient seers, deciphering the secret texts of the Harappan and the Buddha that their line has protected for millennia.

"Pravheet is right to ask," Jov says. "I think it is time we hear from the Player herself." And now, all their eyes turn to Shari Chopra. Jamal takes her hand and straightens next to her, as if he's readying for an onslaught.

"Elders," Shari says, her voice serene. "We needn't look for Sky Key." And sure enough the voices come fast and furious. Shari can make out only snatches of their confusion, their anger, their exasperation.

"But this is Endgame" . . . "What is this blasphemy" . . . "not look for Sky Key?" . . . "lose" . . . "We'll lose" . . . "She dooms us all" . . . "All is lost and the dark is coming" . . . "What does she mean" . . . "Surely she's loony" . . . "She is giving up" . . . "Maybe she knows" . . . "no no no" . . . "How can this child be a Player?" . . .

"ENOUGH!" Jov shouts. Even the cavorting children in the adjoining room stop playing. He holds out his hand, palm up, in Shari's direction. "Please, my Player. Explain."

"We needn't look for Sky Key because we already have it."

These words have the opposite effect on the assembly. Instead of vociferous objection, there is disbelieving silence.

Finally, Chipper says, "Already have it?"

Shari lowers her eyes. "Yes, Uncle."

"Where? When did you go and get it? You can't have gotten it before Earth Key," Helena says, her voice accusatory.

"In a manner of speaking, Auntie, I did."

"What are you saying, Player? Please, speak plainly." It is Pravheet again.

"Sky Key is my Little Alice."

All the adults go deathly quiet, save for Una and Ghala, who both gasp. Paru's voice is quavering as he asks, "B-but how can y-you be sure?"

"It was my clue from the kepler. And it is what Little Alice has told me too, in her own way. She's been having dreams. I've been having them as well."

"But why would the Makers do this?" Chipper asks. "It is immoral to involve a child in this way."

"The Makers *are* immoral, Uncle," Shari says emphatically. "Endgame is immoral. Or rather . . . amoral."

More gasps.

Over half the people in this hall truly believe that the keplers exist on a plane higher than the gods. The gods are *Their* children, after all, and humans are at another remove, the children of the gods. The keplers are the gods of the gods and, for many here, they are beyond reproach.

"I will not listen to this heresy!" Gup blurts. He stands quickly from his chair and stalks out of the room. Short-tempered and slow-witted Gup. No one follows him.

"I do not wish to cause dissension, elders, but I alone have met a kepler. After gaining some distance from it, and considering the clue it gave me, I have come to the conclusion that the one I met was . . . detached. At best. It came to announce the commencement of Endgame, and the coming of the Great Extinction, and all it really did was talk as if it were reciting some kind of history already passed. Don't get me wrong—it was physically wondrous, unlike anything I have ever seen, and it had abilities that go far beyond anything we have learned. Yet for all this power, its message was thus: 'Nearly every human and animal will die. You twelve will fight to figure out who doesn't. Good luck.' Like a child plucking wings off a butterfly. There is no nobility in that."

Shari pauses. She expects another rush of questions. This time, the other Harappan stay silent. Shari continues.

"As for the other Players, they fall into two camps—those who should win, and those who shouldn't. At least half were twisted monsters, poisoned by their vanity, by the knowledge that they are among the deadliest people on Earth. The others were different, more self-aware, perhaps capable of feelings beyond bloodlust. I would say that fewer than half deserve to win. In our brief meeting, only two distinguished themselves—and shamefully, I was not one. The first was the Aksumite, a dark-skinned and regal boy with the bluest of eyes, who begged us to pool our knowledge and work together in an effort to perhaps spare Earth from undue suffering. The other was the Koori, a wild woman of Australia, who saved my life in Chengdu. But mostly the Players were . . . just people. People driven by a purpose they don't—we don't—wholly understand."

Another pause. Shari watches the children in the next room. Some of the older ones have stopped playing and instead stand in the doorway, listening.

She continues. "Helena—you said that I am not a natural killer, and I concede that I am not. But I *have* killed, and I will kill again if Endgame requires it. But I will not take pleasure in it. Do you understand?" Helena makes an audible huff. Shari ignores this. "I will not kill a person who is a true human being, do you see? The boy I killed was a monster. I broke a chair to pieces and drove a wooden stake through his heart."

Shari stands and looks over the faces in the room, meeting the gaze of each of her elders with a sad smile on her lips. She can see that many do understand. Jov and Paru and Ana and Pravheet and Una and Chem especially. She finishes by turning to Jamal. He squeezes her hand tightly. As she speaks, she doesn't take her eyes from Jamal. "I do not tell you of this murder of mine to boast," she says quietly, "but to demonstrate that I will stand for my people. I have stood for my people, and chief among all of you, I will stand for Little Alice. She *is* Sky Key. I know it, and it is only a matter of time before the others do too. They will come for her. We, all of us, every initiated member of our line, must protect her."

"You mean *you* must protect her," Helena says, a desperate bitterness creeping into her voice.

Shari looks lovingly at Helena. "No, Auntie. I mean *we*. I mean you especially. With respect to all of you, please listen. I have thought long and hard on this. The kepler said explicitly that there are no rules in Endgame. I am the Player, and the Event is coming in fewer than ninety days—perhaps even sooner if the kepler wills it. We must prepare. If the keplers have the, the, the"—she searches for the words—"the immorality, the cynicism, to make a child, *one of our own children*, a piece of the Great Game, then I say we can do whatever we like. I propose that we go to the Valley of Eternal Life and take Sky Key with us. We take our people there. That ancient fortress is one of the most defensible keeps in the entire world. Let the others Play the way they want to—by hunting and killing and saying to themselves, 'I am the best, I am the best, I am the best.' We will wait. We will wait for them to bring Earth Key to us, and they will break hard on our walls, and we will take Earth Key. I will take it, and bring it together with my Sky Key for the last leg of the game. But I need you, and want you. *We* are the Harappan, and *we* are going to protect our own. *We* are going to save our line. *We*."

She sits down. Everyone is still. The only sounds come from the very small children still playing in the next room. Shari watches as Little Alice pushes through the legs and arms of her cousins and says, "Did you say my name, Mama?"

Shari's eyes well with tears. "Yes, *meri jaan*. Come sit with us."

Little Alice, precocious and far more confident in her movements and speaking than an average two-year-old, prances across the hall to her mother and father. She is oblivious to all the eyes upon her. As she climbs onto Jamal's lap, Jov says, "I will consider your words before deciding on a course of action, Shari. But I would like to talk more with you, along with Helena, Paru, Pravheet, and Jamal. I want some more assurance that what you say about Sky Key is true."

Shari bows her head. "Yes, Jovinderpihainu."

And as each individual in the room thinks about what Shari has just said, Shari's maid steps into the hall, practically folded in half out of deference, and says with her voice shaking, "Madam Chopra, please forgive me but I have an extremely urgent message."

Shari holds out her hand. "Come, Sara. Stand and don't be afraid. What is it?"

Sara straightens and shuffles forward, the balls of her feet scuffing the floor, and hands Shari a piece of white paper.

Shari takes it and reads.

"It is a message from the Koori," Shari says. "She found me. She found us."

Shari pauses.

"What does it say?" Paru asks.

Shari shows it to Jamal, who stands and carries Little Alice in his arms back to the playroom, whispering silly things in her ear as they go, Little Alice giggling and nuzzling her father's neck. The wall of teenagers parts for them, and they disappear into the next room. The teenagers come back together and stare at Shari.

When her husband and daughter are out of earshot, she says, "The note reads, 'Stay sharp. Your Little Alice is in danger. Grave danger. The others will come for her. I don't know why, but I have seen it. The Old People have shown me in my dreams. I will try to stop them. The keplers have given me a way to do this. Keep her safe. Keep yourself safe, until the end. May we be the last standing, and fight it out then. Two of the good ones. Yours, Big A.'"

Jov claps, and it is like a giant clapping away a covering of clouds.

No more confirmation is needed.

The 893rd meeting of the Harappan line is over.

They must move.

They must Play.

They are going to fight.

Together.

AN LIU

On Board HMS Dauntless, *Type 45 Destroyer, English Channel, 50.124, -0.673*

An's interrogator—still slumped across An's chest—is shut up and *BLINK* shut up *BLINK* shut up and quiet and dead. An needs to get out of *shiverblinkblinkblink* out of his restraints and *blinkblink* and move. He closes his eyes *blink* closes his eyes and sees her. Remembers the smell of her *shiver* her hair and the taste of her breath, *BLINK* full and aromatic, like some kind of ceremonial *blinkblinkblink* some kind of ceremonial tea.

CHIYOKOCHIYOKOCHIYOKOCHIYOKOTAKEDA CHIYOKOTAKEDA

CHIYOKO TAKEDA CHIYOKO TAKEDA CHIYOKO TAKEDA CHIYOKO TAKEDA CHIYOKO TAKEDA CHIYOKO TAKEDA

The tics subside just enough to *shivershiver* just enough to . . .
An wedges his left hand between his hip and *blinkblink* and the edge of the metal gurney. He twists so that the base of his thumb is pressed against the cold metal. Then An pushes all of his weight down, onto his thumb, until he hears *blinkCHIYOKOblink* until he hears the *pop*. His thumb dislocates, flops loose and rubbery against his palm. It is *blink* excruciating, but An doesn't care. He pulls, squeezes his hand through the restraint and pushes his shoulder into Charlie. The interrogator slides to the floor with a thump. An unbuckles the strap on his right. When his other hand is free, he grips his dislocated thumb and shoves it back into place. It is sore, swollen, and bruised.
But it works.
A loud alarm wails outside the door. He works the restraint off his forehead and sits up. Pain surges through his head, front to back, like a

sponge soaking up water. It throbs and fills his ears and pushes at his eyeballs.

The gunshot wound. Charlie said he was concussed.

An must ignore it.

An takes stock of himself. He is wearing a V-neck T-shirt and drawstring scrubs, scratchy fabric, dressed like a prisoner or a mental patient. He unfastens his *blinkCHIYOKOTAKEDAblink* unfastens the restraints from his ankles with both hands, climbs off the gurney, lands next to Charlie, kneels. He pats down *blink* the interrogator for anything useful. He finds a rolled-up sleeve that feels like it contains *blinkblink* contains syringes. This could be more of the wonder drug, the one that cleared his mind. It made An tell the truth too. So much truth. He hopes that the remnants of the drug still in his system keep his tics to a minimum.

So he can *blinkblink* so he can escape.

He rips off Charlie's suitcoat and shrugs it on. He pats the man down a final time, finds a gun holstered under Charlie's armpit. Glock 17. Stupid cocky military *blink* military types. Bringing a gun into a room with a *blinkblinkSHIVER* a Player of Endgame. Might as well shoot himself.

An unholsters it. Releases the safety. Closes his eyes tight. Fights back the pain *blink* and the pain *SHIVER* and the pain *blink* and the image of . . .

CHIYOKOCHIYOKOCHIYOKOTAKEDA

Flat and dead Chiyoko Takeda.

Her name is his now.

In him.

His.

An hears a creak. *SHIVER*. Not the ship shifting on the waves. *Blink.* He looks up.

The wheel on the steel door is turning.

"Chiyoko," he says.

He breaths in and out, in and out.

"Chiyoko."

The storm inside *blinkblink* calms some more.

Time to go.

An pushes up the sleeves of Charlie's coat and gets ready. The wheel on the door stops turning and swings inward. Two men slide into the doorway, rifles ready.

Bang, bang. An fires the Glock from his hip, shoots both soldiers in the face, between the eyes. They fall to the floor, one on top of the other.

An moves. *SHIVERblinkSHIVER.* Moves quickly.

The alarm is louder with the door open. It echoes off the metal walls, down the corridors, in his ears, makes the pain worse, but whatever. An can deal with pain, perhaps better than any of the Players.

He steps toward the two men. *SHIVERBLINK.* He crouches, searches them. The rifles are wedged under their torsos. Voices come from the corridor. Men, angry, scared, excited. At least 10 meters off. Approaching cautiously. He feels the drone of the engines through his bare feet. Guesses which way is aft.

Left.

That's where he'll go. Get to the back of the ship.

The voices are closer.

CHIYOKOTAKEDA. He unclips two M67 grenades from one of the dead men. An desperately pats him down for more of these beautiful little bombs, but there aren't *SHIVER* there aren't any. An stuffs the Glock in the front of his pants and stands, a spherical grenade in each hand. He pulls the wire pin from each with his teeth. He positions himself on the uneven flesh of the men and waits.

CHIYOKOCHIYOKO.

You play for death, she said to him. *I play for life.*

SHIVER*blinkblink*SHIVER

Why? An wonders desperately. *Why did she have to be taken from me?*

BLINKBLINKBLINKBLINKBLINK

He bites his lower lip so hard it bleeds.

"Chiyoko . . ." he says quietly.

The voices are closer. He can make out phrases. "Armed and dangerous." "Fire when ready." "Shoot to kill."

An smiles. He hears the rubber soles of their boots squeaking in the corridor.

I play for death.

He lets the spoon pop on the first grenade. An knows exactly how *BLINK* how much time he has. Four seconds. Waits 1.2 before slinging it out the door.

An whips behind the wall, plugs his ears, the remaining grenade pressed up against his cheek, clenches his jaw, ignores the pain in his head.

He doesn't close his eyes.

SHIVERSHIVER.

The 400-gram, 6-centimeter metal sphere arcs soundlessly through the air. Four men move into position as it comes down. They don't even see it. As soon as it clanks to the floor, it explodes at their feet.

Pressure waves roll through the ship. The sound is deafening. An pulls his fingers from his ears. Transfers the other grenade to his left hand, draws the *blinkSHIVERSHIVERblink* draws the Glock. He hears new sounds.

A man screaming. *Blink.* A steam pipe hissing. *Blink.* The alarm, still going, but fainter since the blast temporarily took some of his hearing.

Blink.

An waves through the doorway, half expecting his hand to get shot off. It doesn't. He peeks *shiverBLINKshiver*. Checks right, where the explosion was, then left *blinkblink* then right again. Sees two dead men and another under them, his arm gone, moving slightly and moaning. A steam pipe over them hisses, a white jet filling the air.

CHIYOKO.

An moves into the corridor, holds his right arm out straight, and shoots. The man stops moaning.

A bit of violence always clears the head.

A bit of death.

He moves aft. The metal floor is cold. The ship tilts. The air is warm and getting warmer from the steam. The corridor goes straight for five meters, has closed doors on either side, turns right at the end. More sounds up ahead. Footfalls, clicks and clanks of metal things. Men, but no voices this time. The men at the forward end of the hall were amateurs. These aren't.

These are *blinkblink* these are special forces.

An takes eight quick steps, his bare feet completely silent, and stops where the corridor turns right. *BlinkCHIYOKOshiverBLINK.* An guesses that the men have assembled around the corner, at the far end. They're waiting for him.

BLINKSHIVER.

They kill the lights.

It is completely black. They killed the lights because they have night vision and he doesn't. But no matter.

BLINKSHIVERBLINKBLINK

An releases the spoon of his last grenade. Counts one second and throws it, overhand and hard, so that it caroms off the wall and hits the floor, bouncing crazily out of sight toward the special-forces men. "GRENADE!" and two quick shots, the slugs ricocheting off the metal with high-pitched zings. An throws himself back the way he came and plugs his ears before the 2nd blast.

This blast is even more deafening than the first. An unplugs his ears before the echoes are done reverberating. He has maybe three more minutes before he loses the element of surprise. After those three minutes they will stop trying to contain him and instead simply contain the ship, making it impossible *blink* impossible *blink* impossible for him to escape, even if it's just to jump over the side and take his chances in the water, which would not be ideal to say the least.

BLINKshivershiverCHIYOKOblink.

Time to go.

He raises the Glock and slips around the corner, running quickly and blind-firing into the darkness.

Twelve rounds, and by the sound of them, three find flesh and bone. No return fire. He runs 5.4 meters and slides like a midfielder trying to steal the ball from a charging forward. He reaches out and feels in the darkness—a head. Just a head.

BLINKBLINKSHIVER

The darkness in front of him is more open, the smoke from the grenade rising and rising. An guesses that he has just entered the ship's hangar.

More moaning. But also a scrambling sound.

An lifts up the head he slid into and *blink* and *blink* and *blink* and gets his fingers around a pair of night-vision goggles. He yanks them free. As An pulls the goggles over his face, he realizes for the first time that his head is *blinkSHIVERblink* is bandaged. He tightens the straps and they squeeze *blinkblinkblink* they squeeze *blinkblinkblink* they squeeze the swollen skin and pull at the fresh stitches across his forehead and his hairline. He winces and stifles the urge to cry out. The goggles are in place, but they aren't working.

"Who has eyes?" a faraway voice whispers, the sound echoing through the hangar.

He's not alone.

"Almost online," a 2nd voice answers, this one closer. "Come ON!"

This voice is only feet away. *SHIVERblinkSHIVER* An sees the soft green glow as the goggles come to life. Only three meters away.

"I see him!" the man blurts.

But he doesn't shoot. He must have lost his rifle in the explosion. The ghostly light frames the edge of his face, his scruffy beard, gnashing teeth. It all surges toward An, who flops to the floor, aims his pistol, and fires.

The man falls against him. Dead. A knife stabs the floor just next to An's ear.

BLINKBLINKshiverBLINKshiver.

Close one.

An pushes the man off *shiver* and feels the goggles *blink* again and finds the switch.

The room turns green.

It is indeed the hangar.

A shot screams from the far side of the room and misses An by a less than a meter. He spots a large *blinkblink* a large man shouldering a rifle. No goggles. He's guessing. Firing toward the commotion. An raises the Glock, takes his time, and fires a single round. It passes through the man's front hand and enters his skull directly over his right eye. He falls.

An pries a knife from the dead man's hand, inspects it. *Blinkblink.* It has a 30-centimeter straight blade with a single edge and no serrations. *Shiver.* It's more like a small sword than a military tactical knife. Probably this man's prize possession, his weapon of choice. His signature.

Not anymore.

BLINKBLINKSHIVERSHIVERBLINK

An slaps himself, runs across the hangar, whispering, "Chiyoko Takeda Chiyoko Takeda Chiyoko Takeda." He bobs and weaves just in case, but no shots come. He finds it *blinkblink* finds it odd. This is a large ship, probably a Type 45 destroyer, and even a skeleton crew would require over 100 seamen. By his count, he's only killed 17. That means more will be coming.

Or maybe it means the rest of the ship doesn't know about An. They don't know what's happening below deck. Maybe An's a secret.

He scurries around an amphibious vehicle and between two pallets stacked with cargo *blinkshivershiverblinkblink* with cargo wrapped in plastic and nylon webbing. Three meters away is an open doorway, a set of stairs inside, going up, up, up.

A Type 45 destroyer has a *blink* has a *blink* has a helipad. Maybe a Merlin Mk1 or a Lynx Mk8.

An has logged 278 simulated hours on the Merlin and 944 on the

Lynx, plus 28 hours in a real one.

An makes for the door.

blinkblinkblinkblinkblink

He hits the narrow stairs and goes up.

One deck.

Up.

Two.

Up.

Three.

The air cools and he smells the *blinkblinkblink* the salty sweetness of the sea and best of all *SHIVER* best of all *SHIVER* best of all he hears the *whomp-whomp-whomp* of a chopper's rotors coming to speed. *Thank you, special forces.*

BLINKBLINK.

An is a few steps below the door that leads to the helipad. It's open. The ship's engines throttle up, as if the hunk of metal and electronics and weaponry is nervous. He feels the first breeze of the rotor wash from the helicopter and pulls Charlie's coat closed around him. He sees the sharp, full moon, the sky clear and the stars bright and the void limitless above.

BlinkSHIVERblink.

Chiyoko would have liked this night, An thinks. *Would have seen the beauty where I can't.*

An rips off the goggles, the straps tearing his bandages and popping a couple of stitches.

He has to get to the chopper.

He peers over the last *BLINK* last step. A Lynx Mk8, just as he hoped. He's lined up perfectly with the cockpit—beyond it is the stern of the ship, and then the blackness of open water. He spies twinkling lights along the horizon. A city in the distance. He glances at the sky. Sees Cassiopeia a few degrees above the Earth. Wonders if the *SHIVERBLINKSHIVER* the keplers are watching him right now, wonders whether they are cheering.

BLINKSHIVERBLINK.

He wants to kill them all for what they did to Chiyoko.

Snuff it all out everywhere for infinity in every direction for all time. All of it.

blinkSHIVERblinkSHIVERSHIVERBLINK.

An moves to the doorway. The chopper's lights are off. The pilot is going to take off *blink* take off *blink* take off dark.

Now or never.

There's a 20-millimeter machine gun in the Lynx's bay that's aimed right at the empty expanse of deck that An has to cross. He hopes the airmen in the chopper won't break every protocol in the book and open fire while still on the deck.

An bolts, firing the Glock at the cockpit, but the rounds bounce away, zinging into the rotors.

At two meters he stops firing, holding three rounds in reserve. The chopper rises off the deck slowly. An reaches *blinkSHIVERblink* the side door just as it's sliding shut. An fires. The copilot falls into the cargo area, his helmet tearing away from his exploded head. An breathes out, leaps up, scrambles in. *SHIVER.* The pilot spins in his seat, his Browning perched on his shoulder, but An fires his last two rounds and the pilot falls to the side.

BLINKBLINK.

The Lynx lurches to port as the dead pilot pulls at the stick.

An drops the pistol and vaults over a long metal box in the cargo area, landing in the copilot's seat.

He gets a strange feeling as he passes the box.

A feeling of calm and peace.

He flicks an array of switches, disabling the pilot's controls, and takes the copilot's stick. Floodlights from the boat illuminate the bridge.

BLINKSHIVERBLINKSHIVER.

"Yaaaaaaaaaaaaaaaaa!" An screams in an attempt to banish the tics.

He can barely hear himself through the cacophony of the helicopter. A dozen sailors, all carrying small arms, spread out under the floodlights and open fire.

BLINKSHIVERBLINK.

Tracers light up the night in multicolored arcs. An smiles. They're too late.

He brings the chopper up 10 meters and sticks back over the stern, flying precisely north-northeast in reverse, putting almost 87 meters between him and the boat in 2.2 seconds. He flicks the weapons on, prays that the Sea Skua missiles are armed, and presses fire.

Blinkblinkblinkblinkblinkblinkblinkblinkblinkblinkblinkblinkblink—

The missiles scream forward and the ship's bridge explodes in orange and black and white and An pulls back hard and spins 180 degrees and jams the stick forward and throttles up and hits 170 knots in 4.6 seconds and the ship is burning and exploding behind him and he is free, he is free. Until they scramble the fighter jets to shoot him down he is free.

Shiverblink.

He flies fast northwest, only meters from the surface of the water to avoid radar, and makes for the flickering lights.

Shiverblink.

He is free.

Blink.

Free.

And I will also declare unto you what is written concerning the pride of PHARAOH. MOSES did as God commanded him, and turned his rod into a serpent; and PHARAOH commanded the magicians, the sorcerers, to do the same with their rods. And they made their rods into three serpents which, by means of magic, wriggled before MOSES and AARON, and before PHARAOH and the nobles of EGYPT. And the rod of MOSES swallowed up the rods of the magicians, for these deceivers had worked magic for the sight of the eyes of men. Now that which happeneth through the word of God overcometh every magic that can be wrought. And no one can find him to be evil, for it is the Holy Spirit Who guideth and directeth him that believeth with an upright heart without negligence.

HILAL IBN ISA AL-SALT, EBEN IBN MOHAMMED AL-JULAN

Church of the Covenant, Kingdom of Aksum, Northern Ethiopia

Many Ethiopians and Eritreans and Somalis and Djiboutis and Sudanese believe that the Ark of the Covenant is kept in a cube-shaped concrete building in the Ethiopian city of Aksum, close to the Eritrean border. The building, which is behind a high iron fence and has a small Islamic-style cupola, is called the Chapel of the Tablet at the Church of Our Lady Mary of Zion. A single ward attends it. It is in plain view for all to see, and everyone knows what is inside.

Everyone is wrong.

Eben ibn Mohammed al-Julan doesn't even know what's in the chapel. It's not that he lacks the authority to find out—it's simply that he doesn't care.

Because he knows where the ark truly rests.

All the initiated members of the line of Aksum know, and have known for millennia.

They know because the Makers decreed them to be the Keepers of the Ark.

They have been its guardians since the fateful year of 597 BCE, when the Babylonians destroyed Jerusalem, razing the Temple of Solomon. It was in the dead of night on 30 Shebat. Nebuchadnezzar II, who was an incarnation of Ea the Corrupted, and his invading horde was less than two miles from the temple. As they advanced, Ebenezer Abinadab and three other Keepers covered the ark in blue linen, took hold of its acacia poles, and lifted. It weighed 358.13 pounds, just as it always had, ever since Moses and Aaron finished building it and the Maker who had spoken to Moses on Mount Sinai had placed his covenant inside.

Ebenezer and the Keepers walked out of the temple, put the ark in a covered cart drawn by a jet-black ox with gilt horns, and drove east across the desert and over the Sinai to Raithu, where they slaughtered the ox and salted his flesh for food and carried the ark onto a small wooden galley to be sailed south on the Red Sea. They took it back on land at Ghalib. These four men, heads down, backs strong, hands never touching any part of the ark save the poles (instant death was the punishment for such a transgression), moved overland on foot for many miles and many weeks. They only moved at night, and avoided all contact with people.

They avoided people out of kindness and respect for life.

For any human—man or woman, babe or elder—who happened to see this sacred caravan of the world's most esteemed travelers was stricken immediately blind and had his or her mind poisoned with raving, blabbering, slithering madness. Ebenezer saw this phenomenon seven times over the course of their 136-day voyage, recording each instance in his journal, and each was more horrifying than the last.

Eventually, Ebenezer and his companions reached their destination in what is now northern Ethiopia. They put the ark in a thick stand of cedar trees, erected the tabernacle around it, making it safe from wandering eyes, and convened with the esteemed members of the line. The Aksumite Uncorrupted Brotherhood. All the living ex-Players plus the current Player as well, a 14-year-old boy named Haba Shiloh Galead.

The underground temples had already been constructed, if not yet converted to churches—the Makers had seen to their creation when the Aksumite line had been chosen for Endgame thousands of years before—and the ark was taken nine levels down, to the deepest and most secure chamber.

This room is the Kodesh Hakodashim.

Once the ark was in place, the entrance to the Kodesh Hakodashim was backfilled by Haba himself with stone and dirt and glimmering rocks, so that for over 2,600 years the only way to reach it has been through a crawl space just big enough for a man to drag himself through on his elbows.

Which is precisely what Eben ibn Mohammad al-Julan is doing right now. Crawling along the well-worn tunnel on his calloused elbows toward the ark.

Crawling there to do something no person has ever done in the history of history.

He thinks of Hilal as he moves. The Player is weaned from morphine and walking and talking, although the latter causes him much pain. Eben left him in his room, sitting in a chair, staring into a mirror. Hilal's injuries have afflicted him with a twisted form of vanity. This is new to Hilal. In spite of his previous and unequivocal beauty, he was never vain. But now he cannot stop looking at his face, and is especially smitten with his red eye and its white pupil.

"The world looks different through it," Hilal said just before Eben left him. The Player's voice was raspy, as if his throat were full of ash.

Eben asked, "How so?"

"It looks . . . darker."

"It *is* darker, my Player."

"Yes. You are right." At last, Hilal looked away from his reflection, turning that red eye on Eben. "When can I Play again, Master?"

Eben has given up on telling Hilal not to call him "Master" anymore. Old habits die hard.

"Soon. You were right about the Event. It could have been prevented. Furthermore, the keplers intervened."

"They are not supposed to," Hilal replied bitterly.

"No."

"What are we going to do?"

"You are going to keep Playing, but I want to see if we can gain an advantage first. Perhaps you can push back at the keplers, as well as do something that will help you deal with the others."

"You're going to open the ark ..."

"Yes, Player. I'll be back. Rest. You're going to need your energy soon."

"Yes, Master."

And Eben left.

That was 27 minutes ago.

He is five meters from the end of the tunnel.

Four.

Three.

Two.

One.

Knock-knock.

The leaden hatch swings into the room, and Eben pushes forward, tumbling into the chamber.

There is no graceful way to enter the Kodesh Hakodashim.

Like the ark it houses, the Kodesh Hakodashim is of specific dimensions. It is 30 feet long, 10 feet high, and 10 feet wide. Every angle in the room—where wall meets floor, wall meets wall, and wall meets ceiling—is a precise 90 degrees. The earthen walls are covered in thick panels of lead, and the lead is leafed in random-length strips of silver and gold. The chamber is lit by a self-powered and undying light of Maker origin, shaped like an inverted umbrella, that hangs from the center of the ceiling. The light gives off an even and pinkish glow with an unwavering 814 lumens.

Two-thirds down the long wall is a curtain of blue and red. In the 10' x 10' x 10' area this curtain creates sits the Ark of the Covenant with the Makers.

The hatch was opened by one of two Nethinim. The one who didn't open the hatch offers a hand to help Eben stand.

"No thank you, brother," he says, working his way to his feet. "Same-El, Ithamar," Eben says. The two men are in their early 30s. Ithamar is an ex-Player, Same-El a trainer in industrial chemistry and Surma-style stick fighting.

"Master al-Julan," they say in unison.

Eben holds up a hand and does something he has never done before—
he closes the hatch and turns the bolt that seals the room.

He turns to the Nethinim.

"It is time?" Same-El asks, his voice shaking.

"Yes, brother. You two have the honor."

Ithamar's eyes widen; Same-El's shoulders shudder. Both look as if
they are about to buckle from fear.

But Eben knows better.

Opening the ark is an esteemed honor for the Keepers. The highest
honor.

Ithamar breaks all protocol and grabs Eben's hand and tugs it like a
child.

"Can it really be that we are so lucky?" Same-El asks.

"Yes, brother."

"We will see what Uncle Moses last saw?" Ithamar asks. "Touch what
he alone was allowed to touch?"

"If the ark allows, yes. But you know the risks, brothers."

Yes, the risks.

The Aksumites know all the tales and more. How the ark, if opened,
will smite even the most ardent of adherents mercilessly and without
fail. How it will unleash hellfire upon the Earth, and pestilence, and
untold death. How it will run rivers of blood and scorch the sky and
poison the very air, since opening it is not the will of the Makers.

The power inside is God's and God's alone.

Not anymore.

God be damned, Eben thinks.

"We are ready, Master," Same-El says.

"Good, my brother. When the Aksumite line survives the end of ends,
you will be remembered among our greatest heroes. Both of you." He
looks the men in the eyes, embraces them, kisses them, smiles with
them, and then helps them prepare.

The Nethinim untie and remove their bejeweled breastplates. Ithamar
hangs his on a peg and Eben takes Same-El's and pulls it over his

torso, a rectangle of 12 wooden blocks attached to one another with iron metal hoops, each set with a colorful and smooth oval stone, all of them different hues.

The Breastplate of Aaron.

Same-El ties it tight for Eben.

It—plus his faith—will be his only protection.

Ithamar pours holy water from a pitcher into a wooden bowl and kneels. Same-El kneels next to him. They take turns washing their hands and arms and faces, their dark, wet skin reflecting the pinkish light in swirling patterns. Eben's head is already spinning.

He envies these two men, even if they do end up being sacrificed.

No, *because* they will end up being sacrificed.

They remove their robes and hang them on the wall and stand, naked, anticipating what is to come.

Eben hugs and kisses each of them one last time. The two men face each other and slap their own thighs until they are red. When they are finished, they slap their stomachs and their chests. They grab each other by the shoulders and yell at each other the names of their fathers and their fathers' fathers and their fathers' fathers' fathers. They invoke Moses and Jesus and Mohammed and Buddha and ask for forgiveness.

Eben asks the same for both blessed men.

Finally, without looking at Eben, Same-El and Ithamar smile and turn toward the curtain. Holding hands, they go forward. Eben turns away and walks to the hatch and presses his knees into it and closes his eyes and covers his ears and waits.

It takes one minute and 16 seconds for the screaming to commence. It is not joyful or enlightened. It is terrifying. These are two strong men, some of the strongest in the entire line, and they are crying like babes being torn by wild beasts from their mothers' breasts.

Seventeen seconds later the air at Eben's back becomes hot, and he can hear the curtain whipping and snapping like an untethered sail in a tempest.

The screams continue, they are desperate, tearing, shrill, final.
Then the light comes, so bright the lids of his squinting eyes turn as orange as the sun, and Eben is slammed into the wall by a heavy wind and he cannot move. His nose is smashed against the wall, which heats up like a stovetop, and he smells his own flesh cooking and hears his own heart beating faster than it's ever beaten, like it's going to sing out of his chest, and he too is going to die.

And still the screams, weaving the horror together like a searing thread.

Then darkness, and the air sucks back like a vacuum and the curtain's metal rings clatter and clank and Eben, eyes still closed, tears freezing in air suddenly turned frigid, has to step back with one foot and then the other to steady himself. His robes pull toward the ark so hard that he thinks they will be torn from his body, or will spread out around him like fabric wings and fly him backward into the howling void.

A full three minutes and 49 seconds after it began, there is silence.
Stillness.

Eben peels his hands from his ears. They are clammy, his fingers stiff, as if he has been gripping something with all his might for hours upon hours. He tries to open his eyes, but they're crusted shut. He digs his fingers at them, wiping away crystals of ice and gobs of yellow, congealed tears.

He blinks. He can see.

He snaps his fingers. He can hear.

He stamps his feet. He can feel.

The pinkish light of the room is unchanged. He looks at the shiny wall, only centimeters from his face, striped with gold and silver. It is unchanged. He can see his splotchy, imperfect reflection there, just as before.

He breathes.

Breathes and breathes.

Holds his breath and turns.

The room is utterly undisturbed. The lamp hangs from the ceiling on its slender rod. The low gilt table, with the bowl and the pitcher, is on his right. The robes hang on the pegs on the wall. The jeweled breastplate from antiquity that Ithamar wore hangs there too.

The curtain is as before—straight and bright and clean.

"Same-El? Ithamar?" Eben asks.

No answer.

He steps forward.

He reaches the curtain.

He drags his fingertips across it.

He closes his eyes and pushes his hand through the parting and walks in.

He opens his eyes.

And there it is. The Ark of the Covenant, golden, two and one half cubits long, one and one half cubits high, one and one half cubits deep, the mercy seat lifted free and leaning against the wall, the cherubim on top facing each other in timeless reproach.

The only sign that Same-El and Ithamar ever existed are two fist-sized piles of gray ash on the floor, precisely two meters apart.

Eben stands on his tiptoes and tries to see past the leading edge of the ark and into the bottom.

But he cannot see.

He edges closer.

And there. Inside, a ceramic urn coiled in copper wire. A stone tablet without any markings. A wrinkle of black silk pushed into one corner. And in the middle of the ark two black cobras, looped over each other in a figure eight, sleek and vigorous, chasing and nibbling at each other's tails.

Eben reaches down and touches the edge of the ark. He is not smitten, not blinded, not driven mad.

He pushes his knees against it and leans forward and grabs a snake in each hand. As soon as his flesh touches theirs, they harden and straighten and transform into wooden rods, each a meter long, and each tipped with a metal snake head on one end and a golden spike on the other.

The Rod of Aaron.

The Rod of Moses.

He slips one under his sash.

He holds the other.

Eben kneels and reaches for the tablet and turns it over with a thump. It is blank on both sides.

Eben huffs and his heart feels hollow. This is the covenant with the Makers.

A blank stone tablet.

Curse them.

He doesn't dare open the urn, which is without doubt the manna machine. The Aksumites will guard it—having a machine that potentially makes food might come in handy after the Event, so long as they can figure out how to work it—but they don't need it yet.

All that's left is the crumpled pile of black silk.

Eben pushes the silk aside with the cane, and there—there it is.

He leans over and picks it up. Turns it over in his hand. Runs his fingers over it.

He shakes his head in disbelief.

Knock-knock.

Someone is at the hatch.

Eben spins and crosses the Kodesh Hakodashim. He opens the latch and lets the person on the other side push it inward.

Hilal pokes his disfigured head into the chamber. "Well, Master? I couldn't just sit there and wait."

"You won't believe it."

"Is it open?"

"Yes."

"Who?"

"Same-El and Ithamar."

"Did they survive?"

"No."

"God take them."

"Yes, my Player. God take them."

"And what was in it?"

"These," Eben says, indicating the snakelike rods. "They are living weapons. The rods of Aaron and Moses, the consuming snakes, the prime creators, the ouroboros. Our symbols of uncorruption, the hunters of Ea. Even if our line never finds the Corrupted One, the canes will serve you well in Endgame."

"And what else? What of the covenant?"

"There is no covenant, Player. The tablet was blank."

Hilal looks to the side. Through clenched teeth he asks, "Was there more, Master?"

"Yes, Player. And that is what you won't believe."

Eben holds it out and Hilal looks.

It is a slender sheath of black metal the size of a large smartphone, curved slightly and etched in one corner with a glyph.

Eben hands it to Hilal, and as soon as the Player of the 144th line touches it, it glows to life.

Hilal looks at Eben.

Eben looks at Hilal.

"To Endgame, my Player."

"To Endgame, Master."

Domini fati in textile temporis
fila ultima nostra texuere

AN LIU

Over the English Channel, heading 0° 12' 56"

Shiver.

He is free.

But exactly *where* he is free he does not know.

He inspects the instrument panel of the Lynx, locates the navigation system and the autopilot. Punches a few buttons on the touch screen and sees the English Channel. The lights to the north are Dover. He does not want to return to England, not ever, not ever *blinkSHIVERblink* ever *blinkSHIVER* ever *blinkblinkSHIVERBLINKBLINKBLINK* not ever. An punches himself in the cheek to knock away the tics.

It works. "Chiyoko Takeda," he whispers. "Chiyoko Takeda."

Blood drips from his nose.

Shiver.

He blows out his cheeks. The adrenaline from the escape dissipates. The pain soaked into every cubic centimeter of his head revs like an engine.

He grabs the stick and arcs the Lynx low over the water, until his heading is 202° 13' 35". He passes the still-burning destroyer three kilometers to the east, and prays that they don't see him and that their guns are disabled, or that they're too distracted by the burning ship to even bother with the guns.

And that's when he notices a section of the controls that he isn't familiar with, and realizes why the chopper was taking off dark, and why he is not at the moment being shot out of the air by a pair of F/A-18s.

It took off dark because it could.

The strange controls are a stealth array, and they are already active. An can use this bird to disappear.

Blink. Shiver.

Why would stealth be active in the first place? If he had been on the Lynx as their prisoner, that would have made sense—he is a Player of Endgame, one of the deadliest people on the planet—but it was scrambling to take off before he'd even reached the flight deck.

So *why* take off dark?

Blink. Shiver. Blink.

And then he lurches forward, as if someone hit him in the back of the neck.

The metal box in the cargo hold.

The metal box the size of a coffin.

CHIYOKO TAKEDA.

An brings the chopper up 50 meters to keep a safe distance from the water and activates the autopilot, punching in a new heading of 140° 22' 07".

He spins out of the copilot's seat and lands right in front of the box.

Shiver.

He takes a step forward and places his hands on it.

He doesn't have to open it to know.

He falls forward on top of the casket, his ear and jaw cold on the metal, his arms draped over the sides.

"Chiyoko Takeda."

The tics have stopped.

He stands, the internal world of the helicopter loud and pressing in on all sides, pain drilling the wound on his head, and he gets his fingers under the lid. It comes up more easily than he expects. He flips it away and peers inside. In the faint light he can just make out the wavy reflections of a rubber body bag. Next to the body bag is a small stuff sack.

An snatches a flashlight from a charging dock by the door and flicks it on.

The body bag looks as if it contains a broad-shouldered child.

An grabs the stuff sack first. Works his fingers into the cinched opening and pulls it open. A black analog watch, a leather sleeve containing assorted shuriken, a small knife, a ball of black silk, an eyeglasses case, some inch-long paper tubes that look like straws, a small plastic container. A thumb drive. A pen. A thin leather billfold. Chiyoko's things.

He closes the sack and sets it next to his feet.

The body bag.

He takes a breath and hooks the metal hoop of the zipper with his finger and slides it down 43 centimeters. The flashlight tumbles into the casket. It shines hard on the face of Chiyoko Takeda. One of her eyes is open and lifeless, dry, the pupil large and black. He touches it with his fingers and closes it. Her skin is pale and tinged blue. Purple capillaries crack over her right cheek in a fractal of jagged lines. Her lips are the color of the sea. They're parted slightly. An sees the dark within, and the thin line of her front incisors. Her hair, black and straight and unchanged, has been combed and pinned away from her face. He puts his hands on her cheeks. Runs his hands over her neck and her collarbones and over the balls of her shoulders, covered in a pale green cotton hospital gown.

An whimpers.

He collapses into the box and his face lands on hers and the moonlight streams through the windows of the darkened chopper churning south-southwest to Normandy and he is blinking back tears and he can see the black filigrees of his wet eyelashes like a shroud of lace that is draped over him, over her, over them.

He works his arms under the rubber bag and squeezes. Hugs her.

"Chiyoko," he says.

A beeping sound from the nav computer.

An kisses Chiyoko's blue lips, her eyes, the little saddle where her eyebrows and nose meet. He smells her hair—it smells alive, unlike the rest of her—and he pirouettes into the copilot's chair. He takes the stick and throttles back, looks out the port window past the pilot's slumped body.

There, 500 meters away, is France. The beach and land rising above it is dark, hardly populated. Not far away, he knows, is the town of Saint-Lô. And in Saint-Lô is a Shang resupply cache. The world is littered with them. He just happens to be near one.

He is lucky.

He brings the Lynx to a hover and punches a new course into the autopilot but doesn't activate it. He pulls on a life vest but will wait until he's in the water to inflate it. He grabs a dry bag. Throws in the stuff sack of Chiyoko's things, four MREs, the pilot's Browning Hi-Power Mark III, extra ammo, a field kit, a GPS, a headlamp. Takes the pilot's knife. Grabs another life vest and a coil of rope. Cuts a long section and ties one end to a loop on the dry bag. Ties the middle to the 2nd vest, which he inflates. Ties the remaining end to his waist. He doesn't seal the dry bag, not yet. He has to put some more things in it first.

He hits a red button with the side of his fist, and the starboard door slides open. Air, cool and fresh and salty, rushes in.

Before jumping into the water, he kneels over Chiyoko, grabs a fistful of her hair, and holds up the knife.

"I am sorry, my love. But I know you understand."

The tics are gone.

He brings the knife down and cuts. He starts with her hair.

iv

SARAH ALOPAY, JAGO TLALOC

London Underground Tunnel near Gloucester Road

They're running. Sarah is in the lead and Jago has made it a point of pride to catch her. He pushes himself, pumping his legs as fast they'll go, and he still can't touch the Cahokian.

No one has followed them.

Sarah's elbows swing and her shoulders sway as she clutches the rifle in her hands. The only light in the tunnel comes from the train signals, red and green at intervals, and the headlamp strapped to Sarah's forehead. It's on the weakest setting, only 22 lumens, a red filter over the white plastic.

The red halo of light bounces along the walls. Jago finds it strangely mesmerizing.

"SAS, you think?" Sarah yells over her shoulder, not even out of breath.

"*Sí.* Or MI6."

"Or both."

"Four at the door, two at the window, sniper support." Jago counts them off. "How many you think in the van out front? Or at HQ?"

"Three or four in a mobile unit. Twenty or thirty at ops."

"Probably a drone too."

"Probably. Which means—"

"They saw us come in here."

"Yep." Sarah skids to a halt. Water pools around the soles of her shoes. The tunnel forks. "Which way?"

Jago stops next to her, their shoulders touching. He memorized these tunnels as part of their escape plan. Went over it with Sarah back in the hotel. Maybe she wasn't listening. Maybe her mind was elsewhere, like it's been these last days.

"We talked about this, remember?" Jago says.

"Sorry."

"North goes to the High Street Kensington station, which is basically outdoors. South is a service bypass," he reminds her.

"Then south."

"*Quizás.* But these tunnels will be crawling with agents soon. It's only been"—he checks his watch—"four minutes and three seconds since we came underground. We might be able to make the station, get on the next train, and disappear."

"We'd have to split up."

"*Sí.* We'd meet at the rendezvous. You remember the rendezvous?"

"Yes, Feo."

They both know this is imperative. Renzo, who's unaware of this little hiccup, will be at the airstrip in the afternoon to pick them up. This was their plan. But now that Sarah and Jago have been made, they need to get out of the UK *ASAFP*. Every extra second they spend in the tunnels will be an extra second that the authorities can use to catch them.

Jago points to the rightmost tunnel. "If we go to the service bypass, it'll take us longer."

"Why?"

Jago sighs. He's disturbed by how much she's forgotten, or how much she didn't listen to in the first place. Players don't forget or miss things, especially things like escape routes.

"Because," he says, "we'd have to use the—"

A slight breeze cuts off Jago.

"Train," Sarah says casually.

Without another word, Sarah takes off into the north fork. Decision made. The wind picks up at her back, the tunnel begins to glow. She sees one of the cutouts used by workers to avoid moving trains. She dashes to it and slides in. It's big enough only for her, but directly opposite is another. Jago fits into it just as the cacophony of the approaching train fills their ears.

The vacuum riding the front car takes Sarah's breath and pulls her hair around her neck. Her eyes are level with those of the seated passengers on the Tube. Sarah picks out a few in the blur of glass and metal and light that passes less than a foot from her face. A dark-skinned woman with a red scarf, a sleeping elderly man with a bald spot, a young woman still dressed in last night's party clothes. Regular unsuspecting people.

The train is gone. Sarah gathers her hair together and remakes her ponytail.

"Let's go."

As they approach the station, the light in the tunnel brightens. She switches off her headlamp. The station comes into view. The train that just passed them pulls away from the platform. From their low angle they see the heads of a few people making for the exits.

They go to the short set of stairs that leads to the platform, being careful to stay in the shadows. Sarah raises her hand, points out the cameras closest to them, one of them hidden behind a grate.

"They're going to see us once we're on the platform."

"*Sí*. We wait here for the next one."

Jago unscrews the small bolt securing the scope to his rifle. He belly-crawls up the steps, as close to the platform as possible without appearing on camera, and peers through the scope.

Just the usual early morning scene. A few people waiting, swiping at smartphones, reading tabloids and books, staring at nothing. A businessman appears in the middle of the platform. Brimmed hat and dark shoes, a rolled newspaper tucked under his arm. He looks disappointed. He's just missed his train.

"Coast looks clear." Jago lowers the scope.

"We'll have to leave the rifles."

"You still got that pistol, though, right?"

"Yep."

Jago rescans the platform. A young mother holding the hand of a three-year-old. A blue-collar worker in a jumpsuit. The businessman, who's now reading his paper.

Jago squints, focuses the eyepiece.

The businessman is wearing what looks to be a very nice suit and black tactical boots.

"*Mierda.*"

"What is it?"

"Hand me your rifle."

Sarah does it without asking. Jago shoulders it, aims, pulls the secondary trigger that fires the undermounted dart gun.

The projectile puffs out of the chamber with a low whoosh and pop. The man is too far away and doesn't hear it. The overhead digital sign several feet past him announces that a new Edgware Road–bound train will arrive in one minute. The man steps back at the last split second, and the dart just misses his neck, clanking into an advertising panel.

The man drops his paper and sets his feet wide, looks left and right. Holds a hand to his ear and says something. Jago pulls back from the top of the steps.

"No good. Gotta go back."

"Someone see you?"

"Don't think so."

"Christ, Jago. You don't *think* so?"

Maybe he's getting sloppy too. Too much forgetting, too much Burger King, too much sex.

Sarah stands and looks, and there he is. Already 20 paces closer. The businessman sprinting, his hat fallen off, a pistol in his hand.

Jago brings the rifle up and without sighting pulls the secondary trigger again. Another dart. It hits the man in the cheek, just below his eye. He recoils and falls, slides along the concrete only 47 feet away. He comes to a stop. He rolls. Paws at his face, the bushy-tailed dart hanging out of it. He fights for consciousness, but it's no use. He passes out.

The young mother screams.

The Players turn and run. The light from the station recedes. Sarah flicks on her headlamp. She's several feet in front of Jago when they feel the air change, the light coming for them.

The Edgware Road train.

Sarah kicks it into high gear. She slams into the safety of one of the cutouts as the train comes into view, her shoulder crunching into the concrete wall.

But Jago's not there. He couldn't run as fast. He's only 13 feet away, but it might as well be a mile. He looks at her. She can see his eyes, wide and white.

Sarah screams, "Down!" as the train barrels by, cutting off her view of Jago.

The train's horn sounds. It doesn't slow. A loud smack and sparks and a small explosion. The rifle being impacted by the front of the train. All she hears after that is the machine churning in front of her, the movable storm of wind, the Doppler effect of the blaring horn.

Again, Sarah looks into the blurred interior passing just in front of her, this time through glassy eyes. And this time there are no people on it. None. Until the last car, which is full of men dressed in all black.

Men with lots and lots of weapons.

The train didn't slow because they saw him. They saw him and they wanted him dead.

The train finally brakes as it disappears around the corner and pulls into the station. She has maybe one minute to get to the other tunnel. She glances into the well between the tracks. Doesn't see any sign of him. Squints. Raises her eyes. There, in the darkness, a piece of cloth floating through the air and settling on the rail.

A piece of cloth that matches Jago's shirt.

She takes a step forward to see what else she might find, but freezes when she hears voices in the distance. Men, frantic and yelling.

No time.

She shakes with fear. No time to see what's left of Jago Tlaloc.

Fear.

She rubs her sleeve over her eyes and vaults onto the tracks and runs away.

Runs away from another death.

Another death of someone she loved.

AISLING KOPP

*JFK International Airport, Terminal 1 Immigration Hall, Room E-117,
Queens, New York, United States*

Aisling has been sitting in the room for one hour and three minutes.
No one has come to see her, no one has brought her water or a bag of
chips, no one has spoken to her over an intercom. The room is empty
except for a table and a chair and a steel ring in the floor and a bank
of fluorescent lights in the ceiling. The table and chair are both metal
with rounded edges and welded joints. Both are secured to plates that
are set in the concrete floor. The walls are blank, painted white with a
yellow tint. There are no pictures, no shelves, no vents. There isn't even
a two-way mirror.

But Aisling *is* being watched. There's no doubt about that. Somewhere
in this room are a camera and a microphone. Probably several.
Because there are no dangerous items in the room, the men who
brought her here didn't even handcuff her. They just put her in
the chair and left. She has not moved from the chair. She has been
meditating since the door closed and the bolts inside the door slid
into the locked position. Three of them. They were whisper quiet, but
she still heard them.

One, two, three.

Shut in. *This*, she thinks, *is worse than the Italian cave.*

She lets the things that come to her mind arrive and pass. Or tries
to, anyway. Just because she's a Player doesn't mean she's an expert
at everything. Shooting, fighting, tracking, climbing, surviving.
Solving puzzles. Languages. Those are what she's really good at.
Centering herself, opening her mind, all that *om om om* bullshit, not
so much.

Although all that shooting practice couldn't help her take down that fucking float plane when it mattered most.

When it might have saved the world.

Let it pass. Let it pass.

Breathe.

Let it pass.

She does. The images and feelings come and go. Memories. The rain lashing her face as she sits on the northeastern gargoyle's head on top of the Chrysler Building. The taste of wild mushrooms scavenged from the Hudson Valley. Her heaving lungs pushing out water when she nearly drowned in Lough Owel, Ireland. The creeping fear that she can't win, or doesn't deserve to win, or shouldn't win, the doubt that every Player who isn't a sociopath must confront. The bright blue of her father's eyes. The spooky voice of kepler 22b. The escape from the Great White Pyramid. The regret that her crossbow bolt didn't skewer the Olmec in the attic of the Big Wild Goose Pagoda. The anger over what the cave paintings showed her in Italy. The anger that the Players are being played by the keplers. The anger that it's not fair. The anger from knowing that Endgame is a bunch of bullshit. The anger.

Let it pass.

Let it pass.

Breathe.

The door whispers. One, two, three. The latch turns. Aisling doesn't open her eyes. Listens, smells, feels. Just one person. The door closes. Whispers. One, two, three.

Shut in.

A woman. She can tell by the smell of her soap.

Light-footed. Steady breathing. Maybe she meditates too.

The woman crosses the room and stops on the other side of the table. She introduces herself: "Operations Officer Bridget McCloskey." The woman's voice is raspy, like a lounge singer's. She sounds big. "That's my real name. Not some cover bullshit, *Deandra Belafonte Cooper* . . . Or should I say *Aisling Kopp*?"

Aisling's eyes shoot open. Their gazes lock. McCloskey is not what Aisling expects.

"So you admit your passport is a fake," McCloskey says.

"I don't know what you're talking about."

"I say *Aisling Kopp*, your eyes pop open. That's an admission in my book, a hundred times out of a hundred."

"What book is that? *Fifty Shades of Grey*? *Letters to Penthouse*?"

McCloskey shakes her head with a look of disappointment. She's in her early 40s. Like Aisling she has red hair, except that hers has a Bride of Frankenstein streak running from her forehead all the way through to the tip of her tight ponytail. She's leggy and stacked and flat-out hot, like a *Playboy* bunny just a few years past her prime. She has eyeglasses with teal frames and very little makeup. Her eyes are green. Her hands are veined and strong, the only giveaway that she's the real deal. She must have been stunning when she was Aisling's age.

"You'd be surprised how often I hear degrading shit like that," McCloskey says.

"Maybe you need a new line of work."

"Nah. I like my job. I like talking with people like you."

"People like me?"

"Terrorists."

Aisling doesn't flinch and doesn't speak. She understands that from a law-enforcement perspective any Player of Endgame could absolutely be considered a terrorist—but what does this woman know about Endgame?

"No more smart mouth? I'll remind you that you've been caught trying to cross the US border under an assumed name."

"Am I under arrest?"

"Arrest?" McCloskey chuckles. "How quaint. No, I'm not with the part of the government that arrests people, Miss Kopp. I'm with . . . *another* part of the government. A small and exclusive part. The one that deals with terrorists. Up close and personal like."

"Well, we have a problem, then, because I'm not a terrorist."

"Oh, dear! So you're telling me this is all one big misunderstanding?"

"Yes."

"So I'm wrong in believing you're a member of a very old sleeper cell that, once called to action, can and will do anything to achieve its goals? That's not you?"

"A sleeper cell, huh? Is this a joke?"

McCloskey shakes her head again. "No joke. Did you hear what happened in Xi'an? You have anything to do with that?"

The mention of the Chinese city causes Aisling's heart to quicken. A shiver runs down her neck. If she can't head off her body's hardwired threat response, then she might break out in a cold sweat. She can't break out in a cold sweat. Not in front of this woman, who already seems to know a bit too much.

"What, the meteor? Is my sleeper cell responsible for that? Lady, if I could control meteors, you can bet I wouldn't be sitting here."

If I could control meteors, Aisling thinks, *the Event would never come.*

"No. We'll get to the meteor soon enough. I'm talking about the dirty bomb that was set off at the residence of one An Liu a little over a week ago."

The name prickles Aisling's ears. Somehow this woman has pegged the Player who is probably Endgame's most dangerous and unpredictable. If Aisling could pick one Player to kill, it would be the Shang. Still, Aisling conceals her feelings as she wrinkles her brow and asks innocently, "Anne Liu? Who's she?"

"*He.* Another member of your sleeper cell."

Aisling's heart rate rockets up, not from nervousness, but from umbrage. It never occurred to Aisling that someone might consider all the Players to be members of the same group. The concept of the 12 separate lines has been so driven into each Player—*I am for my line, and the other lines are not for me*—that the idea that they're essentially the same is blasphemy.

Blasphemy!

And gross. To lump her in with the Shang. That twitchy freak.

"I don't know anyone named An Liu," she says calmly. "And I am not part of a Chinese sleeper cell."

McCloskey sits on the edge of the table and inspects her fingernails. Picks at a cuticle. "Maybe sleeper cell is the wrong term. You—and An Liu—prefer to call them 'lines.' That ring a bell, Aisling Kopp?"

"No," Aisling says too quickly, immediately regretting it.

"Uh-huh. How about this: اقب علل ةيامن!"

Aisling speaks passing Arabic and she knows what it means. She tenses. Pushes so hard with her back and legs against the chair that it creaks audibly.

"I thought so."

Aisling squints. "Whatever you think you know, you don't know anything."

"That's where you're wrong, Kopp. I know there are twelve ancient lines, and that yours is La Tène Celt. I know that An Liu has a line too, called Shang. I know the real names of no less than five more line members, and I know that since the meteors you have all been 'playing' against one another for some kind of prize. And you will continue to play, until the world ends. Which, I'm sorry to say, will be pretty soon."

"You're crazy."

"I wish I were, Kopp. But it's not just that I've read things—some of which were given to the agency by none other than your father, Declan, back when you weren't even out of diap—"

"My *father*? Are you serious? My father was a madman," Aisling blurts. All pretense is dropped now. No more pretending.

"I know that. He was such a madman that his own father, your grandfather, cut him down."

"Yeah. I know," Aisling whispers.

"Good. Thank you for your honesty."

A few moments of silence pass between them. McCloskey picks at her nails, Aisling fumes. She knows she should keep silent, wait this woman out, but . . .

"Why the *fuck* are you holding me?"

McCloskey slides off the edge of the table and places her hands on it, pressing into its cold surface. "I'm going to be honest with you, Kopp. Not because I've been ordered to be honest with you, which I have, but also because I want to be. I've seen a lot of shit in my lifetime. Much more than you can imagine—and I suspect you can imagine a lot. I know what you are, but you have no idea what I am, or the places I've been and things I've done. The people I've hurt. The ways in which I've hurt them. I've seen horrible things. Mystifying things. Things that aren't of this world—literally. I know you know what I'm talking about."

"You sound like my father. You sound crazy."

"Don't be obtuse, Kopp. We don't have time for it. The Event is coming. I know it and you know it. Those twelve meteors, the ones that woke your lines, your sleeper cells, they were just a prelude. Another is coming. And it will bring hell with it."

Aisling's eyes widen. Her thin lips part. This is too much for an outsider to know. "How do you know all this?"

"I told you. Your father gave us some material, and we have other sources too. We've even had a fair amount of contact with the Nabataean line, whose Player is a borderline sociopath named Maccabee Adlai. You know him?"

"Not really."

"Sick, handsome asshole. Dealing with the Nabataeans has been both elucidating and terrifying. The first time we crossed paths with them, we got so close to finding out about Endgame that they took out just about every case agent and operations officer in Jordan, plus a few hundred civilians, including children. Just to keep us in the dark."

"Endgame. So you *do* know."

"I don't know everything, but I know a lot. Most importantly—and depressingly, I might add—I know that there's a huge monster space rock bearing down on our planet, and it's a genie that we won't be able to keep in the bottle, no matter how hard we try."

"Do you know where it'll hit?" Aisling asks, feeling a little desperate to be asking this outsider questions.

"More or less." McCloskey huffs. "There's a team of pencil pushers at NASA that thinks they have it figured out. They just spotted it in the heavens a few days ago, and given our security clearances as well as our extraterrestrial interests, we found out about it quick."

"Where *will* it hit?"

"That's classified."

"Fuck your classified. Tell me."

"Can't. Not yet."

"When can you tell me?"

"After you make me a promise, Kopp."

"What's that?"

McCloskey takes a moment before answering. "You know, Kopp, I didn't want to have anything to do with you. I wanted to go a whole other direction."

"What direction was that?"

"That's also classified. I will say that it involved preventing our alien forebears from ever returning to Earth, though. But then those meteors hit and we knew it was too late and fuck me and all that, right?"

"You have no idea."

McCloskey manages to look sympathetic. "Maybe I don't. I know the kind of training you Players go through, and I've seen what some of you can do, and I'll be the first to say it's impressive. You're more highly trained and capable than any special forces soldier on Earth. And some of you are more ruthless. A truly terrifying group of individuals. Anyway, it's moot now. The game has started. The doomsday clock is ticking, and, to be totally honest, me and my associates are a little freaked out. We talked it over and after a long argument we decided to go with you."

"What the hell does that mean?"

"It means that if this cosmic bad joke really can be won, and if that the winner gets to guarantee the survival of her line members, then we need to make sure that *you* win."

Aisling finally gets it. She smiles. "Because you're La Tène too."

McCloskey puts a finger on her nose. "Bingo. Because we're La Tène too, just like nearly a quarter of all Americans, and about a fifth of Europeans to boot. You, Aisling Kopp, are *our* Player."

Aisling's heart races again. This is all too much. The fact that a government spook—a nobody in the realm of Endgame—knows all this is seriously unsettling.

It means the world is already changing, even before its end.

McCloskey leans forward. "Here's why you're here, Kopp: So I can offer you our help. However, just so you know, you don't really have a choice in the matter. We're tagging ourselves in. Our small team of very deadly, very capable, very connected, very tooled-up people are going to help you find the keys, kill whoever you have to, and win. All the way to the bloody, bloody end."

Aisling sits back. Recoils, actually. She very much wants to be out of this room and away from this woman.

"You could've just said that from the start," Aisling says.

"Nah. We wanted to meet you, get a measure of our star," McCloskey replies, grinning. "Aisling, baby, you crazy-terrifying La Tène Player, we're your number one fans."

MACCABEE ADLAI, EKATERINA ADLAI

Arendsweg 11, Basement Clean Room, Lichtenberg, Berlin, Germany

"It'll take a little time before it works perfectly," Ekaterina Adlai says in the nearly forgotten language of the Nabataean line. A flowing language, interspersed with phlegmy, Arabic-sounding clucks and monosyllables. A language both she and Maccabee are proud to speak. The room is bright and cool, and the faint hum of the HVAC vents can be heard overhead. The first movement of Bach's Double Violin Concerto in D Minor plays quietly over a Sonos sound system tucked in the corner.

Ekaterina is in full scrubs, a clear visor pulled over her face, a pair of surgical loupes flipped over her eyes. Machines whir and chime intermittently. Tubes, liquid, a bag of blood. She leans over a spread of blue sterile cloth, where the boy's arm rests, the skin caked in blood and iodine. Attached to the wrist is a black anodized mechanical hand, complete with fiber-optic wiring and titanium cabling and an ultrathin prototype lithium battery that is good for 10,000 hours. She's finished with the surgical tools that fused the warm flesh to the cold metal and has moved on to diagnostics with a voltmeter and soldering iron.

Maccabee is also in scrubs. He's been assisting Ekaterina.

She prods the fingers with the soldering iron, not to complete any circuits, but to give the fingers a pain stimulus to react to. She touches the pinkie, it twitches. The ring finger, it recoils. She touches the middle digit—a little thicker than a regular middle finger—and it flinches too, a small servo sound emanating from a gearbox in the hand's palm.

"And when it does work," she says, "it'll take your friend some getting used to."

"He's not my friend."

Ekaterina gives Maccabee a knowing look. Her eyes are gargantuan through the lenses of her loupes, all black pupils, like those of an owl on a cloudy night as they search the forest for the slightest movement. She has a beauty mark above her upper lip.

"I gathered as much. . . . The thing we discussed is in there."

She touches the soldering iron to the index finger, but it doesn't move at all. She holds the hot tip there for two seconds, three. Nothing. She places the iron in its cradle and turns to a computer terminal. Pounds away at the keys, rewriting code, reconnecting nerves to wires.

"I'll give you a fob to activate it," she says. "Only do it when you're ready, my dear. It's to your specifications, and I have to say, I don't understand them. A poison nodule or an explosive would be so much more . . . straightforward."

"Both of those could be detected, Ekaterina."

"By this little savage?"

"He is savvier than he lets on. It has to be this way."

She stops typing, grips the iron, returns it to the index finger. It yanks back quickly.

Ekaterina watches the new measurements scroll up the monitor: 3-0-7-0-0. She nods in satisfaction.

"Good work, Ekaterina. Excellent."

"Thank you." She touches the hot iron, all 418 degrees Celsius of it, to the thumb.

Flinch.

The palm.

Flinch.

The heel.

Flinch.

She puts down the iron and pulls off the visor and flips up the loupes. She snaps off her surgical gloves. She takes a folded square of gray cotton and dabs sweat from her face. She extinguishes a bright overhead lamp. She rubs her hands together, kneading out the strain of hours of concentrated work. "All the same, my dear, I wouldn't be too close to him when you activate this fail-safe."

"I won't. What's the range of the fob?"

Ekaterina crosses the room to a shelf, her stomach rumbling audibly. "Not more than seven meters." She opens a small box and takes something out of it. "I'm starved."

"Me too. I have a surprise for you."

Ekaterina spins, a smile on her face. "Yes?"

"I have the best table at Fischers Fritz." He smiles broadly, looks at his watch. "A car is coming for us in an hour."

Ekaterina—who is a little pudgier than she was when she was younger, and more earthbound—jumps several inches in the air, clapping an open hand onto her closed fist. "Fischers Fritz? How did you on such short notice? Do we have a line member there I don't know about?"

Maccabee rubs his index and middle fingers against his thumb. "No, Ekaterina. I got the table the old-fashioned way."

"Well . . ." she says, obviously overjoyed, already thinking of the food.

"Here's the fob." She drops a short metal tube into Maccabee's hand. He turns it over, flips open the top. A red button. "Click it three times quickly." She taps her foot on the floor to demonstrate the rhythm. "And that's it?"

"And that's it. There's no abort. No going back."

"Fine."

Ekaterina inspects the room, looking to see if she's forgotten anything. She hasn't. The machines whir and beep. Maccabee and Ekaterina hear Baitsakhan's steady and regulated breath.

"Fischers Fritz," she says dreamily. "A wonderful surprise."

Maccabee beams. He rests his hand on her shoulder. Squeezes. "Yes, Ekaterina. Just you and me and a bottle of 1928 Krug. A meal fit for the end."

FROM: wm.s.wallace58@gmail.com
TO: lookslikecandy@gmail.com
SUBJECT: Hi—PLEASE READ NOW!
PRIORITY: URGENT

Hey Cass,

It's Will. Obviously. How are you? How're Petey and Gwen and that little mutt Crabapple? Did Joachim finally get that gig at the hospital?

Anyway, I'm writing from my never-used Gmail account because what I'm about to tell you can't come from my NASA address. It's classified. Really, really classified. But it's EXTREMELY EXTREMELY EXTREMELY important. I don't mean to be an alarmist, but it's mortal, even. For you and the kids and, well, everyone near you. Not even near you—it's mortal for everyone who lives within a hundred miles of the Atlantic Ocean. It might be mortal for every single living thing on Earth.

As you know, for the last five years I've been working in the NEO program, on a team that scours the sky for any and all rocks that come within 1.3 AUs of the sun. Most people would find the work boring, but you know me—I love my job. Numbers and the call of space have always been my thing. Always.

At least, until now.

We've discovered something huge, Cass. Something we literally didn't see coming. It's so close, and it just appeared, as if it popped out of a wormhole or got folded out of some crease in the space-time continuum. Really, it is so, so close. It's a monster, and we should have seen it years ago, and if we had, we would have been able to plan and redirect it. But now, there's probably nothing for it. The government's trying to figure out what to do, but they're scrambling—and VERY scared. The scientists at JPL are at a loss. No model they create is sufficient to stop or nudge this thing. The appearance of it—it's been nicknamed Abaddon, which is Hebrew and loosely means "the Destroyer"—has been such a blow that it's caused many of us to question science on its most fundamental and foundational terms. A lot of the others have just

113

stopped coming into the office.

Seriously, Cass—if the calculations are right, it will impact Earth in the next 82 to 91 days. Right now I can say with 95% certainty that it will impact in the northern hemisphere, probably in the central Atlantic, maybe a shade closer to the U.S. than Europe. I can't begin to convey the destruction this thing will cause. It would be like piling up the world's entire nuclear arsenal, multiplying it by 10, and lighting a fuse—and the explosion would happen in a matter of seconds. It will be the end of . . .

It will be the end of everything, Cass. Everything.

You need to plan and prepare. Sooner than later this info will either leak or be released and, once it is, the world will change. I can't predict what will happen, but staying in Brookline is not an option. You need to get in the car—or better yet, rent a giant RV, fill it with food and, I hate to say this, guns—and meet me and Sally in the middle of the country. We can come up with where exactly over the next few days, but I was thinking somewhere remote, and near the Canadian border (there are going to be far too many armed nutsos in this country once this thing plays out). Maybe Montana, or North Dakota.

Please take this seriously. I am of sound mind. Start to prepare now, before the world at large is scrambling and fearful. Abaddon is coming, and it will end the world as we know it.

Call me, and we can talk.

Call me.

XXOOXXOOXXOO, your big bro, Will.

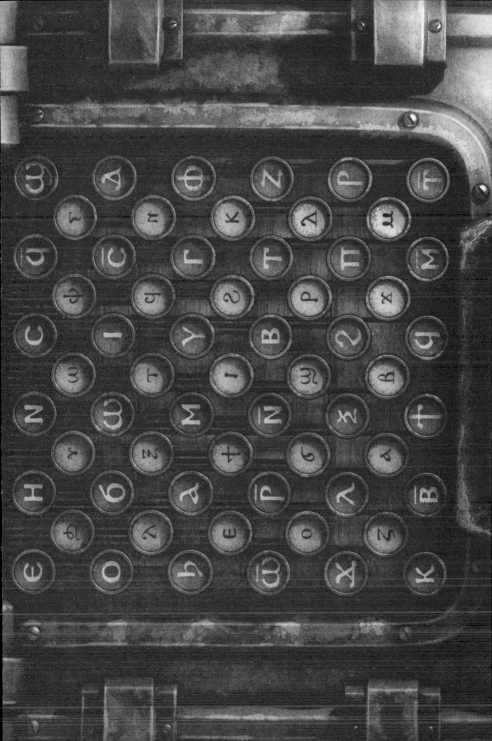

SARAH ALOPAY

London Underground Tunnel near High Street Kensington Station

Sarah runs as fast as she can. She runs and she doesn't think about his death.

Another death.

Jago's.

Was he there? Did he really die? Yes. Yes, he must have.

Yes.

And if he didn't, then the soldiers will have finished him by now.

Another death.

She runs, reaches the fork in the tracks, takes the southern one, the one Jago said led to the service tunnel.

Jago who is gone.

Jago who she loves.

Who she *loved*.

Past tense. Like Christopher before him.

She runs, her feet splashing in puddles, the ribbons of steel reflecting the weak light of her headlamp. She runs. Small details come to her in the form of Jago's voice. Details she didn't pay attention to when he was saying them in the hotel room, but that her trained mind stored away reflexively, automatically.

There is a door. A sewer access point. We can go down it, into a cistern. We'll head through the northern flow for a click until we reach a ladder labeled "Norland Transfer and Electrical." Up and out. We'll steal a car. Sarah, are you listening?

Yes.

Okay. We'll steal a car and drive north. Avoid the highways. We'll meet

Renzo at an old airstrip. RAF Folkingham in Lincolnshire. Say it.
RAF Folkingham in Lincolnshire.

"RAF Folkingham in Lincolnshire," she says as she comes upon the door to the sewer. It's chained shut. She blasts the lock off the door with her FN F2000, the clattering report echoing through the tunnels. That certainly gave away her position. The men are coming. She hasn't seen or heard them yet, but she knows.

Sarah plows through the door to the southeast, descends a set of iron rungs into a low passageway with rank, ankle-deep water. She moves as quickly as she can northeast to the cistern. When she reaches it, she takes a guess and picks a tunnel labeled E15OUTFLOW, hoping the *E* stands for *east*. Before leaving the cistern she tears a piece of cloth from her shirt and snags it on an exposed tip of rebar on the tunnel labeled W46INFLOW. Maybe that will send some of the men chasing her down a blind alley. Just as she leaves the cistern, a large explosion comes from above. A few bits of loose concrete and dust fall from the ceiling.

What happened up there? She doesn't have time to find out. She has to keep moving. Could it have been Jago?

No. It can't be. Hope is too dangerous a thing in this moment. It could slow her, it could cost her the game, her life.

Earth Key!

She pats her pocket. It's still there. Thank the gods, it's still there. After a kilometer of treading through the snaking tube, water flowing in from spillways at waist and shoulder level, she reaches a circular room. Rungs go up. The words NRLND XFER AND ELEC are stenciled on the concrete above a large "7" in red paint. She slings the rifle over her shoulder and, before taking the rungs, cups both hands over her ears and listens. She can hear faint splashing from the direction she came from. Feet.

Again she wonders: Jago?

Or a team of executioners? How many could she kill before they subdued her? Is that what she wants? A brief revenge followed by death?

Or could it be Jago?

No. It can't be. *You can't hope. Hope is a killer. It is death.*

Move.

She moves.

Up, up, up.

She pushes her shoulder into a manhole lid, places her hands on the side of the tube, bunches her strong legs on one of the higher rungs. She pushes with her thighs and knees and lifts the iron disk, gets her fingers around its edge, carefully now, carefully, and works it to the side. It scrapes along the floor. She emerges into a small, dark room. Cold, damp. She listens again for the feet and hears nothing. Perhaps she was hearing things. Yes, that's it. She was hearing things. Hope can do that. She crouches and quietly slides the manhole lid back into place. She looks around. A workbench, a collection of tools, a paper map of the sewer taped to the wall. Two pegs with canvas jumpsuits hanging on them, hard hats.

A door.

She stashes the rifle behind a trio of shovels and pulls down one of the jumpsuits. It's too baggy, but she doesn't care. She pulls it on over her clothes, ties her hair in a bun, and sticks a pencil from the worktable through it to hold it in place. She rolls the cuffs of the pants. She breathes. Faces the door. Breathes.

And that's when she realizes she's crying.

She touches her cheeks, her eyes.

She's *been* crying, for how long she doesn't know.

She slaps herself.

Again.

"Get it together, Sarah. Get it together."

Again.

"RAF Folkingham in Lincolnshire. RAF Folkingham. You're going to steal a car, drive north, stop for a road map"—she can't risk using her smartphone, or any phone for that matter—"and meet Renzo. You're going to leave England. RAF Folkingham in Lincolnshire."

She wipes her eyes, blows out her cheeks, and tries the door. It's unlocked. She cracks it open and peeks outside. No men waiting for her, no antiterrorism units, no APCs, no SAS kill teams.

She steps outside.

Breathes.

She walks briskly, but not too briskly, along a pleasant and quiet residential street. Goes two blocks, doesn't see another person. There are sycamores on one side at regular intervals, the gray bark peeling in irregular chunks that look like the outlines of countries or lakes. Birds chirp overhead. She hears a siren on a far-off street, hears BBC news from an open window. She turns a corner. Walks another block, passes a woman dragging a puffy Pomeranian, its tongue hanging out of its black-lipped mouth, the woman encouraging: "Come along, Gracie. Come along."

The woman barely looks at Sarah.

On the 4th block Sarah tries the handle of every car she passes.

The 6th opens.

It is a Fiat Panda, bland and inconspicuous, a two-door hatchback with a dent in the hood. A perfect getaway car. She gets in and has it running in 18 seconds. Not as fast as Jago hot-wired the car back in China, but respectable.

Jago.

Jago who is gone.

Or is he?

Were those his footsteps?

No, they couldn't have been his. He wasn't as fast as her. He's dead.

But maybe he isn't?

She shakes her head. This kind of thinking will slow her down and get her killed.

Why is she acting like this? Why didn't she look for his body? She abandoned him so quickly.

Too quickly.

She is abandoning lots of things, lots of people too quickly. Tate,

Reena, her mother and father, Christopher, Jago.

Herself. The Sarah she knew. The Sarah she loved.

All in the name of Endgame.

What is happening to her? To her heart?

Shut up. Get it together. Don't hope. Move.

She leans across the car, opens the glove compartment. Pulls out a crumpled baseball cap and a pair of cheap sunglasses. Stuffs her hair into the cap as she pulls it on. Slides the sunglasses on too, realizes that the sky is white, covered by a carpet of clouds, and yanks the glasses off.

As she puts the car in gear, she catches her reflection in the mirror. She is still crying.

Don't fall apart, Sarah. Drive. Don't fall.

She ignores the broken-looking girl in the rearview mirror and pulls out of the tight parking spot and goes. She just goes. After two hours and 23 minutes of driving five miles above the speed limit, she's on the A15, passing out of Bourne, Lincolnshire.

She's almost there.

The car buzzes past an elderly cyclist on the narrow country road. He wears a tweed sport jacket and wellies; there's an umbrella in the basket, a green woolen newsboy cap on his head.

The sky is still gray, but it hasn't rained.

She grips the wheel with both hands, wringing it, her knuckles white. She's almost there.

RAF Folkingham.

She's been crying intermittently throughout the drive. The whole time it's been as if it's one person crying and another person driving. Is that Sarah Alopay sobbing behind the wheel? Or is that Sarah Alopay gripping the wheel, coldly turning her back on the trail of death behind her? The two Sarahs, they don't like each other; they disgust each other.

She has enough sense to realize that something has happened to her. Something messed up. Maybe something profound. Did she hit her head in the fight with the commandos? No. It doesn't hurt at all. Has she been like this since Christopher, since she got Earth Key? Maybe, but this is more intense.

She tells herself that she's just Playing. That's all. She's empty inside and she's just Playing, and now Jago isn't there to help her.

But there's something else that's wrong. It's not just her head. Her chest is tight, and her throat feels dry and rough, and her jaw hurts. She pulls to the side of the road and cuts the engine and looks in the mirror again.

She is screaming.

At the top of her lungs, screaming.

She brings both hands to her face and rubs rubs rubs. Jams a fist into her open mouth.

The screaming stops.

GET IT TOGETHER.

She runs her hands over her thighs and breathes. Her heart races as fast as it does after a long hard run, 127 bpm, which is too high, way too high. Over the next couple minutes she works it down to 116, 107, 98, 91, 84.

When she gets it below 78, she does every centering meditation trick she can think of.

"Okay," she whispers. "Jago is dead and I'm on my own. I have Earth Key and I can win. Renzo will get me out of here, and if he doesn't want to, then I'll make him. I can win. Even if I *have* triggered the Event, I can win. I'm going to go home, see my family, tell Christopher's parents that he's dead, and Play on. I can win. I can win. I can win."

She thinks of Christopher. Not as she last saw him, his torso gone, his legs toppled over on the green grass of Stonehenge. She thinks of him after football practice back in Omaha, in a sleeveless T-shirt, glowing with sweat, the bright golden hairs on his forearms shining in the late afternoon sun. Smiling, walking toward Sarah as she smiles back.

"I'm *going* to win. Because what else is there?"

She listens to her heart—59 bpm. Good. She turns the ignition, puts the car in gear, and goes.

Six minutes later she pulls off the A15, swinging onto an unnamed, sporadically paved road surrounded by fields. Wheat, alfalfa, barley, potatoes—lots of potatoes. She recognizes them all instinctively. She is the Cahokian, after all, and has spent more time in the American High Plains than all the other Players put together.

After a mile the road simply ends at the edge of a field that's carpeted in bright green clover. She pulls the car under the boughs of a weeping willow, hiding it from prying eyes. She peels off the jumpsuit and double-checks that she has Earth Key, which is becoming a nervous habit. She slides the magazine from the plastic-and-ceramic pistol, inspects it. She smacks it back in and makes sure the safety is on before sticking it in the front of her waistband. She lets her hair back down and pulls it into a ponytail. The air is sweet. It smells of soil and water and peat. Some honeysuckle. An undercurrent of manure.

It's good to be outdoors, in the country.

It calms her down.

She cuts across the clover field, the ankle-high grass grabbing at her pant cuffs. The old airstrip should be right ahead.

You can't miss it, Jago said.

Fifty paces later she realizes that he was right.

She sees an old military truck of some kind, rusted out, the paint long since peeled away, its insides black and mysterious. It's almost completely overgrown with vines and tall grass. Decades of exposure have turned it green and gray and brown. It's being reclaimed by the land, one season at a time, and is perfectly camouflaged. Soon the land—burned, irradiated and toxic—will reclaim everything.

As Sarah gets closer, she sees more ghost machines: motorcycles, amphibious assault vehicles like those used on D-day, trailers, tractors. Wings of World War II-era planes, tail sections, giant tires, all manner of discarded metal in every shape and size. The clover field ends and, as if out of nowhere, is replaced with concrete, right in the middle of the field, cracked and patchwork since it's also succumbing to the ravages of wind, dirt, rain, and determined plant life.

Life really is remarkable, Sarah thinks. *It will continue. Come what may, it will find a way to continue.*

And I will too.

Sarah vaults over the front of a derelict tractor. She stands on a rough ribbon of tarmac that extends to her left and right, all the vehicles pushed to the margin. It's not very long—the northern half appears to be completely overgrown—but it's still a few thousand feet, which is enough runway for a turbo prop or even a small jet. She looks for some sign of Renzo or a plane that can actually fly and doesn't see any.

But he has to be here, she thinks. *He has to.*

She moves to the center of the runway and kneels. Runs her fingers over the ground. She finds the black smears of fresh tire tracks going in both directions. There *is* a plane. It landed in the last 12 hours, by the look of the tread marks.

She pulls the gun from her waistband and flicks off the safety and stalks north, keeping close to the vacant machinery on her right.

A breeze kicks over the fields, the trees whisper, and some movement catches Sarah's eye. A tarp billowing behind the skeletal remains of a large truck lying across the northern end of the runway.

A new tarp, covered in a modern camo pattern.

"Renzo!" Sarah calls out.

Nothing. Just the sounds of the countryside.

"Come on! I know you're here!" she yells.

Nothing.

"I've had a long morning," she says at a normal volume, continuing north, the pistol at the ready position.

"You and me both," a voice says, much closer than she expects.

She spins to the sound but no one is there. Just another rotted truck and grass and vines and a line of trees in the background.

"Where are you?"

"Here," Renzo says, his voice coming from her right, which is impossible, since that's just the open space of the runway. "What, you can't see me?"

"No," Sarah says, ashamed, remembering that Renzo is an ex-Player.

"Show yourself."

"Where's Jago?"

"He—"

"Don't tell me he didn't make it. You tell me that and we have a major problem."

"He didn't make it."

"I should kill you, *puta*," he says, now his voice coming from *behind* Sarah.

She wheels, but sees no one.

A ventriloquist.

A rustle, she spins again, and Renzo *is* there, only 10 feet away near the rotted truck, holding a simple, old-school sawed-off pistol-grip shotgun. He looks the same as he did in Iraq—squat and sturdy and sure of himself—minus the jovial glint in his eye. Today he is all business. His cheeks are ruddy. His brown eyes squinting.

Sarah begins to raise her gun—the same one Renzo gave her back in Mosul, the same one that killed Christopher—as Renzo brandishes the shotgun and yells, "Don't even think of it!"

Her arms freeze. She keeps the pistol at the ready position. Without sighting down the barrel she can tell that, if neither of them moves, she could shoot his right foot off instantly.

Of course, he could blow her entire chest away in the same instant, so Renzo has the advantage.

Also, he has the plane.

In a cool, serious voice, Renzo says, "If you level that on me, I *will* shoot. No more talking. We'll both be dead and that'll be that."

"Okay." She doesn't raise the gun.

"You look like hell." She knows it's true.

"Like I said, long morning."

"Where's Jago, Cahokian? And don't give me that he didn't make it crap."

"But he didn't. If it makes you feel any better, I've been pretty torn up about it."

"That doesn't make me feel any better. Tell me how."

She does. She even mentions the explosion she heard in the cistern, but not the faint sound of footfalls in the sewer. She's not sure they were really there. And she can't let Renzo know that she's on the precipice of a complete mental breakdown.

Which is why she also doesn't mention the screaming episode in the car, or the crying, or that she is just holding on, and that maybe a small part of her is considering raising that gun and being done with all of it.

When she's finished, Renzo asks, "So this train passed and you didn't go back to check on him?"

"He wasn't there, Renzo. I looked. I saw a piece of his shirt. He was probably pasted to the front car. There were thirty men coming for me. Thirty killers."

"You're a killer too."

"Yes."

"But you didn't kill Jago?"

"What? No!"

Her gut twists. Her left eye flutters. *Did* she kill him? She killed Christopher. Willingly. Did she somehow kill Jago too?

No. She couldn't have.

Her gun begins to shake. The breeze picks up. She is going to lose it. She is going to lose it. She is going to lose it again.

"What is it, Cahokian? What are you afraid of?"

"Nothing. I told you, I'm pretty torn up. I love Jago. *Loved* Jago. He was . . . he was the only one I'd ever met like me. Who knew *all* of me."

"Love." Renzo makes a sucking sound through his teeth. "I warned him about that."

"I don't think he paid attention."

"No shit. And because of that, now he's dead. Or so you say."

"He's dead," she confirms quietly.

Sarah can see Renzo's wheels turning. "All right. So your play is to come here and get me to fly you away, that it?"

"That's what I was hoping, yes. England is too hot right now. I need to go home. To see my line."

"And then what, you just bid me farewell when we land? Good luck to the end and all that?"

"I don't know what I could give you that you don't already have, Renzo. I can get you money, if that's what you want."

"Don't insult me. I want to live. I want my line to survive, same as you. I want my Player to win."

"I'm sorry," she says, using every effort to conceal the fear growing in her chest.

He's right to ask: What am I afraid of?

"You have Earth Key?"

"Yes."

"So let me get this straight. You're probably being placed on any number of international wanted lists as we speak—FBI, MI6, Mossad, CIA, Interpol—and you're going to take Earth Key *home*? You're made, Cahokian! They came for you in London—what makes you think they won't come for you in America too?"

"I have to go home, Renzo. Before I keep Playing, I have to."

"Sentimental bullshit."

"What?"

The wheels turn some more. "Listen, and listen carefully. Fuck you. I am not taking you anywhere. For all I know, you killed Jago to have him out of the way. For all I know, Jago is still alive, maybe captured, and I need to help him. For all I know, you took Earth Key from *him*."

She doesn't know what to say to this. She wishes that she hadn't been the first Player to possess Earth Key and trigger the Event—more than anything she wishes it. Even more than she wishes that she hadn't shot Christopher. After eight seconds she says, "I'm telling you the truth, Renzo, on the honor of my line, and all its Players, all my ancestors, on the history before history. I didn't take it from him. I was carrying it—

am carrying it—but we . . . we were sharing it."

Renzo shuffles forward a half step, as if he's having trouble hearing Sarah. "You were sharing it." A statement.

"Yes."

"Why would you do *that*? *How* can you do that?"

"You know we were Playing together. We were going to find the other keys together, and try to . . ."

Renzo is so floored by what Sarah is saying that he relaxes his grip on the stock of the short-barreled shotgun. "Are you telling me that you decided to try to win . . . *together*?"

Sarah nods. "Yes."

"*¡Me cago en tu puta madre!*" Renzo yells. This blasphemy is too much. He takes another half step forward, absently lowering the shotgun two inches . . .

All she needs is this moment of inattention. She pivots like a dancer. He snaps to attention, raising the gun again and firing. A loud bang, a small cloud of blue smoke, the razor-like clinks of shot bouncing off the metal detritus on the opposite side of the old runway.

Renzo missed.

Before he can fire again, she is next to him. Her left elbow cracks into his shoulder blade with a pop. He lurches forward, releasing the stock of the shotgun. Sarah pivots again and is behind him. She jams the muzzle of the pistol into his lower back and feels the spinal ligaments crunch.

Renzo moans. He tries to step away from her, but Sarah is too quick. She thrusts her left foot forward and sweeps his feet out from under him, the gun in the middle of his back pushing him down. He puts his hands forward, the right hand still gripping the shotgun. The knuckles of this hand drive into the ground, the gun splaying out at an angle away from his body. He manages to prevent his face from smashing into the concrete, but only by a couple of inches.

He pushes up, but again Sarah is too quick. She drops to her knees and straddles him. She slams the back of his head with her forearm, and now his face does find the ground. His nose breaks in two places, the blood begins to flow, and that sneezy nasal sting invades his sinuses. His eyes fill with tears.

Sarah acrobatically twists her right leg forward, relieving Renzo of his gun, breaking his pinkie in the process. The weapon spins over the ground, stopping 11 feet away.

Renzo ignores the pain coursing through his body and again tries to get up. If he gives her any more openings, he's done for. He feels her ease up with the pistol, feels her weight shift. He will flip over and grab her. He may not be as fast as she is, but he is stronger, and they both know it. All he needs to do is get his hands on her.

He turns quickly, and Sarah topples over. He lunges forward with his arms, and her legs dance out at odd angles. His fingers close as they grab for her shirt, but they come up empty. He catches a glimpse of the pistol. He reaches for her again with his left arm, sees the concentration and the fury on her face. Her left leg bends over his chest, something hard smacks the crown of his head, her hands are behind him pulling at her ankle, and before he knows it she's locked him up in a figure four. His right arm is pinned uselessly beneath him, his left arm sticks straight up next to his ear, his neck and chest constricting, his eyes watering even more. She's under him, her shoulder blades and head on the ground, her butt rising, all of her muscles holding and squeezing. He tries to slip out of it, flails with his legs to throw her off, but it's pointless. She squeezes, squeezes, squeezes.

"It doesn't have to go down like this, Renzo," she says, her voice betraying no effort on her part.

She is a Player, after all.

And Renzo isn't. Not anymore. That much is obvious. To both of them. Renzo tries to say, "Yeah it does. You broke my nose and my hand and maybe killed my Player. It definitely has to go down this way," but all that comes out is, "Yeshoes. Brkmyple. Isway."

She squeezes, squeezes, squeezes. Renzo is passing out.

"I'll let you go if you agree to tell me the plane's start-up sequence."

"Fumptoo." He sticks up the middle finger of his left hand.

"Fine. I'll figure it out on my own."

Squeezes, squeezes, squeezes.

She is so good, so efficient, so capable when she doesn't think or succumb to her emotions. And this is when she realizes just what it is that she is afraid of.

I am afraid of myself.

I am afraid of what I am.

But not so afraid that she stops squeezing.

And she would keep squeezing Renzo, push him past sleep and into death, if not for the fact that, just after his sturdy body goes limp, a figure jumps through the trees and surprises her.

A figure saying, "Sarah, what the hell are you doing?"

Jago Tlaloc, the Olmec.

DOATNet/Decrypted Message/JC8493vhee938CCCXx
FROM: TYLER HINMAN
TO: Doreen Sheridan

D—Just got this from S and wanted to share it with a trusted colleague. This is powerful information and potentially dangerous in the wrong hands. Take good care of it.

<<<<<<<<<<<<<<<<<<<<<<<<<<<<<<<<<<<<

Now that Endgame is coming, I feel compelled to reveal more about the Corruptor-in-Chief. This is the unvarnished truth about Ea.

He is the devil on our shoulder. The violence in our blood. The hate in the pit of our stomach. He IS the corruption. And he came from Out There.

As you know, for far too long he pretended to be my father.

But he is a *monster*.

He came here over 10,000 years ago as an alien, a Maker. He acted as an envoy to the people of Mu. His job was to create the technological and societal foundation that would allow humans to advance to the point that they could serve the Makers forever. In the process, he became something like a demi-god to the Mu. The advancements he taught them were nothing short of magic. He brought them *miracles*. And eventually, the high council of the Mu—the Brotherhood of the Snake—became his acolytes and his fierce protectors.

But to the Makers Ea was expendable, a young volatile brute who had a lot to learn. They hoped that this mission would help straighten him out. Instead, Ea became far too invested in his role as savior, began to believe the lies he fed to the humans, and worst of all, to show insubordination to his superiors.

The Makers decided that Ea should not be saved, and that the Mu needed to be destroyed and its remnants cast to the ends of the Earth. This would implant once and for all the ancestral trauma—the *fear*— that would fester and rot at the heart of humanity, providing the soil in which Corruption could take root and metastasize over the course of thousands of years.

So they brought down a great cataclysm, a tectonic fury of lava and boiling water that submerged the continent of Mu, and left only a few to drift away across the oceans to find their fate. Ea was dead, and his followers mourned.

But Ea's hubris had unwittingly provided a way back for him. Using what he had taught them, that ancient order of the Brotherhood revived him and fused his alien essence to a male human that was sacrificed for this purpose. From that moment forward Ea was outwardly human but inwardly alien. For reasons I still don't understand, his flesh became immortal, and he's existed in this form ever since.

The visitors came back over the ensuing centuries to look in on their other human creations, the original members of the 12 lines. They enslaved many other people, and harvested more gold, and further proclaimed and solidified their godlike status over prehistoric and Neolithic humans. All the while, Ea kept himself hidden, quietly building his power, and cursing those that left him to die on this pathetic planet.

Yet as much as he hated his brothers and sisters, he hated humans even more. He found them petty and small-minded and gullible and tribal and violent. He despised them, and despised even more that he was fated to live among them. He harnessed their fear, their naiveté, and their willingness to commit the most savage violence against one another. He made them his subjects. He taught people that they were nothing, and that salvation could only be found outside themselves, and that things that were different were things that were to be feared and destroyed.

He taught them corruption. And through his teachings he became powerful, and rich, and influential. His resources were, and still are, unlimited. His mind, although poisoned, is honed to the sharpest of points. He IS evil.

Throughout the course of human history Ea has emerged as

consigliore to many prominent people, urging them to ever more sadistic conquests. He was whispering in the ear of people like Pharaoh Thutmose III, Emperor Caracalla, Hugh Capet, Tomás de Torquemada, Adam Weishaupt, and Josef Mengele[v]. He has been at least partially responsible for every single war, religious or otherwise, every genocide, every mass atrocity in the history of humankind.

Every single one.

Yet in spite of his meddling in human development, what Ea has really been waiting for is the beginning of the promised Judgment Day known to the lines, and now to us, as Endgame.

His goal is simple and terrifying. Let Endgame play out, killing as many humans as possible, and then do everything in his power to prevent his brothers and sisters from ever returning to our solar system. He wants nothing less than to have this planet—our planet—to himself. So that he can breed a world solely beholden to him, an eternal, savage playground.

Even though we share Ea's desire to see the Makers vanquished from our corner of the universe, we also cannot let Ea succeed in making his ancient, twisted vision come true. We must stop him. We must find a way. WE MUST.

Yours in Truth,

S.

>>>

ALICE ULAPALA

Lufthansa Flight 341, Initial Descent
Depart: Kuala Lumpur
Arrive: Berlin

Alice wakes from another vivid dream. This one of a forest on fire, all
the animals running out of the billowing smoke to safety.

Running to the open arms of the girl, Little Alice Chopra.

Little Alice was smiling, happy, welcoming—not scared as she has
been in so many of Alice's other dreams. She glowed in beams of gold
and silver, her radiance so powerful that it kept the tongues of flame at
bay as the animals darted into her protective aura.

Glowing.

Like a bright and sunny day.

Like the midday sky.

And Alice understands.

She smacks her forehead. "I'll be snookered," she says, turning to the
man next to her. "Little Alice *is* Sky Key!"

The man—mid-20s, bulky headphones around his neck, baggy pants,
Oakley sunglasses over his eyes, and a noxious breath courtesy of too
many whiskeys during the flight—looks at Alice, who has not uttered a
single word to him otherwise. "Y'don't say."

"Yeah! Those kepler bastards have pulled a little girl into the mix. Can
you believe it?"

The man hiccups, turns in his seat so he can size up Alice. "Y'know,
you look pretty strong."

"Damn right I am. Fit as a mallee bull. You don't know half of it."

The man chuckles. "No doubt." He adjusts his sunglasses and leans
into the corner of his seat. "What'd you say before? A kepler? The hell
is that?"

"A bastard, that's what. Tall and skinny and blue-skinned, like a goddamned Smurf."

"Smurfs are short."

"Yeah well, these ones are tall. Think they run the bloody universe."

"Do they?"

God, I love drunkards, Alice thinks. *Talk about anything. Take it all at face value. Smurfs, for Chrissakes!*

"Yeah, they kinda do run the bloody universe. Still, to hell with them. *A little girl!* And Shari's, to boot."

"So you're going to see one of these kepler guys in Berlin?"

"Me? Nah. They're cowards. At least that's my opinion. They wouldn't be caught dead just walking around on this planet. Not yet anyway."

"Oh, so they're aliens."

"Yeah," Alice says, as if this man is an imbecile. "But I'm in Berlin to see someone else. A boy. He's a lot of things, but not a coward. Little Ned Kelly–type shit."

The man has no idea who Ned Kelly is, but lets it slide. "So this guy's like, what, a boyfriend?"

"Hell, mate. You trying to make me laugh?" A PA announcement interrupts them. The woman says they'll be on the ground in 20 minutes. "Gonna piss."

"Go for it."

Alice makes for the business-class lavatory. As she walks, she becomes more and more aware of the acute signal pinging in her head, marking Baitsakhan, the Donghu.

The beacon is like a three-dimensional map with Alice in the middle. Being in a plane and above the world accentuates the sense of depth. The map extends in every direction, and its edge is defined by the blip. When Alice was on the other side of the world, the blip was far away and faint, but still discernible. Now that she's within a couple hundred miles of the source, it's bright and sharp. The map has shrunk accordingly and feels more navigable. In fact, it's so clear she could probably walk from the airport to Baitsakhan's location blindfolded.

Not that she will, but she could.

Alice unbuttons her jeans, pulls them down, and sits on the toilet.

Alice wonders if Baitsakhan has captured another Player, if he is torturing one of them for information about the keys like he did Shari, if he's made any progress in the game. She wonders if he's hurt, and if so how he found someone to help him. Maybe he's hiding out.

She wonders if maybe he was the one to find Earth Key, and is taking a break to bask in his success, as any sociopath would.

Sociopaths are fun.

Always shocked when they die.

Alice stands, pulls up her pants, and washes her hands. The PA chimes, indicating that it's time for her to return to her seat.

She will be on German soil in less than an hour.

She will go to a hotel and check in.

If the Donghu moves, she will follow.

Otherwise, she will sleep, and tomorrow she will hunt.

"Breaking news today that a leaked email from a scientist at NASA is beginning to cause panic in some coastal communities of New England and the mid-Atlantic states. Covering the story is Mills Power, fresh from his assignment at Stonehenge. Mills?"

"Good afternoon, Stephanie."

"Good afternoon. This supposedly leaked email from NASA scientist William Wallace is causing quite a stir. What can you tell us?"

"Well, I'm here at NASA's Jet Propulsion Lab headquarters in California, and despite numerous attempts I have not been granted access to Mr. Wallace. I have managed to obtain written confirmation that one Will Wallace, a planetary geologist with a doctorate from Caltech, does indeed work at JPL's NEO program."

"NEO is, for our viewers watching at home . . ."

"Near Earth Object, Stephanie. This team looks for asteroids that come close to Earth and figures out the likelihood of an impact."

"Interesting, particularly in light of recent events."

"Indeed."

"And what have they told you about him, or about his allegations?"

"Not much. Other than verifying Mr. Wallace's employment status, NASA has neither confirmed nor denied the existence of the giant asteroid nicknamed Abaddon that is—according to this now widely circulated email—headed for Earth."

"Well, Mills, some folks are interpreting the lack of an outright denial as a confirmation. Is this truly strange behavior from NASA, though? They are a government agency, after all, and with the recent tragedies . . ."

"It might seem reasonable, but practically all the data and imagery JPL and NASA generate is for the benefit of the public—not just the United States, but the world. Typically, all of their discoveries are posted online, and are updated weekly, sometimes daily. If Mr. Wallace's email is indeed legitimate, then JPL is taking the unprecedented step of keeping this information secret."

"I don't want to lend credence to these conspiracy nuts, Mills, but if NASA is withholding this information, could it be in the public's best interest, so that the government has time to formulate, uh, some kind of a response?"

"If developments on the East Coast are any indication—the water hoarding, the mile-long lines at gas stations, the run on cash at the banks, and most tellingly this nascent boom in online gun and ammunition sales—then not knowing the truth could be just as disruptive as knowing it."

"It sounds like people are preparing for the end of the world, Mills."

"I really, really think they're overreacting, Stephanie. This is, after all, one as yet unverified email. But yes, you are correct. These people are getting ready for the end of the world."

vi

AISLING KOPP

JFK International Airport, Terminal 1 Immigration Hall, Room E-117, Queens, New York, United States

That's nice, Aisling thinks after Operations Officer McCloskey makes her grand overture of top-secret hit-squad government assistance. *Only I don't want the help of my "number one fans."*

Of course Aisling doesn't say this. She doesn't fully buy McCloskey's pitch, and she's positive the agent is holding something back. She *is* CIA, after all. Isn't it part of her job description to lie, and often?

But because what Aisling wants more than anything is to get out of this room, she gathers herself and calmly says, "Thanks, McCloskey. I'll accept your offer. Gladly. Armageddon isn't going to be an easy thing to deal with."

"No. It isn't."

"If you don't mind, I'd like to meet your team."

McCloskey sticks out her hand. "Sure. But first we gotta shake."

Aisling stands and takes the tall, attractive woman's hand.

McCloskey doesn't smile. Neither does Aisling.

They shake and the locks in the door whisper one, two, three and McCloskey says, "Let's go."

McCloskey pulls a badge on a thin chain from inside her pocket and slings it over her head. Then she leads Aisling back into the teeming immigration hall. They stop at the same group of K-9 officers who led Aisling in. One of them hands McCloskey a holstered pistol, which she straps to her waist. Aisling stares at the officers, but they don't acknowledge her at all. They're just grunts following orders.

Aisling follows McCloskey through baggage claim to an older man of average height with a scraggly brown-and-white beard. He's wearing circular, gold-rimmed sunglasses, à la Steve Jobs. If Aisling had to pick a spook out of a thousand people, he would be one of her last guesses—which is probably one reason he's a spook.

"This is Case Officer Griffin Marrs," McCloskey says, coming to a stop.

"Hi, Marrs," Aisling says.

"Howdy-hey," he says. Her carry-on backpack is slung over his shoulder and he points at Aisling's checked bag by his feet. "That's a big gun you got in there, man," Marrs says in a pothead's nasal monotone.

"I have an international transfer permit for it."

He raises his eyebrows. "Under a fake name too. Pretty impressive."

"I *am* a Player. We do have our ways."

Marrs looks at McCloskey. "Least we cooked the right chicken."

"Oh, there's no doubt about that," McCloskey says. She turns to Aisling. "Ready to meet Officer Jordan?"

Aisling gives a curt nod. "The sooner the better. Time's a-wasting."

"It most definitely is," Marrs says.

McCloskey goes first, then Aisling, then Marrs. McCloskey hands a piece of paper to the last customs agent before the exit. Except for the CIA seal and a block of text, Aisling can't see what's on it. The agent reads it as McCloskey and Marrs present their credentials. Nobody says a word. As Aisling passes, the agent says, "Have a nice day, miss." They move through the arrival terminal, passing a line of people pressed against a metal railing as they wait for loved ones from all parts of the world. People dressed in T-shirts, jeans, suits, saris, sweats, fatigues. They hold flowers and stuffed animals and little signs. There are children and wives and cousins and grandparents. Aisling and her new friends pass a phalanx of limousine drivers, holding tablet computers or placards with names on them—Singh, X. James, Örnst, Friedman, Ngala, Hoff, Martin. They leave the terminal. An all-black Cadillac CTS waits at the curb. Engine running. An unseen driver behind tinted windows. McCloskey opens the rear passenger door. "After you."

Aisling notices that the car rides low on its suspension—it's armored—and that there's a clear partition separating the back seats from the front.

"Nice ride," Aisling says as she moves toward the open door. "Especially for government."

"I told you—we're tooled up," McCloskey says proudly, one hand resting on the edge of the car door, the other on the butt of her Beretta 92FS.

Marrs puts Aisling's bags in the trunk and walks to the other side of the car. He opens the back passenger door. He's going to ride with Aisling. Maybe McCloskey is too, with Aisling wedged in the middle, keep it all cozy.

I don't want your help, she thinks again.

Aisling steps off the curb and turns casually to face McCloskey. She lowers her butt onto the edge of the seat. Behind her, she hears the *beep-beep-beep* of a shuttle bus moving in reverse, and the vrooming throttle of a stationary motorcycle from the far side of the median.

A fast-sounding motorcycle.

Aisling lifts her feet from the ground, but instead of swinging them into the footwell, she kicks them up and hits McCloskey square in her chest as hard as she can.

I don't want your help!

McCloskey reels onto the sidewalk, gasping for air as Aisling executes a backward somersault through the car and launches out of the other side feet first. She catches Marrs across the jaw and shoulder, and he slams into the car door with a crack. "Hey, man!" he blurts.

Aisling lands on her feet and pivots. She's at top speed in three steps as she darts around the reversing shuttle bus, putting her out of view of the CIA officers for a few precious seconds.

"Stop!" McCloskey strains to shout.

A scream.

Another.

Aisling doesn't have time to look, but she guesses that the agents have unholstered their weapons.

Aisling sprints toward a thin man straddling a black-and-silver BMW S1000 RR sport bike. He's in fully padded riding gear, his helmet on, his bike idling. He doesn't notice the commotion or the girl with the short red hair rushing toward his right side.

Aisling skids to a stop, reaches down, grabs him by the ankle, and lifts. Surprised, he cartwheels off the bike and splays onto the pavement, a muffled shout coming from behind his visor.

"I said *stop!*" Aisling can just barely hear McCloskey yell as Aisling snags the bike and jumps on and takes the grips and guns it.

She's out of the pickup area in seconds, and screams toward the airport exit ramp at 85 mph, weaving between cars and cabs and Port Authority blue-and-whites.

One of these flashes its cherry lights and gives chase.

It'll never catch her.

Aisling works the bike up to 95, 103, 112, 119, humming good in 5th gear at 8,000 rpm. It's just getting warm. It's got another gear and 60 or 70 mph to go before it tops out. Inside a minute she's on the JFK Expressway, snaking through the potholed and confusing interchanges to the Belt Parkway.

Two gray Malibus tear onto the highway in front of her from North Conduit Avenue. Aisling makes them for regular cops, undercover, not part of McCloskey's posse. Aisling zips the bike to the left shoulder, hugging the median, zooming by cars and SUVs. The cops are still in front, trying to block her. Aisling slows to 79 mph and, at the last moment, swerves dangerously between an Escalade and a little Smart car to screech onto the off-ramp at exit 17N, the back wheel skipping and sliding before catching the road and propelling her up the ramp. Aisling changes gears, guns it again, and pops a wheelie onto the streets, heading west.

She blurs past the Aqueduct horse-racing track, pulling two marked squad cars, along with one of the gray undercovers from the highway, into her wake. As she slaloms through the cars at 111 mph in 3rd, not stopping for any red lights, she glances in the mirror and catches sight of the CIA Caddy several blocks back, its front lights flashing, red high beams glaring from behind the grille.

McCloskey is coming, and she won't be happy when she catches Aisling.

You're not telling me something, McCloskey. And you're not gonna catch me.

Aisling kicks it into 4th, whips around a truck, veers onto Linden Boulevard, and finds a long, wide, straight stretch of road.

And midway down that road, a twinkling congregation of police vehicles blocking the way, officers out and guns out too.

Aisling crunches the brake and clutch and cycles down through the gears, turning left onto Drew Street, cutting across two lanes of traffic. She would mash the gas and go go go, but in front of her is an oncoming squad car.

Screw it.

Time to play chicken.

She goes goes goes.

And the squad car goes too.

Neither flinches, neither swerves.

They're going to crash.

Aisling pictures it. She'll go over the bars and probably splatter her brains everywhere. If not that, then she'll almost definitely get caught. And if not that, she'll be so messed up from the crash she'll have no chance of surviving Endgame.

But at the last second the cop car brakes hard, and the laws of physics drive the hood toward the ground, the front bumper throwing sparks. Aisling lifts the wheel again and slams onto the roof of the car and rides over it and up and through the air. She lands 30 feet later, bouncing violently onto the ground, struggling to keep the handlebars straight, two quick gunshots ringing behind her, both clumsy and off the mark. She turns right onto another street and one block later finds herself at the edge of a multiblock housing project.

She skids to a stop by a bunch of kids hanging on the corner in the midafternoon sun, all of them skinny and muscly with straight-brimmed ball caps and baggy shorts hanging off their asses. They don't see too many redheaded white girls riding $20,000 German motorcycles in these parts.

"Yo, top o' the morning to ya!" one kid shouts. His friends laugh. Aisling smiles, yanks the key out of the ignition, jumps off the bike, tosses the key to him.

"Trade my bike for your cap," she says with a wink. She takes off on foot, grabbing the kid's all-black Nets hat right off his head, and leaps over a low iron fence parkour-style, disappearing into the tree-lined project, the boys all yelling, "Oh, shit!" "For real?" "What the—?"

She gets more looks from grandmas and little kids and teenagers as she sprints through the housing complex. She considers scaling one of the buildings and hiding on the roof until things cool off, but that would be too conspicuous and the cops are likely to put out choppers soon if they haven't already.

No. She needs to get home, and fast. If she can get there with some time to spare and grab a bag of toys from the basement safe room, then she'll be able to disappear for good.

Disappear and Play.

Run and not get caught.

Stop the Event if she can. If she can't, win the game.

By myself.

She hits a chain-link fence, scales it, drops down, and is back on the street. She hears the sirens in the distance and, sure enough, a chopper coming from the south. There aren't many people around in this section of the development, but the ones who are watch her with a sort of detached wonder. Like so many city people, they've learned to mind their business.

No one says anything when Aisling walks up to a purple-and-yellow souped-up Honda Civic, jumps through the open window, and hot-wires her new ride in less than five seconds, which might be a street record. A lilting *narco-corrido* track pours out of the sound system. She turns it down and puts on the Nets cap and pulls away from the curb casually, her wrist hanging limp over the top of the wheel. She takes a pair of sunglasses off the dashboard and slips them on.

She drives south a few blocks, a cruiser screaming past her toward Linden, and turns west. She guns it for a quarter mile, goes casual again, and works her way back toward JFK on side streets, hoping that the police haven't put up a blockade anywhere on Cross Bay Boulevard.

They haven't.

Less than half an hour later she rounds the corner onto West 10th Road. The next 10 minutes are critical. Broad Channel is nothing more than a natural bridge in the middle of Jamaica Bay. The police, or this McCloskey person, could easily pin her down. If they block the roads, she could get on Pop's boat to try to escape, but boats are not very good for that sort of thing.

So she crosses her fingers and hopes.

She stops four houses shy of the teal bungalow. No sign of anyone.

She gets out. She pushes her hands into her pockets and trudges forward.

Still nothing. The block is quiet.

She turns up the walk, stops by the garden gnome in the tiny yard, flips his pointy red hat back, and pulls out a little case with a combo lock on it. Puts in the number, 9-4-6-2-9, opens it, and takes out the key.

Aisling goes to the front door. She looks over her shoulder one more time. A 747 angles skyward out of JFK. A starling chirps on the roof's gutter. The bolt in the lock slides open. She pushes the door and slips in and closes the door and locks it.

The house is dark.

She puts her right thumb on an unmarked section of the wall. A red light comes from behind the paint. A drawer in a side table slides open on silent rollers. Without looking, her eyes darting from corner to corner and down the hall, Aisling pulls a silenced Sig 226 out of foam casing pressed into the drawer. The safety is already off. This gun's safety is always off.

"Pop?" Aisling calls for her grandfather.

No answer.

"Pop? It's me. It's Ais."

No answer.

Aisling pads through the hall to the door that leads to the basement. Still watching the corners, searching everywhere, the pistol pointing and waiting for a target. No one is there. She's alone. She stops. Raps a spot on the wall with her fist. A section of wood paneling swings back to reveal a combination safe dial. She spins the dial from pure muscle memory. 59 right. 12 left. 83 right. 52 left. 31 right. The door clicks open.

Aisling opens the heavy door—it looks wooden but is really three-inch-thick steel—and closes it behind her. The lights go on automatically as soon as it bolts shut. She's safe.

She goes down the stairs and passes two racks of guns, a pantry, an empty hazmat suit, scuba gear, and a bulletproof plexiglass closet full of all kinds of hand-to-hand weapons, some of them museum-quality, ancient, and utterly priceless.

She ignores all of it and goes straight for two bags hanging on a wall. One a backpack, the other a duffel. The go bags. They contain everything she'll need.

She turns and stops by the bulletproof closet. Places her eye in front of a retinal scanner and punches away at an alphanumeric, case-enabled keypad. The sequence is 25 characters—GKI2058BjeoG84Mk5QqPlll42—25 characters she has known by rote since the age of seven (she always complained to her grandfather that he should change it periodically, but he never did). The door slides open. She steps into the climate-controlled partition and takes her line's most cherished sword, a curved steel Falcata from the 6th century BCE—the only steel sword in all of Europe at the time, and a weapon that counts exactly 3,890 lives ended on its razor-sharp edge. The La Tène Celts who trace their blood to the ancients, those who received knowledge directly from the Makers, knew how to make tempered steel for millennia, and told no one their secret. A sword of steel in the 6th century BCE was as good as a magical blade.

She slips the sheathed Falcata into the top of the duffel bag and leaves the glass room. Aisling heads back up the stairs, the lights ticking off behind her. She emerges into the hall and closes the door and is about to leave when she's frozen by the sound of clapping.

"Nice escape, Ms. Kopp," a man's voice says from the living room.

Aisling spins. A man in his mid-to-late 40s sits in Pop's favorite Barcalounger. He is exactly average in height and build, if a little thick around the middle. He's an extra on a movie set, a face in the crowd. He has graying hair with a bald spot, and a little bit of stubble on his cheeks. He's plain in every visible way, except for the long scar Aisling can just make out on the side of his face and neck, and even that seems unremarkable on this man's ordinary face. He wears blue jeans and a light gray V-neck and black trail runners.

Aisling wouldn't pay this guy any attention, except that he's pointing a compact model HK416 at her. Right now. The red laser sight is trained on her throat. He was clapping by patting his thigh with his right hand.

A lefty. I wouldn't have guessed.

Aisling doesn't raise her pistol. "You must be McCloskey's boss."

"Bravo."

"Got a name?"

"Greg Jordan."

"McCloskey outside?"

"She's on her way."

"She's probably pissed."

"Actually, no," he says, his eyebrows rising slightly. "She's relieved. Anything less than the stunt you pulled and she wouldn't think you're worth fighting for. Marrs, though—*he's* pissed. He's one of those 'I'm too old for this crap' guys."

"I guess I'll apologize, then."

"Good. He'll appreciate that."

"So the airport—that was a test?"

"What isn't a test, Ms. Kopp? Especially now that Earth Key has been recovered?"

"Good point."

"Can I tell you something about myself? Since we'll be spending a lot of time together."

"Hate to break it to you, Greg, but we're not going to be spending a lot of time together."

"That hurts, Ms. Kopp. What is it—you don't like us?"

"I don't trust you."

Jordan sighs. "I wouldn't trust us either in your position. But here's the thing. *I* trust *you*. I have to."

"Because I'm your Player?"

"Yeah, that. And because I have no other option."

"Sounded like McCloskey would disagree. She seemed to think there *was* another option. She said she didn't want to hook up with me, and that you were the one who convinced her."

"That's true. All of it. See? We're earning your trust already."

Aisling presses, not satisfied with any of this. "What was your other option if you don't mind my asking?"

"It's not important. Now that the asteroid is coming, nothing is as important as working directly with you."

"I'd still like to hear it."

He sighs again. "We wanted to stop Endgame from happening."

Aisling smirks. "And you really thought you could do that?"

Jordan shrugs. "I guess we dreamed big. Crazy, right?"

Aisling lets some of the tension out of her shoulders. In spite of her misgivings about accepting help, she likes this guy. "Totally crazy."

"But listen—you didn't let me tell you that thing about myself."

"Shoot."

Jordan smiles. The irony is not lost on him. He still hasn't lowered his gun. He's got a steady hand.

"I don't like to drop f-bombs. Never have. A lot of station chiefs I've worked for—especially stateside ones—love to drop f-bombs. It's like they live off them or something, like they provide sustenance. Personally, I think an overreliance on f-bombs is a sign of arrested development, a kind of pointless bluster. A few people are experts at using them and using them often—they can pull it off. But they're a gifted few."

"Okay . . ." Aisling says, drawing the word out.

Jordan waves his right hand demonstratively. "That said, a well placed f-bomb—just like a well-placed actual bomb—is very effective. I think of them as finite, you know? I hold them in reserve for when I really need them."

"I think I know where this is going."

"No, I don't think you fucking do."

"That was one."

Jordan smiles again. In spite of his misgivings about this whole Endgame thing actually going down on his watch, he likes this girl.

"We have your grandfather."

Aisling takes a half step forward.

"Ah-ah. Careful," Jordan says.

The gun.

"Go on."

"He's not a prisoner. He's on board with us—he wants you to accept our offer. But you have to understand that what McCloskey told you is true. We're the good guys, but when we need to be the bad guys, we can be very fucking good at doing very fucked-up things. So—if you want your grandfather to live, then you will say yes to us. We will be your best fucking friends to the end of time. That is a promise. But you *have* to say yes and mean it. You're the Player—*our* Player—and we need you so badly that we're prepared to do anything to make sure you accept us. Say yes, Aisling. Say yes and mean it. No fucking bullshit. Understand? Say. Yes."

First McCloskey and now Jordan—these agents love their big speeches. Aisling wonders if they take a training seminar for them. All the same, she feels like Jordan might be more self-aware than his crackpot cohorts. But she also wants to kill him. For forcing her to take his help when, really, she's the one helping him. And for threatening Pop. She could probably kill Jordan now, finish him off before she died from blood loss, but then that'd be it for Pop and for Playing.

So what else can she do?

She shrugs. "I want to see Pop."

"Is that a yes?"

"No, Jordan. It's a fuck yes."

U+2624^{vii}

HILAL IBN ISA AL-SALT

JetBlue Flight 711, Taxiing to Gate D4, McCarran International Airport, Las Vegas, Nevada, United States

No one liked the look of Hilal ibn Isa al-Salt.

No one in Addis, no one at Charles de Gaulle, no one at JFK, and no one on the flight to Las Vegas. They didn't like that half his head was wrapped in bandages, or that these were mottled by rust-colored bloodstains. They didn't like the blue eye next to the dark skin, and they especially didn't like the damaged red-and-pink eye peeking between the wraps. They didn't like that they had to shield their children's eyes, or console them after they began to cry at the sight of the Aksumite. They didn't like his straight white teeth—perfect in every way except that they were housed in the face of this ... this ... this monster.

Which, on the outside, is what Hilal ibn Isa al-Salt has become.

The only people who spoke to Hilal during his trip were those who had to—the desk agents and the flight attendants and the customs officials and the people who shared the misfortune of sitting next to him on the plane. The most recent seatmate, a young African-American woman, simply whispered, "Oh my God," and said nothing else. She spent the entire flight from New York looking away, or sleeping, or pretending to sleep.

Hilal spent the entire flight staring at the back of the seat in front of him. Meditating, accepting the searing pain that will envelop him for the rest of his days, learning to like it.

He also reflected on his new mission.

He has come to Las Vegas for one reason—because the phonelike device hidden for over 3,300 years in the Ark of the Covenant with the Makers told him to come home.

At least that is how Hilal and Master Eben interpreted it.

When the device glowed to life in the Kodesh Hakodashim, it revealed a seamless image resembling bright interstellar background noise, woven with countless strands of darkness and planes of color, an impressionistic tapestry of space and time in three dimensions. Hilal moved the device up and down and back and forth in sweeping arcs, and this background remained pinned in place, as if the device were a handheld window that afforded a view of an alternate universe.

But when Hilal positioned the device in certain ways, it revealed three distinct images.

The first was a data set, a hazy list of two-point coordinates that Hilal discovered he could scroll through by tapping the top or bottom of the device. The list is only visible when Hilal holds the thing with his arm extended to true south. There are well over a thousand numbers in degree-minute-second notation. Virtually all are static, but several change incrementally over time, as if whatever they reference is on the move.

The 2nd image emerged from the cosmic pattern when Hilal raised his arm to shoulder height and pointed the device east-southeast. There he saw a bright orange, spherical light, pulsating with the rhythm of a fast heartbeat. Hilal initially guessed that, perhaps, in this direction, millions of light years away, was the keplers' home planet—but this idea was dashed as soon as he started to move. Hilal and Eben had to go to Addis Ababa that night to consult with a plastic surgeon about Hilal's wounds, and as they traveled south to the Ethiopian capital, he had to adjust the device's orientation, edging it north, to relocate this orange blob.

It seemed as though this bright light marked some stationary object on Earth.

An object located, based on some basic triangulation, in the eastern Himalayas.

An object that may or may not be essential to Endgame.

The 3rd image was not a list of numbers or a blot of light, but a symbol. A staff entwined with a pair of snakes, two small wings sprouting from the staff's top, just above the snake heads.

The caduceus. Representative of medicine to some, of snake oil and lies to others. The sigil of Hermes, messenger of the Makers, who separated the fighting snakes with his rod and taught them peace.

To Hilal and Eben, the caduceus means something else entirely. Something sinister. It is enough for Hilal to pause his Endgame, to delay seeking the shining beacon in the Himalayas, and to fly across the world to Las Vegas. Before Hilal can continue, he must deal with the Corrupter. He of many names: Armilus, Dajjal, Angra Mainyu, Kalki on his white horse.

The Devil. The Antichrist.

Ea.

For this is the Aksumite line's secret: theirs is unique in that it has not one but two purposes. First, like the others, the Aksumites guard the secrets of human creation and stay vigilant in preparing a Player for Endgame. But they must also seek and ultimately use the rods inside the sacred ark to destroy Ea once and for all.

Ea, the leader of the Corrupted Brotherhood of the Snake, must die. And Hilal will be the one to kill him. This is what Hilal knows.

He also knows that it was Ea who poisoned the soul of man. The snake in the Garden of Eden. He steered humanity away from spiritual understanding, hid from them the Ancient Truth.

This Ancient Truth is what Hilal would pass on to what is left of humanity after the Event. Whether he lives or dies, wins or fails at Endgame, Hilal would see Earth be free of the influence of Ea the Corrupter. He has tormented us for too long.

Hilal wants every person to see, to feel, to comprehend that no god or scripture or holy man or temple or kepler or Maker is needed for enlightenment. That the key to paradise resides within each and every human being.

That we are each the god of our shared universe. To know and accept the Ancient Truth is to at last shuck off the psychological shackles forged for centuries by Ea.

But first, Ea must be destroyed.

"This is the Ancient Truth that must be taught to the new world."

Lost in thought, Hilal actually speaks these words as the plane bumps to a stop at the Jetway.

The young woman sitting next to him, the same woman whose only words were "Oh my God" upon seeing him, can't help herself. "What was that?" she asks.

Hilal turns to her. His blue eye. His red eye. The blood-speckled bandages. "Excuse me?" His voice is low, scratchy, rough.

The woman gulps. "I thought I heard you say something about the 'new world.'"

The PA chimes and the seat belts click off. People stand and gather their things. A baby several rows forward begins to cry. One on the other side of the plane lets out a peal of laughter.

Hilal smiles. "I didn't realize I'd said anything. But yes, I suppose I did mention the 'new world,' my sister."

"You don't actually believe it, do you?" she asks breathlessly.

"Believe what?"

"This thing about Abaddon?"

Hilal bristles at the ancient word. "I'm sorry. What thing about Abaddon?"

He knows the word well. In the Tanakh, Abaddon is a reference to hell. But for the life of him Hilal cannot wrap his head around why this woman is saying it now.

Because in the Aksumite line, Abaddon is yet another name for Ea.

"Haven't you been watching the news?"

"No. I've . . . I've been traveling for the last twenty-four hours. And . . . well . . . my burns are fresh. The . . . accident that caused them was not much more than a week ago."

"I can tell."

Hilal sees that she wants to ask what happened. Before she can, he says, "They used to say I was beautiful." He snorts. There is a smell like smoke in his nostrils. "I always thought it was a strange thing to a call a boy—*beautiful*."

The woman doesn't know what to say. She thinks maybe Hilal is a little crazy.

"Tell me more about Abaddon, if you don't mind," Hilal says.

The woman shrugs. If he is crazy, he is at least polite. "It's all over the news. This email leaked from some guy at NASA. He was writing his sister in Massachusetts, warning her that she had like eighty days to get the hell out of there or her kids and her family would all die."

Hilal's interest is piqued. "What would kill them?"

"Abaddon. That's what the NASA dude called it, anyway. Some kind of humongous asteroid on a crash course for Earth. He said it could . . . he said it could kill a lot of people. Like a *real* lot. Change everything."

"A new world," Hilal mutters.

"Yeah, that. But you know, most people think it's a hoax. Least they *want* to think it's a hoax." She pauses. A heavyset man standing in the aisle shoots her a disapproving look. She lowers her voice. "Still, others are starting to worry because no one's denied it yet—and there were the meteors that killed all those people, and that crazy thing at Stonehenge that no one knows what happened. And that freaky guy on the TV talking about some kind of game."

"Yes. That I *do* know about."

"Shit's screwed up, you know? This Abaddon email—everyone's read it and no politician has said one word about it. Not one. That's messed up, right?"

"Yes," Hilal says thoughtfully.

The fat man in the aisle shakes his head, dismisses this conspiracy talk, walks forward.

Hilal could take his turn and stand and say good-bye to the young woman and leave as well. He probably should.

But instead he looks at her seriously.

He leans forward. His eyes blink. One blue. One red.

"Listen to me. What this NASA email says is true. It *is* true. I can't say how I know this—and if I told you, you would laugh—but Abaddon is real. And you should prepare. Prepare for this new world that's coming."

The woman pulls away and gives Hilal a wild look. "Oh, no. I don't need to hear that shit." She waves a finger in the air and stands, pushing her way awkwardly past Hilal's knees. Her purse hits him on the shoulder. It stings horribly, but he doesn't call out. "I don't need to hear that shit *at all*," she insists.

Hilal understands: the truth hurts.

The young woman hustles into the middle of the plane and exits as quickly as she can.

Hilal sits in his seat as the other passengers leave the plane, again lost in thought. Whatever happens with the Abaddon news, whether the world decides to believe it or not, it doesn't matter. Endgame is here, and the world is already changing.

He gets out the device from the ark. Even though it is an ancient artifact of Maker origin, no one gives it a second look. It's just another screen in a world full of screens.

He holds it. It glows to life. He points it toward the city of Las Vegas, expecting to see the caduceus.

And he does.

But his eyes widen and he breathes in sharply.

For now that he is closer to his quarry, the sign is brighter and bigger.

And most alarmingly, it is doubled. There are two. Two signs of the devil, both right here in Las Vegas.

What could it mean?

A flight attendant steps next to him and says, "Sir, will you be needing a wheelchair?"

The question shakes Hilal from his thoughts. "Excuse me?"

The flight attendant indicates that the plane is empty. "Will you need a wheelchair?"

Hilal slips the device into his shirt. "No, ma'am. Sorry."

He stands and steps into the aisle. Reaches into the overhead compartment and removes a small backpack and two canes with snake heads for handles.

The Rod of Aaron. The Rod of Moses.

The weapons that will destroy the Corrupter, if he can get close enough to use them.

He walks slowly down the aisle. The captain is waiting at the cockpit door.

"Have a nice day, sir."

"You too, Captain," Hilal says.

Off the plane, up the Jetway, into the terminal.

A terminal unlike one he has ever seen.

Not because it is designed differently than your average American airport, or because he can hear the bell-like music of a slot machine signing in the distance, but because it is eerily still.

It is late afternoon and the terminal is filled with people, only all of them are frozen, as if zapped by some kind of ice ray. None walk to their gates, none talk on their phones, none chase after children.

They all stand, necks craned, watching the televisions mounted at intervals around the gates.

On the television is the president of the United States. She sits at her big desk in the Oval Office. Her face is dour, her voice strained.

It quavers as she says, "My fellow Americans, and my fellow citizens of Earth, Abaddon is real."

Audible gasps ricochet around the hall. One person wails.

The president continues to speak, but Hilal doesn't need to listen.

This is Endgame.

He has to find Ea.

He takes his canes, and his resolve, and he carries on.

He is the only person moving through the terminal.

The only person moving through this frozen, terrified, new world.

Eighty-nine heads of state give coordinated televised speeches announcing Abaddon. Eighty-nine heads of state solemnly tell their people that they cannot say with 100 percent certainty that the asteroid will strike Earth, but that it is likely. They don't know where it will strike, but if it does, it will affect the lives of every single organism on the planet. They say it will not be the end of the world, but the end of the world as we know it. They say it will mark the beginning of a new era. An unprecedented era in human history.

"Today, we are no longer Americans or Europeans, Asians or Africans, Eastern or Western, Northern or Southern," the US president says toward the end of her speech, her sentiments echoed across the world by each of the other leaders. "We are no longer Christians or Jews, Muslims or Hindus, Shiites or Sunnis, believers or nonbelievers. We are no longer Indians or Pakistanis, Israelis or Palestinians, Russians or Chechens, North Koreans or South Koreans. We are no longer terrorists or freedom fighters or liberators or jihadis. We are no longer communist or democratic or authoritarian or theocratic. We are not scholars or priests or politicians or soldiers or teachers or students or Democrats or Republicans. Today, we are all simply the people of Earth. Today, we are reminded that we are the most remarkable species on the most remarkable planet. Today, every point of contention, every grudge, every single one of our differences has been washed clean away. *We are the same.* A people that can and will unite to meet the challenges of an uncertain and unexpected future. *We are the same.* And we will have to depend on our good graces, our charity, our love—and our *humanity*—if we have a chance of surviving this possible calamity with any measure of success. We are the same, my friends. May God bless each and every one of you. And may God bless this planet Earth."

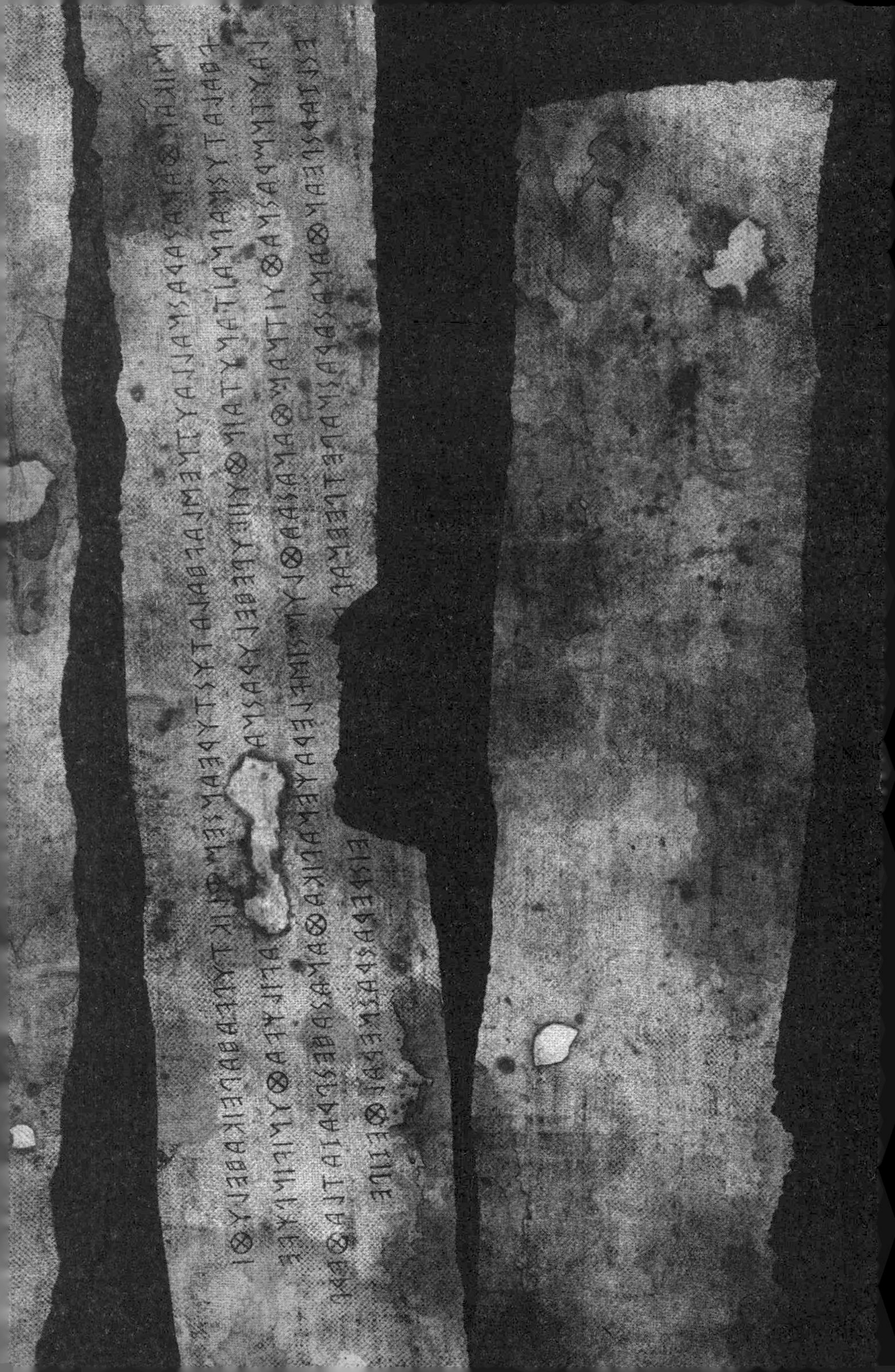

ALL PLAYERS

America. Germany. India. Japan.

Sarah and Jago and Renzo watch the president's address from aboard Renzo's Cessna Citation CJ4. Both Renzo and Sarah were ecstatic to see Jago on the old tarmac back in Lincolnshire, and Jago made sure to smooth over their differences—or at least set them aside. They took off as soon as Jago explained that he'd dived under the train and hid in a large drain under the tracks until the coast was clear. He was not mad at Sarah for leaving him, and told Renzo he shouldn't be mad at Sarah either. They were just Playing, and both had survived the day. They stopped for a day and a night in Halifax, Nova Scotia, to refuel. And now, despite Renzo's protests that it's childish and unsafe, they're heading to a secret Cahokian compound in eastern Nebraska to meet Sarah's family.

She needs to see her parents, explain to them what she did to Christopher, confess what happened when she got Earth Key, and try to explain her mental state. Maybe they can calm her brain, maybe there's one last lesson they can impart to their Player. Teach her how to deal, smooth out her anxieties, bring her back to her senses.

And while she's home, Sarah wants to visit Tate's grave. Her brother. Another casualty of Endgame.

She watches the president's speech with silent tears. When it's over, she excuses herself to the lavatory to cry more.

The president's words do not touch Jago or Renzo. They're ready for Abaddon, and for whatever comes after.

"You need to take Earth Key and ditch her, my Player," Renzo whispers as soon as the bathroom door closes.

Jago strokes the scar on his neck. A habit. He's thinking.

"I can't."

"You must. Time is of the essence. The world will not be an easy place soon. We need to go to our ancestral home. To *your* home. We need to take Earth Key to Aucapoma Huayna and receive her wisdom."

"Renzo, you aren't listening to me."

"I always listen to my Player."

"Cut this obsequious shit. I know you're right, but I won't leave her. And I won't leave you either. I'm going to need your help, not your doubt—do you understand?"

Renzo shifts in his seat. Looks Jago in the eye. Chin up. Man to man. He nods. "Yes. I understand, Jago."

"Good. Now. You're right that we can't waste any more time. But Sarah can't either. Something's wrong with her, and I don't think going to her family will help. She's too fragile. Seeing them will only break her up more."

Renzo stabs his finger at the back of the plane. "Maybe you take her to see a psychiatrist, huh? We got time for that?"

Jago raises his hand. Renzo is silent. "We will reroute the plane for Peru, but we won't tell her, understand?"

Renzo lowers his hand. Gets his emotions under control. "We'll have to refuel again."

"I know. We can stop in Valle Hermoso, in Mexico. Maria Reyes Santos Izil is still there. She'll top us off. Feed us. Let us sleep in comfort and safety."

Sarah angrily pounds something in the lavatory. The wall. The sink. They hear her sobbing.

Jago looks at the door. Sarah's one of the strongest people he's ever met, and yet one of the most vulnerable too. He strokes his scar some more.

Renzo gives him a questioning look. "She's a killer, Jago. I saw that firsthand in England. But she is no Player. Not anymore."

"Enough, Renzo. Leave her to me," Jago says with a twang of bitterness. "Prepare the nav computer and leave her to me."

Aisling Kopp watches from the backseat of the armored CTS as it crosses the George Washington Bridge. Greg Jordan sits next to her, McCloskey is in the front passenger seat, Marrs drives.
"Good speech," Marrs says.
McCloskey snickers. "Sure, but it won't count for anything. Some real Hobbesian shit's about to go down."
Aisling agrees with McCloskey. Jordan and Marrs do too. None of them say so.

Alice Ulapala sits on the bed in her hotel room in Berlin and watches the German chancellor give her speech. Alice speaks German (and French and Latin and Malay and Dutch and middling Chinese, not to mention half a dozen Aboriginal dialects), so she has no trouble understanding. The speech starts at 10 in the evening. It lasts 17 minutes. The chancellor cries at the end. During the broadcast Alice runs a small sharpening stone across the edge of one of her boomerangs.
Over and over.
Back and forth.
Over and over.
"Well, that'll make things interesting."

Maccabee and Ekaterina watch a live stream of the Polish president. They say nothing throughout. Just stare, as rapt as every other person in the world. "I'm glad we had that bottle of Krug when we had the chance," Maccabee says several minutes after the speech ends.
"Me too." Ekaterina pauses. They revived Baitsakhan earlier in the day, but he was still groggy and bedridden. "Should we inform your friend what's happened?"

"No," Maccabee replies, looking at the closed door behind which the Donghu rests. "Baitsakhan doesn't care about this kind of thing. I'm not sure he knows that other people even exist as, you know, people."

Shari and Jamal watch the Indian prime minister give her speech from their simple room in the mountainous Harappan compound, सूर्य को अन्तिम रेज, in the Valley of Eternal Life. If there is one place in the world that can survive an asteroid impact—provided it isn't a direct hit—it is सूर्य को अन्तिम रेज.

Little Alice also watches. While she's only two, she seems to grasp the gravity of the prime minister's words.

So young, so knowing, so understanding. So intelligent, Shari thinks. And the thought chills her to her bones.

"This is about my dream, isn't it, Mama?" Little Alice says partway through the speech.

You mean your nightmare, Shari thinks before she says, "Yes, *meri jaan.*" She squeezes Jamal's hand.

"Will Abaddon hurt us, Mama?"

"No, *meri jaan.* It will happen far from here."

"Your mother and I—your whole family—are here to make sure that none of us get hurt, my little dove," Jamal says.

"Okay, Papa."

The speech goes on. Shari is racked by fear, but not fear of Abaddon. The Makers will see that it hits as far from Sky Key as possible.

For if Little Alice dies, then Endgame dies too.

They are safe for now.

Until the others come, they are safe.

An is in Japan, in Chiyoko's hometown. He watches an illegal stream of the Chinese president on a brand-new laptop. He squats on the floor, looking more like a day laborer on a smoke break than a trained killer. He wears nothing but a pair of black underwear and Chiyoko Takeda's analog wristwatch.

His head is no longer bandaged. A star-shaped cluster of stitches holds his skin in place where he was shot. His ribs curve around his sides like a birdcage. His hand is sore where he dislocated his thumb, the skin purple and blue. He has another bruise shaped like a mango on his right thigh. He doesn't remember how he got that one, but doesn't care.

His eyes are narrow and dark as they watch the bespectacled leader in his pressed suit and red Communist Party tie talk about the impending end of days.

The words do not shock An, or make him sad or nervous or terrified. A giant asteroid is what he expected. He also expected to enjoy this moment. He fantasized about it often during the grim years of his training, the day when everyone's fate would become as bleak as his own, when they'd all look death in the face.

If only he had not met Chiyoko.

If only he had not . . . fallen in love.

Absurd. He. The Shang. Who was incapable of love.

No.

Instead of finding joy in the president's words, he finds anger.

For An, anger is his beating heart. A constant rhythm. But *this* anger is different. *This* anger is new and more intense. More focused. More rooted in the love that he's lost, but that he'll never be able to recover. It's an anger tinged with longing.

For her.

And while he can't get her back, he has a plan. It's unorthodox, but it's right. He knows it is. He knows Chiyoko would think it's right too. He hopes that her line agrees. That they will see the wisdom—the justice—in his plan.

You play for death. I play for life.

Her words.

Chiyoko.

An works something in his hands as he watches the end of the speech. A black braid of silken hair, half an inch thick, a little more than a foot long. In the middle it broadens into a V-shaped net the size of a small hand, woven like a spider's web. Attached to the web are two pale flaps of skin the size of a quarter, and two shriveling human ears.

He holds it up. It is nearly done.

A necklace made of the pilfered remnants of his beloved. Her hair. Her flesh.

He watches the speech.

The Chinese leader, like every leader in the world that day, ends with the same words:

"We are all the same."

The picture fades to black.

An shuts the laptop with a muted clap. He chews a piece of dry skin off his lip and spits it on the floor.

"No," he says in Mandarin. He stifles a barely perceptible *shiverBLINK*.

"You are wrong. We are not all the same. Not even close."

viii

ALICE ULAPALA, MACCABEE ADLAI, EKATERINA ADLAI

Eastern Terminus of Heldburger Straße, Lichtenberg, Berlin, Germany

Alice sits under a neglected linden tree, her back against the trunk, her knees tucked to her chest. She peers through a small but powerful set of binoculars, scanning the area. She whistles "Waltzing Matilda" as her toes tap the time in plastic flip-flops.

The sun rose nearly two hours earlier, at 4:58 a.m. In spite of her odd appearance—an honest-to-goodness Koori is out of place everywhere except the backcountry of Oz—no one has noticed her. The dead end road she's watching is not much traveled. She is tucked away in an abandoned corner of Berlin that only teenagers, vandals, and killers are likely to use.

Killers like her.

That's not to say that this area doesn't have people in it. There are homes everywhere. Past the lots to the north on Sollstedter Straße is a line of four- and five-story apartment buildings. Past the lots to the west are taller, possibly East German–built apartment blocks along Arendsweg.

This is where Baitsakhan hides.

Her internal beacon is precise to the point of being nearly overwhelming. It rings in her frontal cortex like a siren, occasionally interfering with her vision if she moves her head too quickly.

She has to snuff out this Baitsakhan.

And once I do, I'll go look for Earth Key.

She stands and shoulders a large canvas bag. She walks toward the building. The little monster is in a basement 450 meters away. All she has to do is sneak over there, get the drop on him, and finish him off.

Bzzz. Bzzz. Bzzzzzz. Bzz.

Maccabee is woken by a faint noise. He looks at the clock in his sparsely decorated bedroom: 8:01 a.m. He sits up, frowns, whips his head back and forth.

What is that buzzing?

He jumps out of bed wearing nothing but boxer briefs, grabs a gold-plated Magnum Research Baby Eagle Fast Action from the bedside table. In his haste, he forgets his poisoned-needle pinkie ring, which he takes off every night so he doesn't poison himself by accident in his sleep. It stays on the bedside table.

Bzzzz. Bzzz. Bzz. Bzz.

He goes to his pile of clothing, fumbles for his phone in his slacks. No, not his phone.

Bzzzzzzz. Bzz. Bzz. Bzzzzzzzz.

He moves to the center of the room, cocks his ear this way and that. He can't determine the sound's location. First it's on his left, then his right, then behind, then in front. He spins frantically, wondering if maybe he's going crazy, but then he remembers.

The orb.

The one he and Baitsakhan got from the Golden Chamber under Gobekli Tepe.

He grabs a backpack hanging on a hook. The bag shakes shakes shakes. He sticks his pistol in the band of his underpants and thrusts his hand into the bag and wraps his fingers around the sphere that transmits the locations of the other Players. It's vibrating violently, as if it has a wildly spinning gyroscope at its center. He grasps it with both hands, drops the backpack to the floor.

He holds it to his face: a yellow glow streams out of it, creating spears of light between his fingers. The glow dances, zips back and forth across the surface of the sphere, and finally resolves into a single bright dot. It stops shaking. Maccabee peels the fingers of his left hand free and stares into it.

The dot is moving over a crisscross of lines. Maccabee squints.

The lines are streets.

He recognizes them as the streets just outside the building.

"A Player is coming."

Alice reaches the curb of Arendsweg and pauses. Something's been nagging her as she's glided across this open urban space. She hasn't seen a single person or a moving car or heard anyone call out.

In other words, she hasn't had to sneak.

It's just past eight in the morning. Wednesday. People should be going to work, getting in their cars, riding their bikes, moving, doing.

But they aren't.

"Abaddon," she says quietly. "They're terrified of Abaddon." She steps off the curb to cross the street. "Eh, I wouldn't bother going to work either."

She thinks of all the people in their houses, people everywhere who know nothing of Endgame or the lines or the Players or the ancient and hidden history of humanity. People who didn't see this coming, who are not prepared, even if they think they are. Because it's one thing to hoard guns and canned food and water and generators and gasoline, as many Aussies and Yanks have done, but it's quite another to wrap one's mind around the inevitability—no, the *immediacy*—of the end.

"And in a giant bloody fireball, no less," Alice says as she approaches the rear entrance to the building where the garbage is taken out.

The beacon burns bright in her head. He's only 20 meters away. Close. So close.

And still not moving.

Maybe he sleeps.

Maybe he's incapacitated.

Stay sharp, Ulapala. This is a Player. Don't assume shit.

The light in the orb has moved to the center, and the lines of the streets have disappeared. It's completely unlike the time he and Baitsakhan snuck up on the Aksumite, when the orb showed Hilal ibn Isa al-Salt inside, working on a computer. Or when they watched the drama at Stonehenge play out as if they were watching a movie— seeing the Mu crushed, the Shang shot, and the Cahokian and the Olmec running free with Earth Key.

Maccabee wonders why the orb's powers would suddenly weaken, after alerting him in the first place. Maybe this Player is blocking it somehow?

Who knows. Maccabee will find out soon enough. And he'll be ready. He slips into his trousers, pulls on a pair of running sneakers, and puts on a stylish white T-shirt that cost €120 at a shop called the Corner Berlin Men. The clothes fall perfectly over his toned body. He is comfortable, ready. Always ready. He takes the gold-plated pistol and cycles the slide. It doesn't have a safety. The trigger stays full forward, but all he has to do is apply four ounces of pressure and pull the trigger back 2.477 centimeters and the round will fire. If he doesn't let the trigger all the way out, he can repeat-fire quickly with just 0.3175 centimeters of trigger play. That's why it's called a Fast Action.

He opens the door to his room and checks the hall.

No one.

At the end of the hall to his left is Baitsakhan's room, and at the other end is a locked steel door that leads to a flight of stairs. At the top of these stairs is Ekaterina's street-level apartment.

Before doing anything, he has to check on the Donghu. It's possible, though unlikely, that the intruder is already in Baitsakhan's room, murdering him.

Maccabee slides to the wall and creeps toward the door. It's ajar. He hears nothing from inside. He reaches the door and squats, figuring that if someone is in there and they have a gun, they wouldn't be likely to aim low. He peeks into the room. Sees the corner of Baitsakhan's bed and half of his sleeping face in profile. Maccabee then swings around and shoulders the door open. He sweeps his pistol through the room.

No one.

He sidles to Baitsakhan, who stirs at the sudden commotion. The boy's eyes dart back and forth beneath his lids, his lips part, his new hand twitches. Dreaming dreams.

God knows of what, Maccabee thinks. *Probably drowning puppies.* Baitsakhan still needs his rest. The hand works, and Baitsakhan likes it. He even thanked Ekaterina, although Maccabee suspects he won't thank her again. He can't imagine Baitsakhan has thanked anyone more than once for anything.

Maccabee leaves, closing the door behind him and locking Baitsakhan in. To keep him safe.

You're still useful to me, my little killer. Still useful.

Maccabee sprints to the steel door. Keys in a sequence on a number pad and hits #. The door's lock turns, and Maccabee pulls it open and steps into the stairwell. He's about to close it behind him when he hears two quick silenced shots from above. He turns and runs up the stairs, the pistol ready, skipping two steps at a time.

While Maccabee inspects the orb, Alice stands at the apartment building's back door. She drops the canvas sack and pulls out a handmade leather sling and swings it over her shoulders. Her knife. Two bladed boomerangs, another wooden, and one more made of dark metal but not sharpened. She snaps a small holstered and silenced pistol—a matte-black Ruger LCP loaded with hollow tips—to her belt. She wedges the dark metal boomerang into the edge of the door. She pulls hard once. It pops open. She slides inside.

The room is dark, illuminated only by a green exit sign. There are four Dumpsters on the side wall, and a closed door opposite.

Alice takes a whiff. "Fish heads and rotten nappies," she says with a sour look. The knife is in one hand and a bladed boomerang is in the other.

She leaves the garbage room and moves into the building's hallway.

She walks to a T intersection and has to choose.

"Where are ya, ya little bugger?" she whispers.

The beacon is bright in all directions, as if she's right on top of her mark, but as she turns back and forth she gets a stronger signal from her right.

She walks that way. Passes orange metal apartment doors at 15-meter intervals. Hears people inside arguing, the muted sounds of breakfast. Hears a man behind 1E call out, "Hilda!" Hears TVs in the background of every apartment.

Everyone in the world must be watching telly today. Everyone but us Endgamers.

And that is exactly what tips her off. When she reaches apartment 1H she stops. The beacon is brightest here, and if that weren't enough, there is no sound coming from behind the door. Which means the people there are either out, or aren't shocked by this news of Abaddon.

Alice cups her ear to the door and listens. At first, nothing. But then, a toilet flush. Footsteps. Bare feet. Moving right to left and away from the entrance. A creak, like a door on dry hinges.

It's not her mark—that would set her beacon off like crazy—but it's someone. Maybe a Donghu line member?

She tries the handle. Locked, as it should be.

Alice takes a step back. She could break down the door, but that would cause a commotion, and if this is some kind of Player safe house, it probably has an alarm, which would ruin the surprise.

She could try to jimmy the lock, but that might take too long. A neighbor might come out and ask what the hell she thought she was doing, which would be completely sensible. So Alice does what any normal guest would do.

She rings the bell.

The footsteps return and Alice sidesteps so that the person inside won't be able to see her through the spy hole.

"Hello?" a woman asks in German. She sounds middle-aged, maybe 40 or 50, and her accent is unmistakably Polish. Southeastern, near Ukraine, if Alice hears it right.

"Good morning," Alice answers in perfect German with no trace of an accent. "It's Hilda from down the hall. Sorry to bother, but I'm out of tea and I'm desperate. I can't bring myself to go out with all this terrible news. Do you have any?"

"Yes, yes. One moment."

The locks turn, the chain slides free, the door opens.

As soon as Ekaterina sees that it is not Hilda, she tries to shut the door, but Alice wedges her foot in front of it. She reaches forward with the buck knife and places its sharpened tip right under the woman's chin. A small dimple forms on her skin.

"Don't talk. Step inside. Fail to do either and I will kill you," Alice says. Ekaterina is tall, a little plump, has a beauty mark and thin lips and dark eyes and long whitish-blond hair. She wears a dark kimono with long sleeves. She's barefoot. Her toes are perfectly manicured. She was beautiful once, still is. She does not look afraid.

She retreats three steps. Alice moves into the apartment and pushes the door shut with her foot. Without taking her eyes off the woman, she reaches back and locks the door.

"You won't leave here alive," Ekaterina says in English.

"Do what I say and *you* will, all right, sister?" Alice answers, also in English.

"He won't let you."

"There's a girl—thanks for letting me know he's here. Been wondering." Disappointment flashes across the woman's face. Disappointment in herself for revealing information she didn't need to.

"What's your name? Me, I'm Alice."

"Ekaterina."

"Right. Good name. Solid. Now, Ekaterina, I'm going to have to tie you up. Either that or slit your throat. I'll do either in a heartbeat, but would prefer the former. Figure you would too, yeah?"

"*Yaheela biznoot farehee.*"

Alice steps forward; Ekaterina steps back. "Don't know that one. Now listen. We're going to your room. That's it there, yeah?" Alice points her chin to the door on the left. Ekaterina nods. "Great. Turn slowly. Anything sudden and that'll be the end of you."

Ekaterina does as she's told.

"Good girl."

Alice sheathes the buck knife and quickly pats Ekaterina down. No weapons. Nothing. She claps a hand on her shoulder. In her other hand is the knife.

"Go on. Walk."

Ekaterina does. It is only two meters to the doorway.

"You a trainer?"

"*Yaheela biznoot farehee* chint!" Ekaterina spits.

"Ah, yeah. I'm beginning to understand. 'Screw you,' that it? Or something to that effect."

Ekaterina doesn't answer.

They turn into a simple bedroom. A mattress pushed lengthwise against the far wall, a wooden side table, a reading lamp, a desk, a chair, a wardrobe, a bookshelf stuffed with tattered volumes, none of which have any names or titles on the spines. Another kimono is draped over the back of the chair. She'll use this to tie Ekaterina up.

"On the bed, facedown, hands on your bottom. Cross your ankles and bend your legs at your knees."

Ekaterina does as she's told.

"Good girl, again. Real pro, you are. Appreciate that. Really do. The one you're lined up with, he didn't strike me as professional. He's lucky to have you."

Alice reaches for the kimono, taking her eyes of Ekaterina for barely two seconds. Ekaterina moves so quickly and silently that even Alice doesn't notice. She pushes her hand into the gap between the mattress and the wall and comes up with a pistol, a short suppressor screwed to the muzzle.

Alice looks back to Ekaterina just as she's leveling the gun. Alice drops and throws the knife. It's headed straight for Ekaterina's skull.

Two shots. *Thhp-thhp*. One glances off the knife, sending it off course and to the hardwood floor, where it sticks with a *thwump*. Both slugs explode into the wall, missing Alice narrowly.

By the time Ekaterina swings the gun only a few inches down and toward Alice's bulky frame, the bladed boomerang is on her. It zips past the muzzle and over the slide and hammer and her hands and knocks Ekaterina hard across the bridge of her nose. It twirls over her face, slicing her right eye in half, flaying the skin leading to her temple. She yelps and drops the gun. Alice slides forward, pulls the knife from the floor, reaches the edge of the bed, and sinks the blade into Ekaterina's throat.

To the hilt.

Warm blood spills from the wound, coating Alice's hand, soaking the bedspread and mattress.

She pulls the knife free. A straight blade, no serrations or jagged edges. It draws out easily. Alice is face to face with Ekaterina, whose eyes still register life. She gurgles, and would make a noise if Alice's blade hadn't skewered her voice box along with lots of other things in her neck.

"Sorry, mum. Nothing personal. But ya should've listened."

Ekaterina's face fills with fear in the moment before life fades from it for good. Alice closes Ekaterina's eyes.

"Rest, mum."

She stands.

She stands and hears footsteps running down the hall.

Her beacon is going haywire. The mark is near. The Player she's been tracking is almost on her.

But the footsteps are heavy, not light. Heavier than the Donghu boy's would be.

Far heavier.

Alice picks up the bloody boomerang and turns to the door and crouches.

The doorway fills with the figure of a man in dark slacks and a white T-shirt and a golden gun.

The beacon explodes in her frontal cortex and is snuffed out. *Poof!* She's found him.

"You?" Alice shouts, not understanding. She was certain it was the youngest Player, the one who'd left his mark on Shari by cutting off her finger. The one who's been threatening Little Alice Chopra in Big Alice Ulapala's dreams.

Maccabee Adlai is just as shocked. His training fails him. His eyes search the room. He doesn't pull the trigger. He registers Ekaterina on the bed.

Bleeding.

Dead.

Murdered.

Ekaterina Adlai.

His mother.

Maccabee's face lights in anguish. He pulls the trigger, but before he can squeeze all the way, the bladed boomerang clanks into the barrel and rakes his knuckles, cutting them to the bone. He pulls off a shot— *bang!*—but it misses badly, taking a chunk from the ceiling.

He brings the gun back down, but it's knocked aside again, this time by the heavy hilt of the buck knife flying end over end. Both knife and gun fall to the floor and slide behind Maccabee into the hall.

He has a hidden knife strapped to his ankle, but can't take the time to reach for it. Until he can, all he has are his hands. His hands and the biggest dose of hate-and-anger-fueled adrenaline his body has ever experienced, which is saying something. He surges forward.

Four meters separate them.

Alice stands her ground. Hurls the 2nd bladed boomerang.

Maccabee claps his hands, catching it in the air. He whips it back at Alice, but her other metal boomerang—the one without the sharpened edge—meets it with a clunk in midair. They deflect off each other at wild angles, flying to opposite sides of the room.

Three meters separate them.

Alice slings her last boomerang—the wooden one—in an underhand motion. He catches it one-handed without flinching and raises it, rushing toward Alice.

Alice stands her ground.

Without taking her eyes off the Nabataean she unholsters her Ruger in a fluid motion.

She brings the pistol in front of her just as Maccabee chops the concave edge of the boomerang on Alice's left shoulder. It hurts—a lot—but aside from the twitch under her left eye she doesn't show it.

The gun is between them, nearly poised for a point-blank gut shot, but with his other hand Maccabee grabs her wrist and yanks down hard.

Only Alice barely moves at all.

Christ, she's strong, Maccabee thinks.

Their faces are right in front of each other, and before Maccabee can do anything, Alice cracks her forehead into the bridge of Maccabee's nose.

It breaks again.

The 7th time in his life. The 2nd in the last three weeks.

It kills.

But the adrenaline doesn't let him feel it.

Since she's as strong as any man he's fought, he treats her like one. He brings his knee up hard into her groin, very hard, and this causes her to falter for half a second. It even draws out a muted "Oof!"

Maccabee focuses on the gun. He twists the wrist with the pistol and it falls to the floor. He flicks it under the bed with his foot.

But Alice recovers fast, grabs the flesh between his rib cage and his pelvic bone, and squeezes. Squeezes so hard it feels like her fingers are going to cut through him and literally yank out his insides and throw them on the floor.

He lets go of her wrist and zips a left cross over her cheekbone. He can feel it crack below the eye.

"Ack!" she yells, releasing him and hopping backward onto the bed, straddling Ekaterina's lifeless body. She doesn't speak, but her face, smiling wryly, says it all: *Nice hit.*

Maccabee tries to grab her, but she claps a hand on the crown of his head and vaults over him, as gracefully as a circus acrobat. She hits the floor noiselessly, expecting Maccabee to spin and face her. But he doesn't waste time doing that. Instead he sweeps his leg behind him and cuts Alice's feet out from under her. She falls over sideways. She scrambles momentarily, but before she can get up Maccabee's knee crunches into her side and she folds at the middle, crunching to the hardwood floor.

Maccabee jumps on top of her, his knees pinning her elbows, and lands a series of lighting-fast but gut-churning blows to her midsection. She tenses her stomach muscles, pain latticing every fiber, as Maccabee lands his 5th hit. The sound is different this time. More slap than thump. Alice has had worse.

Alice studies Maccabee's face in that split second. It is torn with rage and grief. If he wasn't trying to kill her, she'd almost feel sorry for him. Too many people are going to be suffering from the same feelings soon. Far too many.

Alice thrusts her hips up to try to throw Maccabee. He holds on, but his flurry is interrupted. She works her right arm free and swings up, her hand open, her fingers curled like claws, her nails raking the side of his neck and drawing blood. She swipes again, trying to grab his ear and pull it off, but he whips his arm through the air and catches her wrist. He twists it to the floor and reaches down and pulls out the four-inch blade hidden under the cuff of his pants. It flashes in front of Alice's eyes as it comes down for her throat. He is going to kill her in the same way that she killed the woman.

Your mum, Alice realizes.

She shows a new level of strength as she bucks her left arm, lifting Maccabee's knee off her elbow. The knife slices the air next to Alice's ear, cutting a handful of her curled hair. He doesn't waste any time, though, and brings the knife back, trying to slice a deep gouge on her throat.

But Alice's left arm is now free, and she deflects the swipe away from her neck. She grabs his wrist. He flips the knife in his fingers, point down. He grabs her wrist with his other hand. She snatches this wrist with her hand. He tries to activate the needle in his little ring, but only in that instant realizes that he doesn't have it on.

They are locked up.

The knifepoint is 12.7 centimeters from her flesh.

It is a contest of strength.

For several seconds neither makes any progress. Muscles bulge and twitch. Veins pop on both their faces, a thick one running diagonally from the bridge of Alice's nose and past her pale crescent-shaped birthmark, the vein disappearing into her hair.

Maccabee leans forward, puts his shoulders and back into it. The knife jitters with the effort of both Players. It moves toward Alice's neck, but only 2.4 centimeters.

Alice is silent. Concentrated.

Maccabee screams. Spittle flies from the back of his throat, dotting Alice's face. She blinks one fleck out of her eye, but otherwise stays here, in the moment, her muscles working working working.

Maccabee cannot make progress.

He screams again, this time even more primal and desperate, and rises onto his feet, angles his shoulders so that he can get as much of his weight over the knife, and finally it comes down.

Down.

Down.

It touches Alice's dark skin, pushes in. Maccabee feels the skin give way. He sees the blood. He raises his hips. Pushes down. It pierces her platysma muscle 1 centimeter, 2 centimeters. The blood begins to flow. The first drop hits the floor.

Alice is still silent.

He pushes.

She pushes back.

He pushes.

She grips his wrists so hard that the tips of his fingers are going purple.

He has her.

Alice lets go with her right hand. The knife goes in another centimeter. The pain begins to scream. She doesn't.

She reaches down, in between them, in the space that Maccabee has created by half standing over her. She reaches down and grabs his groin and squeezes as hard as she can.

A sickening popping noise as Maccabee wilts and cries out. She squeezes harder and harder and harder.

She braces his suddenly dead weight with her left arm. Presses a pressure point in his wrist with her middle finger. His hand releases the knife. She twists, throws him to the side, and straddles him, her right hand still in between them, squeezing harder and harder and harder.

Finally she lets go.

Maccabee is panting, crying. He has never felt such pain.

She pulls the knife from her neck and lays it on the floor and balls her fists and methodically punches Maccabee in the face left and right and left and right and left and right and left and right and left.

When she is finished, Maccabee is motionless. His nose is as crooked as it's ever been. His lip is split. His left eye is already swelling shut. Blood and tears and sweat cover his face in a sheen of red. Snot bubbles at his nostrils and pops, bubbles and pops.

Alice kneads her hands. They are bruised but not broken. She touches the wound on her neck. It's bad, but it didn't get anything vital. She'll live.

"Good fight, but you gotta bring more for a Koori."

She picks up Maccabee's knife.

Holds it over his heart.

"See ya in hell, mate."

Yes, Koori . . . In hell. . . . Now Play on . . . Maccabee thinks, still conscious, barely hanging on.

The Nabataean can just make out the contours of Alice's mop of hair and the wistful look in her eyes.

. . . Play on. . . .

Maccabee waits for the warm death of a skewered heart, waits to see his mother in the life beyond, if there is one, wants it even, to see her, to be with her, to have it end. In that moment he is ready to concede— eager, even.

Ready.

But instead of death he sees Alice's head tilt at an impossible angle, rising suddenly and falling 100 degrees to the side, onto her shoulder and past it, blood spattering everywhere.

The knife clatters to the floor.

BAITSAKHAN

Arendsweg 11, Apartment 1H, Lichtenberg, Berlin, Germany

Baitsakhan, wearing nothing but a pink hospital gown, stands over the Koori and the pulped Nabataean, struggling to hold up the dead weight of the huge woman.

All Baitsakhan did was grab and squeeze the back of her neck. His bionic hand did the rest. Maccabee and his mother had explained the hand's functionality to the Donghu, prattling on about pressure per centimeter and augmented grip strength. The Nabataeans and all their words. Baitsakhan didn't pay much attention. He wanted to see for himself.

His hand crushed through the Koori's skin, muscle, and bone like it was a bundle of straw. In 3.7 seconds, Baitsakhan held a squishy rope of pulverized spine.

He releases her. She falls to the side, her head barely attached to a bloody braid of bone and tissue. Her body quivers and spasms for several seconds as the strong life inside fades reluctantly, oh so reluctantly.

She stops moving.

Baitsakhan spits on the Koori's mangled body.

Alice Ulapala is dead.

Her Endgame is over.

Next to her, Maccabee's chest rises and falls. He is battered but he will survive.

"The hand works," Baitsakhan says, as if nothing were wrong with Maccabee. As if Ekaterina were not lying dead only a meter away. "It works well."

Baitsakhan recalls his fight with Kala in Turkey, how Maccabee saved him in much the same way, by sneaking up on the Sumerian and stabbing her in the back.

"We're even now," Baitsakhan says, still staring at his incredible hand. Maccabee can only groan in agreement, his mouth swollen, a broken tooth wedged into his bottom lip. The little monster could finish him off. Two Players extinguished in a few seconds. Maccabee knows this, and is thankful the Donghu has some sense of honor, or gratitude, or whatever code the young beast subscribes to.

He is thankful and surprised. He will lose consciousness soon and will be relying on the Donghu to take care of him, their roles reversed.

Baitsakhan scratches his bare ass through the back of his hospital gown. "I need to pee," he declares, and pads quietly out of the room. His footsteps are much quieter than Maccabee's were. Alice Ulapala was right about that. For all the good it did her.

The lights go out for Maccabee.

But unlike the Koori, he will wake again.

SHARI CHOPRA

सूर्य को अन्तमि रेज, *Valley of Eternal Life, Sikkim, India*

It is Shari's turn to dream.

And dream badly.

She sees the whole thing play out, just as it happened. Alice dying violently in that bedroom on the other side of the world. Shari screams and cries and kicks at the Nabataean and swings at the Donghu with a long stick crowned with a tangle of spikes.

Her blows pass through them like she is a ghost.

Time passes quickly in the dream. Shari watches the boys gather themselves and leave, Maccabee's arm draped over the shoulders of the much shorter Baitsakhan.

Baitsakhan staring lovingly at his peculiar hand.

Alice left behind.

Savaged and cold.

Good Alice. Noble Alice.

Dead Alice.

Shari kneels over her body, tries to give it some dignity, but it's impossible.

Shari realizes that what she's witnessed is no dream.

The Player who is out in the world protecting her Little Alice is no more.

It's a nightmare.

Shari runs from the room to chase the boys, but as she exits the doorway, she's transported somewhere else.

She is neck-deep in cold, cold water in a small stone antechamber.

The water glows blue, and throws undulating light onto the walls and ceiling.

She tastes the water.

Salty.

She wades to a small embankment and pulls herself from the water. She's naked. There's no sound but the whisper of waves breaking in the distance.

Carved into the walls are blocks of words. Sanskrit, Sumerian, Egyptian, Celtic, Harappan, and another language Shari has never seen before consisting of perfectly hewn dashes and vertical lines and dots, some kind of otherworldly braille.

Scattered among the words like mathematical confetti are modern numerals, in a seemingly random pattern: 040113984451340743718763 7845291103656610213196465215829456.

Shari walks along the wall, running her fingers over the writing.

She can read the Sanskrit. A passage from the Mahabharata. The Hindu sacred poem that she memorized in its entirety when she was all of nine years old. The one that tells of Drona and Arjuna, of King Karna and his many victories, of Lord Krishna and the battle at Dwarka, of Sikhandi and Bhishma. Of the great war of Kurukshetra. Of the four human, if not always noble, goals: dharma, artha, kama, moksha.

Righteousness, prosperity, desire, liberation.

The goals that every person lives for, fights for, and that many have spilled rivers of blood for.

As she moves, the light in the water fades, and suddenly all is black. The sound of the ocean disappears.

The numbers light up.

Here and here and here.

Ten of them suddenly fly to the middle of the room and swirl around. 4922368622.

Shari knows these are important. Perhaps, in some way, they are Alice's parting gift to her.

She must remember them.

She tries to grab the numbers, to keep them, but they evade her fingers like butterflies riding a garden breeze.

And then the screaming starts.

In less than a second it grows to deafening levels, and Shari jolts awake. The screaming is gone. Jamal is by her side, still asleep. Little Alice is in her adjoining room in the great stone fortress, also asleep. Shari scrambles to her bedside table to write the numbers down on a scrap of paper. She does. There they are, in the world of the living, a gift from the dreamscape, a gift from Big Alice Ulapala, may the gods take her.

AN LIU

22B Hateshinai Tōri, Naha, Okinawa, Japan

After setting up some just-in-case toys in the backyard, An scales the wall of a four-story prewar wooden residence. It takes him less than a minute to reach the roof. It is 3:13 a.m. The house sits atop a hill, and from the roof An can see all the way down to the water. Naha is asleep, and half-abandoned anyway, since many couldn't bear to live here after the horrors of the meteor that ravaged the harbor.

An is dressed like a ninja. Loose black cotton pants and flat, soft-soled shoes. A long-sleeved black cotton shirt. Fingerless gloves. A hood pulled over his head. A scarf tied over his face. A svelte knapsack slung over his shoulders and tied tightly to his waist so that it doesn't bounce or swing. It contains a few more toys. Two smoke grenades on his chest. A Walther PPQ on his left hip, angled for a right-hand draw. A two-switch remote, the arming mechanism sewn onto the sleeve of his left forearm, the detonator sewn into his right pocket. A smartphone zippered into his left pocket.

And most importantly, the necklace of hair and flesh hanging against his chest.

His talisman. His saving grace. His love.

With him always now.

There are four cameras on the roof. An avoids them, but doesn't go to extremes. He doubts the authorities even care about burglars in light of the Abaddon revelation. All the camouflage probably isn't necessary.

The ninja suit is a tribute. A testament to his beloved. It felt appropriate to wear, considering who owns this house.

This is the Takeda residence. Inside are Chiyoko's people.

He reaches the door on the roof and holds the smartphone over a keypad. The camera overhead surely sees him. Perhaps someone inside is already running to meet him.

To greet him.

Hopefully they will be like Chiyoko and show some restraint. An doesn't want to be killed tonight.

Not yet.

He wants to talk.

He swipes the smartphone's screen and selects a homemade app. It runs through 202,398,241 combinations in 3.4 seconds, transmitting them wirelessly to the door's security keypad. Code number 202,398,242 does the trick. The door unlocks.

An pulls the handle, opens the door, walks inside, closes the door quietly. No alarms, no shouting, no footsteps, no shots fired from the darkness.

Just silence.

The way Chiyoko would have wanted it.

Perhaps the way all the Takedas want it.

Maybe they all are mute, he thinks.

An pulls the scarf and hood from his head. A 2nd tattoo tear is under his eye, fresh and new, glazed with petroleum jelly, ringed with a thin red band of irritation.

He leisurely walks down the stairs, holding his hands out in a gesture of goodwill, just in case he bumps into someone.

He doesn't.

He reaches the topmost floor. A hall light is on. Four sliding doors, three open. He peers into each. Bedrooms. All with futons on the floor. All empty of people. He reaches the 3rd door and slides it open. A western-style bed. A small pewter bell over the doorway, a string leading away from it and disappearing into the wall.

A window overlooking the decimated harbor. A painting on the wall, opposite the bed. A painting of a winding river as seen from a bird's eye, peaceful and serene, like Chiyoko appeared to be.

But An knows that water is always strong and unyielding, and that it seeps into everything.

Like Chiyoko.

He steps inside the empty room. He smells the air.

He can smell her.

This is Chiyoko's room.

He takes a deep breath, holds her scent in his nose, and quickly leaves to continue his search.

Down another flight of stairs—two more empty bedrooms, a study, a bathroom. No people.

Down another flight. A kitchen, a tea room, another bathroom, a sitting room with a Western fireplace, a small orange fire crackling within.

And there, sitting serenely on a round floor cushion, a small bald man in a simple blue-and-crimson-striped *yukata*, his dark, round eyes open and staring straight at An.

A katana, unsheathed, 1,329 years old, rests in a stand just in front of him. A white porcelain plate with crumbs. A cup, maybe empty, maybe not.

"Hello," the man says in Japanese.

An eyes the sword and holds up his hands. "I'm sorry, sir. But I don't speak your language," he says in Mandarin, hoping that since Chiyoko understood it, maybe this man does too.

"That is all right. I speak yours," the man answers in Mandarin. He eyes the details of An's necklace. The shriveled knots of flesh. The ears. The hair.

"My name is An Liu. I am the Player of the 377th line. I am the Shang. I apologize for entering your home in this way. I was afraid that if I rang the bell, you would reject me."

An hasn't been this formal in a long time, and speaking like this takes effort and concentration. More than he expected. It is important that he keep his disdain for formalities in check, that he keep his voice neutral.

"My name is Nobuyuki Takeda. And yes, I would have rejected you. Perhaps worse." He reaches out and takes the hilt of his sword but doesn't lift it.

"Who are you to . . . to Chiyoko?" An asks. "Her father?"

"She is my niece."

"Master Takeda, I am sorry. But I must tell you that your niece is dead." Nobuyuki jumps to his knees. This time he lifts the sword. Even from across the room, An can see tears welling in Nobuyuki's eyes.

"Speak quickly and truthfully. I will be able to tell if you are lying."

An gives him a curt but respectful nod. "She died at Stonehenge. I was there. One of the ancient megaliths fell on top of her when the ground shifted. It crushed her from the waist down. She died instantly."

"You witnessed this?" Nobuyuki's voice is even, not afraid, not sorrowful, but demanding.

And yet a tear rolls down his cheek.

An shakes his head. "No. I was unconscious. Another Player, the Cahokian, shot me in the head." He points to his star-shaped stitches. "If not for the metal plate I have here, I would have died too."

"Were others there?"

"Yes. One called Jago Tlaloc. The Olmec. He was Playing with the Cahokian. And another, a non-Player allied with the Cahokian. He was killed as well."

"And you? Were you Playing with Chiyoko?" Nobuyuki sounds confused. He knows that Chiyoko would never agree to an alliance. She was always a loner. That was one of her many strengths.

An shakes his head again. "Not officially. But we did have . . . an understanding. A relationship."

This last word is hard for him to say.

"You *knew* her? Beyond the confines of the game?"

"Takeda-san"—An uses the Japanese honorific, one of the few words he knows—"there is no 'beyond the confines of the game.' As Chiyoko told me, she Played for life. This phrase, I think, had many meanings for her. Among them, that the game encompasses everything. To go beyond the game is to go beyond life."

Nobuyuki eases back on his knees, but not on his grip of the katana. An's words intrigue him. "Tell me. About your time with her."

"I met your niece while we were Playing—in fact, our first altercation after the Calling was a fight in a hardware store. Neither won. She was incredibly fast. Her chi was unparalleled."

"I know."

"Infectious, even."

"Explain yourself."

"I am sick, Takeda-san. My line has made me so. I suffer from debilitating tics that, at their worst, cloud my thinking and my actions. They are the result of a harsh childhood, a criminally harsh one. They made me into a monster."

"All of you had harsh childhoods."

"Mine was different."

"Yes. Not all of you became monsters."

"You loved her, didn't you, Takeda-san? She knew love?"

"I *love* her, An Liu. Even if she is gone. More so if she is gone."

An lets his chin fall to his chest. He sees her hair that hangs around his neck. Her ears. Her eyelids that he cut free. "As do I," An says quietly.

"And, remarkably, she loved me back. She was the first, maybe the only person, ever to love me. Ever."

"If you are sick, why does it not show? Where are these tics you speak of?"

An raises his head, and gazes into Nobuyuki's dark eyes. The fire cracks. There is no other sound.

"She cured me. Her chi cured me, and her love saved me."

Nobuyuki raises the sword and points it at An's throat. Four meters separate them. "What is that around your neck?"

"It is what I could salvage from your niece. The things she gave me.

The things that continue to save me."

"You *cut* them from her? You *desecrated* her?" Nobuyuki growls.

"I am sorry, Master. But she would have consented. I promise you. I would not have taken them if I knew otherwise."

Nobuyuki's eye twitches. An can hardly blame him. An watches as Nobuyuki suppresses his rage.

The tone of Nobuyuki's voice shifts. "You said that my niece Played for life. I know this to be true. But now I must ask, Shang, what is it that you Play for?"

An sighs. "Not for life, Takeda-san. Life has been cruel to me. Death makes more sense. I would rather snuff out every last Player—myself included—and let the game go unwon than see life go on. I would rather see humanity gone, our alien ancestry wiped away and forgotten, than carry on and perpetuate its lies and hypocrisies and cruelties. There is a big part of me that still wants this. Humanity does not deserve this planet, and this planet does not deserve humanity."

"But . . ." Nobuyuki says, egging on An.

"But . . . then I met your niece, and she lit something in me. I changed, if only a little. And I am hoping that you, and your most ancient and venerable line, perhaps the one most closely related to the Makers, would help me realize that change and make it permanent."

"You wish to propose something? Something mutually beneficial?"

"Yes. I would humbly and respectfully like to renounce my line and Play for yours. Chiyoko deserved to live. To win. I do not. My line certainly does not deserve to inherit the Earth after the Event. I think that yours does. I pledge myself to you, Takeda-san. If you will accept me, I pledge myself to you."

Nobuyuki frowns. An can't read him, can't decide if he's merely caught the old man off guard or if the very idea offends and disgusts him. Either way, Nobuyuki doesn't speak.

"Please, Master Takeda. The only alternative is for me to go back to what I was. I am filled with hatred and rage. Do you understand? It boils inside me, explodes out of me, makes me . . . Your niece could soothe me. She was the only one, but she is gone, and I have done a shameful thing to remain close to her. . . ." An touches the necklace again. Holds his hand there. "I believe you could show me a different way, Master Takeda. Show me Chiyoko's way. I want to Play for the Mu. I want to *be* Mu. The keplers don't care for rules, only for the game and its conclusion. If I can win then I can tell them that I Play for Chiyoko, and for the Mu. They will accept it. I know it. I feel it. Please. I beg you, for the sake of your line, and for the sake of my soul—as tarnished and desperate and imperfect as it may be."

These words exhaust An. There are too many of them, and they are too revealing, pleading, pathetic. But they are true.

Nobuyuki uses the sword like a cane to stand up. He looks labored. Spent. A thousand years old and counting.

"No," the Mu elder says quietly, his voice shaking ever so slightly.

"But—"

"No. The answer is no, Shang."

A hollow feeling grows rapidly in An's stomach. He feels like he is going to cry.

An says nothing.

"I do not make this decision lightly, Shang," Nobuyuki says with effort. "But it must be this way. If the Mu line is to fade, then so be it. What will be will be."

"Please . . ." An begs. His left hand begins to twitch.

Nobuyuki's voice deepens, grows more restive. "You speak of honor, but what do you know of honor? Of respect? You have come uninvited into my house in the dead of night. You have disturbed my meditation to tell me that my dearest Chiyoko is no longer living. You have spoken to me with words that sound respectful, but are nothing more than an ultimatum disguised as a proposition. You do not even bother to learn how to greet me in my mother tongue—in Chiyoko's mother tongue. You come here prepared to renounce the full history of your people, all for your own selfish purposes. Chiyoko may have been young, but she was not selfish. Your trainers were cruel to you. Maybe they beat you and tortured you. So what?"

BLINK.

"What of your ancestors from hundreds, thousands of years ago? Were they cruel to you? What of your line's descendants in the generations to come? Would they be cruel to you? Perhaps they are redeemable, all of them, perhaps *you* can save *them*, now, here, by Playing honorably for your people, as well as for Chiyoko's memory. *That* is how she would have wanted it. This I know. She understood what it meant to be a Player. You, clearly, do not. I am sorry, An Liu of the Shang, but I cannot accept you. Chiyoko may have loved you. I hope she did. But that does not mean that I can, or that any of my people can. If you are broken, then you must fix yourself. I can't save you."

"But . . ." An mumbles, his voice failing. There is nothing more for him to say.

"Now, I would request that you leave, but first there is something that *I* must ask of *you*." Nobuyuki raises his sword and points it once more at An. "If all that is left of my niece—of my beloved Chiyoko—is what you wear around your neck, then I ask that you give it to me so that my line can memorialize her for the hero that she is, and give what remains of her a proper burial."

BLINK.

BLINKshivershiverBLINK.

SHIVER.

An takes *blink* takes a step back. "N-no."

Nobuyuki steps forward and, still keeping the blade raised, bows deeply. "Yes," he says to the floor. "With respect, Player, I insist."

An flicks the arming switch on his left forearm while Nobuyuki isn't looking.

"N-n-n-no!"

Nobuyuki. Still bowed. "Yes."

An reaches across his body and unsnaps his gun's holster. Nobuyuki rises like a giant and lunges forward, covering the space between them in a half second. He slashes the katana at An, who backpedals into the hallway unscathed.

The blade comes again, this time for An's outstretched hand, and, with ease, cleanly slices the muzzle off the gun, rendering its firing mechanism useless.

The sword is angled down, its point in the floor. Without hesitating An pistol-whips Nobuyuki across the cheek. He cries out. An dances over the blade and kicks Nobuyuki's legs out. Chiyoko's uncle falls to the floor. An drops what's left of the pistol and steps on Nobuyuki's sword hand, the bones crunching. The cloth-wrapped hilt comes free.

An bends to pick it up.

Shiverblinkshiver.

"Stand"—*blink*—"stand up."

Nobuyuki stands. Faces An. Skinny, insignificant-looking An, playing the part of a Player.

Chiyoko's uncle rubs his cheek with the back of his wrist. An holds the sword with both hands, high and at the ready.

"Careless, disrespectful boy," Nobuyuki says, blood coating his teeth.

"Enough," An commands. "No"—*blink*—"no"—*blink*—"no more words."

"If you had given her remains to me freely—*honorably*—then I would have reconsidered your request."

The words are *BLINKBLINKBLINKBLINKBLINK* the words are *SHIVERBLINK SHIVERSHIVER* the words are searing.

"A test? You would have"—*blink*—"you would have"—*SHIVER*—"you would have accepted me?"

"Ye—"

But Nobuyuki's answer is cut short as An slashes the ancient sword—sharper than a razor, harder than a diamond—diagonally through the air, cutting Nobuyuki clean in half from his left shoulder to his right hip. The blade is so sharp that for a moment Nobuyuki—every vital organ save his brain and lower intestine completely severed—stands there wearing a look of shock. His face instantly goes pale, and then, after a couple seconds, his top half slides off his bottom half and spills to the floor. Just after that, his lower body falls over sideways.

An breathes hard, his back hunches, his mind reels. He lets one hand off the sword and reaches into his pocket. He clicks the detonator. Outside, in the backyard, a firebomb goes off. The sound of breaking glass and combustion. A blast of air whooshes past An, pulling at his loose clothing. He already smells the burning wood. The old Takeda home will go up in minutes.

An spins to the front door, dragging the katana at his side. Another keepsake. He pulls the black hood over his head, the air growing warmer at his back. He pulls the scarf over his scrunched face.

He walks to the front door and unlocks it and grabs the metal ring and pulls.

There is Naha.

There is Japan.

There is the world.

There is Endgame.

He touches Chiyoko. Her hair. Her skin. Her ears. The tics are gone again.

He walks down the steps.

"I play for death," he mutters.

"I play for death."

JAGO TLALOC, SARAH ALOPAY, RENZO

On Board Renzo's Cessna Citation CJ4, Private Airstrip, Outskirts of Valle Hermoso, Tamaulipas, Mexico

Ever since her crying fit following the president's speech, Sarah has been sleeping. An incredible 19 hours and counting.

Renzo landed the plane in Valle Hermoso, a sleepy but sometimes violent border town in northeastern Mexico, 13 hours ago. Sarah barely stirred as the plane bumped along and taxied to a hangar. Jago let her sleep. He gingerly took Earth Key from Sarah's pocket and placed it in his own. They left her in the plane, posting two armed guards outside with strict orders not to disturb her. Jago also left her a cell phone with a local number on a Post-it so she could call him if she woke up.

She didn't wake up.

While she slept, Renzo and Jago met with the 67-year-old Olmec line member Maria Reyes Santos Izil at her modest adobe home a kilometer away. They had beef-tongue tacos, and poached red snapper with chiles and coconut slivers, and corn custard with creamy poblano sauce. They watched a Mexican football match. Jago showed Earth Key to Maria Reyes Santos Izil. She inspected it from all angles, turned it in her fingers, shone a light on it. *"Es una bolita,"* she said, shocked that such a small thing could be so powerful. Jago and Renzo each drank two beers. They each slept for 6.33 hours. They each said good-bye and thank you to their hostess. *"Vaya con los dioses del cielo,"* she said to them, and then, to Jago, *"Gane."* The men returned to the refueled plane and called Juliaca to let Jago's parents know they would be there soon.

"You'll need to roll out the old woman," Jago tells his father as he stands just outside the plane, running his hand along the leading edge of a wing.

Sarah still sleeps.

Jago goes inside the plane and sits opposite her. He watches her for over half an hour. As he does this, he turns Earth Key in his fingers. Contemplates it, tries to get something from it, anything.

If only this "key" opened some door that would lead to the next passage. If only the keplers hadn't made Endgame so opaque. Of course, that's the point, though. To make us suffer before the suffering really begins.

The more he Plays, the more he hates these bastards from the stars. These so-called gods. He wishes he could eradicate *them*, and not the other way around.

But that's impossible, and he knows it.

Finally, Sarah moves.

Jago places Earth Key in a recessed fireproof compartment built into the bulkhead and locks it shut.

Earth Key is safe.

He watches Sarah again. She brings her fists to her eyes and rubs the sleep away. She swallows. She stretches her legs and her back and flexes her toes.

"Hey," Jago says.

She blinks. Looks at Jago. "Hey yourself." Her voice is raspy, sexy, confident. Jago's happy she sounds like the girl he met on the train in China, like the girl he flirted with, like the girl he was Playing with before she got Earth Key.

Like Sarah Alopay.

"How long've I been out?"

"Little over nineteen hours."

"What?" Sarah props herself on her elbow and looks around, trying to see out the windows.

"*Sí*, nineteen hours. Never seen anyone sleep like that. I once did a twelve-hour lick after a training mission in the Andes, but never more than that."

"I wish you'd woken me when we landed."

"I tried. You were like a rock."

She swings her legs over the edge of the seat. "Well, I'm up now."

He smiles. "I'm glad."

"Listen. About London. I . . . I shouldn't have run like that."

"I told you I wasn't mad at you. I understand. You were scared."

"Yeah, but I shouldn't have left you."

"You thought I was dead. It's all right, Sarah."

"No, it isn't. You wouldn't have left me like that."

"You're right."

Sarah's heart pounds. A lump forms in her stomach. "I shouldn't have left you, Feo."

"It's all right, Alopay. Really. Just don't do it again."

I don't deserve him, Sarah thinks. She tries hard not to think of Christopher. Tries and fails. *I don't deserve anyone.*

"Don't think of him, Sarah."

"That obvious, huh?"

"*Sí.* Don't think about it. You did what you had to do, and you got Earth Key. You Played. What's done is done." He reaches for her hand. She takes it. Squeezes. "I can't help it. Just sitting here like this, with you, reminds me of him. Of what we were."

Jago doesn't know what to say, so he doesn't say anything.

"I did a horrible thing, Jago."

"You have to forgive yourself. You have to find a way. And you will. I'll help you."

Sarah squeezes Jago's hand again and peers over his shoulder and out the window. And that's when she notices the hangar outside.

Her family doesn't have a hangar at the Cahokian compound on the Niobrara River in northwestern Nebraska.

Sarah frowns. "Wait—we're not in Nebraska? I gave you the coordinates. I saw Renzo punch them into the nav computer. I didn't dream that, right?"

"No, you didn't."

"Then where the hell are we?"

"There's been a change of plan, Sarah."

Sarah lets go of Jago's hand and stands, forgetting that there's an overhead compartment directly above her. She bangs her head, rebounds onto her seat. She rubs her crown. Her hair's a mess. Jago likes the look of it—also sexy—but knows he shouldn't be thinking of that right now.

But he's 19 years old, and no amount of training can get that out of his system.

Sarah seethes. "What do you mean, 'a change of plan'?"

"We're at an Olmec airstrip in Mexico. We needed more fuel."

"To go to Nebraska."

He shakes his head. "To go to Peru."

Sarah's face crumples. "What?"

"We need to show Earth Key to a wise woman in my line. She'll know where we need to take it. She'll help us find Sky Key."

"Jago, I don't *want* help finding Sky Key. I *want* to see my family! I *need* to see them!"

"Well, you're not going to see them. Not yet. Abaddon is—"

Sarah lunges across the narrow cabin and falls to her knees in front of Jago and pounds his chest with both fists. He lets her do it. The blows aren't meant to hurt, and they don't.

"Sarah—"

"You don't understand. If I don't see them, I won't make it!" she says.

"Sarah—"

"Something's happened to me, Jago. I don't know what. Something's broken inside me."

"I know, Sarah," Jago says quietly, so that Renzo, if he's eavesdropping at the door, won't hear. "That's exactly why you can't go to your family now."

She pounds his chest again, and he grabs her by the wrists, holds them in place. She's strong, but he's stronger. She collapses, her butt resting on her heels. Opens her hands and flattens them on his chest.

He eases up on her wrists. Lets one of his hands fall on her head as it settles into his lap.

"I'm sorry, Sarah, but you're in no state of mind to make decisions. I have to make them for you. If we could switch places, you'd see that I'm right."

"But you said you wanted to help me. If that's true then let me go to my family. They *can* help me." Her voice is quiet. Plaintive.

"Maybe *sí*, maybe *no*."

"They can. I know it." But she doesn't sound convinced.

"You want to know what I know, Sarah? That so long as you're Playing, you're all right. So long as you're not thinking about Earth Key or Christopher or the Event, so long as you're just reacting to what's coming at you, then you're fine. So that's where I'm taking you. To the game. To Endgame. To Play. You may be ready to give up, but I'm not ready to give up on you. That—that is how *I* am going to help you."

"I want to go home." A whisper.

"I want things too, but I can't always have them." He caresses her hair. Twirls a strand around his finger. She nuzzles her cheek into his thigh. Right now, more than anything, he wants to hold her, kiss her, tear her clothing off.

Right now he wishes Endgame weren't real.

But it is.

"The other Players aren't taking detours to deal with the way they *feel* about what's happening. . . . They're Playing. For all we know, the seven most deadly people in the world—not counting you or me—are using every tool at their disposal to find us, to find Earth Key. For all we know, they are fifty miles away and closing fast. For all we know, one's aiming a sniper rifle at this very airplane, or an RPG, or a telescopic mic and is listening to us talk, right now. We can't let them do this. We can't let them catch us! We can't let them take it, or kill either one of us. We have to stay together, protect each other, hold Earth Key, and find Sky Key. *That* is what we need to do. They are Playing. We *have* to Play too."

She lets one of her hands rest on his knee.

"I could go," she says. "On my own."

His heart flutters at the possibility, but he knows it won't happen.

He knows because: "I have Earth Key."

She pulls away. "What do you mean you have Earth Key?"

"Don't worry. It's safe."

Sarah looks left and right. "Where is it? Where?" She digs her nails into his thigh.

"It's on the plane." He suddenly wonders if he should tell her where he put it. "That's why we're going to Peru. There's an Olmec elder who should be able to help us. *Us*, Sarah, do you hear me?"

She doesn't. "I need it, Jago. You're right about one thing—I can't lose it. I can't be responsible for triggering the Event and then lose the thing that might offer me some way to redemption. Some way . . . some way . . . some way . . ." She trails off, her eyes darting around the cabin in fear.

Jago's heart pounds. She has been poisoned. Did Earth Key do this to her? Is there some defect in her line? Or was she always so fragile right under the surface?

No.

He doesn't think so.

Her nails dig and dig and dig. He takes her head in both hands and lifts her gaze to his. Pushes forward in his seat.

He still sees it there.

The strength.

"It's okay, Sarah. It's okay."

Renzo starts the plane's engines. His voice comes over the PA.

"Leaving in five, Jago."

Jago clicks the all-clear button on the bulkhead.

"I need to see my family," Sarah says again.

"No, you don't."

"I need to."

"You can't. I won't let you."

"So I'm your captive, is that it?"

The plane lurches backward, begins to move into the bright Mexican day.

"Yes," he says. "I won't let you go. I can't."

The engines cycle up.

"Prepare for takeoff," Renzo announces.

"We'll win together?" she says.

"Yes. I swear it." She lifts her head. He pulls her face to his. They kiss, and kiss, and kiss. "I swear it," he repeats, and then they don't say anything else.

ix

AISLING KOPP, GREG JORDAN, BRIDGET McCLOSKEY, POP KOPP

CIA Safe House, Port Jervis, New York, United States

As soon as Aisling saw Pop, she gave him a long warm hug, rocking back and forth. He kissed both her cheeks. They hugged again. She whispered quietly in his ear in their ancient Celtic tongue, "Did they hurt you?"

"No."

"Do you trust them?"

"A little."

"Do you think they can help us?"

"Yes."

"Then let's see where this goes."

"Agreed."

They said it so discreetly and quickly and without even moving their lips that none of the CIA officers noticed.

The following morning Aisling and Pop sit thigh to thigh at the head of a table in a situation room, ready to hear some presentation Jordan's put together. He stands next to Aisling with a clicker. McCloskey sits on the long side of the table at a laptop. Marrs is somewhere else.

"Probably having a powwow with Token D. Doobie," McCloskey says.

Jordan huffs. "Especially after the president's announcement."

Aisling ignores the cutesy pot joke. "But I thought you jarheads knew about the giant meteor already."

Jordan hits the clicker. A screen at the far end of the room lights up.

"Yeah, but hearing it pass the commander in chief's hallowed lips is another level of wake the heck up, you know?"

"And we're not jarheads," McCloskey corrects. "We're spooks."

"Enough banter," Jordan says. "Load up the personnel doc, McCloskey."

Aisling watches McCloskey's body language as she runs her fingers over the laptop. She looks confident and businesslike. No-nonsense. Nothing about her conveys duplicity or intrigue. The same goes for Jordan. They're just two professionals doing something they've done hundreds of times: getting ready to talk about bad guys and what to do about them.

And yet Aisling knows that while body language is a good indicator of intentions, it's not bulletproof. She *knows* these two haven't told her everything.

There's more to these people. But what?

As Aisling ponders this, a low-end graphic appears on the screen. It's a black card with a red target in the background. The title reads ENDGAME PLAYERS.

"You guys make that yourself?" Aisling asks with mock admiration.

"We're not graphic designers, Kopp," Jordan answers wryly. He hits the clicker again, and the graphic changes to two rows of rectangles, six on top, seven on bottom.

Aisling sees herself, from a passport photo. And An Liu, who looks asleep or dead. And Chiyoko Takeda, who to Aisling's surprise is categorically dead. And a grainy picture of Jago Tlaloc on a street corner. And another, much clearer picture of Sarah Alopay in an airport. And a clear snapshot of Maccabee Adlai. And a passport photo of an American-looking kid with blond hair, blue eyes, and light stubble. The other six rectangles are blank and have question marks on them.

"Who's the hunky one?" Aisling asks. "He's not a Player."

"Christopher Vanderkamp of Omaha, Nebraska. Dad's a beef tycoon. He was Sarah Alopay's boyfriend before the meteors."

"Was?"

"Deader'n disco now," McCloskey says. "Blown to bits from the waist up at Stonehenge. We have no idea why he was there, but he was."

"The theory is he puppy-dogged Alopay after she left Omaha," Jordan explains. "He was an all-American quarterback, headed to Nebraska to start. Fast and strong, good student too. He probably thought he could help her."

"Who else was at Stonehenge?" Aisling asks.

"Tlaloc and Alopay, Takeda and Liu."

Aisling knows that Sarah and Jago made some kind of alliance, but she doesn't understand why Jordan paired the other two. "The Mu and the Shang were also together?"

"Absolutely," Jordan answers.

Aisling shakes her head. "I don't see it. Chiyoko was a mute, and An was a paranoid sociopath with a gnarly tic. Neither struck me as the type that was looking for love—or even friendship."

"Well, they were definitely together. The Brits got intelligence that proves it."

"What happened to Takeda?" Pop asks.

"Crushed to death by one of the rocks at Stonehenge," Jordan answers.

"And Liu?" Aisling asks.

"Took a gunshot to the head more or less point-blank. But because of a metal plate he had hiding in there, An Liu is unfortunately very much alive," McCloskey says.

"And you're not kidding about An being bad," Jordan adds. "By which I mean very good at competing in Endgame. British Special Forces had him on lockdown on a Royal Navy destroyer in the English Channel, and in spite of being drugged and strapped to a gurney, he escaped single-handedly. Made off with a stealth helicopter, blew up the ship's bridge, and took what was left of Chiyoko Takeda. Killed twenty-seven, injured fifteen, four seriously. The helicopter ditched and sank in the Atlantic when it ran out of fuel. A remote submersible ID'd Takeda's remains, but no sign of Liu."

"Impressive," Aisling says. "Shame he didn't die."

"You know of any other Players who did?" Jordan asks.

"Only the Minoan, Marcus Loxias Megalos of the 5th line," Aisling says.

"Cocky kid. An killed him at the Calling."

"Good to know," Jordan says. McCloskey types the information into the computer.

"And the Cahokian and the Olmec?" Aisling asks. "Are they alive?" Aisling can't help but think about Italy, when she had a chance to waste them and didn't. And she can't help but wonder: if she had wasted them, then maybe Earth Key would never have been found, and the next phase would never have even begun.

"They're alive," Jordan says. "They neutralized a predawn SAS takedown team that ambushed them in their hotel room. The team had sniper *and* unarmed drone support, but that didn't stop the Players from killing two and injuring everyone else. They escaped, evading the backup team in metro London, possibly the most heavily surveilled city in the world."

"Man, the Brits aren't coming out too good in this one, are they?" Aisling asks.

"Not so far."

"I doubt the Israelis or the Germans or the Chinese—or even you and your associates, Mr. Jordan—could have done much better," Pop says.

"They *are* Players."

"Possibly," Jordan says coyly.

Pop ignores him.

Aisling isn't interested in a pissing contest about the efficacy of the world's clandestine services. She says, "I assume Alopay and Tlaloc have Earth Key?"

"We assume the same," Jordan says. "But we're not a hundred percent on what that even means. I've known about Endgame for a long time but—"

"You mean you've been *obsessed* with Endgame for a long time," McCloskey interjects.

"Haven't we all, McCloskey?"

McCloskey shrugs. "Yeah, I guess so."

Aisling says, "I'll explain the Earth Key thing to you later, but I've been dying to know—exactly how is it that you learned all this? What I mean is, who's your source?"

Pop nudges her under the table. "I've been wondering the same," he says.

"I already told you," McCloskey says. "We got some early and, frankly, very confusing info from your dad, and after that it's been the Nabataeans."

Aisling shakes her head. "No offense, but I don't buy it. Your Nabataean friends wouldn't say, 'Hey, you're La Tène Celt. Go find Declan Kopp's daughter and team up with her. That's the only way you have a chance at surviving what's coming.' No way. If they thought you were useful—and they must have, otherwise they wouldn't have bothered talking to you at all—they would have exploited you. Used you. Tried to recruit you."

McCloskey shifts in her chair. Jordan is stock-still.

There it is, Aisling thinks. *Dig deeper. Now.*

"So who's your source?"

"The Nabataeans *did* try to recruit us, Kopp," Jordan says. "Made a hell of a pitch too. All the same, I said no thanks."

"Don't change the subject, Jordan. *Who is it?*" Aisling demands.

Jordan pauses. Looks at McCloskey. She nods. He sighs. "You ever hear of the Brotherhood of the Snake?"

Aisling frowns. "Stupid name."

"But have you heard of them?"

"No. Should I?"

"Probably," McCloskey says, her voice a little lower than normal. "You being a *Player* and all."

"Fuck you, McCloskey."

Jordan holds up a hand. "Easy, guys. No need for that. It doesn't matter if you haven't heard of them. What matters is that they they know a lot about Endgame."

"But who are they?" Pop asks.

"Truth is we've never met a single one," McCloskey says. "They're shadowy as hell. All of our correspondence was hush-hush and superencrypted. Sometimes they just communicated with us by using puzzle challenges that were really hard to crack. Other times they sent us videos that barely made any sense but that had hidden messages. They're obsessed with combating the, quote, Corruption of Man, unquote, by pledging themselves to some quasi-religion called the Ancient Truth."

"They sound like a bunch of Class-A nutsos," Aisling says. "I realize that as a Player that's a little like the pot calling the kettle black, but still. Nutsos."

"We thought the same thing when they contacted us," Jordan says. "We'd been doing antiterrorism work in the Middle East for years, and when we started hearing about Endgame, we thought it was some kind of massive 9/11 follow-up. When we found out it was something else entirely, we were confused. The Brotherhood tracked us down on their own and helped clear some of that confusion."

McCloskey snickers. "And then this little death match got kicked off and—"

Pop slaps the table hard, and everyone shuts up. "This is not a 'little death match,' miss. Crazy or not, it's real. It's the Great Puzzle, and the Players are tasked with solving it. If one doesn't, everyone will die. And if Aisling doesn't solve it, everyone in this room will die. Guaranteed. So let's stop talking about Aisling's crazy dead father and people who we know are *not* Players and get back to business. Let's Play Endgame, now, in the present, not talk about bullshit organizations that think they know one fucking thing about the past when they don't."

Aisling almost says something to contradict Pop. She liked hearing about Jordan's sources, and is curious about this Brotherhood, but then Pop gives her a nudge and she understands. It's a lesson that these CIA officers surely know: Press too hard too fast and you get crappy information. Play it out, with one person wanting more and another wanting less, and you get better information.

There's an awkward silence as the air clears. "Fair enough, Mr. Kopp," Jordan finally says.

"Call me Pop. Everyone does."

Jordan nods. "Let's get back to the presentation."

"Agreed," Aisling says.

Jordan asks for names and descriptions of the other Players. Aisling gives them. She IDs Kala, who's pictured, and then she tells them about Shari and Hilal and Baitsakhan and Maccabee and Alice, who are not pictured. Aisling gives detailed physical descriptions. She assumes each is alive. She talks about Alice last.

"She's big, very dark-skinned, wild hair, and has a pale curved birthmark above her right eye."

McCloskey takes notes and scans the internet as Aisling talks, and within seconds of hearing about Alice she says, "This her?" A picture of Alice Ulapala's bloodied head pops up on the big screen.

"Yup," Aisling says coolly.

"We knew one of you was aboriginal, so we've been casting a wide net for anything involving border crossings or law enforcement vis-à-vis Australian aborigines. We got this hit from the Berlin PD late last night."

Aisling slowly shakes her head. "I didn't think she'd go so soon. Only met her at the Calling, but she seemed like one of the decent ones. Strong too."

"She didn't go easy," Jordan says. "The crime scene was a bloodbath. A dead woman on a bed, her spinal cord severed between the C-three and C-four vertebra. And there was the blood of a third individual all over the floor. Alice's hands were covered in it, and were bruised and swollen, and one was slightly fractured at the third metacarpal. She pummeled the hell out of this guy—and a pretty big guy, judging by the smear marks on the floor—before a fourth, probably male individual with small bare feet snuck up behind her and, somehow, squeezed her neck with his hand so hard that her head popped off. These two appear to have left the scene as quickly as they could."

"Whoa." Even Aisling is surprised by this. "Any prints on Alice?"

"None," McCloskey says. "But judging by your descriptions, the big bludgeoned guy was our Nabataean friend, Maccabee Adlai."

"Surveillance?"

"No. Whoever Alice was hunting had a camera kill switch for the entire building and every camera for a two-block radius. The apartment was wired something special," McCloskey says.

Aisling suggests that the barefoot one could have been Baitsakhan.

"Maybe the Nabataean and the Donghu are Playing together too? I mean if the Shang and the Mu could team up, why not them?"

"Maybe," Jordan says.

"So that's at least three dead, and maybe two teams. All Playing to win." Aisling says this last thing slowly, pensively.

"As far as we know," Jordan says.

"Why *wouldn't* they be Playing to win, Aisling?" Pop asks, clearly not understanding where she's going.

"Well, to be honest, Pop, I'm just wondering if maybe one or more of the Players is thinking what I'm thinking."

"What the hell do you mean?" Pop asks. And then, with a twinge of fear in his voice, "It's that cave painting you saw, isn't it? The one you called me about. The one your father went to so long ago."

Aisling nods. "It's absolutely that cave painting. I understood it, Pop. I also think I understood what Dad wanted, even if he was crazy."

Pop's eyes narrow.

McCloskey holds up a hand. "Wait—what are you two talking about?"

Aisling turns to McCloskey. "Back at JFK you mentioned that you were going to try to stop this thing before you decided to team up with me, right?"

"That's right," McCloskey says.

"Ais, what are you saying?" Pop interjects.

"What I'm saying is that's what I want too. To stop Endgame, Pop. Because I believe, somehow, some way, that it *can* be stopped."

Pop slaps the table again. So hard that the whole room shakes. So hard that Aisling is immediately afraid that he broke his hand.

Pop doesn't speak.

So Aisling speaks for him.

"I know, Pop," Aisling says quietly. "I know you killed Dad—your own son—for thinking the same thing. It's blasphemy."

"Damn right it is," Pop seethes.

"But this is what I want. No—*this is what's right*. If we learn that there's even a razor-thin chance at ending this thing, then we go for it. We could save billions of lives, Pop. Billions."

Pop doesn't speak for several moments. "So that's it? You abandon your training? Your heritage? Your line?" He pauses. "Me?"

"No. I use all these things to help me, Pop. I use you especially. You especially . . ."

Pop edges his seat away from Aisling.

"I'm not saying we stop Playing," Aisling explains. "We can't. *I* can't. I can't because the only way I'm going to figure out how to stop this thing *is* by Playing. I don't have the slightest fucking clue otherwise. So we hunt Players. We kill them if they're bad and we join forces if they're on the same page. We Play because we don't have a choice. . . . But if we *find* a choice, then we make it. We try to stop Endgame, and we try to make sure these fucking keplers never come back here for any reason whatsoever."

Pause.

Pause.

Pause.

"You sold me, Kopp," Jordan says. McCloskey nods in agreement. And even though Aisling knows he still isn't being all the way truthful, she can tell he means it.

"Good."

"So who do we start with?" Jordan asks.

"An Liu," Aisling says decisively. "He's too unpredictable. And he's definitely not trying to save the world."

Jordan claps his hands and smiles. "We were hoping you'd pick old Liu."

"Why?"

Jordan twirls a finger through the air. "Bring it up, McCloskey." The image on the screen changes to a map of the world, a little red blip labeled 533 moving slowly northward along the curved Japanese island of Honshu. "For all the shit the Brits have eaten the past few days, they did manage to do one thing right. They chipped Liu. Stuck a tracker in his right thigh. And wouldn't you know it? Marrs managed to hack it."

"So we can go right to him?" Aisling asks.

"We most certainly can," Jordan replies. "Better than that, we can reroute our kill team to meet us there."

"Kill team, eh?" Pop asks.

"Kilo Foxtrot Echo," McCloskey says.

Aisling shakes her head. "You guys with your jargon."

Jordan shrugs it off. "Jargon may not kill people—but Kilo Foxtrot Echo does."

What are you waiting for?[x]

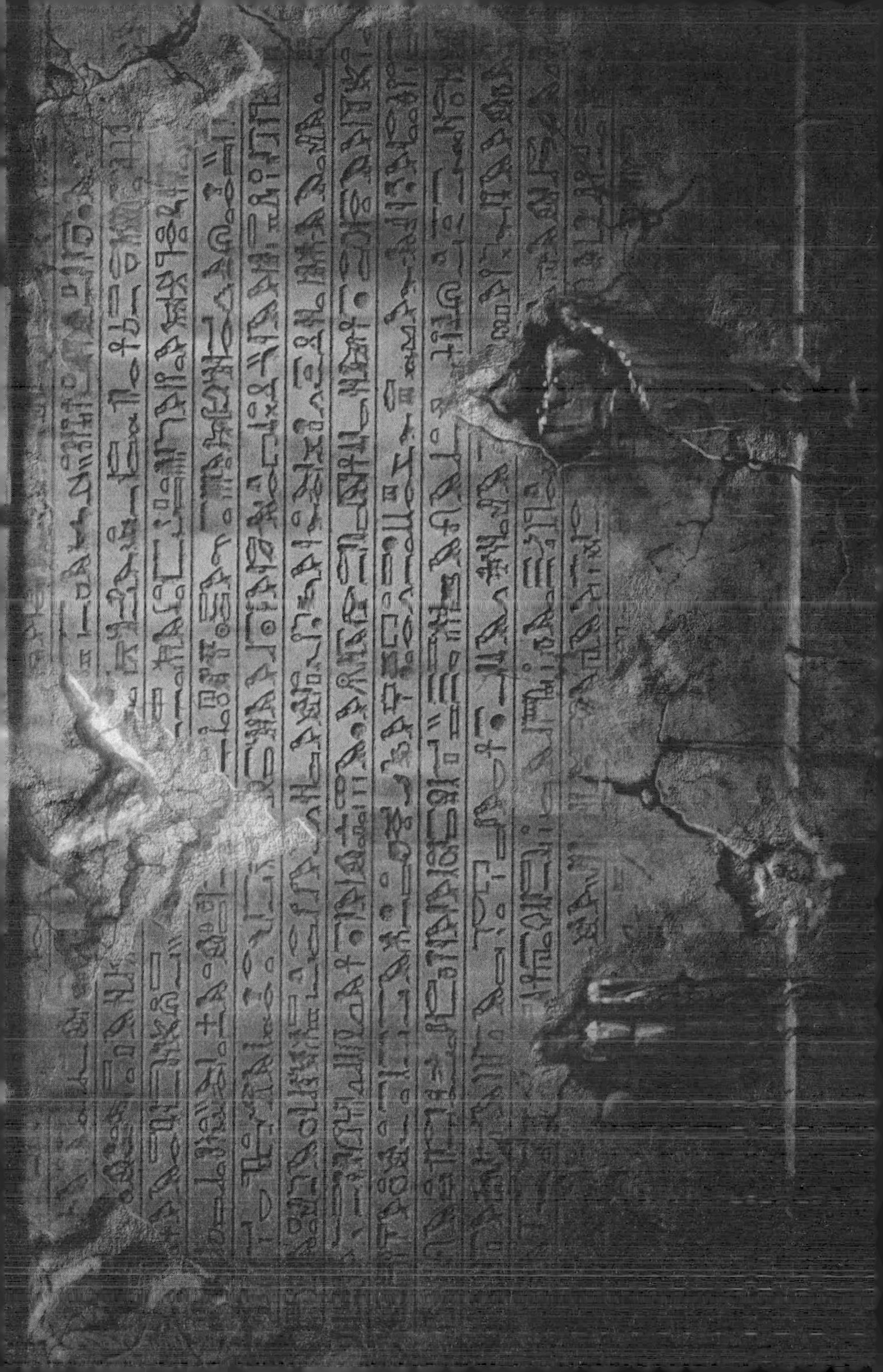

HILAL IBN ISA AL-SALT

Caesars Palace, Suite 2405, Las Vegas, Nevada, United States

Las Vegas is not what Hilal expects. He expects bustle, bouts of
last-minute sin before the end, mayhem and debauchery.
Instead the place is silent.
There is barely anyone on the street or in the casinos. The only cars
on the roads are police cruisers and taxis prowling for fares. The
restaurants are empty, the clubs are empty, the bars are empty. The
lobby at Caesars Palace only has 10 nonemployees in it. From the
casino floor Hilal hears a croupier announce, "Red eighteen," before
sweeping the losing chips away. The lone gambler at the table doesn't
even glance up from his drink. He checks in to a suite on the 24th floor
of the Augustus Tower, takes his bags to his room, lies on his huge bed.
He falls asleep, and sleeps well into the following morning.
He wakes to the sound of a helicopter flying by. He slides the device
from his pocket. It flickers to life. He swings it back and forth, going
from one caduceus to the other, for several minutes.
Why two? Is one Ea and the other one of his surrogates? Has Ea somehow
split himself and inhabited two bodies? Why two? Why two?
He doesn't know.
He inspects the other things the device reveals: the vast cosmic scrim,
the mysterious orange blob in the eastern Himalayas, and the long list
of coordinates. He takes the time to carefully count them twice. There
are 1,493. Virtually all are static numbers, never changing.
But nine *do* change.
One, he realizes as he walks across his large suite to the bathroom,
marks *him*. The Aksumite. The coordinates are to the 1,000,000th

decimal place, so even moving a few meters causes them to shift. *The other eight dynamic coordinates must be the remaining Players,* he thinks. *This is a tracker!*

It is a revelation.

He relieves himself in the bathroom and hobbles back to the bedroom. He gets a pad and pen and his regular laptop from his pack and sits cross-legged on top of the bedspread and gets to work.

He checks all the coordinates in the smartphone. There are three pairs and two solo points, other than his own.

One pair moves quickly, north to south, over Central and South America. This pair must be flying.

Another pair is in a suburb north of Berlin, Germany, and is hardly moving at all.

And the last pair, also practically stationary, is—*ding, ding, ding*—in the eastern Himalayas, in remote Sikkim, India.

Hilal is convinced that the orange blob must therefore be marking one of the Players.

The one that holds Earth Key, he guesses incorrectly.

The two solitary points are in Port Jervis, New York, and Japan, the latter heading north, presumably by train based on the speed, toward Tokyo.

Hilal has no idea who is who, or why three teams would have formed after the Calling. His impressions of the Players were that only four, maybe five, would be open to alliances. And that number includes himself.

It is a mystery, he thinks.

This exercise takes him nearly five hours, and even after the long night's sleep he is exhausted. He flops onto his side. He thinks about the possibilities—the Players, Ea, the strange coordinates, the two caducei—and drifts off to sleep once more. . . .

He wakes with a start in the middle of the night. His eyes widen. He stares at the ceiling. He sits up. His head kills. He swings his legs over the side of the bed and plants his feet on the floor. He looks at the clock: 3:13 a.m. He takes the device—still two caducei, one stationary, the other moving somewhere on the streets below—and goes to the window. Vegas is lit up like a never-ending fireworks show. Multicolored neon, LCD screens as big as buildings with pictures of partiers and showgirls and food, lights of all colors flashing on and off in a choreographed dance. He looks to the Strip. It is still empty.

I need to stretch my legs. Get used to moving without the help of the canes, Hilal thinks, the lights twinkling on his face.

Out of habit, and some precaution, he slips his twin machetes, one labeled *LOVE*, the other *HATE*, beneath his baggy cotton pants. He heads downstairs and steps onto the sidewalk. Walking without the canes is painful but liberating. He can ignore pain.

He only passes policemen, bored and nervous and heavily armed, and a few vagrants and drifters. He turns off the Strip near the Bellagio, its fountains pluming for no one, and meanders southeast until he hits the intersection of East Harmon and Koval. More hotels and shopping areas are to the south, and a sprawling series of vacant, desertlike lots are to the north. He is only a few blocks from the illuminated pomp of the Strip, but here it is as desolate as any bankrupt inner city.

All a show, Hilal thinks of Las Vegas. *All a facade. Even if it were teeming . . . Especially if it were teeming.*

He stands there for several minutes, his eyes closed, the streets empty, the desert air crisp and clean. It reminds him of the air of the Danakil and Eastern Deserts, of his time in seclusion under the unending panoply of stars. And Las Vegas is so quiet, so eerily still, that with his eyes closed Hilal is transported to his home, among the scrub and stars and sand.

Alone.

Whole.

At home.

In peace.

But then his pocket gets warmer and warmer and suddenly hot.

Hilal opens his eyes. He thrusts his hand into his pocket and pulls out the device. It turns cold as soon as he touches it. He holds it up. He swings his arm this way and that, and there, when it is pointed south down Koval Lane, he sees a caduceus, bright and delineated and growing larger.

Hilal squints past the device. About a quarter mile away he sees a car. Its headlights are off, but he can tell as it flashes through the streetlamps that it is moving very, very fast.

Ea!

Hilal looks everywhere for a vehicle. There—in the vacant lot across East Harmon is a dilapidated white van. He slips the device into his pocket and breaks into a dead sprint. The pain in his body sings at full volume, but he does not care.

He is 75 meters away from the van. The car with the presumptive Ea is closing. Hilal is 50 meters away. He can hear the engine of Ea's car. He is 25 meters away. Hilal glances over his shoulder. Ea's vehicle is a late-model muscle car, a Shelby or a Mustang or a Challenger. Hilal moves faster. Is five meters away from the van as the car zips through the intersection. Hilal reaches the van. It is locked. He steps back and stabs at the window with his elbow and the glass spiderwebs and he hits it one more time and it shatters, raining on the concrete like diamonds. He opens the door and brushes glass off the seat and jumps in, stashing his machetes on the passenger side. He works quickly on the steering column and in 19 seconds has the engine running. He turns on the lights, peers at the gas gauge, and says a quiet blessing. It has half a tank.

He takes out the device and wedges it onto the dashboard just as Ea's car disappears around a corner up Koval. Hilal puts the van into gear, and with a creak it lurches forward.

Hilal is inordinately excited. He is close. So close.

Hilal follows Ea, catching sight of the car now and then, moving east then north then east then north then east. The neighborhoods he passes through grow increasingly desolate and run-down, and now he is in an area littered with scrap yards, warehouses, Quonset huts like giant silver insects, sprawling lots overrun with the encroaching desert, and the husks of abandoned houses, trucks, cars. After 30 minutes, Ea turns right off Alto Avenue and heads south on Bledsoe.

Hilal slows. He flicks off the van's lights and turns onto Bledsoe just as the car disappears around a cinder-block wall. The adjacent warehouse glows red with the car's brake lights, then the glow is snuffed out. The car has stopped.

Hilal puts the van in neutral, kills the engine, and coasts to a standstill, the wall on his left, an open desert lot across the street on his right. He takes the device, so bright with the caduceus that Hilal is afraid it will give him away, and secures it in an inside pocket. He takes the machetes and attaches them to his belt. No need to conceal them anymore. He moves to the rear of the van and glimpses around the corner.

Clear.

He slinks along the wall, his hands resting on the hilts of his blades.

He is close.

So close.

When he reaches the corner, he drops to the ground, lies on his stomach, inches forward, peeks. A lithe man in dark clothing, a hood pulled over his head. He slings a knapsack onto his shoulder and closes his car's trunk with a muted clap. He glances back to the street. Hilal doesn't move. He is practically invisible with his head on the ground. Ea's face is completely in shadow, save for the faint dot of his nose. He whips around and walks to the warehouse. Ea's gait is confident, athletic, slightly feminine.

Hilal jumps to his feet and rounds the corner, making for the car. He is completely silent, no footfalls, no breath. He pauses by the trunk and looks under the car. Sees Ea's feet disappear inside the building.

I must try to use the element of surprise.

He sprints to the warehouse, grabs a drainpipe, plants his feet on the wall, and shimmies up to the roof. In spite of all his injuries, Hilal's body feels good, strong.

I am going to need to be strong.

He vaults the parapet wall at the top and silently draws a machete from his belt. The roof is flat and covered in light gravel. There are two triangular skylights and an extension with a door in it that undoubtedly opens onto a staircase. He sees no sign of cameras or microphones. The skylights emit a weak glow. Hilal creeps to the nearest one and, very slowly, looks inside.

He makes out a large room. Painted white. Modern furniture. A wall devoted to computers, a large kitchen with a stainless-steel countertop, a single door leading to another room, a small training area with kettlebells, a heavy bag, a speed bag. Mounted on the wall in this area are hand-to-hand weapons of all kinds: swords, sticks, knives, hammers, a collection of baseball bats.

No sign of Ea.

Hilal is about to move to the other skylight when the skin on his neck prickles. His instincts push him forward, his scarred face pressing into the glass of the skylight. An object whisks over him, grazing the back of his head.

Hilal rolls and swings the unsheathed machete behind him, aiming for his assailant's ankles, but they aren't there. He catches sight of Ea—it must be Ea, no other person in the world could sneak up on Hilal so easily—as he jumps over the machete's razor-sharp edge. Hilal is ready to vault upward but instead must roll defensively as Ea's weapon comes down for his face.

It is one of the baseball bats. Wooden, big barrel. In the dim light and with only a fraction of a second Hilal makes out the word *Slugger* on it, but he has no idea what that means.

Ea's head is still hooded, and as Hilal scrambles sideways, he can't make out any of his features. He feels a tug at his hip, as if his clothing is snagged on something, and manages to get his left hand under him just as the bat comes again for the side of his head. Hilal's weight is distributed perfectly, his legs now tucked beneath him, and he springs a meter into the air. The bat misses. He extends his body and lands on his feet. He brings up the machete and reaches across his waist with his free hand to draw the other blade as well. He will cut this abomination to pieces.

But his hand comes up empty.

Ea straightens, standing three meters away. The bat is pointed at Hilal's chest. Ea raises his other arm and a blade catches the meager light. Ea swiped the other machete. Hilal still can't make out Ea's hooded face, but if he could, he knows he would find a smile creasing his evil lips. Hilal readies himself. How he wishes he had the rods of Aaron and Moses with him now. How he curses himself for being so stupid to leave them behind, so unprepared as he moved into Las Vegas, Ea's stomping ground.

Ea advances with lightning quickness, twirling the bat and machete together like a deadly fan. Hilal backpedals, using his single blade to deflect the blows. Ea's hands and wrists are so fast and loose, faster than any person Hilal has fought or sparred against. The metal clanks, the wood thumps, Hilal dances, Ea dances. Hilal twirls and swipes his feet at Ea's, but Ea dodges. Hilal ducks a blow and parries, but each time Ea steps back at the exact right moment. Hilal brings the blade up in a sweeping uppercut, but Ea knocks it to the side with the bat.

Just when Hilal thinks that Ea is too quick, too serpentine, too limber, Hilal scores a hit as they step past each other. It is a minor hit, the butt of his machete's hilt striking the back of Ea's knee, but it is enough to cause Ea to buckle and drop. Knowing this is his best chance, Hilal brings down his blade with everything he has for the top of Ea's head, the hood swept off in the commotion, his long brown hair pulled into a topknot.

But instead of finding hair and skin and bone, Hilal's blade strikes the bat on an oval logo on the barrel as Ea pulls it over his head. The machete embeds five centimeters into the pale hardwood.

Hilal is about to tug his weapon free when Ea stops him with a simple "Wouldn't do that."

Hilal freezes. The voice. It belongs to . . . a woman.

Hilal sees his adversary for the first time. She is fair-skinned, late 20s, pretty. She has sweeping dark eyebrows over brown eyes painted with black eyeliner, a perfect nose, boyish cheeks, a strong neck and jaw, and on her crimson lips a smile.

She is *very* pretty.

Both breathe heavily, her collarbones rising and falling at the edge of her sweatshirt. Her eyes dart down then up. Hilal looks. The other machete is between his legs, at his crotch, angled slightly. He understands immediately that she is not threatening to castrate him, but instead to nick his femoral artery. All it would take is a little swipe, and given what Hilal has just learned about this woman's speed, he doesn't dare move. Plus, he knows how sharp his machetes are.

Hilal stares at her with his battered and mutilated face. With his red eye, and his blue one. Hideousness staring at beauty.

She doesn't flinch. "Ea send you?" she says, panting.

It is such a ridiculous question. "What?" Hilal asks.

"Did Ea send you? To kill me?" she clarifies.

"Who *are* you?"

"Answer my question, and maybe I'll tell you." She pushes the edge toward Hilal's skin.

"No, he did not send me."

"Need more than that, pal. Why're you here?"

"To *find* Ea."

"Why?"

Hilal pauses. "To find the Corrupted One and kill him," he says truthfully.

A look of wonder passes over her face. But she still holds his life in her hands. "My God," she says. "You're one of them, aren't you?"

"One of whom?"

"The Endgamers. A member of one of the 12 ancient lines."

"How do you know that . . . ?" In spite of the circumstances, Hilal senses some form of kinship in this woman. "You are not Ea," he states flatly.

The woman suppresses a laugh. "No. *Hell* no. Let me guess," she says, suddenly enthusiastic. "Nabataean? Sumerian? No. Aksumite."

Hilal is at a loss.

"You're with the Uncorrupted, aren't you!" she blurts.

A total loss. This woman, who has something to do with Ea but who is apparently not aligned with him at all, speaks to Hilal about things she simply cannot know.

"I am confused," Hilal admits.

She lets the blade away from his leg a centimeter. "Truce?"

Hilal gives her the slightest nod.

"Nice to meet you, Confused," the woman jokes. She lowers the machete to the ground. "Name's Stella Vyctory. I'm Ea's daughter—adopted, thank God. And if you really do want to kill the bastard, I can help. Because, my friend, that's what I want too."

MACCABEE ADLAI, BAITSAKHAN

34 Eichenallee, Charlottenburg, Berlin, Germany

Maccabee and Baitsakhan have moved to another Nabataean safe house in Berlin.

It has been two days since Alice found them. Maccabee's face is swollen. Left eye shut. Lower lip split. Nose busted. All the bones in his face are bruised.

Baitsakhan's hand works well, but his wrist, where the skin is taut over the metal and plastic of the mechanism, is very sore.

They have barely spoken since settling into this latest refuge. It's a nice house in a nice neighborhood with nice people walking the nice streets outside. Some cities have had trouble in the aftermath of the Abaddon news, but Berlin has not been one of them. The German government has decreed that every cultural institution be free, and has given each citizen a voucher for €5,000 to be used in any restaurant, beer garden, or shop, or in any other way desired. Gasoline and electricity are free. Train tickets to anywhere in Europe cost €1, making it easier for people to visit loved ones, or get to the countryside, or see the ocean or the mountains, maybe for the last time. There have been outdoor concerts in Berlin and a pop-up circus for children and even an overnight city-sanctioned love-in.

Maccabee and Baitsakhan couldn't care less about these developments. Instead they have been popping pain pills and trying to heal and cleaning guns and sharpening blades and studying the orb. Baitsakhan still hasn't touched it, not after it burned him in Turkey. He hates that he can't touch it. Hates it.

They've decided that they'll be well enough to move in two days.

Maccabee has already chartered a jet. This safe house has $1,000,000 in cash and 757 ounces of gold. It has plenty of weaponry. All of this will go on the plane.

They will take these things and they will move.

Instead of letting another Player come for them, they will use the orb and go for the Players.

The orb shows An in Tokyo. Shows Aisling moving fast—no doubt on a plane—over northern Canada, presumably on her way to Asia. Shows Hilal in Las Vegas. Shows Shari in the eastern Himalayas. And it shows Jago and Sarah in Juliaca, Peru.

"Tlaloc and Alopay," Maccabee says as he stares into the orb. "The only other Players Playing together."

"And the holders of Earth Key," Baitsakhan says as he runs a stone across his wavy Mongolian dagger.

Maccabee shakes his head.

"Not for long, brother."

"Not for long."

Time to go to Peru.

JAGO TLALOC, SARAH ALOPAY

Inca Manco Cápac International Airport, Juliaca, Peru

The Cessna pulls to a stop in a private corner of the airport. "We're here," Jago says to Sarah. Jago points his chin out his window. "And there's Papi. Guitarrero Tlaloc."

Sarah leans on his lap to look outside. Guitarrero is taller than Jago and much heavier. He's dressed like a rancher, brown cowboy hat and snakeskin boots and bolo tie, and rests the butt of a Kalashnikov on his hip. Next to him is a white Chevy Suburban, a red talon painted on its hood.

"Looks like a lot of bluster," Sarah says.

"It isn't."

She lifts her face to Jago's and gives him a long kiss. "I'm still not happy you brought me here, but I am happy I'm still with you." He smiles. "C'mon, let's go meet your papi."

Renzo lowers the stairway and they exit the plane. The air outside is cool, thinner than what Sarah's used to. Juliaca sits on the Collao Plateau, 12,549 feet above sea level, ocher hills and stark Andean peaks ringing the city in the near distance.

Guitarrero hugs Jago, kisses his left cheek, his right, his left, his right. Makes the cross, holds his hand to the sky, claps Jago on the shoulder. He hugs Renzo. Says something in a language Sarah doesn't understand. The two older men laugh at some private joke. He turns to Sarah.

"What do I say to you?" he asks in English.

"How about 'Nice to meet you,' Papi," Jago says. He takes Sarah's hand. Guitarrero shrugs. Smiles. It's infectious. Sarah smiles too. She does not trust this man, or Renzo. She trusts Jago, though. Or, at least, she did before he brought her to Mexico. Now there are cracks forming in that trust. Sarah wants very badly to believe that Jago is acting in her best interest, that he's right that she's just too messed up to make her own decisions.

Jago squeezes her hand reassuringly.

So she keeps on smiling.

She has to.

They unload the plane—Jago takes Earth Key from the compartment, slips it into a zippered pocket—and climb into the Suburban. They skip passport control and drive a short distance to a chain-link fence. A plainclothes guard hits a button. The gate opens, and the Suburban moves through. The guard waves. Guitarrero flips him off good-naturedly.

"Had to pay him one thousand American dollars for that," Guitarrero says in Spanish. Sarah follows along. She's not fluent, but she manages. "Me! Guitarrero Tlaloc, ruler of this city. Can you believe it?"

"No, Papi, I can't," Jago answers from the front seat, the Kalashnikov across his lap.

Guitarrero drops the Spanish and speaks for nearly a minute in the strange language. His tone is exasperated and punctuated with bursts of disbelieving laughter. The only words Sarah catches that she's heard before are "Aucapoma Huayna." A name.

Jago understands everything perfectly and has no response. Renzo answers instead. His response is short.

"Sí, sí, sí," Guitarrero says.

Jago is still silent.

"What're you talking about?" Sarah asks in passable Spanish, unhappy that they're hiding something from her.

Jago looks over his shoulder, rolls his eyes. "Papi says his protection revenue is down eighty-five percent since the meteor, which we call *El Punta del Diablo*. The city's gone to shit, apparently. All that's left are criminals, opportunists, priests, the desperately poor, and a small contingent of the army—who we've paid off for decades, so they're with us."

"That's good," Sarah offers.

"Yes, except criminals don't pay protection fees to other criminals," Guitarrero says. "Good thing we saved for a rainy day!"

Sarah has a sinking feeling that Guitarrero's lecture had nothing to do with protection revenue. Why would they use their secret language if the topic were so immaterial to Endgame? Why would Renzo, who's been in Iraq for the last 10 years, give a damn? What does Aucapoma Huayna, the revered Olmec elder, have to do with anything?

They're lying to me.

The Suburban reaches the edge of the airport grounds and is joined by two more cars: in front is a large late-model Toyota pickup with a .50-caliber machine gun swivel-mounted in the bed, one man on it, two more men guarding the gunner with M4s. They're surrounded on three sides by blast plates, and the machine gun has an angled steel shield straddling its barrel. All the men wear armor.

Behind the Suburban is a black Tahoe. Both vehicles also have the large red eagle claw stenciled on their hoods.

"Hold on," Guitarrero says in Spanish as the convoy accelerates.

The cars stay in tight formation as they whip through the outskirts of Juliaca, careening toward the western edge of the city. Tendrils of smoke rise above the low-lying brick and concrete buildings in more than a dozen places. Jago points to the one marking the meteor impact, which still smolders.

"Some whoreson torched the water-treatment plant two days ago," Guitarrero says, turning the wheel this way and that to avoid potholes and stray dogs. The men in the pickup fire warning shots, clearing the way. They pass a derelict soccer pitch, drive through an abandoned residential neighborhood, pass into a commercial district with bullet-riddled buildings and smashed-out windows. One bodega is surrounded by sandbags, an elderly man out front, smoking a long cigar, a pistol on his hip. They pass an ornate, Spanish Mission–style church, people milling all around, on their knees, talking, eating, even laughing, the priests in long white robes taking impromptu confessions, handing out bottles of water and kind words, no signs of strife, an island of calm in a sea of turmoil. They pass into a bad neighborhood, low houses arranged like building blocks, flat tin roofs, mongrels pacing barren front yards, armed men and boys everywhere, yelling at their convoy, shaking fists, throwing rocks.

"The Cielos moved in after you left for the Calling," Guitarrero says. Jago explains that the Cielos are a longtime rival to the Tlalocs. They came from Nuestra Señora de la Paz in Bolivia, on the other side of Lake Titicaca. "They know nothing of Endgame," Guitarrero yells over the roar of the engine, "and haven't been much more than a nuisance over the years, but even though they lack the power to contend with us, they've gone all out since the announcement of Abaddon, taking neighborhoods block by block. For the time being we've let them gain a foothold. Endgame is too important to be dicking around with turf battles. We need to be prepared for the Event."

More shots from the men in the pickup. All three Tlaloc vehicles accelerate. Jago whoops and hollers. Guitarrero jams the gas, pulls up right behind the pickup. Gunfire. The thump of the .50-cal firing shots into buildings. They don't slow down. Instead they go faster. They take return fire from small arms. Rounds bounce off them in bright orange sparks like little fireworks. One explodes right next to Sarah's face. Bulletproof.

She doesn't flinch.

The ride is exhilarating.

But then they reach the edge of the dusty Cielo-controlled slum, and Sarah catches sight of a woman in dark jeans and a yellow Nike T-shirt. A baby in her arms. The mother wraps her arms over the baby's head, turning away from the street, seeking refuge.

Both are crying.

This madness is the result of Abaddon.

The result of Endgame.

Sarah fights a sudden bout of nausea.

The gunfire pitters away in the background. They drive another 4.15 miles. The vehicles slow. Stop at a checkpoint manned by men in fatigues. Their two Humvees are painted with the red talon. Sarah is envious of the order and control that the Tlalocs exert over their turf. Her line has been subtler, more content with living in the shadows, ready to act but on a much smaller scale.

This is something else.

The Olmecs are ready for war.

An officer with silver captain's bars on his baseball cap approaches the Suburban. Guitarrero rolls down his window and speaks to him in Spanish. Captain Juan Papan. He leans into the car to shake Jago's hand, nods at Renzo, steals a glance at Sarah. The officer's face is expressionless.

Captain Papan returns to his post, and the convoy snakes up a winding paved road in the brown foothills southwest of the city. Guards are posted every hundred meters or so. Sarah counts five armored Humvees and two pieces of field artillery. The only trees Sarah sees in this barren land are those that surround a smattering of large private mansions, all now being used as military quarters. Every vehicle, every sleeve of every uniform, is adorned with red talons. The road ends at a tall wrought-iron gate in the middle of a taller stone wall. Guards on top. Sarah counts 17. All armed. The gate opens. The Suburban continues up the private gravel drive.

"My home," Jago says proudly to Sarah in English.

"I thought you grew up on the mean streets down there," Sarah says, pointing with her thumb over her shoulder.

Renzo chuckles.

"He did," Guitarrero says.

"This is where we came to get away from it all," Jago says. *"Casa Isla Tranquila."*

And that is exactly what it says on a little hand-painted sign just outside the car, a palm tree and a sliver of blue water framing the letters. Guitarrero spins the Suburban around a hairpin that's been piled high on both sides with thick cement blocks—a last defense in case of a frontal assault—and they pull into a wide, round driveway. A bubbling stone fountain in the middle. Three more SUVs, another armed pickup, a Bentley touring sedan, and a classic 1970 ragtop Pontiac GTO painted yellow with a black 33 on the hood.

"Crime pays, huh?" Sarah says.

Guitarrero pulls to a stop and turns off the engine. *"Sí, señorita."*

They get out. Walking down the steps of the Tlalocs' sprawling Spanish hacienda is a woman in a red-and-purple floral print dress, her dark wavy hair swept back, her feet bare. She has Jago's hair, his chin, his easy manner. She smiles, as if all that's happening in the world is happening on another planet.

Jago holds out his arms and exclaims, *"¡Hola, Mamá!"*

She hikes her dress above her knees and half runs to her son. Embraces him. Kisses him. Says how happy she is to see him alive, still Playing, still representing his line, keeping his people alive.

"I will always do that, Mamá," Jago says, accepting her affections graciously.

"This is my mother, Sarah. Hayu Marca Tlaloc."

"This is the girl I've heard so much about?" Hayu Marca says sincerely in perfect English, as if Jago met Sarah on spring break and brought his American sweetheart home for a visit.

"I didn't know Jago told you about me."

"I spoke with Mamá while you were doing your marathon sleep session on the plane."

Hayu Marca takes Sarah's right hand with both of hers. Smiles at the Cahokian. "I might be concerned that another Player was in our midst, but Jago has vouched for you. And I can see in your eyes that you are good, Sarah Alopay of the 233rd."

"Thanks, Mrs. Tlaloc," Sarah says. "Renzo might disagree."

"I respect Renzo," she says quietly. "But Jago is our Player. You have nothing to fear here."

Hayu Marca is lovely, and despite the fact that Sarah would much prefer to be at her own family's compound, she believes her. Some of the suspicion she felt toward Guitarrero is soothed. Hayu Marca lets go of Sarah's hand and gestures toward the house. "Why don't you let me show you to your room while the boys unload? I'm sure you're travel weary. I've already had some fruit and cheese brought up."

Sarah looks at Jago, her eyes asking if it's okay.

"Rest, Sarah," Jago says. "I will too. I just want to talk to Papi about Aucapoma Huayna first."

"We're flying her by helicopter so she doesn't have to endure that gauntlet down in the city. She'll be here soon enough," Guitarrero says.

"Good," Jago says.

Hayu Marca tugs at Sarah's hand. "Come, Player."

Sarah shoulders her knapsack. The pistol and knife inside clunk against her spine. "All right."

"I'll bring the rest of your stuff in a bit," Jago says.

Sarah looks to Hayu Marca. "Lead the way, then."

They enter the house, walk through a tastefully decorated entry, pass through a sitting room with tapestries and ancient-looking furniture, a huge fireplace at the far end. They enter an interior garden, the house rising around it on all sides. The garden is immaculate, but the flora is dormant for the winter. Guards patrol here and there inconspicuously.

"This place is like a castle," Sarah says.

"I wish you could see it in summer. It's beautiful."

"I'm sure."

They reach the far side of the garden, enter a wide carpeted hall with rooms along one side. Hayu Marca leads Sarah down the hall, talking about flowers and Jago and Lake Titicaca. She stops in front of an open door. Sarah peers in. There's a canopy bed and bay windows looking out on the garden. There's a table set with the promised fruit and cheese and an already-open bottle of sparkling water, a set of fresh towels on the bedspread.

Hayu Marca lays a hand on Sarah's arm. "Sarah, I know that you and

Jago have taken turns saving each other's lives, and that if it weren't for you, he might already be dead. I want to say thank you."

Sarah thinks of how quickly she left him in the tunnel back in London, sure that he *was* dead. How quickly she abandoned him.

She shakes her head. "I'm positive I'd be dead, Mrs. Tlaloc, if not for Jago. He's been good for me. I think we've been good for each other. I wish I'd met him without . . ." She waves her hand.

Hayu Marca looks at her feet. "Yes. Endgame is hard."

"Yeah. Worse than I thought."

Hayu Marca raises her chin. "It will only get harder, Sarah."

"I know." Sarah is suddenly exhausted. "I know."

Hayu Marca takes a step back and looks Sarah over. "I don't think you've showered in days, my dear. Clean up, rest. You'll find some fresh clothing and undergarments in the closet. We'll come for you later."

Sarah smiles. "Thanks, Mrs. Tlaloc."

Hayu Marca shakes her head, holds up a hand. "It's nothing."

Sarah goes into her room. She closes the door. She goes to the table and pours a glass of water. The bubbles pop and hiss. She sips it. The water is good. Sweet. She gulps it.

And as she does, the door is locked shut.

From the outside.

Sarah spins. Runs to the door and tries it. Hayu Marca has shut her in. She pounds on the door and realizes that even though it looks wooden, it's not.

It's steel. Thick and unforgiving.

She unslings her backpack and pulls out her pistol and sights the window overlooking the garden and fires.

The slug ricochets into the room, bouncing everywhere, finally embedding itself in the armoire.

She runs to the glass. Throws herself on it. Pounds it. Screams "Liar!"

She falls to her knees. Hits the glass more. "Fucking liar! Why?"

But no one can hear.

A minute later Jago and Renzo and Guitarrero appear in the central garden, moving toward Hayu Marca, who greets them with open arms.

Jago pays no attention to Sarah—maybe he can't even see her.

The men turn so that their backs are to Sarah's room. The only face she sees is Hayu Marca's. She steps to her son, her only son, the champion of the Olmec line. She gives him another hug. She holds his scarred face with both hands. As she does, she stares at Sarah's room.

Stares at Sarah's room and smiles.

A sinister, sinister smile.

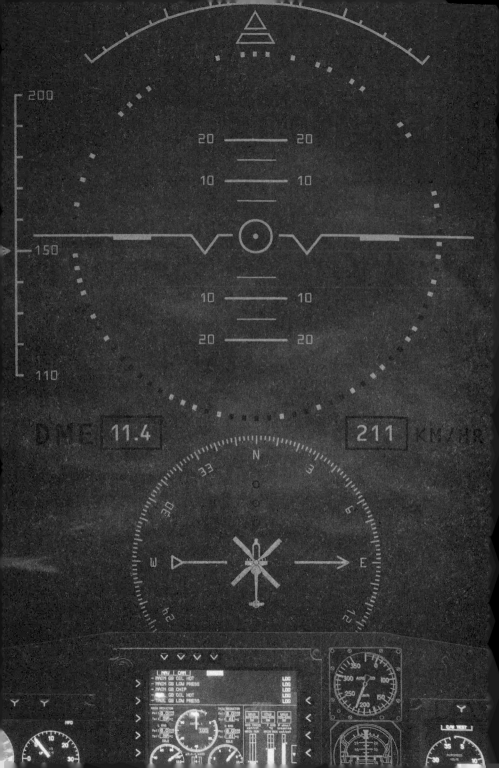

HILAL IBN ISA AL-SALT, STELLA VYCTORY

Converted Warehouse off Bledsoe, Sunrise Manor, Nevada, United States

Hilal sits in a plastic chair at a wooden table. Stella is in the kitchen tending a kettle. She has removed the sweatshirt and is in a simple V-neck and tight black jeans. She has returned the machete labeled HATE to Hilal and even offered him a gun, if it would make him feel better. He said it wasn't necessary.

As she puts tea bags in a pair of cups, Hilal says, "Miss Vyctory, I—"

"Stella. Please, call me Stella."

"Stella—I am sorry, but I have some questions."

"I'm sure you do," Stella says, rounding the counter with two steaming cups of tea. "I do too." She sits opposite Hilal and puts the cups down. "Pick one. Just so you know I'm not trying to poison you."

Hilal points. Stella takes a big sip from that cup, cringing as the hot liquid goes down her throat, and passes it to Hilal. He doesn't take it. Not yet.

Stella leans back, her hands behind her head. Hilal admires her composure. "Mind if I go first?"

Hilal, straight-backed and shamefully a little nervous, says, "Not at all." He is certain she will ask a question about his wounds, but instead she says, "How'd you find me?"

"I am a Player," he says, as if that's enough.

Stella shakes her head. "No offense, but you didn't just luck into finding me. Something led you here. Something that I'd wager is pretty old. Something that belonged to one of Them," Stella says, pointing at the ceiling.

Hilal doesn't respond. He wants to hear what she has to say first.

"Because of Ea I've seen my fair share of strange things. Machines that had no discernable purpose, small rocks that float whenever I touch them, musical instruments made for seven-fingered hands, and an ancient stone map that somehow lights up. So I'm pretty sure you have something like this, am I right?"

"Perhaps."

"I'd like to see it, if you don't mind."

"I am not sure I am comfortable—"

"Did you get it from the ark?"

Hilal is dumbstruck.

Stella says, "Me and my accolytes have been studying the 12 ancient lines for a long time. I know more than you might expect about the Aksumites. So—can I see it?"

Hilal considers this request for several moments before saying, "Yes. You can." He carefully reaches into his pocket and pulls out the device and places it on the table. "This marked you—and him—with the sign of the caduceus. You are familiar with this sign?"

"Does the Pope shit at the Vatican?"

"Um . . ."

"Kidding. Yes, I know the caduceus." Stella looks at the device, leans forward, squints. "Can I touch it?"

"Yes."

She reaches across the table and as soon as her fingers grace the device, it glows to life, just as it does in Hilal's hands. This is validating for Hilal. He becomes slightly more convinced that finding Stella was a stroke of luck.

Or of destiny.

"My, my," Stella says.

"It does not do that for everyone, Stella."

"Count me lucky, then." She picks it up and moves it around the room. "Know what all this means?"

"Come next to me and I will explain what I can."

Stella rises and walks around the table, her eyes never leaving the small screen. She kneels next to Hilal. There is no array of stars and no caduceus when Stella holds it, but there is the list of coordinates, as well as the glowing blob. And there is something else on the device when it's in her grasp: odd glowing glyphs, not unlike the one etched on the device, consisting of straight lines and little dots.

"You know what the coordinates are?" Stella asks, almost like a test.

"The dynamic ones are Players. The rest, I am not sure."

"Interesting. And the orange ball?"

"What do you think?" Hilal asks, curious if she might elucidate him.

"Mr. al-Salt, I think that's your first question. Your restraint is admirable."

"Thank you, Stella. But please call me Hilal."

"All right, Hilal. And I actually know what the blob is: it's what that guy on TV called Sky Key."

Hilal frowns. "But how can you be so sure?"

"I mentioned a map a few minutes ago. It's of the entire Earth and it has this blob on it too. Before Earth Key was found, the blob was over Stonehenge. Now it's in the eastern Himalayas. I'm certain it's Sky Key."

"And you think it will show us where the third key is too, when its turn comes?"

"One would hope, right?"

"Yes. One would hope."

"Stella, if you know this is Sky Key then why aren't you going to it? Don't you want to find the other Players?"

"I'm not interested in Sky or the Players. Not right now, at any rate. You see, I have what you might call a line of my own. Not one of the original 12, but a little army that I've put together. I've been recruiting them for a while now, educating them, learning from them, challenging them, training them. Training *with* them."

"For what? Endgame?"

Stella stands and places a hand on Hilal's shoulder. "No. For war."

"Against Ea?"

Stella shakes her head.

And then it hits him: "The Makers."

"Yes."

And in that moment Hilal's trust grows leaps and bounds for Stella Vyctory. He believes her. Utterly. She hands him back his device and returns to her seat and lets the air clear. She drinks more of her tea. Hilal finally drinks his too. It is delicious. Slightly acrid yet sweet and flowery.

"Why would you fight them?" he asks.

"Not to be coy, but let me answer that with a question. Why is Endgame happening?"

A pain shoots through Hilal's neck. "If you had asked me before it started, I would have told you because the Makers said it would."

"So prophecy. Because God promised it."

"Yes."

"And now what do you say?"

"Because they want it to happen. They want to see us fight each other, see us suffer, and see us die. And—although this is a guess—because they want what we have."

Stella puts a finger on the tip of her nose. "Exactly."

"Earth."

"Yeah. Right out of a fucking sci-fi movie."

"Yes. But why? If they are an extremely powerful race that can travel the stars, why Earth? And why ever bother with Endgame at all?"

"That's the bit I haven't worked out. For now, it's enough to know that they're coming and that we need to stop them." There is a long pause. They drink more tea. Stella puts down her cup and waves a hand, indicating his wounds. "Another Player do that to you?"

"Two, working together."

"I'm sorry."

Hilal shrugs. "I survived. It is part of the game. A part of the . . . war."

Because that is what this really is, Hilal thinks. *Not a game, but a war. How can we have not seen that? How can we have been so blinded by prophecy? Aren't we supposed to be the enlightened ones?*

How?

"This is a lot to take in, Stella."

"I know. Honestly, it's a lot for me too."

"Can I ask another question?"

"Fire away, Aksumite."

"Why do you want to kill Ea?"

"Ah. That one has a long answer. The short version is that I hate him and he's a monster. But I don't want him dead merely for revenge. It's a lot more than that. I know that if humanity is to have any meaningful future—alien invasion or no—then Ea needs to go. He can't have this world to play with anymore."

"That is a good reason. And do not discount hate. It can be a potent fuel in the engine of righteousness."

"I'll have to remember that one. Anyway, Ea lied to me. For years I thought he was my father, but it turned out he'd kidnapped me after arranging for my mother to die in a horrific car accident with me in the backseat."

"That is disturbing."

"Oh, it gets worse. My mother had been an astronaut in the eighties and had her DNA altered in orbit during one of her missions. And this new DNA was not at all human."

"You mean . . . ?"

"Yep. Some of her genetic code became *alien* code—*Maker* code, the same code that runs through Ea's veins." She takes another sip of tea. "And, since I'm her daughter, I happen to be the lucky recipient of some of it."

Hilal's eyes widen. "So you're a—"

Stella nods. "A hybrid. An intergalactic mutt."

Hilal shrugs. "At least it explains why you were marked by the caduceus on the ark's device."

"Yeah, if nothing else it brought us together, which is great. But wait— I'm not done. He spent the next twenty-two years tormenting me in order to keep me compliant. You wouldn't believe some of the things he did. Luckily, it didn't last. Not too long ago I started to learn of things about humanity's old history and, even though I was ignorant of Endgame until it started, about the 12 lines and the corruption of man and about something called the Ancient Truth."

"Did you say the Ancient Truth?"

"Yes. You know it, don't you? Obviously, by the look in your eyes."

Hilal nods. Tells Stella of the Aksumite duty not only to keep a Player ready for Endgame but also to guard the Ancient Truth and to seek and destroy Ea. "But we have never been able to find him," Hilal laments.

"He's a sly snake," Stella says.

"Yes."

"But now you have found him. Or you've found me. And even though I couldn't get within half a mile of him, *you* can."

Hilal's spirits lift. He is suddenly ecstatic. "You will help me, Stella Vyctory?"

"Hell yes, I will. Although I have to say, going after Ea is a suicide mission, and one that's bound to fail. You see, Ea—he goes by the name Wayland Vyctory."

Hilal knows that name. Everyone does. "The hotelier?"

"That's the one. The problem is, the bastard is fucking immortal. Been around for over ten thousand years, and will be around for the next ten thousand too."

"I can kill him," Hilal says, shaking his head.

"Bullshit."

"No. I can."

"How?"

He tells her of the ark, and of the rods of Aaron and Moses. "All I have to do is get close enough for them to strike."

"I can make that happen, Hilal." Stella takes a long sip of tea. "I still think it's a suicide mission, but if your weapons will work, it'll be worth it. Sorry to be so blunt."

"Not at all. I agree. Completely."

"Great. I have a mole who works very closely with Wayland, a woman named Rima Subotic. She's been waiting for a long time, and I think this is it. So what do you say—will you let me help you?"

"Yes, Stella Vyctory. Yes."

"Great. Then let's get you an audience with the inestimable Wayland Vyctory."

AN LIU

Shang Warehouse, 3 Chome-7-19 Shinkiba, Kōtō-Ku, Tokyo Port, Japan

Blink. Shiver. Blink.

An is woken by a slight tic, an echo from a dream he can't remember. He is on a cot at the southern end of a cavernous room. He turns onto his side, stares across the open space. Sunlight fights through three oily skylights. Support columns and desks and tables full of computers and screens and keyboards. Metal chests full of weapons and money and ammunition. A shipping container full of explosives and detonators and switches and electronics, rigged to explode and take out and poison everything for a three-block radius on this man-made block of land in Tokyo Port. Another shipping container housing an IBM z Systems mainframe protected by an intricate, quadruple-redundant firewall of his own design. A Canon 5D on a tripod. A showerhead over an open drain. A sink. A toilet. A full-length mirror. A rolling rack with a small collection of clothing.

His temporary kingdom. One of six remaining Shang headquarters in the world. The palace of destruction from which he will make his next move.

He stands. Naked save for the thing around his neck. Walks across the concrete floor, goes to the sink. Runs hot water. The steam rises. He puts his hands to his chest, smooths the hair and skin necklace of Chiyoko Takeda. Breathes deeply through his nose. He can still smell her. The scent is weakening, but he can still smell her.

He's not sure for how much longer.

Blink. Shiver. Shiver.

The tics are like small aftershocks. Chiyoko protects. Even after what

An did to her uncle. Even though he disrespected her line.

Even after.

That is how much she loves him.

Even now.

An runs his hands under the water. Chiyoko's analog watch is on his wrist. The second hand clicks along.

Tick tick tick.

The seconds pass.

Time doesn't wait.

Tick tick tick.

He slips into a black jumpsuit from the rolling rack. He sits at his main terminal. Bites his nails while the computer comes to life. Bounces his knee. The screen is on. A wallpaper picture of Chiyoko fills the screen, a picture he found from an airport surveillance camera in China. He opens a terminal window, and types a string of commands and a PIN: 2148050023574. He raises his hand, passes it through the air. A Kinect that's hooked up to the computer interprets his gestures. Windows open and close, open and close. Maps, photos, lists of names, coordinates, ancient places, sacred places. He opens a folder full of photos, flicks through them.

There is Sarah Alopay's yearbook picture.

A clear surveillance picture of Jago Tlaloc.

A snapshot of Maccabee Adlai, maybe one year younger, in a black Speedo on the shores of some European beach.

A grainy picture of Baitsakhan from a security archive in Ulaanbaatar.

A clear and smiling picture of Hilal ibn Isa al-Salt, found on an Ethiopian Christian charity's website. His blue eyes, his straight teeth, his perfect skin.

Aisling Kopp in a bikini at Coney Island, her skin as white as snow.

Shari Chopra on vacation, standing in front of a peculiar-looking church, all spires and red stone, that looks like it's been dripped from a giant's hand. Shari holds a baby girl in her arms, her cheeks pudgy, her hair short, her hands tugging at Shari's colorful blouse.

He doesn't need pictures for the dead. Chiyoko. The Minoan. The Sumerian. The Koori, whose battered and lifeless picture he found online.

Four and counting.

He puts the photos into a PowerPoint presentation. He works on his speech. He runs it through Google Translate to get a passable version in English.

When he is ready, he moves to the camera and starts recording. On the 4th try he gets it all the way through without any major hiccups.

"People, my name is An Liu," it starts. His voice is calm. His eyes are vacant. He doesn't sit up straight. And he has a necklace of hair and skin and shriveled ears draped over his chest.

"I want to talk to you about everything that is happening. About the meteors. About Abaddon. About the dirty bomb in Xi'an. About life and death. About something most people have not heard of. A thing called Endgame. I do not care if you believe what I say, but what I say is true. Endgame is real. It is a contest started by these things that are happening. It is contest that has been secret for many thousands of years. A secret guarded by twelve chosen lines of people. People who trace their ancestors to the beginning of time. To a time before time. To the gods themselves. My line is called Shang. Endgame is real and Endgame is here. We fight each other to win, and the winner gets to live. The people in that person's line will also live. Everyone else will die."

He clears his throat. He will edit this out.

"Endgame will make the new world, but it will be an awful world. Endgame will kill most of you. Children. Mothers. Sons. Fathers. Daughters. Babies. If none of us win, Endgame will kill all of humanity and much of life. But, people, Endgame is a contest that can be stopped. And I know how to stop it."

An is lying. He has no interest in stopping it, and if he knew how, he wouldn't tell a soul.

"Abaddon is coming. This is a thing me and other Players call the Event. Our lines have known about the Event for many thousands of years. We did not know what it would be or when it would arrive until only a few weeks ago, but we did know that it would be horrible. Abaddon will be horrible, people. More horrible than I can say or you can imagine. . . . But *you* can stop it. . . . *You* can help *me* stop it. The way to stop it is simple. Me and the Players are people."

When the video is ready, here is where the faces will go.

"The names are Sarah Alopay. Jago Tlaloc. Maccabee Adlai. A boy named Baitsakhan. Hilal ibn Isa al-Salt. Aisling Kopp. Shari Chopra. Four others are already dead. One I killed."

Clears his throat again.

"They are just people. Not all-powerful, not supernatural. But very, very dangerous. All of us are trained for killing, for evasion, for computers, for disguise. Expert pilots, fighters, drivers. Together we are the most dangerous people on Earth. This is not hyperbole. Ask the English Special Forces about me. They will confirm."

He brings his hands together, as in prayer.

"Here is what I ask of you. That you help me kill all of these Players. When all are proven to be dead, I will kill myself. If not, then you can kill me. I will not hide from you. If all of us die before Abaddon, if our lines are all ended, then the game will short-circuit. The gods who put Abaddon in the sky will take it away. Its appearance in our solar system is a mystery. A great mystery. Its disappearance will be just as mysterious, but we will know why it happened if not how."

He leans forward, gets closer to the camera.

"It will happen because *you* did not allow it to. Because *you* worked together and saved life. Life on Earth. Not death. Life."

He holds out his hand.

"Please. Join me. Kill the Players. Save the world. Kill the Players. Save the world."

He pauses, still holding his hand out.

Then, *BLINKshivershivershiverBLINKBLINKblinkblink.*
SHIVERSHIVERshiverBLINK.
BlinkSHIVER.
Shiver.
BLINKBLINKBLINKBLINKBLINKBLINK.
A small torrent of tics. Nothing to fret over. He turns off the camera.
He'll edit it and upload it from an anonymous account to YouTube,
email-blast every single news outlet and government agency and
thousands of independent reporters and internet "tastemakers"
worldwide. He'll hack the YouTube viewer counter so that it launches
with millions of views. In the comments section he'll even write the
last-known locations of every single living Player, a task his web-bots
and aggregators and filters are still working on. Once he has these,
the video will go live, and everyone in the world will watch it at least
once. It doesn't matter if everyone believes it. All he needs is for *some*
people to believe it. All he needs is for the special forces and secret
police and clandestine services of the world's governments to see the
faces of the Players, to learn of their locations, and to think they can
stop Abaddon. All he needs is a little help.
Help from unwitting and foolish people who will still all perish.
To the man, the woman, the child.
All.
As he waits for the footage to download from the camera, he notices
that the second hand on Chiyoko's watch doesn't move. He taps the
face. Pushes a button at 10 o'clock. Taps the face again. The second
hand moves.
Tick tick tick.
He unfastens the buckle so he can wind the mechanism. And as he
does this, something catches his eye. He's not sure, but it looks as
though a small digital blip swipes across the clear face.
What prize did you leave me, Chiyoko?
He picks up a different DSLR camera. Takes a picture. Transfers the file
to his computer. Opens Photoshop.

And there.

A faint, imperfect grid, its squares minuscule but uniform, stretched across the crystal.

Maybe the camera's polarizing filter revealed this grid? He unscrews the filter, takes another picture.

No grid.

He spends the next 2.3 hours writing a macro into Photoshop that will generate thousands of polarizing patterns every second, applying each to the photo of the watch, seeing if any yield results.

And yes. After 17 minutes and 31 seconds of running the macro, pattern number 3,114,867 hits.

He prints this pattern onto a sheet of acetate and stretches it over the camera's lens. He puts it on a tripod, points it at the watch on the table, and feeds the camera's image directly to his computer.

A blip.

Blip-blip.

Three seconds.

Blip-blip.

Stationary for the moment.

A scale at the bottom in tiny letters: D cm = 300 m.

A set of coordinates at the top: -15.51995,-70.14783.

An punches the numbers into Google Maps. The site is blacked out, but it's just south and west of Juliaca, Peru.

Jago Tlaloc?

He clicks the button at 10 o'clock.

The tiny screen swipes. Another blip.

Blip-blip.

Three seconds.

Blip-blip.

This one moving, quickly.

An punches these coordinates into the computer. Another Player, apparently flying southwest from Europe toward South America. Someone going to Jago Tlaloc? Who? Does one of them have Earth

Key? Does one of them have Sky Key? Is the game so far along that it's too late for An's plan to work?

No. The kepler would have announced if a Player had taken Sky Key. He clicks the button again. Chiyoko only tracked two.

Two out of the seven others who remain.

What a gift. What a precious, precious gift.

"Even in death, my love." An strokes Chiyoko around his neck. The video will be ready soon. He will mark these Players for the world, broadcast their locations.

"Even in death."

GREG JORDAN

Gulfstream G650, 37,800 Feet over the Bering Strait

Greg rubs his eyes. Looks wearily around the cabin. Sees everyone else—McCloskey and Pop and Aisling—totally knocked out.

Good for them. We're going to need as much rack as we can get before this thing gets rolling.

He lets out a big sigh. It's been a long couple of days. The news of Abaddon, the alliance with Aisling, the choice to hunt down An Liu, the decision to redirect the kill team Kilo Foxtrot Echo, which he has yet to do, and most importantly the knowledge that billions will die very soon make these the longest days of his life. And he's had some doozies.

But these days. They're the *fucking* longest.

Greg stands, thinking, *If now isn't the time for an f-bomb, then I don't know when is. Shit, I could probably sit in a dark room and just let out an unending stream of f-bombs for a week, and that would be a perfectly reasonable thing to do in light of everything I know.*

He thinks that he'd rather live than just curse into the void, though. Even if the fucking world really is gonna fucking blow up.

And Greg knows that living means helping Aisling now, and not Stella. Not DOAT. Stella and hers can carry on with their mission to stop the aliens from coming back, and God bless them to heaven and hell and back, but right now Greg has to prioritize. Greg has to live. Greg has to help Aisling. If Aisling can figure out some quick way to end the game, great, but if not, then she has to win. That's the plan and he's down with it. He's down.

This means that Greg has to get his crew to Japan and help Aisling figure out the best way to go about killing An Liu.

Greg opens the cockpit door and squeezes into the copilot seat. Even Marrs is sacked out, letting the plane make its way on autopilot.

Greg puts the cans on and fires up the encrypted radio. Puts in the channel and gives it the series of coded clicks that Kilo Foxtrot Echo is always listening for.

God bless KFE, Greg thinks. *To heaven and hell and back.*

After about a minute the line cracks. Per protocol, the woman on the other end says nothing.

Greg says, "This is Gold Leader. Authorization to speak freely is granted. Code is 'hot sauce fifty-nine jays with bunnies,' repeat, 'hot sauce fifty-nine jays with bunnies.' Copy back."

"Hey, Gold Leader," the woman says.

"Hey, Wi-Fi. Where y'at?"

"Still in Amesbury."

"You guys got DOAT wired to deal with Stonehenge?"

"Roger that. Wired and ready. Should only be a few days now. Waiting on word from Stella."

"Ah, Stella. Talk to her lately?"

"Not at all. Gone silent since Abaddon announcement. Shit's FUBAR, yeah?"

"Super-duper FUBAR, Wi-Fi. Listen now and listen good. I have a new mission, effective yesterday."

"Fire back."

"You need to pull up and relocate the team to the Tokyo safe house, stat. We'll be on the ground in under five hours. What time can you make?"

Wi-Fi pauses. "Fourteen hours, sixteen tops."

"Excellent. This is a kill mission, top-shelf. Pack your guts and expect to get wet."

"Can't wait," Wi-Fi says, and Greg knows she means it. Wi-Fi loves a good kill mission. Every member of Kilo Foxtrot Echo does.

"Marrs'll upload everything we got on the mark soon. You can check it

en route. I repeat, Wi-Fi, look hot on this one. Get the boys ready."
Wi-Fi just makes a little giggly noise. The boys are always ready, and
Greg knows it. All she says before clicking off is "See you in Japan, Gold
Leader. Wi-Fi out."

HILAL IBN ISA AL-SALT

Caesars Palace, Suite 2405, Las Vegas, Nevada, United States

Hilal left Stella at her warehouse headquarters 37 hours ago. She told him to be ready to receive a message on this day—the message that would help him gain access to Wayland Vyctory.

He wakes early. He prays to Uncle Moses, Fathers Christ and Mohammed, Grandfather Buddha. Meditates on the divine spark that resides in each human being like a forgotten organ. Asks for guidance and strength.

Does not pray for salvation or redemption. Whatever happens, he is already saved, already redeemed.

Paradise is here, within, not up there, beyond where the Makers reside.

When he is ready Hilal opens a hidden compartment in his suitcase.

In it is the Breastplate of Aaron. The 12 wooden blocks, the 12 colored stones: Odem, Pit'dah, Bareket, Nofekh, Sapir, Yahalom, Leshem, Shevo, Ahlamah, Tarshish, Shoham, Yashfeh. The same piece of ancient armor that protected Master Eben from the mortal ravages of the ark in the Kodesh Hakodashim.

Hilal pulls it over his body, ties it tight so that the ancient panels press into his skin.

He hopes that it will protect him too.

He hangs his twin machetes from a sash. Covers these with a pair of loose cotton pants, hiding them from the world. Puts on worn leather sandals, a baggy white shirt that obscures the Breastplate of Aaron.

He pulls on the necklace he wore to the Calling. Even after all that has happened, he still believes in good fortune.

He is going to need it today.

He lays the device from the ark on the bed, and his smartphone, and five bundles of $10,000 in crisp $100 bills. All of these will go into his black leather shoulder satchel.

Last, Hilal picks up the canes, the Rod of Aaron, the Rod of Moses. He activates each by caressing the back of its snakelike head. The brown wood transforms instantly into scaled skin, the things writhe and twirl around Hilal's forearms. He looks into the cobras' black eyes flecked with gold.

The snakes flare their hoods. Show their teeth. Snap at each other. Hilal coos to them. Blows on them. Speaks to them.

"Today is the day that you will fulfill your purpose," he says. "Today is the day that you will devour the being that betrayed you so many eons ago. Today is the day that you will give human beings back that which Ea has taken from them."

The snake of Aaron shoots forward and runs across Hilal's shoulders.

"Today is the day that you will restore innocence to man."

AISLING KOPP, POP KOPP, GREG JORDAN, BRIDGET McCLOSKEY, GRIFFIN MARRS

Sheraton Grande Tokyo Bay Hotel, Adjoined Suites 1009 and 1011, 1-9 Maihama, Urayasu, Chiba, Japan

Aisling and her newly formed band of CIA spooks arrived in Japan two days ago and checked into a pair of grand Japanese-style suites overlooking Tokyo Bay. An's hideout is only a few clicks to the west. Marrs is at a computer, sucking on a fancy Japanese lollipop shaped like a chainsaw. Jordan is with him. They talk quietly. McCloskey is on the floor cushions, poring over a large map of the northern islands of Tokyo Port, a wooden platform of half-consumed sushi and Japanese pickles weighing down one corner of the map. Aisling stands at the floor-to-ceiling window. Pop is at her shoulder. Winds, funneled through the Uraga Channel from Sagami Bay, buffet the glass in gusts and whooping howls. The bay is a dark expanse plied by ships of all sizes, surrounded by islands stuffed to capacity with buildings and golf courses and hotels and marinas and shipyards. In the distance, to the southeast, is a white space-age structure that looks like the headquarters of a Bond supervillain. To the west is the Tokyo skyline, limitless and twinkling, the largest city Aisling has ever seen.

"What a place," she remarks to Pop in their Celtic language.

"Yes. I've visited twice. Both times I was floored."

Aisling and Pop have not had a proper chance to talk about whether or not they should have accepted the help Jordan and his team offered, mainly because they haven't been left alone for even a second. So they take this chance, in this huge room, the wind howling outside, to talk quietly.

"What do you think they're not telling us?" Aisling says in their guttural yet singsongy language.

"That they wanted to kill you—and every other Player—before they decided that they had to team up with you," Pop says flatly.

Aisling nods. "That's what I think too."

"However, I think they mean to help you now. I believe them when they say they're scared."

"I believe that too."

They watch the movements of the ships on the bay.

"Aisling," Pop says slowly. He doesn't have to say another word for her to know what he's going to ask.

"I told you why already. I wasn't lying in Port Jervis."

"I know you weren't, but I can't accept that."

"You have to, Pop. I'm the Player and this is my call. You know once the game begins I can't be replaced. So you're stuck with me, and this is the way I'm Playing it. Stop the game if possible, win if not."

Pop doesn't say anything.

"I'm sorry to put you in this position, Pop, and I'll cut right to it." She takes a deep breath. "We have to do it this way to honor Dad. To honor your son. To make sure his death was not in vain." She lets these words sink in. "I know you were ordered to kill him, and I commend you for following that order. Not because I agree with it, but because that's how it had to work. Our line demands order. That's our way. But now that it's all begun, and it's real and not a thing we've imagined for all these years, now that the *planet* is on the line, we have to do this. We have to. If you want to make Declan's death mean the *right* thing, Pop, then this is absolutely what we have to do."

She looks at his profile as she speaks. His jaw twitches. His eyes well up.

Aisling puts a hand on his arm. "I love you and I forgive you, Pop. Now you have to forgive yourself too. I think that this is the best way for you to do that."

He still stares out the window. Reaches across his body and takes her hand. Squeezes it. Hard.

"Are you with me?" she asks, barely above a whisper.

"Do I have a choice?"

They both know the answer. She doesn't have to say it.

"I will always be with you, my Player."

"Good." She slides her hand down his arm and they stand, shoulder to shoulder, watching Tokyo. The water is mesmerizing. Aisling half expects Godzilla to rise out of it and start roaring at helicopters. But it's not time for Armageddon. Not just yet.

"Good news," Jordan announces, breaking up the moment she and Pop share. "KFE is online with eyes on Liu and ready to strike on your count, Kopp."

Aisling squeezes Pop's hand one last time and spins to Jordan.

"Excellent. Let's see what they can see."

Jordan briefed Aisling on Kilo Foxtrot Echo after he called them up. The team consists of six men and one woman. Four former SEALs, one ex–Delta Force, and two CIA assassins. Their code names are Duck, Wi-Fi, Zealot, Charnel, Clov, Hamm, and Skyline.

Aisling and Pop join Jordan and Marrs while McCloskey continues to inspect her maps.

Marrs works a joystick that controls the cameras the team has set up. He tilts left and down. Pushes a red button. An image on his laptop zooms in. "There, in all his glory, lies An Liu," Marrs says, the lollipop still in his mouth.

An sleeps on a cot along the wall. He's covered by a sheet, his emaciated back exposed.

"That's him?" Pop asks. "He looks like he's in a concentration camp."

An rolls over and they see his face. The tattooed tears. "That's him," Aisling says.

"According to Wi-Fi, he's been busy," Marrs says. "Hacked Google, Twitter, Facebook, Anonymous, Dropbox, Instagram, the NSA, the DIA, the CIA, the NGA, NASA, Russia's FSB, MI6, Israel's Unit Eight-Two Hundred, China's MSS, and god-knows-what else."

"She's already in his system?" Aisling asks.

"No, that's based on visual. To get into his system, we'll have to go in and physically tap it."

"So we wait for him to leave," Jordan says.

"He'll only leave if he's never coming back is my guess," Aisling says.

"No. We have to take him out."

"I agree," McCloskey says from the floor.

"Good old McCloskey, always ready to jump in feetfirst," Jordan says.

McCloskey stands and stretches. "*Pop!* One shot and out."

"I'd take that shot with a smile on my face," Aisling says.

"I don't know, man," Marrs interjects. "We might want to get in his computers first. Wi-Fi thinks he has some choice intel."

"Can we talk to her?" Pop asks.

Jordan shakes his head. "No. KFE protocol is to shut the hell up when they're casing. I can have her move to comm distance, though."

Aisling considers it, but then says, "You sure they can get in there without Liu knowing?"

McCloskey says, "KFE could climb up a kitten's asshole without it knowing."

"Thanks for that image, McCloskey," Aisling says.

Pop ignores the joke. "We could sedate him and check his intelligence to see if it's developed enough. If it is, we kill him. If it isn't, we let him wake up and carry on."

McCloskey shakes her head adamantly. "We've had a shit ton of experience with serums. No matter how engineered they are, the mark knows something was done to him. Remember that kid in Bahrain?"

Jordan rolls his eyes. "Farouq al-Nani?"

"Old Two-Left-Feet Farouq," Marrs says. "Couldn't walk a straight line for six months after we hit him with that cocktail."

Aisling clicks her tongue. "I agree that sedation is too risky. Besides, I want to see KFE in action. I mean, they are going to be my personal black-ops super death squad, right, Jordan?"

"Damn right they are."

"Can they go in tonight?" Aisling asks.

"They can go in in two minutes, if you want," Jordan answers confidently.

Aisling shakes her head. "I think we should all be there on support. I'll take a cover sniper position on this building to the west, and you guys can split up to block the roads off the island north and south—just in case it gets hairy. Otherwise, let's get KFE on the horn, and let's see what these badasses of yours—I mean, *ours*—can do."

My blood will I take and bone will I fashion
I will make man, that man may
I will create man who shall inhabit the earth,
That the service of the gods may be established, and that their shrines may be built.
But I will alter the ways of the gods, and I will change their paths;
Together shall they be oppressed and unto evil shall they . . .
And Ea answered him and spake the word:
. . . the . . . of the gods I have changed
. . . and one . . .
. . . shall be destroyed and men will I . . .
. . . and the gods . . .
. . . *and they* . . .

HILAL IBN ISA AL-SALT

The Vyctory Hotel and Casino, Las Vegas, Nevada, United States

Stella's message comes at the appointed time. A young porter delivers it and disappears down the hallway. Hilal opens the envelope. The single sheet inside reads, *Tell the clerk with the yellow flower "Our mutual friend is Rima Subotic."*

Cryptic but straightforward. Hilal likes it. Gets his canes, burns the message, and leaves Caesars. He will walk to the Vyctory.

The streets are not as empty as they were on his first night. As Hilal travels the Strip, he passes makeshift kiosks that hawkers and madmen and entrepreneurs have set up on the sidewalk. Their signs say things like: *Are YOU Prepared?* and *How to Make Sure You Have Water!* and *Your DOG and Your GUN Will Be Your Best Friends* and one sign that simply says *How to Kill.*

A man stops Hilal and literally tries to sell him salvation: "An investment in the Lord Jesus Christ, on the Day of Judgment, when the sky turns black and the rivers run with blood, and what comes after!" Hilal admires the man's pluck but tells him he is not interested and leaves the man behind. After 15 minutes, Hilal reaches his destination. He pauses in the street. The Vyctory hotel[xi] is a 75-story mirrored cone that reflects the skyline and the mountains and the clouds and the sun. The word *Vyctory* is emblazoned vertically over the southernmost side, covering more than half of the lower floors.

Hilal passes a cordon of armored vehicles belonging to a private security force and goes into the ornate lobby, the plush red carpeting, the warm lighting, the glass chandeliers of all colors and shapes. The place is busier than Caesars but not hectic.

Hilal pulls the device from his satchel and holds it overhead. And there, almost directly above him, is the caduceus marking Wayland Vyctory.

Hilal eyes the clerks. None wear yellow flowers. In fact, there is a dearth of flowers in the whole lobby. If this Rima Subotic person is his key to reaching Ea, then he will just ask another clerk for help. He walks to the main desk and picks an Asian woman in her late 40s, her long hair pulled into a tight bun on top of her head. She has red lips and dark eyes. The name on her tag says CINDY.

"Hello, Cindy," Hilal says. She was engrossed with something under the hood of the desk—a computer, her phone—and didn't notice him.

"Hell—oh!" She brings her fingertips to her lips and breathes in sharply.

"I am sorry for my appearance."

"No, it's . . . I mean, I wasn't expecting . . ."

Hilal waves his hand. "Think nothing of it."

"Are you checking in?"

"No. But there is someone here I wish to see."

Cindy punches something into her keyboard. "Very well. Room number?"

"I don't know it. Her name is Rima Subotic. She is a friend."

Cindy looks left then right before whispering. "You want to see Ms. Subotic?"

"Yes," Hilal says simply. Apparently people do not ask to see Rima Subotic—or, he guesses, Wayland Vyctory.

Cindy straightens. "I'm sorry, but that's not possible."

"Yes, Cindy, it is. When she learns I am here, it will absolutely be possible."

She shakes her head. Punches something else into her keyboard. Hilal notes some movement in his periphery.

Security.

"Anyway, Ms. Subotic isn't here at the moment."

Cindy is an awful liar.

Hilal's voice is low, gravelly, ominous-sounding. "I know that is not true. I can assure you that she will want to see me, and I can assume that her boss—*your* boss—will not be happy when he finds out that you tried to shoo me away."

Cindy looks up. She is clearly scared.

Security gets closer.

"My name is Hilal ibn Isa al-Salt, the Aksumite. A mutual friend sent me to see Ms. Subotic. Tell her that. Understand?"

She nods slowly. Holds up a hand.

Security stops moving in.

Cindy makes the call from a phone out of earshot. She hangs up. "Wait here, Mr. al-Salt."

"Thank you, Cindy."

Three minutes later two very large guards appear. Without saying a word they take Hilal to the bank of elevators past reception. They escort him to a private carriage at the end of the hall that they access with an old-fashioned brass key. It has two buttons on the silver panel: UP and DOWN. The bigger of the two guards—a man who Hilal estimates to be 202 centimeters in height and 127 kilograms in weight—presses UP. The other man indicates that Hilal should raise his arms in order to be searched.

Hilal docs so.

The carriage begins a fast ascent.

The guard checks Hilal's satchel, ignores the bundles of cash, and holds up the device from the ark.

"Do either of you speak?"

One of the guards shakes his head, opens his mouth.

His tongue has been cut out.

Hilal nods. "You're Mr. Vyctory's Nethinim, yes?"

Without so much as a hint of surprise, the guard nods. He shakes the device.

"I am here to present this prize to Mr. Vyctory. It is harmless. You can hold it if you wish, but you must hand it to him when I say so."

Expressionless, the guard slides it into one of his pockets.

The elevator comes to an abrupt stop. The doors open. Hilal is ushered into a bright white foyer, a single table on the far wall, on it a vase exploding with yellow lilies. Mounted on the wall behind the flowers is a photograph of deep space. Hilal recognizes it as one taken by the Hubble Space Telescope. The guard frisks Hilal, starting at his feet. He removes Hilal's machetes and hands them to his counterpart, and continues up to Hilal's chest, feeling the thing under his shirt. His eyes widen and grow fearful. He grabs the collar of Hilal's top and rips it open, revealing the Breastplate of Aaron.

Hilal says, "It is not—"

"What you think," an androgynous voice says, cutting Hilal off. "It's quite benign, Kaneem. A memento from a bygone age."

A tall woman ambles through the doorway on the left. The woman's skin is relentlessly pale, as if it has never seen the light of day, and its paleness is accentuated by her black, silky, straight hair. Her eyes are larger than usual, as if they have also spent countless hours in the dark and have grown bigger in order to take in more light. She is svelte, graceful, as young as 25 or as old as 50. She is dressed in a form-fitting light-green business suit, a thin red belt hugging her waist. Silver flat-soled shoes. No jewelry of any kind.

If Hilal didn't know better, he would think that she was part alien.

He bows to the woman. "Miss Rima Subotic, I assume?"

"Yes, Aksumite," she says. "Please, state your business."

Hilal understands that as Stella's mole, Rima must keep up appearances. He plays along. "Ms. Subotic, I humbly present myself to you. A Player of Endgame, the member of the Aksumite line. I bring a gift for the Lord Seer and Father, the Chief Scion of the Old Order, the Heliach. I bring him a most unexpected gift."

Subotic betrays no emotion. Joins her hands at her waist. "Why should I believe you, Aksumite?"

Hilal keeps his head low, watches the floor at the woman's silver-shoed feet. "This is your choice, sister, whether to believe me or not. But I come here because I know that our Lord Seer, he who is called Ea, would like to participate in the Great Puzzle."

"And how would you propose he do that?"

"Please, Nethinim, show Ms. Subotic what I have brought."

The woman holds out her hand, and Kaneem hands her the device. She takes it, turns it over, runs her fingers over it. It does not function for her.

"What is this?"

"It is from our master's long-lost cousins. My line opened the Ark of the Covenant with the Makers, and this was inside." The woman's eyes widen, but she doesn't speak. Hilal thinks, *She's good. Convincing.* "It will enable Ea to communicate with his brethren, and help him see that the game ends however he wishes it to end. Here. Let me show you."

Hilal holds out his hand. The woman passes it to him, and immediately it glows to life, showing the bottomless well of stars and space. He swings it toward one of the doors, and the caduceus comes into view. "That is Ea," Hilal says. He moves it so that its heading is 236° 34' 56". The throbbing orange ball fills the screen. "That is Sky Key." The woman gives Hilal a mischievous smile, takes the device back from him. It falls into darkness. "So you used this to find Master Vyctory?"

"Yes." Hilal doesn't dare mention Stella or the other caduceus that marks her. Nor does Subotic.

"All right, Aksumite, you have earned your audience, but it will be closely monitored."

"Naturally."

She makes a perfunctory bow. "You can keep on the witch doctor's vest"—she points a disturbingly long index finger at the Breastplate of Aaron—"but the canes will have to stay."

Perhaps too convincing. Doesn't she know that if I am to succeed, I must be allowed to keep them?

"Ms. Subotic, look at me. I was nearly killed by a pair of Players not long ago. I need my canes."

Rima Subotic shakes her head. "I'm sorry, but they could be used as weapons. As you and I both know, your line excels at a martial-art form of stick fighting, am I right?"

"Yes, although I prefer my machetes, which this man has already taken. Please, you are free to inspect them," Hilal says confidently. "They are harmless."

Rima Subotic gives the unnamed Nethinim a curt nod. He takes the canes and disappears for nearly four minutes. Hilal leans uncomfortably against the elevator doorway, shifting his weight from foot to foot.

The man reappears. He hands the canes to Rima Subotic.

Nods.

She looks at them. "They're clear, Aksumite."

"I know."

She runs her fingers over the carvings, over the vacant eyes. "Snake heads, hm?"

Hilal smiles. "Did the snake not tempt man?"

She passes Hilal his canes. "Yes, he did, Brother al-Salt."

Subotic presses a series of unmarked points on the wall, a hidden panel beneath glowing red then green then purple then blue then white. The door hisses open, sliding away. Another white room beyond.

"Now please, Aksumite. Follow me. Master Vyctory awaits."

xii

AISLING KOPP, AN LIU, KILO FOXTROT ECHO

Shang Warehouse, 3 Chome-7-19 Shinkiba, Kōtō-Ku, Tokyo Port, Japan

It is 4:17 a.m.

Aisling lies prone on the roof of a two-story building one block west of An's warehouse. She holds her beloved bolt-action sniper rifle, the Brügger & Thomet APR308, a barrel-like silencer screwed onto the muzzle. She has on a black jumpsuit guarding her from the cool wind blowing off the water. She has unobstructed sight lines of the streets to the south, east, and north. To her right is a high wall she can vault over and take cover behind. To her back, 75 feet away, is the edge of the building, which dives straight down into the water.

Over her left eye is a Griffin Marrs–modified Google Glass monocle mounted on a hinge.

She flicks through video uplinks on the monocle. Charnel is opposite from her, bearing 85° 42' 39", 716 feet away, covering the eastern side of An's warehouse with his own sniper rifle, a suppressed M91A2. Clov and Hamm are on the roof of An's warehouse, each sighting An's slumbering body from opposite sides, ready to rappel into the warehouse if needed. Duck, the demolitions and communications expert, is covering the bay doors from the street. Zealot is covering the rear exit in a back alley. Skyline is assisting Wi-Fi. Wi-Fi, clad completely in black, is already hanging on the line that dangles inside An Liu's domain. Aisling flicks two more times. Sees Marrs's array of computers. He's in a van several blocks to the north. Jordan's with him. Flicks again. Sees Pop, his hands folded serenely over the top of an M4 carbine in the passenger seat of another van, this one several blocks to the south, McCloskey at the wheel.

Jordan's voice comes over Aisling's earpiece. "All units double-check sync time. Nineteen seventeen and thirty-five seconds Zulu."

Aisling checks: 19:17:35 and ticking.

"One click from all units for go."

Aisling clicks her monocle—her note is F-sharp—and hears the distinctive, multitoned clicks of the others.

"Roger. All counted, all ready. This is a go on Shang. Repeat, go on Shang."

An's sleeping body is curled and turned to the wall, his fingertips gracing the strands of Chiyoko's hair and her shriveled ears.

Wi-Fi descends from the ceiling. She lands bottom-first on the floor without a sound. She unclips her rappel line and flips onto her stomach and edges forward. She reaches An's desk, slides under it, finds the slumbering Mac Pro that acts as the central station for all of An's computers.

Wi-Fi pulls a black box no bigger than a pack of cigarettes from a pocket on her thigh. Grabs a roll of soft plastic from a pocket on the other thigh. Props herself on her elbows and gets to work. The black box is a very small and very powerful solid-state computer. She takes the only cord leading from it and carefully plugs it into the Mac Pro's high-speed data port. Wi-Fi's little black box is programmed with a special protocol that will not wake up the tapped system: the Mac Pro continues to sleep.

She unrolls the soft pad of plastic. A silent keyboard.

She types. The black box works. She sees the display in her monocle. She establishes the uplink. From his perch in the communications van, Marrs scours An's system, transferring as many files as he can until he hits pay dirt: the video An recorded and the accompanying information he gathered on the remaining Players of Endgame.

A seagull cuts over Aisling as she watches Wi-Fi's feed. Once she's established the link, Wi-Fi sits cross-legged under the desk and draws an HK Mark 23, also silenced, and levels it squarely at the center of An Liu's back, a faint dot marking his spine and lung. Aisling watches as An's shoulders rise and fall under a thin dark sheet.

Aisling and Wi-Fi and all of Kilo Foxtrot Echo wait.

Wait for Marrs to do his thing.

An Liu dreams of Chiyoko. She is alive, swimming in black inky water, her hair cut haphazardly, her ears missing, her lips smiling, her head and neck and white round shoulders the only part of her that are visible. A breeze pushes across the water's surface, causing little ripples. Chiyoko's face fills with alarm. She raises an arm. Goose bumps speckle her shoulders. She points. Opens her mouth and screams.

But no sound comes.

Just an open rictus, screaming silently, getting bigger and bigger and bigger.

A warning.

An Liu's eyes shoot open. His slow breath continues.

In out.

Up down.

He blinks. The wall is only centimeters from the tip of his nose. He smells the sea. He feels a faint whiff of fresh air coming from above.

One of the skylights is open.

He did not open it.

He is not alone.

Marrs says, "He has intel that puts the Aksumite is in Las Vegas, and the Harappan somewhere in northeastern India. He thinks Aisling is still in New York, which isn't a vote of confidence on his intel, but whatever. Best of all he's tracking two of them. Based on elimination, he's pegged these as the Olmec and the Nabataean. The Cahokian is with the Olmec, which is what British intelligence says too. He's not sure about the whereabouts of the Donghu. I'm copying the files now. Need one minute fifty seconds. But this is an affirmative. An's been a busy boy, and we got what we need."

"Proceed on my mark in approximately one minute forty-eight seconds," Jordan says. "Copy back, one click each."

Aisling clicks. Hears the others.

Click click click click click click click click.

An slides his hand along the edge of the metal bed frame where it meets the wall.

He feels it. A button, no bigger than a coin.

A Player is here for him. How, he doesn't know. But a Player is here.

He pushes the button.

In 0.06 seconds the bed frame flips toward the wall, and he's thrown into a dark crawl space, the bed now flush against the opening, shutting him off from the room.

Clank! Clank! Clink!

Three shots, all from different directions, two of them rifle caliber.

BlinkSHIVERblink.

An shimmies forward quickly. Something metal jams into the crease at the edge of the bed. He doesn't bother looking. He knows it's a pry bar. He double-times it.

SHIVERSHIVER.

Crawls into a slightly bigger space, large enough to sit in, with a weak red light illuminating everything. Other gunshots dot the wall outside, in his exact position.

They can see him, even behind his cover.

They can see him.

And maybe—can they track him too?

Yes. He overlooked something. His friend Charlie from the British Special Forces must have had the paranoid foresight to chip An when he was still on that destroyer in the English Channel.

He will need to get rid of the chip when he has a moment.

More sounds from the bed. The metal panel screeches as it gives way, revealing the space. An looks just as a hand appears and lobs something in his direction.

He hits another button. A steel partition zips up from the floor. The thing clatters into it on the other side.

He covers his ears.

An explosion. The walls shake, but not much. This little armored room protects him. And besides, he can tell by the sound that it was a small grenade with a limited blast radius, meant to harm only whoever was right in front of it.

The kind of grenade he might use in certain circumstances.

The kind of grenade that requires special modification.

A crafty Player. The Donghu maybe, or possibly the Celt. One of the two that he has the least amount of info on.

And, based on the multiple calibers and shooters, this Player isn't alone.

Very *SHIVERshiverSHIVER* very crafty.

An slips into a vest. It's covered with bombs and remote triggers and a pair of semiauto pistols. He flops onto his back and pulls on black cotton pants. He sits. Caresses Chiyoko.

Right over his shoulder comes the chattering cry of a hammer-action power drill.

He has to move.

But first, he has a little surprise for whoever's outside his little *blinkblink* outside his little hidey-hole.

Aisling watches An disappear and the rest of the team spring into action.

"Jordan, this is Aisling, over."

"Copy Aisling," Jordan says, his voice anxious.

"I'm going in."

"No," Pop says. "Not yet. Be patient. Keep your gun ready."

"Pop's right, Aisling," McCloskey adds. "KFE will handle themselves. They always do."

That's what I'm worried about, Aisling thinks. *That they're experts, and they think they know what they're dealing with.*

Aisling hears a burst of automatic gunfire, and Clov calls out in pain. She flicks to his feed. He's on the ground, writhing. On his vitals display in the lower right corner, his heart rate skyrockets. If she could see the look in his eyes, she would see the anger there, the anger that he's been shot.

And the confusion.

They don't know what they're dealing with.

Wi-Fi and Hamm jump to the side and look at the floor. An slid open a little slot near their feet and fired on Clov, whose ankles are mangled and spouting blood. "Phase two," Wi-Fi says urgently over the comm. Skyline, still on the roof, throws a rope through the open skylight. She catches it, clips it to Clov. "Evac now," Wi-Fi says, and just like that Clov is being dragged across the floor and up through the air to Skyline, and to safety.

In the meantime, Hamm picks up the drill and resumes his work. His eyes scour the wall and floor for another hidden door, expecting one to slide open and for a gun to peek out at him.

Wi-Fi jumps back several feet and sights the wall, moving her pistol all around. As she does, a muzzle pokes out near Hamm's feet, and Wi-Fi fires on it. Slugs zip along the floor, the pistol is yanked back.

Hamm keeps drilling.

Another panel opens, this time 10 feet to the left. From it seven black spheres drop and roll across the floor in seven different directions. "Fire in the hole!" Wi-Fi shouts. Both she and Hamm turn and run as fast as they can around the desks and the computers. On the roof, Skyline slings the injured Clov over his shoulder and runs too.

The explosions come quick—*bangbangbangbangboombangboom.* Only two are incendiary; the rest are smoke and light. The real ones send shrapnel flying indiscriminately through the space, grazing Wi-Fi on the hip and missing Hamm altogether. Both are knocked to the floor, though, as is Skyline on the roof. He's unharmed. He looks at Clov, who is losing blood through his ankles. "I'm fine. Get that fuck," Clov says, and Skyline nods. "Roger that."

"All secondary units hold positions," Jordan says over the comm. "That means you, Aisling. If Liu emerges, take him out. Repeat, *take him out*."

Inside the warehouse, Hamm leaps to his feet and takes cover behind a column. Wi-Fi ignores her flesh wound and takes cover too. Hamm signals to Wi-Fi—a fist, three fingers, a thumb sticking left.

The message is clear.

An Liu is not going to emerge.

He is going to die.

Aisling fights every urge to move. But the others are right. As much as it pains her, she has to stay put. An could show up anywhere, and if she's not there to take the shot, it will be a major missed opportunity. She hates it, but she has to wait.

She hates it.

As soon as the bombs go off, An slides into the main room, now filled with smoke and the acrid smell of sulfur. He doesn't need to see. He knows where everything is.

Everything except the people who hunt him.

He makes it to the desk in 4.7 seconds. He reaches out, finding the edge of his laptop. He flips down the screen, yanks out its cords, and slips it into a large sleeve in his vest.

He pats the top of the table some more, here and here and here.

He finds it too.

Nobuyuki Takeda's katana. He slides it through a loop on his pants.

The *slith-slith-slith* report of a suppressed rifle. A burst of gunfire zips through the smoke, pulling little contrails in its wake. The shots miss An, but barely.

An draws both pistols and fires blind, four shots with each gun in a syncopated rhythm. He aims for the columns at the other end of the room, which is where he would take cover if he were them.

All eight shots hit the metal beams, and he can't see just how close he comes to blowing Wi-Fi's head off or putting a massive hole through Hamm's neck.

Wi-Fi and Hamm slide to the floor.

Skyline skids along the roof, adjusts the settings on the HUD in his monocle. Adjustments that will reveal An's location via his British tracker instead of his heat signature.

Skyline just needs a few more seconds. Then he will send the settings to Hamm and Wi-Fi and everyone else, and Kilo Foxtrot Echo will have An Liu dead to rights.

While Skyline works, An stalks through the smoke in the direction of the shipping containers. He flips a trigger guard on a little box on his vest. He presses and holds the red button underneath. When he releases it . . .

Aisling receives Skyline's HUD modifications and—*pop!*—just like that she can see An Liu's tracker, which she knows is embedded in his thigh, swinging back and forth as he walks through his warehouse.

Player to Player.

The way it's supposed to be.

She applies the first ounce of pressure to the trigger. Lowers her head. Breathes. The rounds in her gun are armor-piercing, and will have no problem boring through the building and into An's body.

No problem at all.

But just as she is ready to shoot, the street to the west lights up, and her face grows hot, and buildings and sky and windows glow orange and red, and her ears fill with noise. She pulls the trigger reflexively.

The shot hits An's warehouse, pierces the wall, misses the Shang by two feet, and bores through the armor, skin, bone, lung, bone, skin, and armor of Hamm's chest before embedding in the concrete floor. Hamm slumps and dies instantly in the smoke-filled room.

Aisling flops down, covers the back of her head with her hands.

The bomb went off just outside the bay doors of the warehouse. It throws debris and shrapnel at Duck, driving a foot–long shard of steel through his cheek and the base of his brain, severing the very top of his spinal column.

Another down.

On the roof, Skyline is flattened but still unhurt, and Clov, who is in and out of consciousness from blood loss, doesn't even register the blast.

Wi-Fi crawls to Hamm. Skyline says he's going in. Zealot abandons his cover in the back alley and moves in too. Aisling lifts her head, scans the side of the warehouse, fire raging, car alarms going off. She hears the far-off moan of a ship's horn in the bay, completely unattached to what's going on here, now, in Endgame.

She recovers and gathers the rifle and throws the bolt and breathes, ignores the cries over the comm link, ignores how everything is going to shit, ignores Jordan's orders for Skyline and Zealot to stay put so that Aisling and Charnel can fire at will.

Ignores it.

She squints through her monocle, tries to get a bead on the tracker that's in An's leg. At first she doesn't see it, but then, yes. A purple blip. She sights down the muzzle. She squeezes, adjusts, squeezes, adjusts, squeezes.

And fires.

A large round cuts through the smoke and misses An's right leg by only a centimeter.

He walks faster.

Another round, from the opposite direction, misses him by several feet. *Yes, they are tracking me. That bruise on my leg. It is there. I must dig it out when I get the chance.*

He runs.

Another large round from the better marksman misses again by only a couple centimeters. The running motion is putting them off.

The better marksman.

The Player, An thinks.

Several smaller rounds zip by him. Shots from within the room. He lays down cover fire in that direction as he runs even faster.

Another sniper shot from the rear, still several feet off.

Another from the front, only three centimeters away.

And now, fire from above, medium caliber, from a suppressed carbine. He reaches the container with the mainframes just in time. Its doors are open. He steps inside and yanks them shut, throws a bar that will hold off his assailants for a few moments.

Aisling fires at will, and then, *poof,* An Liu's tracker disappears. She fires three more rounds until Skyline calls to hold. Wi-Fi says, "I have visual. He's in the westernmost container. We have him cornered. Moving in."

Skyline and Zealot move in too. Charnel sprints over the rooftops, whispering the Lord's prayer.

Aisling pushes up, gets to her knees, stands. She is about to vault over the edge of the building and slide down a drainpipe to join the others when the image of Marcus Loxias Megalos zooms to the front of her mind's eye.

Marcus, the first casualty of Endgame.

An, the first one to kill.

An, the one who used the gathering in the Qin Lin Mountains to try to kill as many as he could.

An, the one who blew up his hideout in Xi'an with a very large dirty bomb.

Aisling stops.

"Wait—" she says over the comm.

Pop asks, "What is it, Aisling?"

"Why did he corner himself?"

"What d'you mean, kid?" McCloskey demands.

"What if—"

An moves deeper into the container. More rounds bounce off its armored husk from all directions. They make an almost pleasant high-pitched song. An ejects the magazines from his pistols and reloads each. He holsters them. Someone bangs on the door. The firing stops. An pushes over one of the mainframes, crashing it into the door. Sparks fly as the thing comes undone, its circuits crackling. He spins to the rear of the container. He walks toward a hazmat suit, inserts his legs, his arms, makes sure Chiyoko is comfortable around his neck, pulls up the zipper. Straps on the helmet, lowers the hood over the helmet, secures the hood to the rest of the puffy astronaut-like suit, emblazoned with the exact colors and markings of the Tokyo Fire Department. He flips the gloves over his fingers, opens a panel on his left forearm, pushes a series of buttons. The air begins to flow. He lies in a metal capsule and hits another button on his arm. He hears the doors of the container being torn open. The capsule closes. He puts his arms at his side. Airbags inside the capsule inflate, pressing on him from all sides.

I Play for death, my love. For death.

He pushes the last button, on the heel of his right hand. Before releasing it, he closes his eyes.

Here comes salvation.

I Play for death.

"What if he's about to set off another dirty bomb?" Aisling yells.

"Oh shit," Jordan says. "All units, abort. Repeat, abort, abort, abort!"

Aisling abandons her rifle, runs across the roof toward the water. Runs so fast, the wind screaming in her ears, her breath churning, her feet slamming, her thighs like rocks, her calves like springs, her blood pumping and pumping and pumping. She is scared, but invigorated.

Running from what would be certain death were she stupid enough to be lured into An's trap, which she almost was.

The running excites her. Endgame fills her with fear.

This is Playing, even if, in this moment, she only has a slender chance of surviving.

She runs so fast.

Fifteen feet to go.

So fast.

Ten feet.

So exciting.

Five.

She opens her mouth, fills her lungs.

One.

She leaps over the edge.

Brings her hands together, pitches her body forward, dives.

The sky lights up so so bright just as she hits the water and shoots into the depths. She swims down and down and down. Kicks and scoops at the cold darkness as things of all sizes land above her. She spins, goes to the submerged structure that supports the man-made island above. Pushes her back against it, holds herself in place, her hands pushing into the pilings. All she can see is black below and muted orange above, slashed here and there by white as things splash down and sink. She hears bubbles and her own heartbeat. Her personal record for holding her breath underwater is three minutes and five seconds.

She will need every one of those seconds tonight.

Every single one, and more.

SARAH ALOPAY

Casa Isla Tranquila, Private Room, Juliaca, Peru

How could he do this to her?

How?

She's going to kill him. She's going to kill him. She's going to fucking *kill* him.

It has been 25 hours since that queen bitch brought her to this room.

Sarah has slept for only three. She has sat cross-legged on the floor, staring at the door, hoping that one of the Tlalocs comes in.

Hoping that *he* comes in, the Olmec, the Player, her friend, her lover, her confidant.

Her betrayer.

She is going to fucking kill him.

He hasn't come in.

She has sat and paced and screamed at the door and the window and the people in the garden, who either ignore her or can't see or hear her.

She tries to stay calm, tries to reason out what's happening. She lies on the bed and tries to sleep in 10-minute spurts. She doesn't want to miss one of them coming in, and she knows they do, because sometimes when she wakes up there is fresh food.

She doesn't eat it.

When she's feeling groggy or generous or sporadically calm she thinks: *He's doing this on purpose. He wants me in here. He hasn't betrayed me. He loves me.*

But then she remembers that he has Earth Key, that he took it from her while she was sleeping, defenseless, powerless.

No.

She seethes and paces, seethes and paces. Like an animal.

She hates him.

Hates him.

Hates.

She is going to kill him when she sees him again.

Fucking kill him.

JAGO TLALOC

Casa Isla Tranquila, Juliaca, Peru

Jago doesn't pace his room—the room where he broke his foot when he was seven while jumping off the bed, and sliced his hand open when he was nine while sharpening his knife, and shared his first kiss with his second cousin, Juella, when he was 12 and she 14. He doesn't curse the walls or forgo the comforts of home or scheme about who he's going to kill next and how and when. He doesn't forgo sleep. He doesn't refuse to eat. He doesn't convey worry or fear.

He can't. If he did, it would be too dangerous for her.

For Sarah.

For the one he loves and has pledged himself to.

For the one he has temporarily betrayed.

He's been thinking of her since his mother and father imprisoned her against his wishes. Thinking of when he should break her out. Because he has to break her out. Even if it violates the pact he has with his blood and his line. Sarah and he are together now. A team.

And she is a Player.

Like him.

She needs to Play.

He is angry with his mother and his father, so angry, but he can't show it. If he did, they would kill her. He has protested—not protesting would also be suspicious, and would probably result in her death as well—but he has also pretended to agree that Sarah needs to be held. His parents seem to have accepted Jago's acceptance. Either that or they're willing to accept his lies, which amounts to the same thing.

But inside he knows: he will not Play without her. He made her a promise. Unless something unexpected happens, he won't leave Isla Tranquila without Sarah Alopay.

He won't.

But first he has to see the Olmec elder.

First he has to see Aucapoma Huayna.

Now.

A knock on his door.

"Yeah."

Renzo wedges his head into the room. "She's ready."

Jago rises. Smooths his hands over his thighs. Crosses the room and picks up Earth Key—so small, so seemingly insignificant—from a mahogany bowl and wraps a fist around it. He and Renzo go to the inner courtyard. Jago doesn't look for Sarah at her window. They're met by Guitarrero, smoking a cigarillo by the fountain. Guitarrero asks if Jago is ready and Jago answers, "Of course."

They leave the courtyard, enter the guest wing of the sprawling house, go toward Aucapoma Huayna's room.

Five doors down, at the end of the hallway, is Sarah Alopay.

Jago can almost smell her anger.

They reach Aucapoma Huayna's door. Guitarrero takes a pull of his thin, brown smoke. "She has requested that you go alone, Jago."

Good, Jago thinks. "Very well," he says.

He puts a hand on the door. "Papi, if I have to leave Sarah in Peru, will you . . . look after her?"

"I will."

"You swear?"

"I do."

Jago, the human lie detector, can hear that Guitarrero lies to him. His own father. Lying.

Again.

"Thank you," Jago says, and he means it this time. He needed to know what his father's intentions were. He pushes the door all the way open and disappears into the room.

The shades are drawn, but the lamplight makes it bright and pleasant. Some tinkling classical music plays over a small radio. Aucapoma sits at a round table, waiting. The woman is stooped and frail—more bone than muscle—and her skin is as wrinkled as a raisin's. She wears a light blue silk robe and puffy slippers on her feet. Her thin wrists are covered in silver bangles. She looks straight at Jago—through him, almost—and says with a sweet voice in the Olmec's old language, "Come, child. Sit."

Jago does. "Thank you for making the trip, Aucapoma Huaya."

She waves a hand in front of her face. "Think nothing of it, child. This is what we have all been waiting for, isn't it?"

"It is."

"Now, I am old—as if you couldn't see that!—so let's get down to it, hmm?"

Jago appreciates her directness. "Agreed. Do you want to see it?"

She turns her hand over and holds it open. "Very much so."

"Here." Jago drops Earth Key onto her creased skin.

"Ahhhhhhh," Aucapoma Huayna breathes. "So light . . . yet so weighted."

Jago doesn't speak.

"The Sky People are infinite craftsmen—or I should say, craftsbeings!" She laughs at her own poor joke, a small, birdlike laugh.

"They made us, didn't they?"

Aucapoma Huayna wraps her fingers around Earth Key and points a long index finger at Jago. "Indeed they did. And they ruled us—especially the Olmec—favorably for many generations."

"Aucapoma Huayna. You possess the wisdom of King Pachakutiq. You know more about the ancient history and its truth than any living Olmec. Tell me. What do you know of the game?"

"I do know much about the ancient history, Jago. As if I was whispered facts by the Makers themselves. I know of the ancient gold mining and genetic experimentation, of specifications for pyramid construction, about how the Makers would concentrate the energy fields found all over Earth to their purpose. I know the secrets of the last ice age and the Great Flood that ended it. I know of the ancient flying machines and the connections between the continents in prehistory—between China and South America, between India and Africa. I know of epistemology and the subjugation of people through systems of belief. I know how to kill people in every conceivable way. I know dozens of languages, both forgotten and dead. I am the missing anthropological link." She pauses.

If this is getting right to it, then Jago is glad she didn't want to sit and have a long conversation about all that's happened.

"And now that I have seen this Earth Key, I know exactly what to do with it."

Here we go, he thinks.

She stares at the small black ball as she says quietly, "Earth Key was sourced from the great sunken quarries of the older-than-old settlement found beneath and among the late-antiquity city now called Tiwanaku, south and east of the great high lake covering the Crag of Lead. There you will find the Gateway of the Sun. I know it intimately, from top to bottom. Take Earth Key to it and put it in the southernmost side of the archway precisely two *luk'a*—one hundred and twenty-one-point-two centimeters—from the ground. Then and only then will the Player see the location of Sky Key."

Jago sighs. "Tiwanaku."

"Yes, my Player."

"Fucking Cielo territory—I mean, sorry for the language, Aucapoma Huayna."

The old lady chuckles again. "Please. I am old. There is nothing virginal about me—especially regarding my ears and my tongue!"

"And do you know anything about the third and final key—Sun Key?"

"No. Nothing."

Aucapoma Huayna smirks before falling into a light coughing fit. When she is finished, she holds out her hand and returns Earth Key to Jago. Her eyes are glassy from the coughing.

Jago stands and composes himself with an air of propriety. "Thank you, Aucapoma Huayna. Please continue to safeguard our ancient knowledge. I may need it again. Now, if it's all right, I have to Play."

Jago spins on his heel and takes three steps but is frozen as Aucapoma Huayna hisses, "Stop!" Her voice is different—strained from whatever caught in her throat and made her cough. "I need to tell you about the girl," she growls.

Jago turns, though much more slowly this time. "What about her?"

She takes a sip of water from a small, gold-leafed glass. "What has she told you about her line?"

"Not much. I get the impression they're not as prepared as we are— they thought they were more 'normal' than the other lines, for some reason. Don't get me wrong—Sarah's as capable a killer as any Player, but her line seems to lack the . . . resources of ours and some of the others."

Aucapoma nods slowly. "There is a reason for this, my Player."

Jago steps forward. "Yes?"

"You did not know about any of the lines when the game began, but I have known about the Cahokians for many, many years."

"What about them?"

"They are alone as the only one of the twelve lines that, in the history of history, stood up against and fought the Makers."

Jago falls into his seat. "Xehalór Tlaloc mentioned something like that to me a long time ago. Something about a battle between humans and Sky Gods. So it's true?"

"Yes."

"When?"

"In the year 1613 of the Common Era. The Makers were done mining Earth for gold by that late year, but the Cahokians owed them a thousand of their youths as their end of an old bargain. And when the last contingent of Makers on the planet asked for these children before their departure, the Cahokians refused."

"Didn't they fear the Makers' wrath?"

"No. By then they understood that the Makers weren't gods but mortal, and that their abilities were due to technology and not divine power. The Cahokians had the hubris to think they could use powerful technology the Makers had given them—essentially, projectile energy weapons—to repel the Makers. What they didn't account for was that the Makers had kept other weapons in reserve, and after three days of battle that saw grave losses on both sides, the Makers simply obliterated the battlefield from orbit, without even bothering to safeguard their own soldiers. No Makers survived. Only two male Cahokians lived, plus a scattered group of women and children."

"So that was the price they paid. Near annihilation."

"They paid a dearer price than that. As an ultimate insult, they were made to forget the true name of their line—which translates simply as 'The People.'"

"*Dio*," Jago exclaims.

"There's more. The Makers are afraid, my Player. They are afraid that, given another hundred and fifty years or so—but a fraction of a blink to the Makers—that we—"

"Would become something more like their equals."

"Yes."

"Which I believe is why Endgame is happening now. Not merely to fulfill the prophecy, but to reduce our numbers, to stunt our progress."

They share a silence.

"You must kill her, Jago," Aucapoma Huayna orders blithely.

"What?"

"An alliance with her is folly. The Makers will not allow her people to win. They simply won't. And they won't allow one of her allies to win either. They especially won't allow her lover to win."

"I . . ."

"You must kill her, by your own hand. You must show the Makers that you would go to any end to win."

"But why? You just admitted that they're mortal, and implied that they're petty."

"No more or less than us. It is true that we are made in the image of our creator." Aucapoma Huayna takes Jago's hands. Her cheeks are suddenly red, her lips quaking with urgency. "But they are still to be feared. That is the lesson of the Cahokian rebellion. We can't test them, Jago Tlaloc."

"What if the game can be stopped?"

"It can't," she insists, leaning ever closer. Jago can smell her breath—an unpleasant and heady combination of coffee and vitamins and stomach acid. "The Event has been triggered. Nothing can stop it now. You must Play. And you—*you!*—must kill the Cahokian."

xiii

HILAL IBN ISA AL-SALT

The Vyctory Hotel and Casino, Personal Suite of Wayland Vyctory, Las Vegas, Nevada, United States

Hilal follows Rima Subotic down a featureless hallway, the two Nethinim behind him.

This is what it all leads to, Hilal thinks. *Not Playing the way I thought that I would. But this.*

Destroying the Corrupter.

His nerves shake and rattle. He thinks of sand and wind and sweet dates and cool water. Those physical things that bring him peace. They still his heart.

Barely.

"Another question, Aksumite," Subotic says over her shoulder.

"Yes?"

"Why have you forsaken your line and come to submit to Master Vyctory?"

"I have not forsaken it in the least, sister," Hilal says plainly.

"Explain yourself."

"Not long after the Calling, I learned that the Players could save humanity and prevent the game from even beginning."

Subotic reaches the end of the hall and stops. There is no door, no window, no opening of any kind. Hilal senses that the Nethinim have stopped moving as well. Subotic gives Hilal an inquisitive look.

"All we had to do was stop Playing," Hilal continues. "If one of us had not retrieved Earth Key, then the Event would not have been triggered, and Endgame would not have progressed."

"Yes. The Maker said as much in its announcement."

"Precisely. I tried to inform the other Players of this, but my efforts were thwarted by a coronal mass ejection that, by the hand of the Makers, only fell on our little corner of Ethiopia. I was simultaneously attacked by two aligned Players and suffered these wounds. Not thirty-six hours afterward, Earth Key was found, and the Event triggered. After spending many hours in consultation with my master, we realized that the Makers had intervened in the game. . . . They are not supposed to intervene."

"No. They are not. But that still does not explain why you are here, pledging yourself to Master Ea."

"We decided that if the Makers were going to violate their pledge to us, then we could at least return the favor by opening the ark and seeing what powers lay within. Two Nethinim died in the task."

"The ark is a powerful tool."

"Yes. In it were two cobras, each chasing the other's tail." Hilal grips the snake heads of the canes. His palms sweat. He knows that Ea is watching and listening to this conversation, and Hilal is on the razor's edge where truth meets falsehood.

"The ouroboros, in the flesh," Subotic says.

"Yes. Consumed by anger at the Makers, my master took up each and whipped their heads on the edge of Father Moses's vessel. Both died and frittered to ash. The only other things in the ark were a pile of dust, the manna machine, which he didn't touch, and the device that you hold."

Subotic turns it in her hand.

"It was lifeless in my master's grip, as it is in yours, but as soon as I—a Player of Endgame—touched it, it sprang to life. Its message is simple, and presented me with two paths: play the game by chasing after the keys, or seek out Master Ea. After learning that the game was folly—that the Makers could affect the outcome of the Great Puzzle after they had promised since time immemorial that they would not—we decided that we needed help. Pure and simple. We know that

Ea hates his Maker brothers and sisters more than anything, so what better person to help than the most powerful living being on Earth? Who better to ally ourselves with than the enemy of our enemy? Understand, Ms. Subotic. The other Players are not my principal concern anymore, not even the ones who did this to me." He passes a hand over his face. "The *real* enemy is the Makers, and Endgame itself."

Subotic nods slowly. "It is a convincing argument, Aksumite. And one that I accept. Please, follow me."

Yes, she is very good at concealing her true allegiance, Hilal thinks. So good that it briefly occurs to him that perhaps Subotic is not a mole at all, and that he is walking headfirst into an elaborate trap.

He dashes these thoughts from his mind.

Trap or no, he is about to meet Ea face to face.

Subotic turns to the wall and walks forward. Even Hilal is somewhat surprised when she simply passes through it, as if she were a ghost. He hesitates, but one of the Nethinim prods him from behind. Hilal sets one foot after the other and, like Subotic, he walks through the wall as well.

It is nothing more than a holographic projection.

Hilal finds himself in the entryway of a grand room. The floor is solid marble; the ceiling soars 13 meters overhead. The walls to his left and right angle outward in a wide V, and are leafed with silver and adorned with all manner of exotic plants and flowers. A dark wooden cage on his left is filled with over a dozen parakeets, yellow and blue and orange and pink, all twittering happily. Opposite the birds is an ancient book of several hundred pages on a waist-high stand. It is bound in dark leather, and open to a section in the middle. Hilal can barely see its markings, and they are unfamiliar and foreign.

Several meters away is a tall tree made of multicolored glass, illuminated from within, glowing with every color of the rainbow. Arranged around the tree are plush chairs and couches and low tables. Past this sitting area, at the widest part of the V-shaped room, are the windows, floor-to-ceiling, looking over Las Vegas with its fantastical buildings devoted to the god called Money and a limitless sky and the jagged red mountains as a backdrop. And there, standing at the window, facing Hilal, is Wayland Vyctory.

He looks to be about 70. His eyes are bright, his smile plastered on. He appears to have had a lot of plastic surgery. He wears a hand-tailored suit and shirt and no tie. He has a gigantic gold-and-diamond ring on his left pinkie.

"Master Hilal ibn Isa al-Salt, welcome to my home." When he speaks, the skin on the left side of his face barely moves.

Subotic steps aside and lowers her head.

"My lord," Hilal says, moving toward his enemy. "Thank you for receiving me."

The Nethinim follow silently.

Hilal and Vyctory are 10.72 meters apart and closing. Hilal grips the canes. Gets ready to activate them. He just needs to be less than a meter away and the ancient snakes will do the rest.

Only 8.6 meters.

Vyctory stops by the colorful glass tree. "I can see your pulse, Player Aksumite. What troubles you?"

Hilal keeps walking. Pushes his diaphragm down, tries to feel the weight of his legs, his guts, his heart. "Nothing, lord. I am, well . . . excited. Strange things these days, amazing things. No amount of training is sufficient. I never thought Endgame would start. And I especially never thought I would find you!" Hilal stoops deferentially. While Hilal looks to the floor, he catches Vyctory making a small gesture to his Nethinim. Hilal looks up. Vyctory smiles. "I am excited too. I was wondering when—*if*—a Player would find me. I am glad that it is you."

Vyctory's voice is mellifluous and intoxicating. Hilal must resist it. All his training has been for this.

Only 7 meters.

"I am sorry that you have had to endure so much so soon, Master al-Salt," Vyctory sings, indicating Hilal's wounds. "If things go well today, know that I can fix your appearance."

"That would be wonderful, lord."

Six meters.

Five.

This is it.

Hilal moves his thumbs over the hoods of the snake-headed canes.

It will be quick. It will be very quick.

Vyctory smiles and smiles, his mouth growing grotesquely long, as if his face has the ability to stretch like a comic-strip superhero's. His fingers stretch too, and he nods, and he puffs his chest.

Come, his movements say. *Come to me and bask.*

They are three meters apart. Two.

But just as Hilal is about to bring the canes to life and let them attack, the Nethinim kick the canes out from the floor. He falls onto his knees. Each Nethinim claps a hand on one of Hilal's shoulders and forces him down, while, with their free hands, they bend forward and grab the canes and twist them out of Hilal's strong grip.

Hilal's fingers spread on the floor.

The canes remain wooden as they splay over the marble. The snakes will not appear or attack.

Subotic does nothing. She has betrayed him. Or perhaps, in order to maintain her cover indefinitely, she simply cannot help.

Vyctory grabs Hilal under the chin and squeezes so hard that Hilal can't talk. It is excruciating.

"Did you really think that you could fool me? I *taught* men how to lie in the dark days of antiquity!"

"Uhr," Hilal manages through clenched teeth.

"Quiet, Aksumite. I heard everything you said to Rima. I only allowed you in here so I could witness your patheticness firsthand, and so I could see this 'prize' you've brought to me."

Hilal says nothing.

"I don't know why, but I pity you." Vyctory spits the words. "I will make your end quick, when the time comes. And it will come shortly."

Vyctory releases Hilal's chin, and the Nethinim grasp his wrists and pull them up and back, torquing his arms unnaturally in their sockets. His torso pitches forward, and the side of his face slams into the floor so that in order to see any part of Vyctory besides his feet Hilal has to strain his neck and roll up his eyes.

Vyctory: "Show me this prize of his, Rima."

Subotic tosses the ancient device through the air. It claps into Vyctory's hand. He gives an impressed-sounding whistle. "My, my. This is an old piece of tech. I have one just like it somewhere. Do you know what this is, al-Salt? What its intended use was?"

"Stuffing up your backsides?"

"Hmph. I don't appreciate the human inclination to vulgarity in times of duress, al-Salt."

"In truth, neither do I."

"Then shut up and tell me what you think it was for."

"It was for this, for finding you. Like an alarm housed in a glass box: break in case of emergency."

Vyctory shuffles his feet. "No. This is what Moses used to converse with my cousins on their ships before they all—or mostly all—abandoned this sorry corner of the galaxy. As you know, the ark was thought to be a kind of transmitter—the mercy seat, the cherubim, the gold-leafed box of shittah wood—but it was just for show. This was the real transmitter. It's what they gave Moses, and it's what he used during his forty days on top of Sinai to talk to his god."

Hilal would scoff at this blasphemy if he didn't know the truth of the world.

And this *is* the truth.

"Were you able to converse with the one up there now?" Vyctory asks.

Hilal's shoulders burn; his knees are like pins pushing into the marble. He tries to reposition himself to get just a little more comfortable. The Nethinim tighten their grip and punish him for it.

"No," Hilal manages.

"Do you know why you were not able to do this?"

"No."

"Because you are not Moses, Aksumite. You are nothing but a Player."

"Perhaps. But I'm a Player who nearly got close enough to kill you, Master Ea."

"Kill me? What ancient books have you been diddling? The only one that tells the real truth is right over there, on that stand. It has all the knowledge of antiquity in it. *All* of it—plus your Makers' rules for Endgame. The rules you'll never see or know."

"Thank you for letting my eyes rest on it, then, master. If even for a moment."

"Bah, I am tired of you, but I am glad you brought me this. I will use it to talk to my cousins when their ships next visit this corner of the cosmos, which should be soon." He looks at the Nethinim. "Kill him."

Vyctory spins on his heel. One of the Nethinim moves his hand from Hilal's shoulder to his nape.

An unexpected calmness washes over Hilal. One way or another, it is all about to end. This is his last chance. "Don't you want to know *how* I was going to kill you?" he asks.

Vyctory stops. The Nethinim pause.

"I was going to get close enough to drive one of my ancient canes— handed down from before the days of D'mt and Ezana and Na'od and even Menelik, held by each Aksumite Player's hands—I was going to drive one through your mouth and throat and gut. And with the other I was going to impale you through your chest. I was going to make the sign of the cross inside you, and burn your Maker essence out, and cast it away forever and ever. That was how I was going to kill you, Ea. That was how."

Lies. But with the threat of imminent death giving him strength, Hilal makes them sound completely truthful.

Vyctory laughs through his nose. He spins back to Hilal. "The *sign of the cross*? Has your line learned nothing over the millennia? Signs only have meaning because meaning is ascribed to them. It is all falsehood, Aksumite!" Hilal can practically hear Vyctory shaking his head. "I am glad Endgame is finally here and all of these lines will be wiped out. Yours especially. There is nothing worse than someone who is initiated but who still clings to some shred of belief."

"Perhaps. But I was at least going to *try* to kill you. That is more than any others of my line have done since the year 1200."

"And the same thing will happen to you that happened to her. You will try and you will fail. Canes, Rima! Can you understand it?"

"No, master. I cannot," Subotic says hollowly.

"Nor I. Show them to me, Jael," Vyctory says, finally naming the other Nethinim.

Yes, Hilal thinks.

He closes his eyes and says a silent prayer.

Yes.

His heart slows. His breath evens out.

Jael lets go of Hilal and picks up the canes, and Hilal is able to relax a little. He sees Ea reach out for the rods of Aaron and Moses, a scowl on his face.

Yes.

As soon as Ea graces them, they change and the snakes surge forward. The device drops to the floor and slides away. Jael reaches after the serpents, but the snake that was the Rod of Moses is too fast. It dives straight into Vyctory's gaping mouth and disappears in a fraction of a second, going down and in. The other, the one that was the Rod of Aaron, wraps three times around Vyctory's neck and squeezes, its hood flared, its fangs dripping and stabbing in lightning strikes at Vyctory's face. Vyctory raises his hands to his neck, trying to work his fingers into the snake's coil. Jael tries to do this too, but it is simply too strong.

Kaneem, equally shocked, loosens his grip just enough for Hilal to shift his weight under his body, flop onto his back, and sweep the guard's feet from under him. He drops to the floor, right next to Hilal, who raises his elbow and strikes at Kaneem's Adam's apple.

But he is fast, and he catches Hilal's arm before his throat is crushed.

Hilal jabs Kaneem with his other hand and breaks three ribs. Hilal can hear Vyctory gasp and squeal as the Moses snake wends its way through his innards.

Hilal jabs Kaneem again and again and again, breaking more ribs, and Kaneem lets go of Hilal's elbow and Hilal raises it and brings it down into the Nethinim's throat and everything inside his neck breaks and Kaneem is dead.

Hilal hears the pad of Subotic's shoes rushing toward the fray. He hears the slide of a pistol charging a round. He rolls. A shot rings out and glances off the marble and into one of the windows, causing it to spiderweb, but not break.

She is shooting at Jael and at Vyctory.

She did not betray him.

Hilal vaults toward Jael and Vyctory as Subotic fires three quick shots, one striking Jael in the thigh. Hilal wishes she would stop and let the snakes do their job. He slides past Jael, snagging the machete marked *LOVE*, but he is not fast enough to corral the other one as well.

Hilal comes to a stop and scurries around the back of a couch. He will let the snakes finish before confronting Jael.

But as he listens to the struggle and to Vyctory gurgling and choking, he hears the words "Kill them both!"

Hilal peeks over the top of the couch as Jael releases Vyctory and twirls around the glass tree. Subotic shoots again, and it breaks into a million shards of rainbowed colors.

Jael hurls the other machete in that instant, the air full of glass, and Subotic barely reacts before the blade slices violently across her hip and stomach. The gun falls free, and both she and the blade crash to the floor. Her face drains of what little color it had.

Hilal looks to Vyctory. Jael should confront Hilal now, but instead he turns his back and returns to Vyctory, his beloved master, who is in the final throes. Hilal sees the desperation in Jael's actions as he fruitlessly tries to yank the snake free of Vyctory, but it is too strong. Hilal stands and stalks toward the pair. Vyctory sees Hilal approaching, and fire lights in his eyes, but Jael doesn't catch it. When Hilal is less than a meter from Jael's back, he raises his machete and makes two quick strikes across Jael's shoulders, severing both arms. The blood flows, and Jael falls, and Hilal kicks him to the side with his feet.

Hilal stands over Vyctory for several seconds. He is on his knees, his eyes full of fear. Hilal doesn't smile, he doesn't gloat, he doesn't lick his lips in triumph.

He just watches.

Hilal places his machete's curved end on Wayland Vyctory's chest. The man grabs it with both hands, his face swollen with venom and purple with asphyxiation, little dots from the fangs on his face like bleeding freckles. He grips the blade tightly. Dark blood wells between his fingers. Hilal snaps his wrist 90 degrees, and Vyctory's grip is loosened, the insides of his fingers skinned.

Hilal pushes the man with his blade's tip, and he falls back against the couch.

Hilal lets the machete fall to his side. He feels suddenly exhausted. After five seconds the victim seizes and shudders and the legs go straight and Wayland Vyctory dies.

His head falls back on the couch, the mouth open and motionless. The snake of Aaron comes free of the neck and sits on Vyctory's chest. His Adam's apple moves up and down and the mouth opens and the blue tongue spits out and the dark snake emerges. It rises four inches out of Vyctory's mouth and looks around. When it sees the other snake's tail, it takes it in its jaws and swallows it and then slithers all the way out of the dead man's lips, sheened with blood and bile and mucus.

"You have it?" Hilal asks eagerly.

But for all its power, this ancient creature can't answer. It is only a snake.

Still, Hilal knows that it does have it. It has swallowed the alien seed that is Ea.

As the snake of Moses gobbles up the other's tail, the snake of Aaron looks around for the tail of its counterpart. When it finds it, it takes it in its mouth and swallows as well, forming a living, writhing, flopping, serpentine circuit that falls across Vyctory's motionless chest.

The pair works in unison to each consume the other, and to keep their prey contained.

"The living ouroboros," Hilal says quietly.

When each snake reaches the midpoint of the other, they stop and become utterly still and rigid and slide down Vyctory's chest and stomach and across his silk-covered thigh and to the floor with a clatter.

They are wood again. They form a ring. The line on their inside a perfect circle, 20.955 centimeters in diameter.

A circle.

Like the clue that kepler 22b gave him.

An end.

A beginning.

An orbit.

A planet.

A sun.

A circle.

A beginning.

An end.

The death prison of the thing called Ea.

Never to be opened.

Hilal slides the machete into the belt under his loose pants. Picks up the ring of snakes.

It vibrates in his grip. Gently, pleasingly.

He has done it.

He has done it and he has lived.

He inspects the object. It is simple, beautiful. The scales are perfectly rendered, the black eyes flecked with gold, the weight ideal. He slips it over his hand, and as soon as he does, the ring shrinks. He moves it to the center of his forearm, and the thing gets smaller and smaller until it presses comfortably into his skin.

He will wear it. Guard it. Keep it.

He slides it up his arm; it adjusts its girth. Over his elbow, his bicep, and to the muscular depression between his upper arm and his shoulder. The whole time it changes so that it fits exactly.

He will wear it.

Guard it.

Keep it.

Hilal turns from Vyctory's vanquished body. Takes the device from the ark. Takes the brass elevator key from Kaneem. Walks toward the exit and stops by Rima Subotic. He assumed she was dead, but now he sees that she still breathes ever so slightly. Her eyes are vacant, and her arm is extended. Her lips quaver and move. Hilal kneels next to her. Takes her hand. Pushes sweaty hair out of her face. "Thank you, sister."

Her lips move. No sound.

"I am sorry I could not save you."

Her lips move. No sound.

"What is it?"

"B . . . buh . . . buh . . ."

Her eyes widen and Hilal spins and he sees it.

The book.

Hilal understands. "I will take it, sister. I will take it to Stella. Ea is dead. The Ancient Truth lives. Your death is noble, sister. So noble. Thanks be unto you."

A smile creases her lips. Her eyes close. Hilal bends and kisses her forehead. She dies. He picks up the other machete from the floor, the one marked *HATE*. He rises and takes the book from the stand. Pauses one last time by the body of Rima Subotic. Shakes his head.

Rest, sister.

He walks out of the room. Down the hall. Into the elevator. Turns the key. Goes down. Into the lobby. Nods at the clerk, Cindy. Out of the lobby. Walks north and east. A young injured man with a book and a million untold secrets.

A proud, young, injured man.

Who, in his way, is still Playing.

He walks north and east.

To Stella.

MACCABEE ADLAI, BAITSAKHAN

Calle Ucayali, Juliaca, Peru

Maccabee and Baitsakhan sit in a Ford Escort taxi they bought right at the Juliaca airport with a single one-ounce piece of gold. Since the announcement of Abaddon, the price of precious metals has soared.

Last they checked, gold was selling for $4,843.83 an ounce.

Maybe a bit much for a beat-up Escort, but since it's a local cab, and therefore completely inconspicuous, worth every single gram of the soft yellow metal.

Maccabee is behind the wheel, Baitsakhan in the passenger seat. The sun has just dipped below the horizon, but both wear sunglasses: Maccabee a fine pair by Dolce & Gabbana, Baitsakhan a cheap pair of light-blue Wayfarer knockoffs that were in the Escort's glove box.

Maccabee looks like his face was run over by a motorcycle. It's been several days since his thrashing by the Koori, and he's definitely on the other side of the healing process, the side that is less about pain and more about trying to feel normal again, but she really messed him up. If anyone ever thinks he's handsome again, it will be because they like tough-looking dudes who've clearly been through a wringer.

Which is just fine by Maccabee.

Wedged between the dashboard and the top of the steering wheel is the orb, their Maker-tech tracker. Glowing faintly on its surface is the sign for the Olmec, the sign for the Cahokian.

Maccabee and Baitsakhan are close.

But they cannot go to their adversaries.

Because it would be too dangerous.

Both Players stare down a long road, brick buildings lining the street. Several blocks away is a cordon of black military vehicles, red talons painted on their hoods. The men are in black uniforms, some of them with their faces covered by balaclavas. All are heavily armed. They check everyone who tries to pass.

They don't let many pass.

Both Players know what's up that road.

Jago Tlaloc.

Sarah Alopay.

Earth Key.

Baitsakhan shakes a pill from a small plastic bottle and pops it in his mouth. Crunches it into a bitter powder, swallows it. Holds the bottle out to Maccabee.

"Want one?"

Maccabee takes a pill and swallows without chewing.

They've been pounding antibiotics since leaving the flat in East Berlin. With Baitsakhan's surgery and Maccabee's wounds they can't risk infection. Baitsakhan rests his feet on the dashboard. Taps his toes. Holds his bionic hand in front of his face, fans his fingers, closes them into a fist. He smiles. He thinks of the Koori, of how her muscle and bone gave way so effortlessly. Thinks of how her blood flowed over his digits. He loves his new, death-blessed hand.

"How much longer?" Baitsakhan asks.

"Don't know."

"They can't stay up there forever."

"We haven't even been staking them out for two days, Baits." On account of his wounds, Maccabee has to speak out of the right side of his mouth. His nasal passages are still inflamed. His voice is garbled and twangy.

Baitsakhan punches an imaginary adversary in the air. "So?"

Maccabee shakes his head. "They'll come down. They have to. Even if they bring a small army with them, they'll move. They're going for the keys. They're Playing." Maccabee coughs. Winces. It hurts. "They'll move," he repeats.

"And when they do, we'll follow them."

"Right. Just like we said. Going up there would be suicide. Plus, you and me aren't exactly fit for battle right now."

Baitsakhan bristles. He is always ready.

Maccabee continues. "We'll follow them, bide our time, and kill them." Pause.

"A small army . . ." Baitsakhan says slowly.

Maccabee turns to the boy. "What're you thinking?"

"You speak Spanish?"

"Of course."

"Then I'm thinking you and me would look good in those eagle-claw uniforms."

Maccabee smiles. A local disguise. It's a good idea. A great idea. "If you can't beat 'em, join 'em, eh?"

Baitsakhan frowns. "What?"

"If you can't beat 'em, join 'em."

"What kind of stupid talk is that?"

"It's an expression," Maccabee says flatly. "What I mean is that we'll jump a pair of those guys, take their clothes and their truck, and blend seamlessly into the environment. Then, when the time is right . . ."

Maccabee draws a finger over his throat.

"That's what I'm trying to say," Baitsakhan explains.

"Christ. Never mind."

"Fine. But we *will* ambush them and take the key, right?"

Maccabee fights the urge to roll his eyes. "Yes, Baitsakhan. That's the plan."

The Donghu smiles. He likes it. "And then, my Nabataean brother, we will go and kill the Harappan and the Aksumite."

Maccabee doesn't say anything. He understands Baitsakhan a little better than before, how revenge for the deaths of Bat and Bold and

Jalair clouds his judgment—the same happened to Maccabee when he saw Ekaterina slaughtered by the Koori—but all the same he's growing tired of the Donghu.

Yet Maccabee still sees some wisdom in their alliance.

"Take kill win, Baits," Maccabee says, echoing Baitsakhan's clue from the Calling. "Take kill win."

FOR IMMEDIATE DSTRIBUTION

AUM.

THE CLUB OF GODS AND HERMITS, seeing in the lightness of the darkness, and that which has been prophesied by our leader for forty years and counting, it is time. Our hand on this morning to act. We cannot be outdone by charlatans and posers, these unnamed fighters for freedom and desolation who like cowards take no responsibility for the explosion and radioactive poisoning at Tokyo Port early this morning.

We cannot be outdone.

AUM.

This arrival that the Beast calls Abaddon will be loud.

The death that precedes it, today, my people, in this frail nation's most traveled port. The death that precedes it will be quiet.

Look east, sinners of Tokyo, to where the sun rises over the faded false empire.

Look to Narita.

AUM.

KYODO NEWS—BREAKING

At 8:37 a.m. local time, five compact hydrogen cyanide devices were detonated in the HVAC systems of Terminal 1 at Narita airport. Three minutes prior, a press release was issued by the terrorist organization Aleph, also known as Aum Shinrikyo. In the interval, evacuation was begun at both terminals. This procedure proved inadequate. Hundreds are confirmed dead, hundreds more suspected dead. Gunfire, presumably from security forces, has been reported as well. It is advised that all people, foreign and domestic, remain free of Narita and environs for the time being.

It is not known if this event has anything to do with the explosion and release of radioactive material at Tokyo Port earlier this morning.

Effective immediately, all mass transit in Tokyo is suspended. Officials are declaring martial law for central Tokyo, Chiba, and Narita.

This is a developing story.

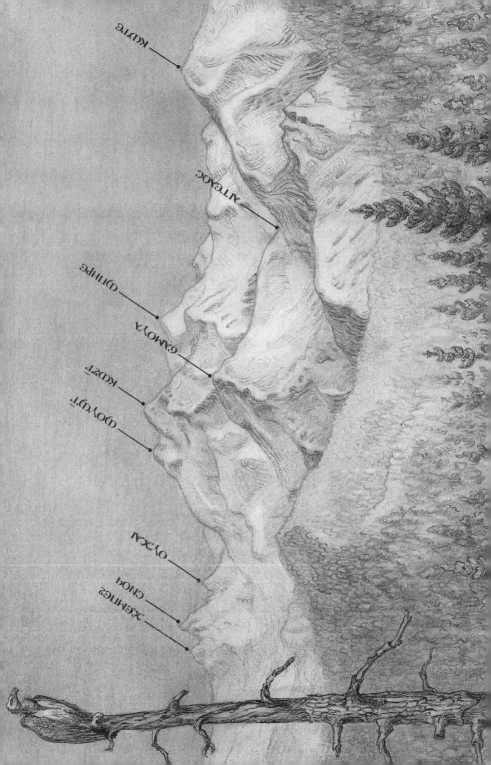

AISLING KOPP, POP KOPP, GREG JORDAN, BRIDGET McCLOSKEY, GRIFFIN MARRS

県道55号線, *Headed West-Southwest*

After An's explosion, Aisling did indeed need every second of her breath and then some.

She held it hot and hollow in her chest under the water for four minutes and fifteen seconds, a personal record, one created by fear and desire and determination but mostly fear. When her lungs lit with fire and her stomach clenched for life and her heart beat so loudly that she could hear nothing else, she surged upward and surfaced, screaming for air.

Air that was black and poisoned and thick.

But it was the only air available, and there was oxygen in it, along with pulverized concrete and plastic and glass and metal and god-knows-what isotope of what element—probably cesium 137—and so she breathed.

And breathed.

And breathed.

She pulled herself from the water and breathed.

The bomb An Liu detonated was massive. It destroyed every building for three blocks, and damaged many more past that. It left a crater at ground zero 104 feet across and 37 feet deep and smoldering and black as pitch.

Aisling didn't dare go to look. Nothing could survive that blast. She needed to find her grandfather and Jordan and his team—or what was left of them.

She wandered south along the shoreline into the wind blowing off the water, trying to get a signal out of her waterlogged radio. She got nothing. She abandoned the radio.

She avoided the smoky plume that flowed over Tokyo Port. She rounded a corner and found Pop and McCloskey sitting on the edge of a curb, their arms draped over their knees, McCloskey talking to Jordan and Marrs on her comm link. They were behind Aisling, only a few minutes away.

All four had been just outside the blast radius and they'd survived. Aisling hugged Pop. And hugged him and hugged him. When they were done they sat on the curb, utterly exhausted.

"You're soaked," he said.

"Took a morning swim."

"Was it nice?" McCloskey asked.

"Wonderful."

Silence.

Aisling broke it. "That was . . . not good."

"No. It wasn't." McCloskey continued to fiddle with her radio, trying to establish some contact with the KFE team. Aisling and Pop just sat. Still. Quiet. Sirens in the far but audible distance.

"We need to leave," Aisling said.

McCloskey pointed. "Here they come."

Jordan and Marrs rounded the corner, clambered over a capsized car. They were covered in soot. Aisling and her group rose to meet them. Jordan and McCloskey hugged. Marrs lit a cigarette and let it dangle from his lower lip. Pop and Aisling leaned on each other.

The group turned from the destruction and walked over a causeway, still toward the open bay, looking for transportation.

"Kilo Foxtrot Echo?" Aisling eventually asked.

But she knew the answer.

They all did.

Jordan said, "Dead. Every one."

"Least An Liu is dead too," Aisling said.

"True. I saw the blast site, and it's textbook. No one's walking out of it," Jordan says, confirming what Aisling already knew.

They continued south. In the parking lot of an out-of-place golf course they stole two compact cars and left. No one had seen them. They took a circuitous route back to the hotel, avoiding police and any official entanglements.

When they got to the suite, Jordan passed out potassium iodide pills and everyone stripped and they threw out their clothes and they showered and they got rid of the few weapons they had, since they could have been contaminated. Aisling was glad that she hadn't brought her ancient Celtic sword with her to the op. It wouldn't have been very auspicious to have to discard such a priceless and dear artifact.

After they were clean, the news wires lit up and the television blared with horror, not only for what had happened in the shipping port, but of what was happening at Japan's largest and most important airport. Run-of-the-mill terrorists were getting in on the action.

This is one way the world ends, Aisling thought.

Aisling declared that they had to leave Japan, and no one argued with her. They talked about where to go. McCloskey said South America, to chase the three or maybe four Players they could still track. Aisling overruled her. "No. It's true that one of them has Earth Key, but we might as well let them fight over it and kill each other in the process. They clearly don't know they're being tracked, so we can go to them when the time is right. I say we look for Sky Key, and also for a way to stop this madness."

Pop asked where they might do that.

"Stonehenge," Aisling answered. "I'm guessing you can access the site, right, Jordan?"

"Of course I can. I even know the NATO CO personally. He's kind of a bastard."

"Great. Stonehenge it is."

"You sure about that, Jordan?" McCloskey asked, and Aisling wondered if she was slowly getting closer to whatever it is they're not telling her.

"Sure I'm sure, McCloskey. You know we'll get the grand tour. We'll just tell them you're a new case officer, Aisling. Langley's latest virtuoso, don't let her young looks fool you. How's that strike you?"

"Fine. Now let's go. I don't want to stay in Tokyo one second longer."

They agreed and gathered their things and moved out that afternoon, before martial law could be fully implemented.

And now they drive north in another van, looping around the vast metropolis. Their next destination is Yokota Air Base, only 19 miles from the center of Tokyo. Jordan's Gulfstream waits, fully gassed and loaded with weaponry and some new equipment and armor and food. With uncertainty high and the trains shut down and martial law looming, Tokyo's citizens pour into the countryside. Traffic crawls. They sit in the van for over two hours, and by Marrs's estimation have another hour to go. Aisling is in the back on her laptop. Pop is next to her, running a sharpening stone over the Celtic sword. The others are in the front.

Aisling scours a folder of An's files, the files they stole before the op went to shit. She looks for anything regarding Stonehenge or other ancient sacred sites like Carahunge or Carnac or the Egyptian pyramids—anything that might help her locate Sky Key. *Anything.* But she finds nothing. Apparently, An Liu didn't give a shit about Endgame—at least not about its heritage, or about the Makers, or about humanity's strange history. All he cared about were the Players—especially Chiyoko Takeda—and about bombs, destruction, and death.

He Played for death, Aisling thinks. *And that's what he got.*

The van inches along the smooth Japanese highway. Jordan and Marrs and McCloskey have been quiet for most of the ride, and have reverted to their gallows humor only sparingly. Losing Kilo Foxtrot Echo has knocked their confidence down a peg or two.

They pass a tall Shinto temple on the side to the road, its stacked stories and curved roofs a remnant of another age, a golden age.

Pop drags the stone over the blade. He nudges Aisling's shoulder. He doesn't break from sharpening the sword. A sword that's already one of the world's keenest, a sword that doesn't need the attention.

"You're wondering again if you should have teamed up with them?" he asks very quietly.

Aisling frowns at the front of the van. She doesn't want to them to hear. She opens a new Gmail window and types her answer there.

A little. Just before everything went bad, I asked myself that. Sure, it has its advantages, and with the world already getting unpredictable, those advantages can't be ignored, but . . . I don't know . . .

Pop puts down the sword and stone. Moves his hands to the keyboard.

Types: *I agree about the advantages. But that mission did not go well.*

They take turns.

No. It didn't. Still, Liu is dead.

Pop pauses. *I'm not convinced he is.*

Aisling shoots Pop a look. *Why? You saw what happened back there. Besides, Marrs says his tracker is kaput.*

So? An's a Player. The most dangerous of all, perhaps. Until you know, I would assume he's alive.

Pause.

Shit. If he IS alive, if he meant to do that in order to escape, then I think we SHOULD stay with them.

They do have access to transportation, and weapons.

Pause.

Aisling writes, *Yes. But if we stay, I have to take charge. These calls, they have to be mine. I don't care how much experience they have.*

Agreed.

Aisling highlights everything and deletes it.

McCloskey looks to the back of the van. "You guys all right back there? Awfully quiet."

"Yeah, we're fine. Just tired."

"Tell me about it."

McCloskey turns back to the road. The van stops and starts as Marrs works it along. Pop goes back to sharpening. Aisling goes back to the

Shang's files. She checks An's tracking programs. Both blips are in Juliaca, Peru, about three miles from each other, and both are virtually motionless.

One is watching the other.

One is going to surprise the other.

Soon, most likely.

Just as she's about to close her laptop, a Google Alert pops up in a window. Her breath is dashed and her heart races and she clicks the link hastily. Either from beyond the grave or by his own living hand, An Liu has posted a video on YouTube.

The title is simple and direct:

ENDGAME IS HERE. KILL THE PLAYERS. SAVE THE WORLD.

AN LIU

Fishing Boat 冷たい風, *Sagami Bay, Heading 204° 45′ 24″*

It *is* by his own living hand.

His bomb-proof capsule was thrown clear of the blast, sailed 100 meters in the air, traveled 1.2 kilometers south, and landed on the fringe of the green of the 10th hole of Wakasu Golf Links, where it rolled and rolled until it tilted into a sand trap. It was a jarring trip that knocked An unconscious for 12 minutes and 15 seconds. After he woke, he blew the explosive bolts, the door blasted off, and he emerged from the pill-shaped vessel. He walked south along the fairway in his hazmat suit. He reached the marina, removed the suit, and climbed into his dinghy and slipped along the water to his escape boat.

Now, An Liu is on the bridge of his 35-foot Yamaha pleasure cruiser, the 冷たい風, the morning sun pouring through the windows. Oshima Island is in the distance, a wispy plume rising from the island's volcanic crater. The heading is locked into the boat's computer, the speed a steady 10 knots on glassy seas. No wind, no clouds. The conditions are ideal.

He needs to get rid of the tracker the Brits put in him.

He uses a specially rigged voltmeter to get the weak reading from the transmitting chip inside his thigh. He washes his hands and puts on surgical gloves and takes a scalpel and digs at his skin and hair and veins, parting muscle and pulling up red and pink chunks and placing them on a white sheet of plastic next to the computer keyboard. Digging and digging until he finds it and pulls it out with a pair of sterilized needle-nose pliers. It is a long slender thing, like a hair with a black teardrop of metal and plastic on one end. He wads it up in a ball of gauze and slides open the window and slings it into the water.

He is not being tracked anymore.

Whoever was hunting him will not be able to chase him so easily.

He pours iodine over the wound and cleans it up and sews it shut.

As soon as this impromptu procedure is finished he turns his attention to the video. He runs the script that will post it, along with all its built-in fake views and all its pings and all the links to other sites and all the emails to journalists and news outlets. He hits send and he watches it move and build and seep into the still-connected world—

"Because it won't be connected for long, Chiyoko. No, it won't."

He knows that people will devour it, and that it will go viral.

He knows that he is not being tracked.

He knows that he is free.

Safe.

And he knows that the other Players *SHIVERblinkSHIVER* the other Players are not.

"With the world shifting so fast since the announcement of Abaddon, our attentions here at Fox News have shifted as well. With all that is going wrong in the world—with the terrorist attacks in Japan; with Pakistan and India falling headlong into a full-scale war overflowing with nationalistic and religious fervor; with Russia invading Georgia and Kazakhstan; with Iranian fighter jets flying over Riyadh last week in a show of Shia force; with a low-scale "preppers' war" erupting on the Montana-Saskatchewan border between armed militias; with the deadly race riots in Los Angeles and Saint Louis and Jackson, Mississippi—we at Fox News have been going out of our way to report on many of the good things that have developed in the shadow of the asteroid that will impact our planet.

"We've brought you news from Washington, which has not ceased to surprise us. It seems that Abaddon's first American victim has been partisanship of all kinds. The men and women of the US capital have been very busy doing something that we have not seen in recent memory—cooperating on nearly everything. They have—literally at times, as we saw during last Friday's vigil at the Lincoln Memorial—come together and held hands, praying for the graces of god and man, proclaiming America's importance as a positive force for good in the harsh world that we will inhabit. There simply does not seem to be a Democrat or a Republican left—only Americans, only leaders. It has been remarkable.

"We have brought you the story of the veteran Kansas City police officer who has tirelessly gone door-to-door in the rough neighborhoods he's patrolled for the last twenty years, checking on every single family and elderly woman and man and every kid who's home alone, making sure they're okay, giving them anything he can—money, food, time, a ride to the clinic or a relative's house—and how he has already saved three lives in the past week. How he told us that this was how he should have been policing for years.

"We've told you the story of the social-media billionaire who's paid the cost of reuniting any family for any reason and without asking them to prove that they can't afford it.

"We've shown you the strange story of the commune in northern Wisconsin that's offered what they are calling, quote, 'free love to anyone who needs it.' At first derided as not much more than a sex scheme, what's developed is a place teeming with people who want nothing more than hugs and good food and personal contact before the end.

"But our next story is not one of these feel-good stories. Without further comment, here is Mills Power."

"Thank you, Stephanie. We live in a mind-boggling moment of history. Maybe even the end of history. As a reporter, I have to say that it sometimes feels like a blessing, but mostly, and quite frankly, I'm terrified—"

"Me too, Mills."

"Yes, well . . . I'm here to talk about a video that appeared only yesterday on YouTube. It already has over eleven million views. In the last hour alone, eight hundred and ninety nine thousand and thirty-four people have watched it."

"I've seen it. The young man in it is very . . . disturbing."

"Yes. But my sources at the CIA and the FBI told me that An Liu is legitimate. He was at Stonehenge when it . . . changed. According to my most trusted source, he was drugged and strapped to a gurney but still managed to escape from a British destroyer all by himself, killing dozens of sailors, stealing a stealth-equipped helicopter, and nearly sinking the ship."

"My God."

"So what I'm saying is this: Believe this Shang 'Player' called An Liu. Believe this crazy thing he's calling Endgame. Believe that there are eight teenagers, including him, who need to be killed to stop Abaddon. Believe him. Scream his message from the rooftops. Translate what he said and what I'm saying now into every language and tell everyone. Use his information. If you are military, law enforcement, or even a criminal organization, please help to hunt these people down, and help to kill them all. Maybe what he's saying is not true, but even if it has a one-hundredth-of-one-percent chance of being true, shouldn't we try? Shouldn't we sacrifice these eight souls and pray that it will save billions? . . . Shouldn't we try, Stephanie?"

"Yes. Yes, Mills! We should! We should try to kill these people! Kill them! Please, people of Earth! Kill them all!"

Visita Rectificando Interiora Lapidem

HILAL IBN ISA AL-SALT

Converted Warehouse off Bledsoe, Sunrise Manor, Nevada, United States

When Hilal arrives at Stella Vyctory's headquarters, he finds her door open. He goes inside. Calls for Stella but gets no reply. On the table is a laptop, its screen frozen on a login page, a pink Post-it on its metal edge. Written in Amharic, the note reads, *The weight of the ark.* Hilal knows this figure—358.13 pounds—by rote. He enters it into the computer's login page but it rejects him. He tries again, spelling the number out, and this time the screen glows to life. On it is a PDF document also written in Amharic. He settles into a chair and reads:

> *Hilal—I am sorry, but I had to leave at the last minute. My army is embarking on an operation that requires my attention, and I had to travel from Las Vegas immediately.*
>
> *But Hilal—I know that you were successful and . . . There are not words. I cannot begin to tell you the feelings that I'm having, all of them good and full and spilling over with joy. You are an honor to the Ancient Truth. If it lives through the dark days to come, it will be because of you, the Aksumite, Hilal ibn Isa al-Salt.*
>
> *You have killed Ea, and I am overcome with happiness.*
>
> *Thank you. A thousand thank-yous, ten thousand, a million, an infinite cosmos of thank-yous.*
>
> *There are not words.*
>
> *Please, treat my home as your own. Rest for a while, if you can. Use anything, take anything, eat anything. Arm yourself for the next round.*

I will reach out to you in the days that come, but for now I will be incommunicado. My current mission is essential. I will tell you more about it when we speak.

I hope Rima told you to take the book, which I forgot to mention earlier. Study it before you move. I wish I could tell you more about it, but the truth is I don't know much. All I know is that it is important—to you, to Endgame, to stopping the Makers.

Eternally and unconditionally yours,
Stella

Hilal is saddened that Stella is not there, but he does as she suggests. He draws a bath in her large, modern tub and takes off his clothing and his bandages and stands at the sink and stares at his reflection in the mirror. The steam swirls around the room and fogs his reflection. His skin grafts are stretched and scarred and curdled, his entire head is hairless, and his right ear burned completely off leaving only a hole, like a lizard's. This is to say nothing of the eyes, still mismatched, and the perfect teeth accenting all of it, still straight and glaringly white. He is monstrous.

But he is still here. And he is the Aksumite champion. The hero of Endgame that no one will know or appreciate. The young man who has given humanity back their innocence.

He hopes that humanity will find it.

He turns off the water. Slides into the tub. Stifles a scream by biting his forearm as his burned shoulders submerge. Takes a breath and submerges his head. He screams there, bubbles blowing, at the top of his lungs. Screams for pain and for victory.

For Vyctory.

He comes out of the water. He positions a washcloth behind his head and lies back and closes his eyes. "There is no healing without pain. No cleanliness without filth. No forgiveness without death."

He sits there for 28 minutes and 42 seconds and, except for the rise and fall of his chest, he doesn't move.

He gets out and puts on a robe and takes Ea's old book and sits on the edge of Stella's king-sized bed. He uses the remote to turn on the television. He looks for a news channel—finds Fox News—and mutes it. He watches the images there—ones of death and destruction and fear, and ones of hope and beauty and love—for a few minutes, all in silence, the book heavy on his thighs.

He thinks of Eben, of home, of his line. He needs to call his master, but first he needs to figure out what Vyctory has given him.

Hilal turns his attention to the book.

He leafs through the pages. They're made of a kind of plastic or vellum that feels indestructible, immune to time or the elements. He tries a corner and finds it impossible to tear or crease. Yet they are indisputably ancient. None of the strange writing inside makes any sense to Hilal, and even though Ea said that the volume contains all the wisdom of the ancient world, Hilal can't find any languages he recognizes.

And there are the pictures. All exact and perfect, as if drawn by a robot. There are diagrams and plans for all kinds of ancient structures and city layouts and stone monuments and spaceship tethers and strange portals and landing strips and gold mines and refueling depots. He recognizes many structures from his studies of antiquity, and fails to recognize many, many more, all swallowed by time or water or war or the plants and vines of jungles or the shifting sands of deserts or the rippled ground of earthquakes. And there are pictures of machines that he doesn't understand, of schemes that look mechanical or genetic in nature, of constellations and spirals and three-dimensional webs depicting mysterious connections of unidentifiable things—perhaps earthbound energy grids, or the interrelationships of species, or dark-matter pathways linking the stars, or the messy bush of evolution that belongs to the genus *Homo*. The book is unquestionably a treasure, but to Hilal it is completely impenetrable.

Opaque.

His skin shivers: *I should show it to the device from the ark!*

He retrieves this and it glows to life and he puts the book back on his lap and he holds the device over the writing.

And the device does something unexpected. Whenever it is pointed at the book its screen is black, as if the book interferes with it somehow. Hilal swings the device through the room, sees the familiar throbbing ball that marks Sky Key in the Himalayas, sees the list of coordinates, including those of the remaining Players, sees only one caduceus, which he now knows is Stella, wherever she might be.

Hilal slides the book to the floor and, still holding the device over it, starts at the beginning and flips through page by page. One by one. Every now and then the blackness flickers with light, yet it gives him nothing. But after he's flipped for nearly 20 minutes, something happens.

Over one page and one page only, a language appears on the device's screen. It is ancient Egyptian, which Hilal knows fluently. As he moves the device across the lettering, the hieroglyphs change as well.

It is translating.

He reads:

And we will talk of the Great Puzzle, the Endgame, and it will be originated when we so decry, for reasons unknown and unknowable to the humans of Earth, but it will be just and right and final. And the Endgame will have three stages. And at each stage it will be told that the game can continue or be stopped.

Hilal's heart skips several beats when he reads this.

Is there still some hope?

He reads on.

The Beginning Stage will be marked by the Calling, when the twelve will come and meet. The Beginning Stage will end when the first Player finds Earth Key and triggers the onset of the second stage. If during this first stage all the Players decide not to Play, then the game will not continue.

Hilal pauses. He wonders: If the others had listened to him on that fateful night in the Qin Lin Mountains and sat in peace and talked to one another about their histories and shared their knowledge, then would they have decided to take this course of action? Not to Play? Could they have come together then, really come together, in mind as well as body, when Earth needed them most? Could they have chosen wisdom over history, over violence, over training?

But he remembers the Shang, and the Donghu, and the Sumerian with her velvet tongue, and the brash Minoan, and Hilal knows: *No. We had to Play.*

There was too much pent-up violence there. Too much hubris. Too much eagerness to kill. He keeps reading.

The Middle Stage will begin with the announcement of the uncovering of Earth Key and will continue until the living Sky Key is united with Earth Key.

The living Sky Key?

This will initiate the End Stage, which will rain destruction on the race of humans for many, many Earth years. But if a Player can destroy the living Sky Key before it is united with Earth Key, then the game will be ended. This is not expected to pass, for the living Sky Key will belong to one of the Players. The living Sky Key will always be an innocent, a child, and his or her sacrifice will not come easily. If this child is not sacrificed on the altar of the game, then the Event will come quickly, and the End Stage will begin.

A lump forms in Hilal's throat. He looks up from the book, his mouth agape. Could this innocent . . . could this poor innocent child who is in the Himalayas be with Shari Chopra?

He does not read on.

He stares blankly at the wall, the mirror, the television, the muted news. Will Hilal have to kill a child in order to save the world?

And as if to answer his question, there, on the television, appears an animated title reading ENDGAME: IS IT REAL? And there is An Liu, crazed-looking and sunken-eyed, a dark necklace clinging to his neck and chest strung with—Hilal squints—yes, strung with human flesh and hair.

The Shang's lips move.

He speaks.

Hilal hastens to turn up the volume. An is calm and insistent and assured. No sign of the tics he showed at the Calling. Were they an act? Was he fooling them? Hilal listens, as rapt as the now 145,785,934 people who have watched the video.

He listens.

He sees the pictures of the other Players, including him.

And he is afraid.

Not for himself—Hilal is so disfigured that no one will recognize him, and he should be able to Play without this video affecting him at all.

He is afraid because of what this means.

The game is not private anymore.

It has been blown wide open.

The newscast plays the video again.

And again.

And Hilal watches again.

And again.

And he gets an idea. He fumbles with the remote—can he pause the television? Yes.

He waits until he sees the pictures of the Players that An has dug up, and pauses on Shari Chopra, the last Player Liu mentions. She stands in front of a church that Hilal recognizes immediately: the Sagrada Familia in Barcelona, Spain. The masterwork of the Catalan architect Antoni Gaudí.

The Harappan is smiling.

In her arms is a baby girl.

And the baby smiles too.

On a hunch, Hilal takes the device and holds it up to the television, hoping that nothing will happen, hoping that it will be full of stars or nothingness.

But instead it fills with the pulsing ball that marks Sky Key.
He stands, walks to the screen bolted to Stella's bedroom wall. Holds
it directly over the girl. The ball remains. He moves it only a few inches
to Shari. The ball disappears. The church in the background. Nothing.
A tree on the edge. Nothing.

The girl.

The orange ball.

Sky Key.

Hilal drops the device and collapses to the floor, his legs folded
underneath him.

To stop the game, a young girl will have to die.

A young girl that the Harappan loves, and will defend with everything
inside her.

He prays for the girl, for the Players, for all of them.

They need to know.

It is the only option.

He gets out his smartphone. Launches YouTube. Finds An's video.

146,235,587 views and counting.

People are devouring it.

He creates a new account, logs in, encodes his message, posts it.

And he is afraid.

Afraid of what he has done.

And of what will be done still.

didyouseekeplertwentytwob posted 1 minute ago

On the pad write the next twelve in sequence.

WO Mzncdvj-Huqf mw bnl Tcwpqvhr. M xxzex BEYLL. Dj
lhq knac xs azvi yvy Vashk huir sose hui viryloie gn Pmimm
Qusovr-GUM VW XYS BWG-Icp: xosniiwr.amisfmlssnnhlzkl
uq mflpoiakcx.gmfyvfqkxayviwwki. Tob eain. M qt vjx. SVLHA.
Gwqt ols tmkh goii mov asetq.

AN LIU

Karaya Road, Beck Bagan, Ballygunge, Kolkata, India

"Nearly there, love. Nearly"—*BLINKBLINK*—"nearly there."

It's midmorning. The sun is a diffuse yellow ball hung in a featureless blanket of gray clouds. The disc inches higher over the low buildings of this teeming city. An wonders how our star—92,956,000 miles away, its light taking a full eight minutes to cross the frozen expanse of space before reaching Earth—can sometimes feel like it gives so much heat. Especially on days like this.

Days that are already hot. How can they get hotter?

The air is thick with diesel fumes. An's shirt—the same he's been traveling in since he flew from Okinawa to Hong Kong to Kolkata, all on small charters that cost a fortune—is soaked through.

An rubs his nape with a white handkerchief, pushing the strands of Chiyoko's hair necklace aside, working his fingers under it.

The handkerchief comes back wet and black from soot.

"Nearly there. Nearly there."

He walks with head bent to the ground, a heavy backpack nearly as big as him strapped to his shoulders. Four more blocks of these nameless narrow streets and he will be at his next safe house. According to the Shang manifest, it is not as well stocked with weapons, but it is full of up-to-date computer and communications equipment. It even has a dedicated Ku-band SatLink teleport terminal that will enable him to link with any communications or mapping or weather satellite in the sky. And of course, this being India, where power is never assured, it has its own underground generators and a hidden solar array on the roof. It has water and food and a bulletproof Land Rover Defender and a supercharged Suzuki GSX-R1000.

It will be the perfect seat from which to monitor the next act of the game.

One he will merely observe.

Observe what he has put in motion.

Observe and see *SHIVERBLINKBLINKBLINK* observe and see who is killed.

When.

And how soon.

Because it will be soon.

"Yes. Soon, love."

He walks along the uneven sidewalk, dodging people here and here and here. So many people, just like in China, but different from China. More entropy and disorder. Contrast everywhere. High and low and rich and poor and clean and filthy and past and present and profane and sacred, so much odor and sound and spectacle and sensory overload.

No wonder this is a land that breeds ascetics, An thinks. *It is too much to take in.*

A mutt crosses his path. A one-armed boy covered in filth asks for money. To the boy's left is a white cow, standing in the middle of the road, ankle-deep in food wrappers and empty water bottles and newspapers and shit. Opposite the cow a woman sits cross-legged on the curb, holding an English sign that reads *I will save your soul for Rs 1000*. Next to her is a thin man in a loincloth shaving another man with a straight razor. Someone yells something from up high in a building. Horns honk. Engines churn. People cry or laugh. And they talk. They talk and talk. Not just in English also but in Hindi and Urdu and Bengali and Assamese and Oriya and who knows what else.

An barely understands a word.

He puts his head down and tries to block it all out and rounds a corner onto a quieter side street and gets out his smartphone and looks at the map to double-check where he's going. He's on track.

Nearly there.

Nearly *blink* nearly there.

"Chiyoko."

He touches her ear around his neck. It is so dry now, so lifeless.

"Chiyoko."

He rubs the backs of his hands across his eyes.

Even though she is always with him, he needs to get his mind off Chiyoko. Off what her *shiverBLINKBLINKBLINKshiver* off what her *SHIVERSHIVERSHIVERBLINK* off what her uncle said about her.

And about him.

About An.

The Shang loads up his video and swipes his finger across the screen, swipes his finger, swipes his finger, swipes his finger, and there it is. He stares at the phone as he walks.

Stares at the message posted by one of the Players.

Because only a Player would have an account name like that.

He stares at it and *SHIVERblinkSHIVER* stares at it and smiles.

The code is elegant and strange, like a rarely seen bird.

An swipes at his phone some more, punches in a string of characters, and manages to break the code easily. Discovers that it was the Aksumite who posted it. His clues were generous. All the Players would make quick work of it, so long as they had been paying attention at the Calling.

An memorizes the decryption since it would be foolish to write it out on his phone or anywhere else, to leave a record of it.

He stares and smiles.

"Uncle Nobuyuki didn't see this, did he, my love?" So much bitterness for that old man, next to so much adoration for his departed beloved.

"They will be driven together, and it will be a slaughter."

AISLING KOPP, POP KOPP, GREG JORDAN, BRIDGET McCLOSKEY, GRIFFIN MARRS

Gulfstream G650, 42,000 Feet over the China-Mongolia Border

"I got it. That's it. That's it!"

Aisling holds up the laptop. The others lean in and read Hilal's decoded message. They read it again and again.

"Well, I'll be," Jordan says.

"Sky Key is a . . . ?" Pop says quietly.

Aisling isn't as surprised. "Why wouldn't it be an innocent? I believe the keplers are about suffering, first and foremost. Why not have a Player suffer even more by making a loved one a target? It's kind of brilliant, if you think about it."

Pop says, "That's not how I would put it, but I see your point."

Aisling's eyes narrow. "So it's a little girl, and she belongs to Shari Chopra. And if I'm remembering my UTM correctly, those coordinates are somewhere in India."

Jordan checks his laptop. "Affirmative. In the middle of a tiny Indian state called Sikkim. Never been, but heard nice things."

"We need to go there. Now. Yesterday. Last week." Aisling plops the laptop on her thighs. She punches the screen with her index finger. "We scratch this Stonehenge idea. India's a hell of a lot closer anyway. How far are we—a thousand miles, two thousand, tops? Everyone else is far-flung. We can beat every other Player there!"

"Whoa, whoa, whoa," McCloskey says. "Did it not occur to you that this al-Salt dude could be waiting for us? That this might be a giant ploy to get the drop on other Players? Christ, he might have the site wired to blow as soon as the first Player shows up."

Aisling bristles. "An would do something like that, but not the

344

Aksumite. I'm telling you, al-Salt is nowhere near India, I guarantee it. He wants what we want: to stop this thing."

"What makes you so certain?"

"He was the only one at the Calling who asked for calm, who pleaded for reason. The only one. He didn't want all of this . . . horror. This madness. Besides, his post is less than a day old, and if he was in this Sikkim place he'd have found the girl already. He'd have killed her. He wouldn't need help. He wouldn't need to use that message. No, he's somewhere else. Somewhere far, far away."

"A long time ago, in a galaxy far, far away?" McCloskey asks. "Gimme a break. I'm not Princess Leia and you're not Luke Skywalker."

Jordan holds up his hand. "Can it, guys. Marrs, we need you!"

Marrs ducks through the cockpit door. "You will not believe what just came over the wires, man."

"What?"

"Stonehenge was just blown away. Huge explosion. Possibly a tiny nuke, even. Nothing's left."

There's a moment of silence, not just because they're shocked, but also because, for Aisling and Pop, Stonehenge was a La Tène monument, a piece of their ancient past.

"Who did it?" Pop asks.

"No one's come forward, but it looks like common terrorists, just like back at Narita," Marrs says.

"Fuck," Aisling says. "Guess we *have* to go to India now."

"I don't know," McCloskey says. "Stonehenge getting totaled sucks, but you can't say you didn't see it coming—people are scared, and when people get scared they start destroying the things that are scaring them. I wouldn't be surprised to discover that some of our esteemed colleagues at the agency were behind it, to be honest."

"So where would you have us go, McCloskey?" Aisling asks.

"I don't know. But just because Stonehenge is gone doesn't mean we should blindly follow the suggestion of another Player. Like I said, it could be a trap—or it could simply be a diversionary tactic.

Something to shake us off the real trail . . ."

Aisling doesn't buy it. "But what if it *is* true? And what if the Event happens and we didn't try to do this thing that the Aksumite says will stop it? Chopra didn't strike me as one of the evil Players, but I wouldn't hesitate to kill her or her daughter or her whole fricking line if I thought it had the potential to save billions of lives. Shit, I'd kill you or Jordan or Pop or even myself if I thought it might save humanity."

McCloskey crosses her arms. "Duly noted, Player."

Aisling sits. "Jesus, McCloskey, I'm not threatening you. I *need* you. And we need to go to India. All due respect, but I have to be in charge. I should have been the one in that room with An Liu, not the KFE team. At the very least I should have been in there *with* them. If you want to Play for me, McCloskey, then you have to do what I say. Plain and simple."

"I don't have to do anyth—"

But Jordan cuts McCloskey off: "Bridge, she's right. We screwed that mission up. We all know it. Aisling's a resource. We're a resource to her, and she to us, but we have to serve her in this thing. That's the bottom line. We have to suck it up and listen to her. *Follow* her."

McCloskey doesn't say anything.

Aisling says, "Thanks, Jordan."

Jordan claps his hands. "It's settled. India." He leans into the cockpit and says something to Marrs, and almost immediately the plane banks hard to the south.

A new heading: 206°14'16".

"Fine," McCloskey says. "I just hope you're right, Aisling. I hope this al-Salt Player—this *opponent* of yours—isn't outmaneuvering us." She pulls a small pill out of a shirt pocket and swallows it. She tucks her feet under her butt and wraps her arms over her ankles and closes her eyes. "I'm gonna take off to Planet Xanax and conk out. If we really are going to assassinate a little girl, I'm going to need some rest."

She doesn't say anything else, and in less than a minute she's snoring. Loudly.

Aisling, Jordan, and Pop huddle over the desk, and for the next hour they pore over satellite images and road maps and topographic charts of Sikkim. Jordan summons Marrs and asks him to reposition one of the National Reconnaissance Office's top-secret Spectacle-class imaging satellites to get a closer look at the location given by the Aksumite, "Because this Google map ain't showing us squat."

"Man, any excuse to dance with the octopus!" Marrs says, clearly giddy.

"He loves it when I tell him to play with the NRO's toys. They got this logo of an octopus hugging planet Earth—"

"I've seen it," Pop says. "'Nothing is beyond our reach.'"

While they wait for Marrs, they go over a plan of approach. The location Hilal has given them is challenging. The only way to get into the Himalayas from Siliguri is to drive. They'll have to figure out a way to buy two jeeps, load them up, and leave ASAP, but even then it will take them no less than 10 hours of driving on bumpy roads. Once there, they'll have to find a place to stage, drive what's sure to be a dirt track into the mountains, tool up, and start hiking. Jordan figures that the whole trip, from their spot in the air to the exact point on the map, will take 30 hours, minimum.

According to Hilal, Sky Key is located on the side of an unnamed valley, 12,424 feet high in the eastern Himalayas. The satellite image shows no sign of any of settlement or structure—no road, no solar panels, no discernible radio tower. The location is nothing more than an exposed wall of rock. Knuckled fingers of tree-covered stone surround it in every direction. No-man's-land. The valley runs more or less east to west, originating in a snowcapped section to the west and terminating at a raging river to the east labeled Teesta, a cold-water tributary to the mighty Brahmaputra.

Pop shakes his head. "It's as blind an alley as I've ever seen. If no one's there, it'll be a colossal waste of time and effort."

"If there's something there, the octopus will see it." Jordan looks at his watch. "How much longer on the sat, Marrs?"

"Right now," Marrs announces, stepping into the cabin. "And I think this Hilal guy might be right, man." He squeezes between Aisling and Jordan to take control of the computer. He changes the input on the screen—*snap!*—and they see a very close, very live, very high-definition shot of the Himalayan valley.

And there, without question, carved into the side of the rock, are windows and doors and bridges and walkways. All hidden from a distance, all plain to see up close.

"It's a village," Pop marvels.

"No. It's a fortress," Aisling corrects.

"She's right about that," Marrs says. He punches a few buttons and fiddles with a mouse and the image changes. It goes dark, except for little webs of green filaments and dots moving here and there like ants.

"Those are . . . people!" Aisling exclaims. "Right?"

McCloskey snores again.

Marrs nods. "Yep. The little lines are heat trails. Power's probably geothermal, with some generators and gas lighting." He indicates several points on the image that look like green fires. "They seem to be venting steam—probably from small turbines—along this corridor here." He zooms out and overlays the satellite image with the infrared image. A faint but discernible line zigzags south of the fortress and extends to the east, along the valley floor, terminating at the Teesta. "My money says that's a path."

Aisling stabs the river intersection with her finger. "That's it. That's where we go in. Sky Key is there. Chopra's gotten a bunch of her people together and taken them up to this fortress. . . . She's *guarding* Sky Key. She's *waiting* for the other Players."

"She'll know we're coming, then. We won't have the element of surprise, Ais," Pop points out.

Aisling stares at the screen. "You can feed this into those monocle things, right, Marrs?"

"Hell yes."

She turns to Pop. "They may know we're coming. But we'll know exactly where they are at any given moment. I can promise you, they don't have anything like this." She beams and throws an arm over Marrs. "This is amazing. Really amazing. I don't suppose this satellite has a laser on it or anything? So we can smoke people from orbit?"

Jordan laughs. "That kind of thing is just for the movies."

"Or the Makers," Pop says.

"But we're not fighting them, are we, Pop?" Aisling says.

McCloskey snores again, a three-parter, deep in the throat. She turns her body. One of her feet falls to the floor.

"Got one more thing for us too," Marrs says. "Packed away in the hold is a drone."

"Shit! I forgot about Little Bertha," Jordan says.

Aisling asks, "More eyes?"

"Sure, but that's not the best part. The best part is it carries two lightweight but very powerful air-to-surface missiles. One laser-guided, one heat-seeking."

Aisling beams even more.

Pop can see what she's thinking.

Boy, I'm glad I didn't ditch these people.

She shakes Marrs's shoulder, like he's her best oldest buddy.

I am really fucking glad I didn't ditch them.

JAGO TLALOC

Casa Isla Tranquila, Juliaca, Peru

It's been two nights since Jago spoke with Aucapoma Huayna. He's still at his parents' estate. He's still waiting to Play, to take Earth Key to Tiwanaku. But what the elder told him about the Cahokians and Sarah has confused him, made him pause.

He's not used to feeling confused.

He hasn't told his father all of what the elder said, but he has told Renzo everything. He needed to tell someone. And they talked about it. And they decided.

And now that they've seen the Shang's video, they know. They've not discovered Hilal's message, but it doesn't matter. Jago can no longer wait. He's marked. They all are.

Jago and Renzo watch the video a 2nd time.

A 3rd.

They don't speak.

They don't watch it a 4th time.

Jago navigates to his laptop's music app. Finds a track by Behemoth. Plays it. Loud and driving and pounding and evil-sounding.

Jago loves it.

"Are you with me, Renzo?" Jago asks, the music drowning out his words.

"Now more than ever, my Player. You're going to need my help."

"You're sure? If you cross me, I'll kill you."

"I'm sure."

"You know I can."

"I know I'm too old to stop you."

"And too fat."

"Screw you."

They laugh uneasily, the music assaulting their eardrums. Jago's diamond teeth flash in the light. "Get our stuff ready, but be quiet about it. Guitarrero can't know."

"Of course."

"Papí will be out late tomorrow night for a meeting about the Cielos. At three fifteen that morning, we act. And deal with Sarah."

"Three fifteen."

"You won't cross me?"

"On our line and on Endgame, I swear it."

"Good. Tomorrow night we Play."

xiv

MACCABEE ADLAI, BAITSAKHAN

Unnamed Gravel Road, San Julian District, Juliaca, Peru

Maccabee and Baitsakhan do not see An Liu's video or Hilal's message. And they probably wouldn't give a rat's ass if they did.

Instead, they wait for the right time to pluck some low-hanging Peruvian fruit. Two mercenaries who they've been following for the afternoon and evening. One short, like Baitsakhan, the other big, but not quite as big as Maccabee.

"His uniform will be snug on you," Baitsakhan says wryly, apparently trying to joke.

"Here they come," Maccabee says, ignoring the poor joke.

The Tlaloc mercenaries emerge from a rough cantina called El Mejor. It's in a low-slung wooden building that must be 100 years old. They're drunk, they bob and weave, laugh, their breaths are visible on the cold air. Their rifles sway under their arms.

"The Olmec would not approve of their state," Baitsakhan judges. The boy who has never had a drink in his life.

"They're standing on the edge of the world, Baits. We all are. Everyone needs to have fun now and then, right?"

"I don't."

"No. Of course you don't."

The men approach from the east. Their truck, a large Chevy that for some reason lacks the red-talon emblem, is across the street to the north. A woman rounds a corner out of a blind alley. She wears a long dress over petticoats, a thick sweater, a red and blue and yellow poncho, a dark felt fedora, its crown popped out and up like a rounded top hat. The drunks set on her immediately. Poke her clothes. Squeeze her arms. The shorter one tries to lift the hem of her many-layered dress with his rifle, but she pushes it down. She shakes her head, waves a hand, tries to protest. She's scared. The taller one looks around the barely lit street. No one.

No one to hear her.

No one to help.

He raises his rifle and points it at her head.

Maccabee says, "He's telling her not to scream or he'll kill her."

She doesn't scream.

Her shoulders begin to shake.

The larger soldier backs her toward the alleyway. The smaller one licks his lips and slings his rifle behind his back. He reaches for the woman, she recoils, the man persists. He stabs his hand toward her face and grabs her hat. He smiles as he places it on his head. The larger one backs her into the alleyway. She disappears from view. The smaller one runs after her. The larger one looks around one more time, nervous, excited. Still no one.

He disappears as well.

Maccabee opens the Escort's door and puts a foot on the hardscrabble ground.

Baitsakhan blurts, "What're you doing?"

"I've seen enough."

"I thought you said they should have some fun."

Maccabee winces. "What the hell, Baits? They're going to rape that woman. Both of them. You think that'll be fun for *her*?"

Baitsakhan shrugs. "I wouldn't know."

Maccabee steps out of the car. "No. You wouldn't."

Maccabee is about to close the door when Baitsakhan holds a Kel Tec PLR-22 across the inside of the car. "You'll want this."

Maccabee pulls his ancient and sharp blade from his hip, flashes his deadly pinkie ring. "I don't need that to kill a couple of sex-starved drunks." He runs toward the alley. Baitsakhan kicks his seat back and lays the gun on his lap. Maccabee rounds the corner in seconds and disappears. The orb sits in the car's open ashtray above the gearshift. It glows brightly. How Baitsakhan wishes he could touch it. If he could, he would do away with the Nabataean. And he would enjoy it. This new hand that Maccabee foolishly gave him would make killing him easy. A single rifle report comes from the dark alley, the sound disappearing into the cool night. Baitsakhan rolls down the window with the manual hand crank. Takes a deep breath. The air is sweet, crisp. He loves the cold, wishes it were colder. It reminds him of the open Gobi and his beloved horses.

He misses his horses.

The shorter man emerges from the alley, trying to run while holding up his pants. A bright thing slashes the air and strikes him in the back of the neck, and he falls face-first and dead onto the ground.

Seventeen seconds later Maccabee is back in the street, his arm draped around the woman. She's crying. Their faces are close.

Maccabee consoles her. She looks at the corpse.

Curses.

Spits.

Maccabee takes her hand, puts something in it.

She looks at his face, stands on her toes, and kisses his cheek.

Maccabee says something else and points. He looks insistent. She kisses him again, stuffs what Maccabee gave her—surely an ounce of gold—in the top of her dress, hikes up her skirts, and runs away as fast as she can. Within seconds, she's swallowed by the night.

Maccabee watches her for a few seconds and disappears back into the alleyway. When he reappears, he holds the rifle and the man's clothing. He stops next to the smaller man. Reaches down and pulls his precious blade from his neck. Takes a fistful of hair and drags the body toward the Escort. Baitsakhan leans out the window and enjoys the air some more. He closes his eyes and thinks of his horse cantering across the steppe, throwing dirt from his hooves and spittle from his lips. He hears Maccabee's footsteps, and the man being dragged across the gravel. Maccabee stops.

"Get off your ass and give me a hand."

Baitsakhan doesn't open his eyes. "Coming."

Maccabee crosses to the pickup and throws the man in back.

Baitsakhan takes the Kel Tec's grip and, still lost in his reverie, reaches with his new hand for the orb and wraps his mechanical fingers around it.

And it doesn't burn.

His eyes shoot open.

It doesn't burn.

He looks at the Chevy, the engine running, Maccabee already inside blowing heat into his hands.

It doesn't burn.

He slips the orb into a cloth knapsack and gets out of the car, suppressing a smile, pushing down his excited heart rate.

Maybe, once they get Earth Key, Baitsakhan *can* do away with the Nabataean after all.

Yes.

He can.

Parate ad finem

SHARI CHOPRA AND THE LEADERS OF THE HARAPPAN LINE

सूर्य को अन्तमि रेज, *Valley of Eternal Life, Sikkim, India*

The Close Council of the Harappan sits in a room cut from the gray rock of the mountain, just as every room at सूर्य को अन्तमि रेज is carved from stone. They sit on colorful cushions arranged in a circle. A thick Nepalese rug covers the floor. The center of the rug depicts a four-armed humanoid figure with the head of an elephant—Lord Ganesha—and the wizened figure of Veda Vyasa. The ancient sage dictates the Mahabarata to Ganesha, and the deity dutifully writes everything down. The words of the epic encircle the figures in a spiral that spins out to the rug's tasseled fringe like the scribed arms of a galaxy.

Ganesha, lord of knowledge and letters, placer and remover of obstacles, the being that governs the forces of the bhavacakra.

Obstacles, Shari thinks.

Obstacles.

The council discusses the developments of the Shang video and the Aksumite message.

The message that, they must assume, every Player has seen and decoded.

"And you are certain it gave our location?" It is Helena, sounding excited and a little scared.

"Absolutely," Peetee says. "Somehow the Aksumite has found us. I don't know how. But we are dealing with the mysteries of the mysteries, and as we all know, anything is possible. It is only a matter of time before the others will find us too."

"My family," Shari says, "we knew this was coming. We should not argue over the whys and the wherefores."

The older heads nod. Shari adjusts her position, feels the bulk of the pistol she keeps hidden under in her bright green-and-blue salwar kameez. The gun that belonged to the cousin of the Donghu and that she took from the warehouse where they tortured her. The place where dear Alice Ulapala came and rescued her.

The Koori, the Makers take her.

The gun Shari originally, and foolishly, loaded with three bullets. One for Jamal, one for Little Alice, one for herself.

But then she realized that it is nonsense to put names on bullets. And that killing is hard work, especially this kind of impossible killing, and that more bullets might be needed. What if her hand shakes so much that she misses? What if the first shot doesn't kill her beloved? What if she has no bullets left to kill herself when she is done?

She does not like thinking of these what-ifs.

All the same, she has loaded the pistol to capacity, and strapped herself with two more magazines to boot.

If it comes to the impossible, she *will* be ready.

These thoughts fly through her head, and she doesn't dare mention them. "How are the preparations, my sweet?"

Jamal says, "Good."

"Please, tell us," Jov says.

Jamal squeezes Shari's knee. "As we all know, there is only one path that leads to सूरय को अन्तमि रेज. It is well guarded. We've made two checkpoints along the trail from the river. Each is manned by six men, all heavily armed. There is a third checkpoint at the Elbow"—a hard, angled turn at the end of a switchback trail that can only be passed by going through it—"and if any make it that far, then they will be cut to pieces by the M61 Vulcan mounted in the mountainside adjacent to our keep's only entrance."

"They will not make it that far," Helena says.

Jov looks to Shari. "Helena has offered to go to the second checkpoint to oversee defensive operations." Jov smiles, no teeth, all joy.

"And I will personally man the Vulcan," Pravheet says, the ex-Player, the man who has promised never to kill again.

"What?" Jamal and Paru ask together.

"What of your vow?" Shari begs, betraying a tinge of desperation.

A big reason that she's eschewed violence throughout her training, to the consternation of many, most notably Helena, is because of Pravheet and his vow. Shari has spent countless hours meditating with him and listening to him teach the principle of compassion and the power of love and patience. Her mind is as sharp as it is because of Pravheet. He is the reason she has learned to overcome physical pain and find good in any circumstance—real, tangible good, not just a fool's imaginings. He is the reason she survived her ordeal at the hands of the little animal called Baitsakhan. Pravheet is the reason that she thinks, if it's needed, she will have the inner strength to do the unthinkable: kill her own daughter in order to prevent another Player from taking her away, to the Makers, to the end of the game.

Pravheet stares deeply into Shari's eyes. "If I am ever to break my vow, now is the time, Shari. When you rallied us in Gangtok, you spoke repeatedly of 'we,' the mighty and ancient Harappan, working together to win. I believe that you are right, and that we *should* try to win, and I know that I am prepared to do anything to see that we do—that *you* do. I still love peace and mindfulness, but if this senseless Event is going to happen, then we should be the ones to survive it. That is what we have been told, that is what we know. I would break every vow to see it happen ten times, twenty times, a hundred times. And when the Great Puzzle is over and you have won and the Earth is scarred, I will return to peace, and that is where I will stay. But for now, I am ready to kill. To kill them all."

The room is silent for a few moments before Helena belches. "Nice to have you back, Pravheet."

"There is nothing nice about it, Helena," Pravheet says quietly.

Jov brings his hands together like he's going to pray. "I agree with our esteemed ex-Player, and I for one am glad of your decision. There is no shame in your reversal, Pravheet."

"Thank you, Jovinderpihainu."

Some more silence. A servant is heard whistling the popular Bollywood tune "Pungi" as he walks down the stone hallway outside the room, his feet slapping the cold ground in time.

"We are ready, then," Paru says.

Shari shakes her head. "There is one thing we haven't mentioned." She points a toe at the picture of Ganesha that is woven into the rug. "The elephant in the room."

Her tone is grave, but nonetheless they share a light chuckle at her joke. Jovinderpihainu leans forward. He breathes heavily. "You mean: What if the Aksumite is right."

"Exactly," Shari says. "What if we could stop all of this by . . ."

Jamal cringes. "Don't say it."

A long pause.

"The Aksumite may *be* right," Pravheet whispers apologetically. The heads swing to him. He talks slowly, methodically. "I don't know much about it, but their line guards a deep and ancient secret that none of the other lines are privy to, and their knowledge of certain spiritual aspects of antiquity is unparalleled, even by our standards. There *is* a chance that he speaks the truth."

"You mentioned him before, Player," Jov says. "Can you remind us?"

Shari presses down on her knees, as if she is trying to suppress something horrible inside her. Finally she says, "Hilal ibn Isa al-Salt struck me as being unassailably honest."

"By the Makers," Jamal says angrily. "You can't be suggesting that we kill our own daughter, Shari, can you?"

"No, of course not!" She takes a deep breath, wipes her eyes. She's afraid. Afraid because she might be lying.

This is not the time for lying.

"Jamal . . . I . . . don't know. Countless people—men and women and children and elders—were sacrificed to the Makers in the history before history, and countless times the Makers approved of these sacrifices, asked for them, needed them. Why wouldn't they ask for one now? Doesn't that seem like the whole reason for making Little Alice into Sky Key in the first place? To be grotesque, to allude to the peculiar violence of our shared past with the Makers? Like a coda of Endgame, of our existence, of our ancestry? The human race is born of many things, but chief among them is violence, extreme and supreme violence. Isn't that what this is? Don't they *want* me to do this unspeakable thing?"

Paru and even Helena go pale, and Peetee stares at the picture of Vyasa on the rug. Jamal yanks his hand from his wife's leg. "Shari, I can't believe you're saying this."

"I'm only bringing it up as a possibility, my love."

The gun hidden in the folds of her clothing suddenly feels heavier than the sun.

Heavier and hotter and more absolute.

"I have no intention of hurting even a hair on Little Alice's head, and I will guard her with every fiber of my being and every ephemeral ounce of my soul," Shari says. "But billions will soon die, love. This is guaranteed. This is the promise of Endgame. The question must be asked."

More silence.

Jovinderpihainu breaks it. "You are right to ask, Shari. But there is a difference between being honest and being right. Honest men lie all the time, believing that they tell the truth. Much evil is borne on the back of honesty."

"So you think Hilal is wrong, Jov?" Shari asks. "That he is being misled?"

"I don't know if he is or he isn't. But I do know that if we follow his advice and sacrifice our beloved and innocent daughter and the Event still happens, then there will be no possibility of you winning. You will be utterly destroyed on the inside, hollowed out and empty—we all will be. This is a possibility too. That the Maker, which you took pains to point out seemed petty and even bored at the Calling, was merely a living creature. Not a god. Maybe in spite of all the wonderful things they are capable of doing, they are still weak at heart, and vindictive, and cruel. Maybe their motivation for planting this seed in the Aksumite is simply to see us suffer, and to see you break and go mad and take the life of your own child, for the sake of an entertainment. I say it again: If we're to do what the Aksumite asks of us and the Event comes anyway and the game somehow continues, then how will you win?"

Another silence, its end definitive:

"I will not," Shari says.

The wise elder frowns. "And for that reason, you won't sacrifice Little Alice. Not now or ever. None of us will. We will surround her."

All the heads nod. Shari is so thankful for this logic. It is sound. It is right.

"Bless you, Jov . . . And in a strange way, bless Hilal ibn Isa al-Salt. He has sent these Players to us. He has sent them to their deaths."

"Yes," Helena hisses.

Shari brings her fingertips together and forms a circle with her arms and chest. "We will surround her, as planned. We will surround her and we will win."

Shari stands, and the others stand too. Pravheet helps Jov to his feet. Shari takes Jamal's hand. She gives it a loving caress. He doesn't respond.

They file out.

And as they walk, Shari fills with eagerness and fear and hope and terror.

She cannot tell him.

She cannot tell him that she will keep the gun on her person, always, and that even though she won't sacrifice Little Alice to stop the Event, Shari *will* kill her if it means stopping one of the others from taking away her one and only baby.

SARAH ALOPAY

Casa Isla Tranquila, Juliaca, Peru

Sarah is not asleep when she hears her door open at 3:17:57 a.m.

But she looks asleep.

She's in bed on her side, facing away from the door, gun in hand.

Whoever is in the room is silent—or likes to think that he or she
is silent. The person has had some training in stealth, but it is not
enough to evade her senses.

Meaning it's not Jago.

Sarah waits for this servant to pick up the tray with the empty plates
and glasses, and when he or she picks it up, she will kill and run out
of the room and fight her way out of the Tlaloc compound. She has
thought long and hard about whether she should hunt down Jago, but
has decided that it would be suicide. Not because she couldn't beat
him, but simply because the most important thing for her is to get
away, to live.

Even if it means losing Earth Key for a little while.

Even if it means leaving that which she fought so hard for—which she
killed Christopher for—behind.

The person creeps farther into the room. She waits for him or her to
stop at the table and take the tray.

The person doesn't stop by the tray.

Sarah adjusts her body like a sleeping person would.

Waits.

The person reaches the bed. Comes to her side. Stops. It is a man. She
can hear his breath.

The breath belongs to someone heavier than Jago. Someone older.

She wheels her legs, throwing off her covers, and catches the man across the chin and shoulder with her heels, makes good contact, hears a healthy and painful-sounding *pop!*

She vaults up and is quickly standing in the middle of the mattress, her gun pointed down and ready to fire. But before she does, the man swipes at her ankles. Her legs go out and she falls onto her side, but the gun does not go off.

The man stabs a hand forward and takes the top of the pistol and pushes it down into the bed and hisses, "Stop it, Sarah. If they hear, they'll come for us. *Both* of us."

It's Renzo.

"What are *you* doing here?" she says at full volume.

He leans in to her. She can smell his breath. Wine and cheese and cigarillos.

"Please, whisper." She can see Renzo's chubby face in the dim light. His bulbous eyes. His thin mustache.

"Why should I? I can smell Guitarrero Tlaloc all over you."

"Forget about Guitarrero. Jago wants to see you. *Needs* to see you."

"Why isn't he here, then?"

"He's busy. And if you want to live through the night you need to shut up and come with me."

"Why should I trust you?"

"Because I believe in the sanctity of the game. And I believe in my Player. And he asked me to come for you."

Sarah lets go of the gun and, so quickly that it even surprises her, she reaches and grabs Renzo by the Adam's apple. She squeezes.

"Not good enough."

Renzo's eyes pop and water. He can't speak. She steals a look at the door. It's open. She could do away with this man for good and get out of this room.

She could escape.

She squeezes.

He makes a rasping sound, releases the gun, takes her shoulder, digs in his nails, and holds out a fist, knuckles up, in front of her.

He shakes it.

She doesn't let up.

He opens his fist. A small thing inside drops free.

Earth Key.

She doesn't squeeze his throat as hard.

He plants a hand on her chest and pushes away, taking three steps back, holding his neck, gasping.

"He . . . he . . . he told me to give that . . ." He inhales sharply.

Sarah doesn't speak. She picks up Earth Key from the bedcovers.

"He told me to give that to you." Renzo straightens. Wipes his eyes. He recovers quickly, showing his training. "It is a token of goodwill. He didn't want you to be held like this, but he had to go along with it so he could do what he came here to do."

"Aucapoma whatever-her-name-is?"

"Yes. Now please, we *have* to leave. It's not safe for you here anymore—"

"It was before?" she blurts sarcastically.

"It's even more unsafe now. There's been a development with the Shang. You'll see. But we have to move. Jago's taken the guards watching your room out for a smoke. I sat in for them and watched the monitors before running here." He points to a spot on the wall, indicating where the camera is hidden. "We have to go. Now."

Sarah tightens her fingers around Earth Key. She can feel its energy course through her. She can feel her desire to Play.

"Why not just kill me?"

"Believe me, part of me thinks we should. But like I said, I believe in my Player, and he told me not to kill you."

"Yet . . ." Sarah says.

"He told me not to kill you," Renzo repeats, not saying more.

He ushers Sarah off the bed and arranges the pillows and the covers to make it look like she's still sleeping in it. He gives her the pistol and takes her by the wrist. He looks at his watch. "We have ninety seconds to get out of this house. Are you coming?"

Her gaze hardens. She squeezes the grip of the gun. Earth Key gets warmer and warmer. She smells the fresh air from the garden, from the world, still alive, still strong.

She is these things too.

Alive.

Strong.

"Yes, Renzo. Lead the way."

BAITSAKHAN, MACCABEE ADLAI

Peru-Bolivia Border, Carretera Puno Desaguardero, Desaguardero, Peru

"That better be them," Baitsakhan says. He's in the driver's seat, which is pulled all the way forward so that Baitsakhan, all five feet two inches of him, can reach the pedals. He's been driving since the village of Acora, south of Juliaca, so that Maccabee could navigate with the orb as they followed the Olmec's car at a safe distance. Baitsakhan has stuck with his plan not to tell the Nabataean that his new hand can hold the ancient transmitter.

He has to pick the right time to reveal his secret.

The right and deadly time.

They sit on a side street staring at the bustling but modest border crossing. It is 7:17 a.m. It took just over two hours to get there, including the brief stop they made to dump the body that Maccabee had thrown in the bed of the truck. They'd passed through the barren but striking landscape almost without speaking a single word, which suited both of them.

They were tired of Playing like this.

Of not fighting.

Of not killing.

That was one reason Maccabee had helped that woman the night before. Not merely to get the uniforms off Tlaloc's men, but to stay sharp, to keep the taste of blood on his tongue.

Baitsakhan isn't the only one who loves murder.

But for now they're forced to wait. And watch. And wait.

It doesn't suit them. Hence the bickering.

"'Better be'? Are you threatening me?"

"I just mean I don't want to lose them." Baitsakhan lowers a pair of binoculars from his face. He sees the taillights of the Olmec's car, a nondescript Mazda, as the driver talks with the Bolivian border guards.

"Baitsakhan, we've tracked people across the globe with this thing. We're not losing anybody."

"We should be crossing now, with the Olmec—if that *is* the Olmec. He looks different. Why did he do that to his hair?"

"He was tired of it being black? Who knows. Just calm down. You sound like a woman."

"I'm no woman!"

"You're not even a man, Baitsakhan."

"You're barely a man yourself! What are you—eighteen? Nineteen?"

Another person guessing wrong about Maccabee, who is 16. How he enjoys it. But he doesn't answer. He won't spur the Donghu any more.

"It was only a joke, Baitsakhan."

"I don't like jokes."

"No kidding."

"I mean it."

"All right. Just shut up, okay?"

"Fine. But you too."

"My pleasure."

And they both shut up.

Baitsakhan digs a smartphone out of his pocket and swipes it on. Puts in a pair of earbuds, messes around on the internet.

Maccabee watches the border crossing. Men and women stream into Peru from Bolivia for work. The tourist trade here seems intact, even thriving. Maccabee thinks the people coming here must be rich wanderlusters embarking on their last grand tours, crossing special places like Lake Titicaca off an end-of-days bucket list. In a sense, they're like the tourist equivalents of Baitsakhan or himself. Players playing a different, and far less lethal, game.

Life goes on.

"Look at this!" Baitsakhan interrupts Maccabee's thoughts, thrusts the smartphone across the cab of the truck. Maccabee is wary that Baitsakhan is trying to show him snuff pictures of blown-up people or decapitated animals. Baitsakhan shakes it, yanks out the headphone jack. "Take it."

Maccabee does. There, on the little screen, staring back at him with dark eyes, is An Liu.

Maccabee hits play. Baitsakhan leans across the middle of the cab, practically putting his head on Maccabee's shoulder so they can watch together.

And they both watch.

Only once.

"That son of a whore," Maccabee says.

Baitsakhan pulls back to the driver's seat. "That was a real nice picture he found of you in your underwear."

"It was a bathing suit."

"Not like any bathing suit I've ever seen."

"All Europeans wear them. But Baitsakhan—"

"It's not good. Not good at all."

"And it has almost two hundred million views!"

A destitute-looking man crosses the street in front of them, wearing a sandwich board and ringing a bell. The sign reads, DIOS Y LA MUERTE ESTÁN CERCA. ESTOY A LA ESPERA DE HEREDAR LA TIERRA.

One of the meek ones.

One of the faithful ones.

One of the stupid ones.

He disappears around a corner, his bell tinkling away.

"You think Liu's right?" Baitsakhan asks.

"That killing us will stop Abaddon?"

"Yeah."

"Of course not. He just wants help doing his dirty work. He wants to win, like you or me," Maccabee says, not fully comprehending what the Shang wants.

"Then it's a pretty smart move."

"It sure is."

As they talk, Maccabee scrolls through the comments. Most brim with fear or righteousness or stupidity or cynicism or zealotry or doubt. Many look to be written by people with the mental capacity of a sheep. A full battalion of trolls mocks every kind of post.

But one that nobody has seemed to notice catches Maccabee's eye.

The username is a dead giveaway.

He takes a screen shot.

"The Mazda's moving, Maccabee."

The Nabataean looks up from the encoded message. He'll have to crack it later, when they're not hunting. "Let's go. And let's hope the border guards in this backwater don't have you and me on their stop list."

Baitsakhan puts the truck in gear and drives toward Bolivia. "Now we know why he dyed his hair, I guess."

"Yes. Now we know."

They move to the crossing and get lucky. None of the guards give them a second look. If anything, because of the eagle-claw uniforms, they get the kid-glove treatment.

The two Players pass into Bolivia.

Life goes on.

What will be will be.

HILAL IBN ISA AL-SALT

Los Angeles International Airport, Tom Bradley International Terminal, Star Alliance Lounge, Los Angeles, California, United States

Hilal left Stella's, stole a car, and drove to California. Now he sits in a private cubicle, his regular smartphone pressed to his ear. His predawn flight for Bangkok—the closest he could get to India, given the state of the world—leaves in an hour. He wishes he were in Asia already, but flights have been canceled and moved and shuffled, and there doesn't seem to be a private plane left in Southern California— everyone with the means has left and is holed up somewhere remote and private. Having defeated Ea is a real consolation, but he would rather be closer to the Harappan, closer to the girl, closer to her death. May the Makers allow it.

A dead little girl.

He prays that one of the Players can find the strength to do it.

He is not sure, in his heart of hearts, that he would have this strength.

So to Bangkok. Barring any unforeseen circumstances he will be there in 19 hours and 34 minutes. He will make his way farther west from there. But before he boards the plane, he must speak with Eben ibn Mohammed al-Julan. It is overdue. He must tell him of Ea. Of Stella. Of everything.

The phone rings. Eben picks up almost immediately.

"Hilal? Is that you?"

"It is, Master."

"By the fathers, where are you? Are you all right?"

"I am in Los Angeles. I am fine."

"Have you crossed paths with any of the others?"

"No. They Play on."

"And what . . . what of the Corrupter?"

Hilal lowers his voice to a whisper. "I found him, Master. I had help, but I found him. . . ."

"And . . . Can it be?"

"Yes. I confronted Ea. I spoke with it."

"You *met* with him?"

"Yes. It was the only way I could get close enough to do it."

"And wha—"

Hilal cuts him off. In a stream of words he tells Eben of Stella and her relationship with Ea and her hatred for him and her help in defeating him. He tells him everything. He finishes with "Humanity will be free of his evil for all the days to come."

"I have a hundred questions, Hilal. A thousand, especially about this Stella and her army."

"As do I. She will contact me when she can."

"What do you think she is doing?"

"I have thought about this constantly, Master. My guess is that she and her army are behind the destruction of Stonehenge. She has no love for the Makers, and less still for Endgame. I think, in her way, she too is trying to stop it. All of it."

"I want to meet her," Eben says a little shakily.

"And you shall."

"Hilal—come home. Endgame is so different from what we expected. Come home so we can regroup, and especially so that we can secure the ouroboros that holds Ea's essence in the ark. I beg you."

"No, I will keep it. It is safe with me."

"Only so long as you live, Hilal! I am sorry, but you should come here and return the serpents to the ark so we can guard it. Or, if Endgame wipes out our line, so that Ea can be forever buried in our kingdom and forgotten!"

Hilal looks over his shoulder. A man in a business suit stands behind him, four meters away, staring shamelessly. Hilal has decided to forgo the bandages from now on, to present his disfigurement to the world. One look from Hilal and he scuttles off. Just a curiosity seeker. Hilal has learned by now that having the face of a monster attracts a lot of attention—but also that when he uses his face, it scares off most anybody.

"I agree, Master, and I will return."

"Good."

"In time."

"What do you mean?"

"I must carry on. I must Play. Either to stop the Event, hopefully with the aid of my fellow Players or Stella or both, or to win. Until then, I will carry Ea. This is how it needs to be for now, Master. Please understand."

Hilal's voice is confident, convincing.

"I understand that time will not wait, but I still implore you to think it over, and to return to Aksum as soon as you can. The snakes must be returned to the ark, Hilal. They must."

"Yes, Master. But in the meantime, I need to find Sky Key." He pauses. "And somehow I need to find the depraved and irrational strength to kill a little girl."

Dark young pine, at the center of the earth originating,
I have made your sacrifice.
Whiteshell, turquoise, abalone beautiful,
Jet beautiful, fool's gold beautiful, blue pollen beautiful,
Reed pollen, pollen beautiful, your sacrifice I have made.
This day your child I have become, I say.
Watch over me.[xv]
Hold your hand before me in protection
Stand guard for me, speak in defense of me.
As I speak for you, speak for me.
As you speak for me, so will I speak for you.

AISLING KOPP, POP KOPP, GREG JORDAN, BRIDGET McCLOSKEY, GRIFFIN MARRS

Approaching Harappan Checkpoint One, near the Valley of Eternal Life, Sikkim, India

They made it to the Himalayas, and Marrs was right: There is a path. A path recently traveled by many pairs of feet.

And now their feet travel it too.

They have not spoken since they left Sakkyong Hill Station and the river Teesta. Not a single word. But there have been sounds. Their staccato footsteps, the rattle of gear, the measure of their labored breath, the pittering of drizzle on their helmets and the leaves and rocks and trees. Aisling can safely say that she has never been anywhere like the Himalayas. The Alps were like foothills in comparison. Everything about their surroundings—the expanse of the mountains, the steepness of their slopes, the scale of their summits and their valleys—is grand.

She could stay.

She could lose herself.

She could be happy.

If it weren't for Endgame.

She could stay.

But for the little girl.

The little girl she has to kill.

She's suddenly nervous. Will she do it with the rifle? The pistol? The sword? Her bare hands? She knows what she said to McCloskey— that she would be willing to sacrifice anyone, herself included, if she thought it would spare Earth the Event—but Aisling is beginning to have doubts.

Killing myself would be much easier. But a small girl . . . Will I be able to do it?

She knows that doubt is the seed from which failure grows, so she forces these thoughts from her mind and focuses. Pop is several paces behind her, effortlessly keeping up, even at his age. Jordan and McCloskey keep pace too, but with much greater effort. Marrs, Aisling can see on her HUD, appears to be having an easier time.

For her part, Aisling is holding back. Neither the elevation nor the weight of her equipment bothers her. She could go on like this for hours without stopping.

A warning beep sounds over the comm link. Two red dots that Marrs marked as potential booby traps glow brightly on her HUD. She stops. Holds up a fist. The others stop too.

"Marrs, hold," she says.

"Roger that," he responds, several hundred feet behind them.

Aisling takes a knee. "How's the drone?"

"Droney, man. Ready for anything. It'd be nice if it could get a visual so we can see what kind of hardware we're up against, but this cloud cover isn't helping. Over."

"It'll be fine. Just keep it airborne. Over."

Jordan takes a step forward. "I'll check the trip wires."

Aisling holds out her hand, palm down. "No. I will. This is my mission, Jordan. Besides, when was the last time you disarmed an IED?"

Jordan smirks sheepishly. "2010. Fallujah."

"Exactly. I'll take this. If there's two, I'll disarm one and detonate the other. Stick to the plan and don't engage until detonation."

They're professionals, so she doesn't have to remind them what the plan is: Jordan and McCloskey on the right, Aisling and Pop on the left, Marrs hanging back on sniper and drone support. The forward teams are each responsible for anyone on their side. Only once the flanks are clear will they take the center position, which is likely an RPG, sniper, or machine gun—or one of each.

"Ready?"

They're ready.

"Go."

Jordan and McCloskey move off the path to the northwest, disappearing into the cover of the woods.

Aisling and Pop move to the opposite side.

After 50 paces Aisling says, "Marrs, when we engage, come up fast and take the first clear line up the trail you can find, but stay low and hidden."

"Roger that."

Another 20 paces. Aisling mutes her comm. Pop, who is on her left, does too. "How's that for taking charge?" she asks.

Pop doesn't look at her, just keeps his eyes keen on what's around them. "I'll let you know if we survive the next ten minutes."

"Ha. Fair enough." She unmutes her comm.

The green dots on the HUD that mark the Harappan—purple dots mark Aisling's team—float in front of her right eye. Aisling wonders who they are—trainers, ex-Players, soldiers, young, old? Are they also nervous, as they sit and wait for whatever it is that's coming to find them? They must be. They *are* human. No amount of training can take away fear completely.

She swipes her hand through the air, indicating to Pop that she's breaking off to deal with the traps. The drizzle has changed to light rain. Water droplets form on the muzzle of her rifle. Her gloved hands catch a sudden but brief chill. She finds the path again. It continues west before bending left and disappearing over a rise. The green dots are on the other side of that, less than 150 feet away. She slings her rifle over her shoulder and inches forward, scanning the ground for anything unusual. Her heart is like a drum. She sees nothing. No depressions, no fishlines, no wires, no pile of leaves, no scattered mounds of dirt.

Where is it?

She inches closer.

Nothing. Water drips from the edge of her helmet.

Stupid goddamn rain. Everything is muck and mist.

Wait.

There.

A foot away.

So close.

Droplets, now big enough to see, are getting cut in half by an invisible thread.

Aisling kneels. Sees it. Runs her eyes to the right, then to the left. Yes. *Thank God for the rain,* she revises. She wouldn't have seen it if it were dry.

She traces the line to the left, where it's tied to a tree, and runs back to the right and sees it. A simple lever trigger attached to a bundle of C4 that's covered in leaves.

She searches the ground for a twig, and without taking the time to think too much about it, she pinches the line with one hand and inserts the twig into the lever, jamming it in place.

She cuts the line. It doesn't blow.

She moves forward 12 feet, keeping low. She can see by the purple dots that the rest of her team has stopped moving and taken position, waiting for the signal.

Aisling moves forward cautiously, searching for the next rain-splitting wire. She finds this one easily now that she knows what she's looking for. She steps over it, kneels, removes a spool of her own thread from a cargo pocket. She takes the free end and makes a big loop around the trip wire, ties a nonslip bowline knot. She runs a zip tie through the spool's eye and closes it and loops the tie over her pinkie. She lets out two feet of this line—a snagless Teflon-coated monofilament— and lays it on the ground. She sets a fist-sized rock on the thread and tests it gently. It will hold until it's given a good hard tug, slipping free of the rock and yanking the trip wire and setting off the bomb.

She walks 10 paces forward to the edge of the forest, where a large boulder overgrown with moss and lichens abuts the path. She moves around the rock and puts her back to it and hunkers down. She checks her HUD. Pop is in the woods, 126 feet in front of her. Jordan and McCloskey are 230 feet behind her.

The green dots are still in place.

Waiting.

"Fire in the hole on five. Confirm with one click."

Four separate clicks, one from each member of her team.

She drops her head. "One. Two. Three. Four. Five."

She yanks the thread hard, feels it slip from the rock, and for a split second feels the tension on the trip wire, but then—

The explosion is not very big, but the forest sings with shrapnel. Clinks and clatters from the other side of the boulder as ball bearings and nails and screws and shards of metal shred the forest. Chunks of bark, bits of leaves, slashed branches—all of these rain down.

The blast only lasts a second, then it's quiet again. Aisling stands and checks her HUD. Two green dots are already on the move, headed her way, one from each flank.

Aisling places her guns—a new Brügger & Thomet along with an FN SCAR—on the ground and quietly draws her sword. "Marrs, come to my position. The rest move on the flanks now. Acknowledge."

Four clicks.

She sees her purple dots move.

The two green dots are closer.

Only 65 feet away.

Both hands on the Falcata. She waits. Faces the path they've already walked up.

She hears them clear the rise, and the green dots are practically on top of her. She flips up the monocle so that it won't interfere with her vision. She crouches, rests the tip of her sword on the ground, waits.

A man swings around the boulder, a Kalashnikov on his shoulder, the muzzle pointed at a spot just above her head.

In one motion she stands, leans forward, thrusts the sword between the man's legs. The Kalashnikov lets out a signature burst, the shots flying over her shoulder. The man's face registers shock and terror as she swings the sword upward in a great arc, catching the man in the groin and completely severing his left leg at the hip. Aisling elbows him in the chest and throws him into the boulder, and he drops his rifle and goes into shock. Aisling jumps sideways into the path as a thirtysomething woman with a shotgun rounds the boulder. The woman manages to pull the trigger just as Aisling brings the edge of her sword down on the shotgun's barrel. The blast kicks up dirt between their feet, the buckshot chewing a hundred little craters into the path. But Aisling's strike hits, and the shotgun is useless, its barrel lopped off.

The woman drops the gun and swipes at Aisling's throat with a blade that emerged soundlessly from the cuff of her jacket. Aisling leans far back—the knife just misses her—and then surges forward with the sword. She cleaves it into the Harappan's sternum, right through the heart. Aisling places a foot on her victim's hip and pulls the sword free. The Harappan falls to the side, motionless.

She flips her monocle back down. Sees her dots on the move, the four remaining green dots in a cluster. In 4.6 seconds she hears the report of rifle fire—the telltale slithering sound of the SCARs, the clatter of more Kalashnikovs, three charging bursts from an M60 machine gun. She recognizes each weapon's voice, its character, its part.

The shots ring out for 17 seconds.

As a crescendo she hears the airy pop of Jordan's grenade launcher, followed by a large incendiary explosion.

Silence. The purple dots move. The green ones, their vital warmth already fading, don't.

Threading it all together is the whisper of the rain, the push of a slight breeze, her breath.

Her heart is racing.

"Aisling clear, report back, over."

"Jordan clear."

"McCloskey clear."

"Pop clear."

"I'm nearly there," Marrs says, forgoing jargon.

Checkpoint one is theirs.

Aisling wipes her face. Sees blood on her glove.

Not her blood.

Marrs approaches at her back.

"Jesus," he says when he sees the carnage surrounding Aisling.

Her eyes are wild.

Her face flush, alive, vibrant.

She sheathes her sword. Picks up her two guns.

"Come on, Marrs. This is just the beginning."

SARAH ALOPAY, JAGO TLALOC, RENZO, MACCABEE ADLAI, BAITSAKHAN

Camino Antigua a La Paz, Just West of Tiwanaku Municipality, Bolivia

It's been a long and uncomfortable morning for Sarah. Renzo escorted her through the Tlaloc house, into the kitchens, down a narrow passage to a storeroom dug out of the hillside, into a secluded delivery area outside the estate's walls. The guard who normally patrolled here was slumped against a wall, dead to the world.

"Had to tranq him," Renzo explained.

Renzo took Sarah to a Mazda hatchback and opened a rear passenger door. The seats were folded down. Underneath them was a smuggling compartment.

A small one.

"Just like the 307, huh?" she asked.

"I wish. This one's only good for smuggling."

"What, no weapons? No night-vision HUD?"

"None of that. Now please, get in."

Sarah hesitated. At that point, she could easily have dropped Renzo, stolen the car, and made a break for it. But then she remembered the small army of mercenaries the Tlalocs kept outside their compound. No way she would have gotten through them all, not in that car. And besides, Sarah wanted to hear what Jago had to say for himself. So she threw her bag into the opening, climbed on top of it, folded herself up, held on tight to Earth Key. Renzo pointed to a tube next to her head that led to a reservoir of cold water. He shut her away, got behind the wheel, and drove.

Fast.

The ride was so rough that Sarah was convinced that Renzo was driving straight into potholes in order to punish her.

To needle her.

Irk her.

Anger her.

Which it did.

The ride lasted two and half grueling hours. Sarah was glad that she'd endured so many deprivation trials in the past. Like the time she was locked in a coffin for 62.77 hours. Or when she lived for three full days in an igloo where she couldn't stand or lie down as she waited out a brutal snowstorm—and had to dig herself out from under five feet of snow. Or when she was tied into a chair that was bolted to the floor and left alone, water and food on a table only feet away, a high-pitched chirp sounding every 0.8 seconds, torturing her, until she managed to undo her bindings, which took 14.56 hours.

This car ride was not much different. As in those trials, she turned her mind inward. She pictured fields of autumn wheat and remembered the pleasant ache of her legs after a long run and recalled playing with Tate when they were kids in the tree house on the Niobrara River. But then the car jostled and her legs tingled and she realized that she couldn't feel her feet and that her neck was like a piece of crooked wood. And that made her think again of the coffin, and that made her think of Tate—dead—and Christopher—dead. When her mind went to these places, she became terrified that she would break, that the insanity that had infected her after retrieving Earth Key would return. When these moments came, she turned to the rubber tube and drank the water. And drank and drank until her stomach knotted and her bladder pressed, the discomfort and the pain keeping the crazy at bay.

They stopped only three times. The first, Sarah guessed, was to clear a checkpoint at the bottom of the Tlalocs' hill. The 2nd, she could tell by how the car shifted, was to pick up Jago. And the 3rd was about

40 minutes ago. This stop lasted the longest, and even though her cramped and pitch-black compartment was completely soundproof, Sarah guessed correctly that they were crossing the Bolivian border. And now they've stopped a 4th time. She feels the car rise as two passengers get out. She hears the latch unclick on the smuggling compartment.

The door opens.

The daylight cuts at her eyes like a knife edge. She braces her forearm over her face. She sits up. Blinks and blinks. Her back screams. She rolls her neck. The vertebral cracks echo through her skull. A figure stands before her.

"Can you lift my legs? They're completely asleep," she says, lowering her arm, still blinking.

The figure leans forward and says. "*Sí*, of course."

Jago Tlaloc. Thin, strong, his face shadowed by a hood pulled against the chill of the morning.

Sarah wipes the corner of her mouth, slips Earth Key into a pocket. He takes her legs at the thigh above the knee. He pulls them out and sets her feet on the dirt. She sees no sign of Renzo. Jago kneels, takes the calf of her left leg between both hands and massages it. "I'm sorry about . . ."

The light is less intense. She can make out his features now. The scar. The eyes. The chiseled jaw. Sarah Alopay punches him hard in the cheek. His head whips to the side. Even with the punch, he doesn't stop kneading her aching muscles. He turns back to her. Flashes his diamond smile. "Need to do that again?"

"Yes."

She punches him harder, straight on, snapping his head back and knocking the hood off.

He keeps massaging, deeply, attentively, as if his hands don't share the same body as his head. A drop of blood appears in the corner of his mouth. He ignores it. Looks at her intently.

"Again?"

She sighs. "No . . . maybe later. Christ, Jago. What'd you do to your hair?"

"You like it?"

It's bleached so blond that it's practically white.

"It's awful."

"I had to. How're your legs?"

"Tingly as hell . . . Feo . . . Why did you let them take me?" Her voice softens, even though she wishes it wouldn't.

"I didn't want to. I never would have brought you to my home if I'd known my parents were going to do that. Not with the way you've been . . . feeling."

She doesn't speak. She realizes that, in a way, being imprisoned was good for her. It took her mind off her guilt.

Jago wants to ask her if she's feeling better, but he reconsiders. Instead, Jago pays attention to Sarah's knees, her ankles, her feet. He switches to the other calf. She twiddles her toes. Jago decides that maybe it's better to get to business. Save the personal stuff for later.

"We've been outed, Sarah. Every one of the Players. The world has seen us."

"What? How?" she asks sharply.

"An Liu made a video, showed pictures of each of us. Millions have seen it. Hundreds of millions. He said that if the people of Earth could come together to kill the eight players that remain, including himself, then Abaddon would go away."

"No."

"_Sí._"

"And they believe him?"

"Some do."

"So your hair—that's a disguise?"

"Not a very good one. There's no hiding this scar." He pulls the hood back over his head.

Sarah leans out of the car and peers around. The landscape is bare and desolate and empty. "I think you're safe. This place is dead."

"There are eyes everywhere, Sarah. You know that."

He kneads some more.

His hands feel so good.

"I'll cut my hair," she says. "First chance I get."

"*Bueno.*"

"Dye it black, maybe. Wear some colored contacts."

"*Bueno.*"

She takes his cheeks in both hands. "Jago, I . . . I was going to kill you. If you'd been the one to come for me, I was going to kill you. No questions asked."

Jago hears fear in her voice. And shame. Fear and shame at what she's capable of.

"I know, Sarah. That's why I sent Renzo. I figured you'd at least let him talk, even if only to get a bead on me."

"I . . . I'm sorry."

"What? No. *I'm* sorry, Sarah. That will never happen to you again. Never."

Jago hesitates. He wants to say more, but can't find the words. He thinks of their pursuit of Earth Key, how torn Sarah was between him and Christopher. How torn she was between her old life and the life of a Player. And he thinks of her ancestors, how the Cahokians fought against the Makers, fought for independence, for their lives, for normalcy. They were stronger, in their way, than any of the other lines. Just like Sarah. Maybe this duality he's seen in her, which Sarah is so scared of, maybe it isn't weakness at all.

Maybe it is something to aspire to.

"I will try to be better" is all Jago manages to say aloud.

She smiles. "I might still kill you."

He smiles back. "I don't doubt it."

"My legs feel better. Man, I gotta pee."

He helps her out. She moves around the back of the car and undoes her jeans and lowers herself to the ground, leaning against the bumper. He waits, pushes his fists into the pockets of the hoodie, stares down the road toward their destination. A pickup truck bumps along the road in their direction, but he doesn't pay it any mind. He's thinking about An, and about disguises, and about Earth Key, and about Playing.

Mostly he's thinking about Sarah Alopay.

"But why *did* you let them take me, Jago?" Sarah calls from behind the car.

The truck is close now. Jago is lost in thought. The vehicle bearing down on them finally registers, and he whips his head around as it zooms past, throwing dust and dirt.

Sarah stands. The truck is gone.

She does a little jump as she pulls up her pants. Comes around the side of the car.

"I had to," Jago answers. "They would've killed you outright if I'd put up a fight."

She comes right up to him. Puts her hands on his hips. Grabs the points of his pelvic bone, feels the lean muscles attached to it that lead to his stomach. She presses into him. "Which means Guitarrero and his soldiers will be coming for us this morning, won't they?"

"Without a doubt."

"Then let's get hopping, Feo."

She leans all the way forward and plants a kiss on his lips. A real kiss. Full and wet. She pulls his hips tight. He keeps his hands in his pockets, pushing them into her stomach just below her breasts.

They part.

Jago has never wanted anyone so badly.

Sarah has never wanted anyone so badly.

But now is not the time.

Their faces are inches apart. They can taste each other. Feel each other's heat.

Both of them are so happy to be back together.

So, so happy.

Jago forces his libido down. He answers, "That's why we're out here. To Play." He points his chin across the reddish-tan landscape. "We need to take Earth Key over there, use it, and then get the hell out of South America."

"What's over there?"

"Answers, Sarah Alopay. Answers."

A few minutes earlier, inside the pickup truck. The Mazda comes into view, sitting on the side of the road on the outskirts of a small Andean outpost. Maccabee points. "There they are." Two figures in the distance, one next to the car, the other hunkered behind it, the pudgy man nowhere to be seen.

"The Cahokian *is* with them!" Baitsakhan pushes the gas pedal. The truck, already barreling down the road, accelerates from 109 kph to 131 kph. "Let's run them down."

"Are you crazy, Baits? We could die just as easily."

"We have seat belts. Airbags." Now 141 kph.

The Olmec and the Cahokian are 865 meters away, 22 seconds.

"Get off the shoulder, Baits! Don't do it."

"Why not?" Baitsakhan grips the wheel harder.

"They're here for a reason! They're going to do something with Earth Key, and we need to see what that is!"

"Who cares?"

Now 478 meters, 12.14 seconds.

"I said get off the shoulder, damn it! You could destroy Earth Key."

"No way. It's indestructible."

"But we're not!"

Now 70 meters. Less than two seconds.

"Here we go!"

At the last moment Maccabee reaches across the cab and jerks the wheel to the left and the truck screams past the couple, fishtailing as the wheels jump back to the middle of the dirt road. Jago and

Sarah are lost in conversation, and barely notice the truck. They certainly don't notice who's in it.

Maccabee and Baitsakhan continue toward the settlement, Baitsakhan pounding the dashboard in protest.

Jago and Sarah sit shoulder to shoulder on the Mazda's hood. Renzo is at the caretaker's house across the road, offering a bribe to keep the ancient tourist site of Tiwanaku closed for the morning. They watch An's video on Sarah's phone, and Sarah quickly, almost instinctively, finds the message from didyouseekeplertwentytwob.

"Do you understand it?" Jago asks.

"No, but I'll be able to figure it out. Whichever Player posted this left enough clues here and here." She points to lines in the text that are incomprehensible to Jago. "I think I may be able to break it pretty easily, actually."

"Go for it. You're definitely better at codes than me."

Jago gets her a pad and paper and she starts writing immediately—a string of numbers. Twelve of them, just like there are 12 Players. Jago recognizes the numbers, he'd gotten that far himself. He just didn't know what to do with them.

But she does.

Once she's got the numbers, she takes her phone and navigates to a password-protected site and finds the page she's looking for. "A special decrypter. This kind of code is impossible to break if you don't have"— she taps the numbers—"the key phrase." She punches the numbers into one field and Hilal's gibberish into another, but the result is more gibberish. She reads his post again and again and again. She bites the end of the pen. Jago watches, her tongue playing with the little tip of plastic.

He would rather not be Playing right now.

Not at all.

Sarah snaps her fingers and goes back to her browser and changes the string of numbers and then—presto!—the message changes. They lean together to read what Hilal wrote about Sky Key. About Little Alice.

"*Hijo de puta.* Do you think he's right? Do you think Sky Key is . . . a person? A child?"

"Either that or al-Salt has a major ax to grind with Chopra. But let's assume it *is* true. If he's right about Sky Key, is he also right that killing her will stop Endgame?"

"Only one way to find out."

"Yeah, only one way."

They fall silent. Renzo can be seen half a kilometer away, emerging from a low brick house. He immediately begins trotting toward them.

Sarah says, "Jago, what exactly *are* we doing here?"

Jago tells her about Aucapoma Huayna and what she revealed about Earth Key and how it should tell them the location of Sky Key with far more reliability than some other Player's coded YouTube comment. He says nothing about the Cahokians or about Aucapoma Huayna's order to kill Sarah. He won't kill her, and now's not the time to talk about her line's history.

When he finishes, Sarah says, "So we're here to take Earth Key to this Gateway thing . . ."

"And verify if al-Salt is at least right about Sky Key's location."

"Bingo." Sarah points across the road. "Here's Renzo."

"It wasn't cheap," he says, "but we'll have the place to ourselves for the next two hours."

Sarah and Jago slide off the Mazda's hood and don't bother telling Renzo about Hilal's message. India is on the other side of the planet, and they have work to do.

They get in the car. Drive directly east, the early-morning sun shining into their faces. Sarah eyes a vulture turning wide circles in the northern sky.

A few minutes later they pull into a parking spot near a barricade. Beyond are the ruins of the once-great pre-Incan city-state of Tiwanaku.

They sit for a moment and stare across the plain.

"Am I the only one who's suddenly nervous?" Renzo asks.

"No," Jago and Sarah say together.

"Good."

AN LIU

Shang Safe House, Unnamed Street off Ahiripukur Second Lane, Ballygunge, Kolkata, India

Could it be? Is it *blinkBLINKshiver* is it *BLINKBLINK* is it working?
An leans forward, rubs the necklace between his thumb and index finger. The tics subside. He squints.

Could it really be?

He sits alone in a low-ceilinged room, the only light coming from a collection of glowing screens. He has a keyboard on his knees, a trackball on his chair's armrest, Chiyoko's uncle's sword leaning against the desk. On the back of his monitor, a black 13 is crudely scrawled in permanent marker.

Alone in a blacked-out room and adorned with explosives, the virtual world at his fingertips. No matter where An might find himself, this is the setting in which he's most comfortable, most at ease, most happy. It will be a sad day for An when the Event thrusts humanity back to the dark ages. Other Players worry about their families, their lines. They mourn the extinction of a species.

An mourns the extinction of his internet.

He rubs a lock of Chiyoko's hair between his thumb and index finger. Yes, it *is* working.

As soon as An reached his latest base of operations, he locked himself in and set up his security and armed himself with the Takeda katana and a shoulder band of grenades and a Sig 226 and activated his lair's self-destruct mechanisms and checked his vehicles and made a bowl of rice and had a Coke.

He got right to work finding the others. He entered his PIN: 30700. There were the two blips—the Olmec, who he knows was with the

Cahokian, and one other, probably the Nabataean—that were still in South America. They were on the move, and seemed to be headed toward a showdown. An was able to isolate the IP address Hilal had used to post his encrypted message—a warehouse in an industrial suburb of Las Vegas. After that the Aksumite's trail went cold.

That left the Donghu, the Celt, and the Harappan. An assumed all three were still among the living.

The Donghu remained a complete mystery. Aside from the one poor photo An had dug up, it was as if the boy named Baitsakhan didn't even exist. He gave up trying to find him.

He guessed that the Celt was probably behind the attack in Tokyo, but he wasn't sure where she was now.

As for Chopra, if what the Aksumite had posted was true, than she was undoubtedly at the coordinate location in India.

Sitting and waiting and guarding her precious daughter.

Watching over Sky Key.

An set his attention on these coordinate points. When he searched the skies for a satellite he might use to get a good look at Sikkim, he was *very* pleasantly surprised.

Because for some reason the United States had recently positioned a reconnaissance Spectacle-class satellite over that part of the world.

An knew he had no hope of gaining control of it, but he did know how to access its feed. Which means that now An is seeing what Aisling and her team are seeing.

And what he sees is remarkable.

An can't tell who's who, but he witnesses two groups of humans, five on one side and six on the other, engage in a firefight in a no-man's-land halfway up the Himalayas' eastern range. He sees an explosion, and sees two approach one, and watches as the one dispatches the two quickly at close range. Immediately after, there's a firefight 50 meters to the west and another explosion. The group of six is dead; the other five regroup and move higher into the mountains.

He sits and watches.

Rapt.

He doesn't want to miss anything.

An counts seven people guarding the next flashpoint, which is situated at the opening of a steep-walled valley that leads to the exact point revealed by the Aksumite in his coded message.

And on two other monitors he sees Chiyoko's tracked blips, now in Bolivia, only a kilometer between them. They do not have one hundredth the detail of the action in India, where he can occasionally make out arms and legs and heads, but they're still there. And when one—or both!—of these blips dies, Chiyoko's tracker will register it and tell him.

What luck.

He feels like a god.

He swivels to a small refrigerator and retrieves another can of Coke. Snaps its tab. The hiss of the soda and crack of the seal. He brings the can to his mouth, smells the effervescent sweetness. He sips. His heart rate is so low, he is so calm, he is so happy. He smiles.

"Chiyoko, we will watch, my love. We will watch them fight." His smile grows. He pinches her dried eyelids. Holds them up so she can see. "Look, love. Look at it. They are going to die."

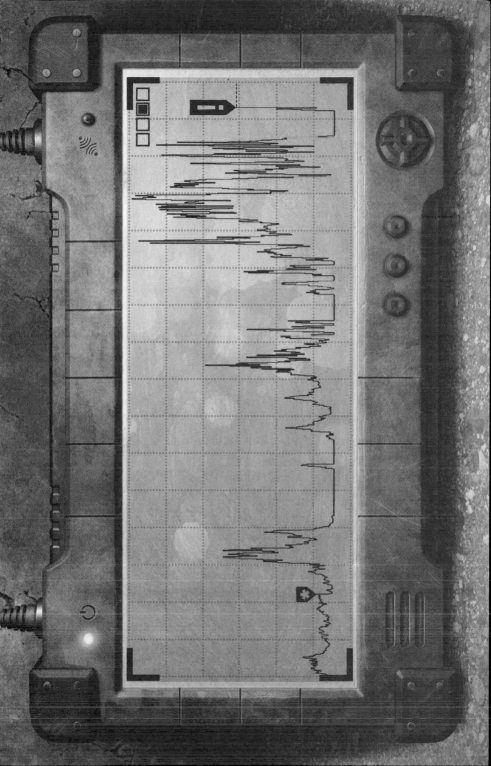

AISLING KOPP, POP KOPP, GREG JORDAN, BRIDGET McCLOSKEY, GRIFFIN MARRS

Approaching Harappan Checkpoint Two, at the Mouth of the Valley of Eternal Life, Sikkim, India

"Hold," Aisling orders.

The others stop. In 50 feet the path makes a left turn, bending from almost due west to southwest.

"What's up?" Pop asks.

Aisling adjusts her monocle. The green dots are a little harder to discern this time. "How many you count, Marrs?" She trusts the observational and technical skills of Marrs the most.

"Seven."

"Me too."

"No question about it. Three in the central location—probably another machine gun, just like before. Two pairs in flanking positions, the northernmost team pretty far from the machine gun. Maybe at foxholes in the woods."

"What're you thinking?" Jordan asks.

"That last machine-gun position was vulnerable from the front. It has to be clear enough for them to shoot, after all."

"You want to put it right down their gullet, huh?" Pop says.

"Yep." She pats the side of her Brügger & Thomet. "Come on, McCloskey. You can be my spotter."

"Just two girls taking a walk in the woods," McCloskey says, rising to follow Aisling. Jordan and Pop sit tight.

The two women disappear into the trees and come to a depression surrounded by oak, alder, and a cluster of tall silver firs. The ground is soft. Fallen leaves are black and purple with rot. The wind whispers through the evergreen needles. Aisling unburdens herself of every unnecessary item and makes a neat pile on the ground. McCloskey does the same. They clamber up the side of the depression toward the fir with the thickest trunk. When they reach it, Aisling lies down, props herself on her elbows, shoulders the rifle, throws the bolt, and peers through the scope. McCloskey is on her left. She uses a Leica laser range finder to spot. She fiddles with the dials and sweeps the area slowly, slowly. "I think I got . . . Yeah. Seven-point-three degrees up; heading is two seventy and thirty seconds. I'll tag it. Your scope should pick it up."

Aisling flips down her rifle's muzzle support and sights the position. At first it just looks like a pile of moss-covered stones, but then she sees it. McCloskey's target, glowing faintly in her scope, has pinpointed the machine gun. It slowly swings back and forth, sweeping the path, searching. And for one brief second during each sweep, when the gun is pointed more or less at them, Aisling catches a glimpse of flesh and hair.

"Mark our location for Marrs. I want him in this spot when we move up."

McCloskey puts down her range finder and enters something on the soft keypad on her forearm. "Done."

"You see that, Marrs?"

He answers, "Crystal. Over."

"Marrs, double-time off the path and take up this position," Aisling says. "I want you right here on sniper support. I'll leave my rifle, if that's all right. I'll be lighter, and it'll already be set for you. Over."

"Roger that. Already hoofing. ETA is three minutes and twenty seconds. Over."

"Pop, Jordan—start your approach from the south flank. Do not engage. Hold when you're two hundred feet shy. Give me three clicks on the comm when you reach position."

"Got it, Ais. We're moving now."

A moment of silence in the woods. Aisling raises her head from the scope and looks around. "Beautiful out here, isn't it?"

McCloskey doesn't look around but says, "It is."

"I've done a lot of training at altitude, but that was all in Alaska or the Canadian Rockies. This is a whole other ballgame. You ever been here before?"

"No offense, Aisling, but when I'm staring down huge machine guns that want to kill me, I generally don't feel like small talk."

Aisling puts her eye back to the scope. "Fair enough." Pause. "It is beautiful out here, though."

Aisling isn't much for small talk either, and she hates herself for even doing it. But she's doing it for a reason. She's doing it to avoid what she really wants to say: *I hope I get to snipe this little girl too. I hope I can take her life from a distance. I don't want to do it up close, McCloskey. I don't know if I'll be able to.*

Her thoughts are interrupted by Marrs on the comm. "Coming up behind you." Fifteen seconds later he stops in the depression. "Here," they hear him say at their backs.

"Sit tight," Aisling says over her shoulder.

"Will do."

Aisling asks, "How many dots in the nest, Marrs?"

"Still three."

Maybe we'll get lucky, Aisling thinks.

Click. Click. Click.

"That's the signal. Ready, McCloskey?"

"Ready. Eyes on."

"Okay. Game time."

McCloskey tags the target again. Aisling sees it clearly. She puts her finger on the trigger, applies the slightest pressure.

The Harappan machine gun sweeps across the path from left to right. She catches the patch of skin and hair. Doesn't fire. Waits. The gun stops, begins to move back.

She pushes the air from her lungs. Squeezes so slightly. Just another millimeter and the round will go. She prepares her shoulder for the recoil. Empties her mind. Forgets about the beauty of this place, forgets about the Chopra girl they're here to kill.

The patch of skin. The hair. The trigger. *The shot.* The clap of the hammer, the hiss of the suppressor. The instantaneous spray of blood half a kilometer away. The slumping machine gun.

Aisling throws the bolt reflexively, readies another round, squeezes, squeezes. Doesn't breathe. Doesn't fire.

McCloskey blurts, "There! To the—"

But Aisling has already seen it. Another clap. Another hiss. Another spray of blood as one of the people in the nest did the unthinkable and in their shock and confusion stood for the briefest of moments.

It was all Aisling needed.

"Two down!" Aisling says. "Pop, Jordan—go! McCloskey and I will take the northern position."

Without saying another word, Aisling spins and slides into the bottom of the depression. McCloskey follows, but she's not nearly as fast. Aisling flips her HUD monocle into place, snags the SCAR assault rifle, takes off at a dead sprint. Branches lash her face and arms, leaves and grass bunch around her ankles, dirt gets in her boots, rainwater in her eyes. A few seconds later, a response comes from the machine-gun nest: only 11 shots, probably firing blind to flush out Marrs. Two quick suppressed reports of her sniper rifle answer, splitting the damp air. Marrs says over the comm, "Missed! But no one's getting on or off that gun without me hitting them! Get in there!"

Nine seconds later, Aisling hears Pop and Jordan clash with their enemies. A patter of gunfire rings through the valley. The mute on Pop's comm flicks off for a moment, and Aisling hears him grunt. He's either been hit or he's fallen or he's fighting them up close and personal.

She hopes he's all right.

She is only 60 feet from her pair of adversaries. She sees them. A woman and a man in a metal blind wedged between two giant birch trees. They're scanning the trees, but not in her direction.

She unhooks a smoke grenade and pulls the pin and lobs it toward them. It arcs through the air, already pluming, and hits the ground between them, creating a cloud. Aisling turns hard right, going down a slope, runs 20 feet, turns left toward their position, and kicks her sprint into the highest gear as the ground levels out. They fire through the cloud, at where she used to be.

They're doing exactly as they're supposed to.

She sees the birches, comes up behind the two Harappan soldiers. The woman catches Aisling in her periphery and spins, prefiring with her M4. Aisling returns a quick burst in full auto. The SCAR is an amazing rifle. Fluid and a little heavy, but almost no recoil. All her shots—a burst of three—hit the target.

The exposed neck of the Harappan woman.

Her body is thrown into the metal wall of the blind.

Aisling drops and slides forward, like a runner going hard into second base, as a burst of bullets zing overhead. She slides into the blind, right next to the man. She overestimated how close the sheet of metal was, and her feet slam into it. The man is quick. He stomps down on Aisling's rifle, driving the receiver into the ground, pinning her right hand and arm.

The man swings his own rifle around. As he does, Aisling walks her feet up the metal partition, vaulting into a shoulder stand. Her feet smash into the side of his face before he gets a bead on her, but his gun goes off, and several rounds penetrate the ground less than two feet from her head. Her ears ring. Dirt and rocks are thrown everywhere. Several pieces strafe her face painfully.

The man stumbles and Aisling pops up. He's ready, though, kicks her in the arm and knocks the SCAR from her grip. She punches him in the throat and he stumbles. She reaches out, stops him from falling by grabbing his rifle, and wrenches it out of his hands. Before she can bring it around, he kicks again, striking the rifle's stock. It's knocked out of Aisling's hands and clatters against the trunk of one of the birch trees. Aisling reaches over her head with both hands to grab the hilt of her sword. But this is another miscalculation. The man lunges and grabs her entire face, his long and powerful fingers wrapping her cheeks, his palm smashing her nose. He throws her against the other tree, her head snaps back, and she's stunned. He keeps one hand on her face, the heel just under her chin, pushing back and up, fingers digging into the hollows of her cheeks. With his other hand, the man pulls a knife and—

"HEY!"

The man's eyes flick toward the woods.

And a blast as loud as a cannon. Even though he's wearing an armored vest, the man's chest explodes and Aisling is splattered again with blood. He loses his grip on her and falls, dead.

Panting, Aisling turns to see McCloskey holding up a giant Colt Peacemaker, its barrel trailing a blue wisp of smoke just like in the movies.

"Thanks," Aisling says.

"Don't mention it."

Aisling picks up her rifle and moves out of the blind. She readjusts her helmet and the HUD over her right eye.

"North flank taken," Aisling says with relief. She raises her eyebrows to McCloskey. The meaning is clear—Aisling got lucky.

McCloskey shrugs. "We knew we'd need luck today. So far so good."

"Southern flank taken," Jordan says. "Pursuing a lone bogey."

As if on cue they hear more gunfire from the south—two bursts from a SCAR and the *pop-pop-pop-pop-pop-pop-pop-pop* of a pistol being emptied, followed by another burst of rifle fire.

They hear Pop cry out over the comm. Aisling's heart skips a beat. "Pop!"

Pop heaves. "Just . . . in . . . the vest." He takes a deep breath. "I'm fine. Get that bitch."

Aisling and McCloskey angle toward the green dot moving through the woods. They'll converge with Jordan at the machine-gun nest. As they get closer, Aisling can see there's still one more Harappan holding that position. He must hear them coming. He pokes his head out, and

403

then there's another muted report from the 338.

Marrs howls, "Ha-ha! Gotcha, you bastard! Nest is clear!"

"Nice!" Aisling says. The remaining green dot zigs and zags like a confused rat in an ever-shifting maze.

"Almost on her!" Jordan says.

The green dot turns due west.

But then it stops.

And disappears.

"What the?" Aisling says as she and McCloskey burst out of the woods right by the machine gun. Three bodies lie there. Pop jogs out of the woods on the other side.

"She's underground!" Jordan says. "Come 'ere!"

Pop joins Aisling and McCloskey as they run forward. Aisling gives her grandfather a concerned look, but his eyes and a wan smile say that he's fine, that he's had a lot worse.

Thank the Makers, Aisling thinks.

After a few more seconds they reach Jordan. He's inspecting the ground with a small handheld device, a discarded and racked PPK near his feet.

"Where the hell is she?" Aisling asks as she skids to a stop next to him.

"A tunnel. Right here. She wasn't armed."

Sure enough, they see the outlines of a metal trapdoor in the ground. Aisling kneels next to Jordan. "Was it Shari?"

"Couldn't tell," Jordan answers. He looks at his device. "I'm not detecting any bomb residue."

Aisling thrusts her rifle into McCloskey's hands and draws her sword. She holds it in her left hand, point down like a dagger, and unholsters a Beretta pistol on her thigh. She brings her hands together and says, "Open it. I'm going in."

Pop places a hand on her forearm. "One of us shou—"

"No, one of you shouldn't. *I'm* the Player. This is the way it's gotta be. Open the damn door, Jordan."

Jordan doesn't say anything. Just grabs the iron ring and lifts. A hole in the ground, three feet across, eight feet deep, a tunnel, weak orange light inside. "Radio will work down there but not your HUD," he says. Aisling pulls off her helmet and hands it to Jordan. "Won't need it." She peers down. "See you in a minute."

And then she jumps in and disappears.

Tiwanaku

No one knows what the native inhabitants of this ruin called their impressive city-state. No one knows because the people are gone, vanished, spirited away.

What is known is that they flourished over 2,000 years ago, though some maintain that their culture, and certainly the roots of their culture, go back many thousands of years before that.

They were masters of agriculture. They conquered not through war but through soft power: culture, religion, trade. They ritually sacrificed men to their gods, disemboweling them and quartering them alive and leaving their remains for the people to see and marvel at atop their high-stepped pyramid.

They worshipped Viracocha, who looked over them from the lintel of the Gateway of the Sun, and another god whose name is unknown, a being with 12 faces, who is always depicted as being worshipped by 30 faces. The god of the seasons, of the march of time, of the calendar, of the wheeling stars and the solar disc.

And they were grandmasters of stone. Cutting exact and intricate angles from andesite, demonstrating their advanced knowledge of geometry and, by the placement of their stones, the stars and moon and the planets and the Earth itself.

No one knows how they quarried their rock, or transported it over great distances without use of the wheel, or worked it into such intricate and massive structures.

No one knows how they learned all of this, or who taught them.

But some.

But some—somewhere, sometime—some do.

MACCABEE ADLAI, BAITSAKHAN, SARAH ALOPAY, JAGO TLALOC, RENZO

Tiwanaku, Bolivia

"What're they doing?" Baitsakhan asks, bouncing in his seat. His anger over not being allowed to ram the others into vehicular oblivion has faded, but he's still itching to kill.

They took the pickup off-road north of the monument and parked it next to a low rise of earth, obscuring the truck from three sides. Maccabee leans out the passenger window with the binoculars.

"They're talking. Getting weapons."

"What kind?"

"The usual. Guns. Knives. Looks like the Cahokian has a hatchet. Don't see any explosives."

"I hope the hatchet's sharp. I'll scalp her with it."

"That'd be fitting."

"Scalping an enemy is always fitting," Baitsakhan says, apparently unaware that some Native Americans were famous for taking scalps after a battle. He flexes his robotic fingers. "After I have her hair, I will crush her skull and brains in my new hand."

"Wonderful," Maccabee says sarcastically. He lowers the binoculars. "We'll go on foot. If we stay to the west, we'll be at their backs. Once they reach the temple, we can skirt east and get close, using the road and the ruins for cover. Then we can surprise them."

"How do you even know they're going to the temple?"

"I guessed." Maccabee has had about enough. He can't understand why Baitsakhan knows so little of their ancient history, of the Makers, of the origins of humanity. "This is Endgame, Baitsakhan," he tries to explain. "And this place might have been the greatest city ever built and used by the Makers."

"To do what?"

"You really don't know?"

"No."

"To visit us. To teach us. To *change* us. And to launch themselves back into the cosmos."

"I don't like to think about those things."

"No kidding. Now let's get off our butts and do the things you actually *do* like to think about."

"Yessss . . ."

Maccabee slips the orb into his backpack and jumps out. Swings around to look in the bed of the truck. A fat black fly skitters over the dried blood left by the Tlaloc mercenary he killed.

Buzzes.

Feeds.

Maccabee unzips a black duffel bag. Opens it. The fly takes off. Inside are guns. All new. All perfect. All ready. They tool up. They each have their ancient blades, forged in antiquity, wielded by hundreds of ex-Players over the years, their peerless edges combining for 7,834 kills. They each take a Glock 20 and an HK G36. Rigged next to each rifle's scope is a compact parabolic mic that has a range of 200 meters. Maccabee hands Baitsakhan an earpiece, takes one for himself. They turn them on. Test the mics.

"One two, one two."

They check out.

They leave the truck and bend low and start toward their prey.

Jago and Sarah and Renzo approach the ruin from the southeast, passing the massive Akapana step pyramid on their right. Cut and dressed stones are strewn around the site as if dropped from the hands of giants. Everything but the sky and clouds is a shade of light red or ocher or dusty yellow.

"You should see it in the summer," Jago says. "The ground is carpeted in green grass and bright yellow flowers."

Sarah wishes she could.

They walk farther and come upon the wall of the old temple. It's a patchwork of red sandstone cut into squares and rectangles.

They reach the corner of the wall, only seven feet high, and Jago holsters his pistol and grabs the stone and climbs, as agile and effortless as a cat. Sarah and Renzo do the same, Sarah just as gracefully, Renzo with more effort.

Sarah expects the other side of the wall to also be seven feet tall and for them to drop into an enclosure, but instead it's only a few inches to the ground. The wall is more of a retaining structure than a barrier. They find themselves at the corner of a wide courtyard, 425 feet east to west and 393 feet north to south. The ground is level and clean but covered in a fine dusting of red dirt. Footprints from tourists and guides are everywhere, and also from the small animals that inhabit this place at night. To their right is a tall carved-stone statue surrounded by a low chain-link fence. The statue is of a man with rectilinear features, his feet together, his hands on his stomach, his block-like head topped with a hat.

Jago points at it. "The Monolith of the Frail, or the *Ponce Stela*. And down there"—he indicates the wide courtyard-within-a-courtyard sunken in the center—"is the Kalasasaya. The central temple and meeting point of ancient man and the Makers."

Sarah takes a few steps forward. "It's pretty impressive, Jago. The Cahokians don't have anything like this. Aside from a few earthen mounds, it's all been buried or lost."

Lost, Jago thinks, recalling the fate of the Cahokians. *Lost and destroyed in punishment for your line's insolence. No, its bravery.*

Jago shrugs. He can't bring this up now. "It isn't the Great White Pyramid or anything, but yeah. It's pretty impressive."

Renzo walks north. "Come on. No time for an ancient alien architecture lesson."

Jago nods and points across the courtyard. Sarah follows with her eyes. "We're going there," the Olmec says. "The Gateway of the Sun."

Maccabee and Baitsakhan drop to the dirt and crawl behind a berm. Baitsakhan says, "I don't think they saw us."

"No. If they had, we'd already be fighting."

Baitsakhan brings his rifle to the firing position. Sights through the scope. "One, two, three, done. Pop pop pop. Take kill win."

Maccabee pushes Baitsakhan's rifle's muzzle into the dirt. "Not yet."

Baitsakhan blows out his cheeks. "Fine. But one of these days we're going to do something my way."

"Patience," Maccabee says, knowing it's like telling a tornado to be patient. "We have to see what they see." He clicks the power switch on the parabolic mic mounted on his rifle. "And hear what they hear."

AISLING KOPP

Underground Tunnel, Valley of Eternal Life, Sikkim, India

The air is warm and damp. The dirt walls are close, the ceiling low, the ground uneven.

Aisling walks straight for 54 paces. A trio of pipes run the length of the wall next to her ankles. The pipes give off heat. There are small lightbulbs on one wall at head height every 15 feet, their looped filaments giving off a pleasant orange glow. When she passes through these illuminated sections, she sees many footprints in the dirt.

But she sees the newest prints too.

A small foot in smooth-soled shoes. Light. Unburdened. But hasty.

Aisling moves quickly. Maybe it *is* Shari Chopra.

The tunnel turns slightly to the left, revealing a larger room. The left wall is carved from the rock of the mountain, and it extends into the room 12 feet. On the far side of the room is a tangle of larger pipes, valves, and wheels. This must be some kind of way station for whatever they're pumping into or out of the fortress—heat, water, sewage. The room opens to her right. If the Harappan stopped and is waiting to ambush her, this is where the trouble will be. Aisling knows it, and the woman she's chasing knows it too.

Aisling crouches and advances slowly. More of the room comes into view. More pipes pretzeling around one another on the back wall. A bright fluorescent light on the ceiling. No sign of the woman.

Aisling is at the edge of the tunnel. She spins to clear the room. Aims. Is ready to fire.

But no one is there.

A dead end.

"You see her topside?" Aisling asks over her radio as she continues to sweep the room.

"Negative. Nothing," Jordan answers.

"I don't—"

She's cut off by a clank and then a loud hissing sound as a plume of white steam shoots from one of the pipes. She ducks and flinches, shielding her face with her shoulder. She's scalded on her ear and part of her neck but not badly.

As she spins away from the steam, something hard and metal smashes across her hands. The pommel of the sword and the top of the Beretta take the brunt, but it still hurts like hell. The gun sails into the tunnel and the sword falls too, landing point-first in the dirt and standing upright.

The next swing is aimed at her face. Aisling spins away from the steam and into the room, backed up on the far wall.

Trapped.

There, emerging from the shadows and the thicket of pipes, is an older woman. She blocks the only escape. She wields a pipe roughly the size of a baseball bat. The woman—mid-60s, but strong and vital and substantial-looking—lunges at Aisling, swinging again, this time for the body.

Aisling's only option is to duck, but that would mean she would get hit in the head instead of the ribs. So she raises her arm and lets the pipe slam into her. She feels two ribs crack, even through her bulletproof vest, and she's going to be bruised as hell, but she's had worse.

At the moment of impact, she clamps her arm over the pipe, pinning it against her side.

With her free hand, Aisling reaches across her body, pulls a knife from its sheath on her left forearm, and slashes at the woman.

But the older woman is fast.

Very fast.

Without letting go of her end of the pipe, the woman slaps Aisling's knife hand. The blade drops to the floor.

Aisling snags another knife from a sheath on her thigh. Stabs forward.

This one finds flesh. Aisling buries it deep in the woman's shoulder. Aisling tries to twist the blade, but the woman jerks backward and takes it with her. It hangs out of her shoulder. She doesn't release her end of the pipe.

She doesn't even cry out.

Instead, the woman smiles.

She says, "You won't find her, Player. You won't take Sky Key."

The woman pushes the pipe, trying to back Aisling against the wall.

"I'm not here to take Sky Key. I'm here to destroy it."

The woman seethes. "You mean you're here to kill a *little girl*?"

Aisling's foreboding hits her again, but she beats it back. "Yes. That's . . . that's exactly what I mean."

The woman spits, "You're a monster!"

She pushes into the pipe with all her strength, which is more than Aisling can handle. She releases her end and squirts between the woman and the wall, making a break for her Falcata. She ducks instinctively when she hears the wet sound of ripping flesh just before her knife flies overhead. She slides onto the dirt floor, grabs her sword from the entryway, and pops back up.

The woman is right on her, swinging the pipe wildly.

Aisling is quicker this time. She parries the pipe and plants her back foot and thrusts. The blade slides into the woman effortlessly, through skin and ribs and heart and out her back.

Aisling tightens her grip and pushes the blade all the way to the hilt.

They are face-to-face. The woman drops the pipe. It clunks on the ground. The steam hisses. Blood flows from her mouth and nose.

"I'll see you in hell," the woman chokes.

Aisling's green eyes are wide. She thinks of the girl she's going to kill, of the haughtiness of the Makers, of her father's madness and his prescience, of the unfairness of it all, of the supreme perversion of Endgame.

"No, you won't," Aisling seethes. "We're already here."

xvi

SHARI CHOPRA, JAMAL CHOPRA, JOVINDERPIHAINU JHA, PARU JHA

Operations Room, सूर्य को अन्तमि रेज, Valley of Eternal Life, Sikkim, India

"Helena!" Shari cries, her chest heaving, her knees shaking. Helena and Shari didn't always see eye to eye, but she was an esteemed member of Harappan line and Shari loved her.

"I will kill the Celt! I will kill her myself!"

The rest are dumbstruck.

They stare at a very large flat-screen bolted to the stone wall. Its image is subdivided into 14 sections. Each subdivision on the screen shows the vital signs of Harappan men and women sent out to guard सूर्य को अन्तमि रेज.

To guard Sky Key.

A set of small speakers broadcasts the audio of everything that's happened. Shari and Jamal and Paru and Jovinderpihainu have heard it all. The explosions, the gunfire, the splintering bones, the severed limbs, the cries, the moans, the death.

All of it on their side.

Jamal is next to Shari, his teeth clenched, his heart pounding. Jov is in a chair, straight-backed, still showing strength, not despairing. Paru leans on the desk, pushing it so hard it seems like he might crush it. Helena's heart rate has just flatlined.

"We're being slaughtered," Paru observes. "How is this happening?"

"It's as if the Celt's people can see us, like they know where we are," Jamal says, his voice dripping with fury, bitterness, fear. "Chem and Nitesh were sniped before they even fired a shot!"

"And yet Helena met the Player face-to-face. She had a chance to kill

Kopp," Shari points out, her anger subsiding, her training kicking in. She allows the horror and the tragedy and the disappointment to flow through her. She does not resist. *Let it flow.* This is her strength. To be able to bend. She knows it. She must stay here and not give in to anger.

The others are not as resilient.

"But how are they doing it?" Shari's father demands again.

Jov bobbles his head in the Indian fashion. "We've underestimated our enemies."

"No." Shari claps to get their attention. Her voice is already cool. She's surprised by how quickly she's able to compartmentalize Helena's death. All of these Harappan deaths. "*They* have underestimated *us*. They've waltzed past the first two checkpoints. Next comes overconfidence. And with that comes mistakes. We will hold. They will experience death this day, I guarantee it."

Jov nods. Shari continues. "Whatever their advantages may be, we still have the upper hand. They are but five people. We will not let the Celt murder my child." She looks each of them in the eye and repeats, *"We will hold."*

At least one of them agrees with Shari. It is Pravheet, sitting in his machine-gun nest outside the fortress. He says over the radio, "They won't pass the Elbow. I will wait for all of them to enter that alleyway and mow them down where they stand."

His baritone voice booms in their ears, a complement to Shari's timbre, which is strong but high and thin and young.

They listen to Pravheet. The disavowed killer. The one whose blood runs like ice.

And what they all know is that he and his Vulcan cannon aren't even the last line of defense on the path to सूरय को अन्तिम रेज. If the Celt manages to reach the courtyard that marks the main entrance of the Harappan fortress, she will be met by 42 more Harappan soldiers standing shoulder to shoulder.

417

Ready to fight.

Ready to die.

"They will not reach our Player or our precious daughter," Pravheet proclaims.

Yet even with her calm restored, one thing still bothers Shari. The Celt was surprisingly forthright when she spoke to Helena. She is not here to win. She is here to kill Little Alice. To try to stop the Event from ever happening.

Shari understands that this desire makes Aisling one of the good ones. One of the Players who recognizes the keplers as petty, and that the game should be stopped at any cost.

Which, by inference, makes her, Shari Chopra, one of the bad ones.

One of the ones who might allow billions to die to save one life.

Jov made a convincing argument for why they cannot sacrifice her beloved Little Alice, but there is still a small part of her that wonders: *Should I not try to end this myself? What if the Aksumite is right? What if?*

She feels the gun on her hip. Heavy. Hidden. Ready.

She knows that Little Alice is only a few rooms away.

Shari could go to her now.

She could do the unthinkable.

No.

No.

No!

"Jamal," Shari says, the tone of her voice betraying none of her inner turmoil, "take Little Alice to the Depths. Neither the Celt nor any other Player can reach her, my love. No matter what happens, none can be allowed to reach her."

And Shari's stomach feels empty and her throat hollow and her heart nothing more than a machine that pumps blood.

Because she knows what the rest of them do not.

That by "any Player" she might also mean herself.

Jamal sees none of this. He nods and takes his young, brave, steely, and beautiful wife by both wrists and squeezes and kisses her full on the lips. "I will. And I will see you when those people are dead, my love."

Ψ

ℓ SIᴄᴧINᴧ ᴧⱭᴨᴋᴧᴧ ᴧꟻᴛᴨMISᴛℓNᴧ Ψℓ ᴧIⱭ
ᴦᴧMᴇᴧIΨℓ IN ᴋᴧᴈᴧI MᴇINᴧI· Nᴨ ʙᴧᴨᴧM
ᴧI MIᴋᴧℓN SᴨᴍᴧN ꟻᴧᴧᴋᴇINIS
MᴇINIS ΨᴧᴛᴧINᴇI SᴧıhS Nᴧᴨh ⱭIⱭᴧIᴈᴇ·
ⱭᴨᴋΨᴨᴍ ʙᴇᴨᴍᴧNᴧI NI ꟻᴋᴧᴍ MIᴋᴧᴧᴍᴧ
ᴄINᴋᴧNᴈᴧ ᴈᴋᴧᴨhᴛᴧ ᴧᴋ ꟻᴋᴧᴍ ᴋᴨʙIᴛᴧᴨ
ᴛᴧıhᴨN ᴧʙᴋᴧNᴇ ᴦᴧᴈᴋᴧᴨhᴛᴇ ΨᴇI ΨᴧᴛᴧINᴇI
ⱭIᴧᴈᴇᴧᴨN ᴦᴧᴛᴧᴋNᴄᴧN ꟻᴧᴈᴋᴇIN MᴇINᴧNᴧ
ꟻᴋᴧᴍ ᴧ ΨᴧNᴧ ʙᴧᴧᴨ ꟻᴧᴨᴋᴧ
ᴧIʙᴧIN ᴧIΨΨᴧᴨ ᴈᴧᴨΨᴨ· ⱭᴇᴍᴨN ᴨS Ψᴧᴍᴍᴧ
ⱭISᴛᴧ MIΨ SᴧᴋⱭᴧM ᴋᴨᴍℓNᴇ ᴧᴋ ʙᴇᴋᴨN Ψᴨꟻ
MIΨ Iʙᴋᴧ ᴄᴧh ᴧᴋᴧ ᴄᴧh ᴧINᴧᴍᴍᴧ Ɑᴧᴨᴋᴧᴧ,
ᴦᴧMᴇᴧIΨᴧ IN ʙℓᴋℓM ᴋᴨᴍℓNᴇ ᴧᴋ IN MIS
ΨᴧN ᴋᴧᴈᴧI· hᴧᴨhᴧʙᴧ ᴄᴧh
hᴧᴨhhᴧIᴋᴛᴧʙᴧ ʙᴇᴋᴨN ΨᴧNᴧ Ψᴨꟻ Iᴈᴇ ᴇI
ⱭᴇIS ᴋᴨᴨNᴇIMᴧ Sᴧ ᴨNSIS ꟻᴋᴧⱭISᴛᴧᴈᴧ·

SARAH ALOPAY, JAGO TLALOC, RENZO

Gateway of the Sun, Temple of Kalasasaya, Tiwanaku, Bolivia

The Gateway of the Sun.

Cut from a single 10-ton andesite slab, 9.8 feet high, 13 feet wide.

The arch is cracked clean through at the top, and for many centuries it was broken into two great pieces and lay neglected. It has since been restored by archaeologists and erected in this corner of the Kalasasaya.

It does not stand in its original spot. No. 4,967 years ago it watched over a great field a short distance to the south and west, on the edge of what is now called Pumapunku. Men and women and Makers alike would pass through the Gateway, like a metal detector at a modern airport, on their way to the field beyond, where the Makers had built Earth's greatest prehistoric spaceport.

On the flattened field there was a structure, a two-mile-long set of steel rails that were tied to the Earth with the great interlocking stones that the Makers had trained the men of antiquity to craft. The rails, long since dismantled and destroyed, traveled due west toward the point on the horizon where the sun set on the summer solstice, and they angled up 13.4 degrees, east to west. The westernmost end of the railed ramp rose 2,447.28 feet into the air, and from this perch the Makers' ships were launched into the sky, and into space. Some of the humans who passed through the Gateway in those days were placed on these ships as guests of the Makers, as vassals, as companions. These people were exalted, and celebrated in songs and stories. Songs and stories they would never hear.

For none returned to Earth.

Jago can't help but be impressed as he walks closer to the Gateway, even though it's not nearly as illustrious as it was so many thousands of years ago. Anyone can walk under it now.

Renzo posts himself on the far side of the monument and keeps watch for any sign of Guitarrero or anyone else who might come around to stick their nose in business that doesn't concern them.

Renzo sees nothing but the countryside, vast and empty. He doesn't see the two other Players hiding behind a low hill only a short distance away.

"We're good," Renzo says.

Jago and Sarah get to work.

She gives him Earth Key, and he stands in the opening, his head and shoulders scrunched in order to fit. He pulls a tailor's measure from a pocket, unfurls it, counts the centimeters on the inside of the southern upright. Counts to 121.2 centimeters, two *luk'a*, just as Aucapoma Huayna instructed. He runs the orb laterally across the rock at this exact height, and yes, there, it shakes and jumps from his fingertips and finds a magnetic home in a thumb-sized divot.

He pulls his hand away and hopes and waits.

Sarah cranes her neck. "Anything?"

"*Nada.*" He lets out a long sigh.

Renzo pops his head around the rock. "Why doesn't she try?"

"Good idea." Jago steps from under the arch and Sarah replaces him. She reaches for Earth Key, and as her fingers draw closer, the ball vibrates and spins in place on a gyroscopic axis. It throws heat, a lot of heat. Sarah keeps reaching.

And she touches it.

The far side of the archway goes completely black, as if the air is suddenly full of ink. This startles all three of them, Renzo most of all. One minute he's looking at Sarah, and the next she's blotted out. He runs around the other side to check on the Players, finds them awestruck but unharmed.

After a moment Jago mutters, "You did it."

"I did *something*. But it's just a black space." She raises her hand, moves it toward the surface but doesn't dare touch it. The air directly in front of it is so, so cold.

She turns to Jago. "What do we do now?"

"I . . . I don't know."

As soon as the blackness appears, Maccabee says, "Come on." He and Baitsakhan jump up and sprint. They're only 27 meters away. They keep the archway between themselves and the others, the solid darkness in its center all the cover they need.

Maccabee keeps the rifle raised so that the mic is pointed at the arch. They can hear Sarah and Jago talk.

"It reminds me of the Great White Pyramid," she says of the blackness.

"*Sí.* That portal that teleported us back to the pagoda . . ."

It reminds Maccabee of that too.

Now 15.3 meters.

They hear the other man, the pudgy one, say, "We haven't got much time. Guitarrero's sure to be here soon."

Now 12.1 meters.

Jago says, "If it's a portal too then we have no idea where it'll take us. It could lead anywhere, Sarah. It could drop us off in space, for all we know."

Sarah says, "Or maybe it'll show us something. Let's both touch Earth Key."

"*Sí.* The power of two Players."

Now 8.7 meters. Maccabee and Baitsakhan pass over another ruin. They slow down and move soundlessly.

The other Players still don't know they're not alone.

"Okay, let's give it a try." Jago squeezes next to her, and their fingertips grace Earth Key at the same instant.

And then—

* * *

424

Only 3.7 meters and the blackness changes.

"Look!" shouts the pudgy man.

The Nabataean and the Donghu are only 2.9 meters away. They flinch, ready to shoot, worried that the darkness in the archway might dissipate as suddenly as it appeared, blowing their chance at an ambush.

Instead, a figure appears in the blackness. Both sides show the same image.

Maccabee's eyes go wide as Sarah says, "It's . . . it's a girl."

Jago says, "Is that the girl from An's video . . . the one the Harappan was holding?"

She's chasing something. A peacock. The background changes. It resolves from blackness, turns red and blue. A tapestry hanging on a wall.

A room.

"Oh my God," Sarah says.

"The Aksumite wasn't lying," Jago says slowly.

"No. He wasn't."

Since Maccabee hasn't decrypted Hilal's message, he doesn't know what they're talking about.

But all the same he has a strong, unshakable feeling: *this girl is important.*

And as if to answer just how important, Sarah breathes out, "She really is Sky Key."

And Sarah realizes that maybe she really can stop the game. Stop the horror that she put in motion.

Maybe.

All she has to do is kill this little girl. This one little girl. She already killed her best friend. No reason to think she can't do this too.

It would save millions of lives.

Billions.

To save the world, Sarah must give herself over and become a monster.

Forever.

To save the world.

Maccabee doesn't know what they're talking about, and he doesn't care.

All he cares about now is the girl, this Sky Key.

He must take Earth Key from the stone archway and unite it with Sky Key and Play on. He is so close.

The Donghu understands this too. In that instant both Baitsakhan and Maccabee wonder how much longer their alliance will last.

Baitsakhan stabs the air with his rifle. Maccabee nods. They advance slowly, silently.

They will take Earth Key.

Take it and kill these others.

Now.

Take.

Kill.

Win.

Now only 2.3 meters.

Only 1.5 meters.

Only 0.8 meters.

The Nabataean and the Donghu are poised to shoot, the Olmec and the Cahokian and Renzo completely unsuspecting. All five of them practically standing under the Gateway together.

Maccabee knows that Earth Key is stuck to the side of the stone on his right, just on the other side of the image.

He will take Earth Key.

Now.

The Nabataean. The descendant of Eel and Laat and Obodas, the only son of Ekaterina Adlai. Maccabee Adlai.

He inches forward. Releases the stock of the rifle with his left hand.

Keeps steady, oh so steady. The muzzle is 21.3 centimeters from Sarah's face. Separated by the image of a child, oblivious, smiling.

The girl is right in front of Maccabee. Her dark hair, her smile, her bright eyes, her innocence. And his hand and the muzzle are about to pierce the image. And he is going to have Earth Key and find this girl, this Sky Key, and *he will win!* And he remembers the little tube in his pocket, the thing that can send a signal to Baitsakhan's robotic hand and activate the code embedded there.

He'll have to do that soon.

His fingers are only millimeters from the image when Little Alice's face grows frightened. She glares at Maccabee. Points. Retreats. Opens her mouth. And screams.

She can see all of them.

LITTLE ALICE CHOPRA, JAMAL CHOPRA

The Depths, सूरुय को अन्तमि रेज, *Valley of Eternal Life, Sikkim, India*

The Chopras brought Tarki, Little Alice's favorite companion, to the fortress from their home in Gangtok. He runs from Little Alice. The girl and the bird are in the deepest part of सूरुय को अन्तमि रेज. The most ancient part. The part that was once dug out of the mountainside by Makers and humans together. Jamal told Little Alice that things were happening outside, and that it would be safer here. Little Alice did not question him. She was not afraid.

But now she is.

Little Alice's nightmares have come alive before her eyes. The people chasing her in her dreams and killing Big Alice and hunting her family, these people are in front of her with guns and malice and desire and, yes, even shock and fear on their own faces. And she spins away from these phantoms as her father rushes toward her to sweep his daughter into his arms and hold her and ask her what is wrong and chase away her demons. And Little Alice points at a low and ancient doorway the Makers used thousands and thousands of years ago to travel deep into the heart of the mountain, but that has been filled in with stone for ages.

At first Jamal sees nothing. The peacock zips out of the room as Little Alice points and yells. "There is Earth Key! There is Earth Key! *There is Earth Key!*"

The rock changes.

And Jamal *does* see. A large man with dark hair and a crooked nose and a battered face stretches his fingers through the wall, and a girl with long auburn hair also reaches out, and the wall isn't solid

428

anymore, and Jamal sees other people behind the first two, and beyond that red rocks and the limitless sky filled with the light of the sun.

And then—

SARAH ALOPAY, MACCABEE ADLAI, JAGO TLALOC, RENZO, BAITSAKHAN

Gateway of the Sun, Temple of Kalasasaya, Tiwanaku, Bolivia

Sarah can almost hear the girl scream. She can see her and the young man holding her as they spin away and follow the peacock out of the room.

And in that instant Sarah knows.

The Gateway *is* more than a gateway. It doesn't just look like the portal in the side of the Great White Pyramid; it *is* one of these portals.

And she reaches out and touches the image and

and at the same moment Maccabee touches the image of the terrified girl and

and as soon as they touch the void these two Players are pulled forward. Both disappear from Bolivia, from Tiwanaku, from the Kalasasaya, from the Gateway of the Sun and

and Jago sees Sarah now in this room, fallen unconscious to the floor, another figure mysteriously slumped near her, and Jago calls after the Cahokian and he runs forward and he disappears too and

and Renzo chases his Player faithfully into the portal and

and Baitsakhan sees each of these four idiots tumble across space and time into this room, all four of them unconscious on the floor.

And he's the only one who can see their folly.

He.

Baitsakhan.

Folly because all these people have used this portal without first securing Earth Key.

Baitsakhan calmly walks around the Gateway and slings his rifle over his shoulder and takes a packet of smelling salts from a pocket. He breaks the packet open. The vapors burn his nostrils, but he doesn't care. He tucks the fuming thing into the front of his shirt, right where it opens at the collar, his eyes watering. He holds his left hand over Earth Key and spreads his right hand over the image of the room.

He eyes Earth Key. He breathes. He puts his palm so close. So close to the portal's surface. It is ice cold.

He counts back from five. His eyes streaming with tears from the salts.

Four.

Three.

Two.

One.

And at the same exact moment he grabs Earth Key and touches the image.

And he too is gone.

All that is left is a grand ruin of the ancient world.

Nothing more than a misunderstood tourist attraction for the uninitiated.

An empty archway of stone.

ALL PLAYERS

Kolkata. Over the South China Sea. Sikkim.

An Liu double-takes.

One of the blips in Bolivia disappears for a few seconds as the tracker recalculates its position and then, pop, just like that, it reappears in Sikkim, India!

Not far from where the Celt and her team are headed!

And the other blip in Bolivia disappears as well, and reappears in India as well. An has no idea how it is happening, but these Players are being driven together. And after they fight and beat and kill one another, An will chase what's left of them.

"Let them have each other today, love. Let them do our work for us."

Hilal ibn Isa al-Salt's plane is an hour from its initial descent into Bangkok. He sleeps soundly and knows nothing of what's going on.

If he did know, he would be just as rapt as the Shang.

Just as invested.

Just as hopeful for death.

Except he would be rooting for the good ones. For Aisling. For Sarah. For Jago. The ones who are in India to kill a little girl. The ones who, like him, dream of stopping the game.

But no. Instead he sleeps soundly, the ouroboros on his arm, the device from the ark in his pocket, his ally, Stella, somewhere in the world also Playing, in her own unknown way . . .

The portal set in the wall is closed and gone.

The Maker tech that transported them takes a physical and mental toll.

It hurts.

Numbs.

Stupefies.

Maccabee is out cold. He's facedown on the floor, his rifle under him.

Jago is out too, but his eyes flutter. Consciousness creeps into him slowly.

Sarah rolls back and forth, bumping into Maccabee on one side and Jago on the other, but she is also unaware of what's happened or where she is.

Renzo is awake but barely cognizant of his surroundings. He's on his knees, his forehead to the floor, his head pounding, his ears ringing.

Baitsakhan is up. The smelling salts did their trick, but the portal still asked a price. He bumbles around the far side of the room, his arms loose, his steps unsure, his rifle on the floor, his mechanical fist still wrapped tightly around Earth Key.

He's like a zombie, but coming around.

Coming around more quickly than the others.

He blinks. Blinks. Blinks. The salts burn his nasal passages. His eyes water. *What's that smell?* he wonders. The spike of ammonia. And he remembers. He shakes his head from side to side. Spits on the floor and slaps the salts out of his collar. He spins wildly, still doesn't have full control of his body. But he sees the others.

He won't be a zombie for long.

Aisling rejoined her team and continued up the path into the mountains, and now she and Pop and Jordan and McCloskey and Marrs stop 20 feet short of a switchback on the path.

The last switchback.

A rock wall rises sheer and smooth on their right, and up ahead is a cutout in the stone. The path turns in to it and disappears. The rain has stopped. The sky is gray and growing darker with the setting sun. Marrs takes a knee and consults his field computer.

"Little Bertha confirms it," he says of the drone that's been moving

433

above them the whole time. He points at the cutout. "That's the only way in. A straight shot up to the fortress' courtyard."

"Whoop-de-do," Jordan says. He eyes the little green dot on his HUD. The one that's around the next turn and higher up the mountain, the one that hasn't moved an inch since they started their trek. "Poor guy's been waiting a long time, hasn't he?"

"Yeah, man," Marrs says.

"How big you think his gun is?" McCloskey asks.

Jordan holds out his arms as far as they'll go. "Bigger than this. He's probably sitting up there thinking how grand it'll be to turn us into mincemeat."

Aisling stares skyward, tries to pick out Little Bertha's underside as it floats high above. But she can't. "Let's straighten him out."

Marrs says, "Roger that."

McCloskey already has the range finder out. She screws a long and slender periscope to its lens. "I'll paint the target."

Aisling shifts her attention to the conglomeration of dots farther up and in the courtyard. "That big group of people must be waiting for us too. Just in case we pass this next flashpoint, right?"

"Who knows," Jordan says. "Maybe they're knee-deep in some kind of ritual. Maybe they're communing with the aliens. Whatever they're doing, I can't imagine they'll be too jazzed to see us when we *do* get up there."

"Exactly what I was thinking," Aisling says. Then she snaps her finger and asks, "Marrs, how sensitive is that heat seeker? Could it hone in on the collective body heat of that welcome party?"

Jordan smiles. "Absolutely. We used one to torch an Al Qaeda camp in the middle of the night in Bahrain a few years back, didn't we, guys?"

"Sure did," Marrs says.

McCloskey grins. "Warmest thing that night was a bunch of broke-dick terrorists farting to keep themselves toasty. That was a good mission," she says wistfully.

"So it'd work here too?"

Marrs nods. "It should. We'll have to do them first, though. If we do it the other way around and blast the guy on the gun, the heat seeker will go there."

"Let's do it," Aisling says. "Take out the courtyard first."

Jordan claps her on the shoulder. "I like the way you think. You'd've made a hell of a case officer, Kopp."

Aisling shrugs. "Maybe in another life, Jordan. Maybe in another life."

"They're here, Shari! They're here!" Jamal yells over the radio. He's running. Little Alice is babbling and crying in the background, saying "Earth Key! Earth Key! Earth Key!"

"What?" Shari asks, still in the operations room with Paru and Jov. "Who's here?"

"I saw three for sure, maybe more."

"Three what?"

"Players, Shari! They used some kind of . . . some kind of *teleporter*!"

"But that's impossible!"

"I'm telling you, they're here!"

"Which ones? What are they doing now?"

"I don't know. I grabbed Alice and ran!"

Shari looks at Paru and Jov frantically. "Take her to the storeroom, Jamal. Lock yourselves in. Don't open it for anyone, do you hear? No one but me."

"I'm nearly there," he says, the signal on his radio getting weaker. "Do you hear me?"

"I . . . h— yo—"

"I'm coming, Jamal!"

"I—lo— ou—"

His voice cuts out.

Jov says, "Go, Shari. Take the guards standing in the hall."

"I'm coming too," Paru says. Shari doesn't want her father to walk headlong into so much danger, but how can she protest? They're fighting on two fronts now, and the Harappan line hangs by a thread.

Jov says, "I'll radio Ana in the courtyard and divert as many as I can to the Depths. Pravheet will hold them off at the Elbow. Fear not, my love: Pravheet will hold them off."

Shari kisses Jov on the forehead. "All right." She looks to her father. "Come." And then she spins and runs out of the room, grabbing the two large and heavily armed men standing outside the door.

As they run, she works her hand into her clothing and pulls out her pistol.

Is the Donghu here? she wonders.

A not-so-small part of her hopes that he is.

LITTLE BERTHA

2,003 Feet over Aisling Kopp, Valley of Eternal Life, Sikkim, India

Little Bertha paddles gently on the breeze. A mindless sentinel waiting for instructions.

Little Bertha gets its instructions.

Little Bertha rises 1,436.7 feet to acquire its target.

Little Bertha spins in place 48 degrees counterclockwise.

Little Bertha arms missile A. The heat seeker.

Little Bertha recalculates. Sends its targeting info to the ground to reverify.

The target is reverified.

Little Bertha releases missile A. It falls 45 feet and ignites, its tail dropping before it levels out and swings in an arc and looks for the low heat signature it's been told to search for.

Missile A finds the signature and zips straight down into the crowd of people who are lined shoulder to shoulder under the only entrance to सूर्य को अन्तिम रेज. Lined up, armed, waiting. Not mindless sentinels, but unsuspecting ones.

They didn't plan for Little Bertha.

The crowd doesn't even register the missile. The warhead explodes 15 feet before impact. The air ignites, and a spherical shock wave pushes out in all directions, throwing shrapnel and phosphorous and fire.

Dirt and stones and weapons and clothing and straps and shoes and bodies and ears and limbs fly everywhere.

Silence follows.

Fifteen are killed instantly. Seven more will bleed out. Six are unconscious and severely concussed. Only two survive and are awake.

And one of these has lost his right arm just below the elbow.

Ana Jha, Shari's mother, is among the dead.

She'd just spoken to Jov. She was going to send 20 Harappan warriors to the Depths to defend Sky Key from the other threat.

But the warriors are not coming to help Shari or Sky Key.

Little Bertha waits for its next set of instructions.

If Little Bertha could peer through the mist, it would see Pravheet rising from the Vulcan cannon as soon as the explosion goes off, his heart pounding, tears streaming down his cheeks. It would see McCloskey lying on her stomach just at the edge of the Elbow. It would see her slide forward, push the periscope that's attached to her range finder around the corner. It would see her adjust, search, seek. It would see that 544 feet away from McCloskey is a giant gray Gatling gun.

She paints the gun with the laser just as the man sits back down and takes the gun's handles.

A fraction of a second later Little Bertha gets its next set of instructions.

Little Bertha spins again. Sends the instructions back to Marrs's computer for reverification. Receives reverification.

Little Bertha releases missile B.

This one drops free and ignites and makes a corkscrew in the air and then takes off for the tagged position.

There is the very brief but unmistakable drill-like sound of the Vulcan spraying 76 rounds in just 0.7 seconds. And there is a 2nd explosion.

The Vulcan is silent.

The Harappan are routed.

Little Bertha doesn't care.

Little Bertha drops back to 2,003 feet directly above Aisling Kopp, where it hovers and waits. A piece of mechanized metal, the decisive factor in a battle it can't know or understand.

A mindless sentinel.

It hovers and waits.

AISLING KOPP, POP KOPP, GREG JORDAN, BRIDGET McCLOSKEY, GRIFFIN MARRS

The Elbow, सूरय को अन्तमि रेज, *Valley of Eternal Life, Sikkim, India*

Aisling and Pop and Jordan and Marrs run toward the opening to get McCloskey and carry on into the Harappan fortress.

But when they reach the turn in the path, Aisling stops dead in her tracks.

The others stop too.

"BRIDGE!" Jordan yells. He falls forward, drops to his knees.

McCloskey is on her face, her shoulders soaked with blood.

Jordan rolls her over, but there's no point.

Her eyes are open.

Vacant.

Gone.

The Vulcan was destroyed, but its single burst of fire hit the rocks near McCloskey. And even though she wasn't in the line of fire, the huge rounds ricocheted and broke off hunks of stone and sent them flying in every direction.

Dust still hangs in the air.

"Bridge!" Jordan wails again, probing the top of her head with his fingers. He grabs her, holds her, wipes smeared blood from her cheeks. He fights back tears, but they're there, wanting to come out. Marrs moves next to them, kneels, puts his hand over McCloskey's face and closes her eyes. Aisling removes her jacket and drapes it over McCloskey. She puts a hand on Jordan's shoulder. She doesn't have words for this situation. In truth, it's less McCloskey's death that stings as the humanity on display from Jordan, his sarcastic veneer set aside.

These are people—assholes, sometimes, allies, ones she doesn't fully trust, but ones that have pledged their lives to her nonetheless.

Aisling steps around the Elbow and sights down her rifle five degrees east of due north. She gazes at the fire raging where the missile exploded. The path is before her.

It is safe.

They can continue.

Jordan lowers McCloskey gently to the ground. Wipes the back of his hand across his face. Aisling breaks the silence. Her voice is steady and cold. "We all knew what we were getting into. We have to make sure she didn't die in vain." Pause. "We have to make sure none of these people did. We have to honor Bridget and all of these Harappan. We have to honor the lines by stopping the game. Today. Now."

Aisling Kopp starts walking, at first slowly, then faster, finally breaking into a run toward the fortress.

Pop follows her immediately.

Marrs looks at Jordan. "See you up there," he says before following too.

Jordan leans over and kisses McCloskey's forehead through Aisling's jacket. "Don't you fucking move," he says, trying to disarm his grief with the humor he and McCloskey shared so many times in the past. "I'll be right fucking back."

This is Endgame.

SHARI CHOPRA

Descending to the Depths, सूरय को अन्तमि रेज, *Valley of Eternal Life, Sikkim, India*

The stone walls fly past. Her clothes flutter behind her like banners. The guards keep up easily, their shoes squeaking as they spin around corners. Paru runs hard but keeps up too.

Little Alice! Little Alice!

Shari sees her sweet daughter's face in front of her eyes, the impenetrable fortress already fallen. Players on the outside coming in. Players on the inside already searching. Players everywhere.

How could she have been so small-minded? How could she have underestimated them so thoroughly?

The Players are hunters. Resourceful. Skilled. Merciless.

The Players are killers.

The Players are psychopaths.

Little monsters.

Not just Baitsakhan, the torturer. But all of them.

Monsters.

Little Alice!

I am not a psychopath, Shari thinks. *I am not,* meri jaan. She turns to go down the last flight of stairs. She grips the pistol harder, harder, harder. The guards keep up. Paru falls behind.

I am coming to you, meri jaan. *I am coming to fight for what I love.*

I am a mother first.

My bullets are not for you.

xviii

BAITSAKHAN, MACCABEE ADLAI, SARAH ALOPAY, RENZO, JAGO TLALOC

The Depths, सूरूय को अन्तमि रेज, *Valley of Eternal Life, Sikkim, India*

Baitsakhan gets his bearings.

Finally, he thinks. *Let the fun begin.*

He shuffles to the Cahokian. Takes her by the hair and drags her to the other side of the room. She moans but doesn't resist. He grabs the Olmec by the wrist and pulls him to the girl and props them against each other like sacks.

Renzo is semiconscious and balled up on the floor. Baitsakhan ignores him. *Not a Player,* he thinks, trying to prioritize. *Not as important.*

He goes to Maccabee. He hasn't moved. He kicks him in the side. Nothing. He kicks him harder. Nothing. He kicks him harder still.

He finds another packet of salts. Breaks it open and places it in front of Maccabee's face.

That does it.

Maccabee pops into a push-up and shakes his head. "Wha?"

"We're not in Bolivia anymore," Baitsakhan says.

Sarah moans.

Rifles are strewn around the floor. Baitsakhan picks one up.

Maccabee gets to his knees. "Wh'are we?"

"Don't know. The archway moved us."

Maccabee remembers. "To Sky Key?"

"Think so."

Maccabee looks left and right. "Where's it? Where's she?"

"Don't know that either."

Maccabee slaps his own face. "Earth Key?"

"Got it." Baitsakhan had slipped it into a pocket on his leg and zippered it shut.

A wave of relief passes over Maccabee's face. "Th'others?"

Baitsakhan points his chin at the two Players. Renzo is between them, still being ignored.

Maccabee's body is a mess, but his mind is clearing quickly. "You haven't killed them yet?"

Baitsakhan shrugs. "I thought you might want to watch."

He points the rifle at Sarah, at Jago.

Maccabee gingerly gets to his feet, a hand planted on the wall. "My head's swimming." He drops back to his knees and picks up the salts and smells them some more.

Baitsakhan grunts and sights the Cahokian. The muzzle makes a little circle. "Mine too." He tries to steady his HK G36. Sarah's head lolls to the side and her eyes flutter. She's coming around.

The Olmec is still out.

Baitsakhan aims for her neck. If he can't handle the recoil yet, then it will force the gun up and take her head.

But just as Baitsakhan pulls the trigger, the man on the floor rises and leaps into the air. The report is loud and drives into their aching heads like a power drill. Every single round strikes the man, and he falls back to the floor, his arm, shoulder, neck, and chest all hit. Some of the bullets find the resistance of Kevlar. Two tear through flesh.

The gunshots jog Sarah. She jumps to her feet and ignores the pain in her head and the noodles she has for limbs. She'll have to operate on rote muscle memory. She'll have to lean on her training.

But she's not ready for that, and like Maccabee she falls back to her knees.

A stunned Baitsakhan backpedals. The man who flew into the line of fire is badly injured. *Not a threat,* Baitsakhan thinks, still struggling to prioritize. Then he catches sight of the Cahokian, and his mind registers: *she's awake!* He retrains the gun on her, but she's throwing something at him. And there it is, heavy and metallic, and it hits the rifle hard, knocking it from his hands.

The hatchet.

Both weapons clank to the floor.

Throwing the hatchet took every ounce of effort from Sarah. She slumps forward, her hands and knees on the floor, her head hung low, her eyes closed. Renzo's blood oozes across the floor toward her.

MOVE! she yells to herself. *This is it! You will die!*

But she can't move.

Maccabee tries standing again. His knees feel like balls of wet paper towels, his feet like cinder blocks. He rises as Baitsakhan stalks toward Sarah.

Sarah hears Renzo choking on his own blood. She turns her head and blinks. Her vision is blurry, but she can make out Renzo's face. His gaze is purposeful. He moves his lips. Tries to speak. No words come.

But she understands.

Kill them. Stop game. Stop Makers.

And she understands more than that. Renzo sacrificed himself for her. Line to line. Ex-Player to Player.

She closes her eyes again. Her head pounds.

Baitsakhan stands over Sarah. He lowers his robotic hand. Unlike the rest of him, the hand isn't sore or weak or woozy.

Maccabee knows what's coming. The crushing grip. The thing that killed the Koori. The thing Ekaterina gave him. The thing Maccabee arranged for Baitsakhan to have, and that maybe was a terrible idea. And then Maccabee remembers: the little tube with the switch. *I need to Play alone,* he thinks. He fumbles for the transmitter that will send the signal to the hand, and brings his other hand to his nose and inhales the salts sharply.

They clear his head some more. A colorful flash catches his eye in the open doorway. A woman running past. But he can't think about her, because immediately two other figures storm into the room, rifles ready. Maccabee lunges for cover.

Baitsakhan, not yet grasping the Cahokian, wheels to the door and rushes the men. They open fire. Startled by the ferocious boy, their aim is slightly off. Baitsakhan's ear is grazed by a bullet but he keeps coming. One shot hits Sarah in her left forearm, making a clean hole, but the rest of the bullets miss. She falls over and pushes herself to the far end of the room. The pain is intense, but serves a purpose.

She is finally awake.

Everything goes clear.

Maccabee unholsters a pistol with lightning quickness and blasts one of the men—tall, fit, caramel skin, black hair, intense eyes—right through the head. The victim spins on one foot and slumps against the wall. Another man sprints through the hallway just outside the room, an older man. He glances at the action, his expression fraught and worried.

Baitsakhan crashes into the other Harappan guard. The Donghu is shorter by a foot and half, and 60 or 70 pounds lighter, but quicker and more flexible.

And he has his special hand.

He grabs the muzzle of the guard's rifle and squeezes. The man pulls the trigger, but the weapon backfires and kicks into the man's hands. He drops the rifle and lashes out at Baitsakhan, who throws the ruined firearm to the floor. Maccabee slides toward the open doorway, his pistol dancing here and there as he tries to get a bead. But it's too difficult. Baitsakhan jumps like a pogo stick, continually taking away Maccabee's shot.

Baitsakhan catches the man by the arm and wraps his left hand around it. The man cries out and falls to his knees. A series of snaps ring through the room. Sarah knows that sound well enough—the muted crackle of splintering bone. The man screams louder. She sees the boy in profile. He smiles. His metal hand is going to rip the man's arm clean off.

And with the *pop* of Maccabee's pistol, the man's head explodes, as the Nabataean puts him out of his misery.

Baitsakhan shoots Maccabee a piercing look. "He was mine!"

"Forget him. Sky Key is out there!" Maccabee says, pointing urgently at the hallway.

Pain radiates through Sarah's arm. She is fully conscious, but she has watched this short and brutal battle from a prone position on the floor in a pool of her own blood.

She wills her eyes to go blank and doesn't dare move.

Baitsakhan takes a half step toward her. He sees her blood and draws his own conclusions. The Nabataean grabs the Donghu by the shoulder and yanks him away. "They're done. The priority is Sky Key. It's right here, Baits! Let's take it."

And with that Maccabee pivots out of the room, his pistol already firing. From down the hall, a volley of rifle shots sails over his head, but Maccabee hits his mark. Sarah knows because the return fire stops. She hears Maccabee's footfalls pound out of the room.

Baitsakhan lingers. Sarah hears his breathing, and feels the caress of his metal finger along her hairline. She has stilled her breath, willed her heart to a whisper. She is excellent at playing dead.

Baitsakhan buys it. He turns and follows Maccabee. He can't let the Nabataean beat him to Sky Key.

When he has both keys and his partner is killed, Baitsakhan will return for the Cahokian.

He will have her scalp yet.

SHARI CHOPRA, LITTLE ALICE CHOPRA, JAMAL CHOPRA

The Depths, सूरय को अन्तमि रेज, *Valley of Eternal Life, Sikkim, India*

Shari shouts "Jamal!" and he opens the door and Shari spills into the room and falls into her husband's arms. Paru closes the door behind them and locks it shut and Little Alice calls "Mama!" and Shari hands Jamal the pistol and she drops to her knees and hugs Little Alice. Shari buries her nose in her daughter's hair. It smells like cinnamon and warm milk.

"I'm scared, Mama."

"I'm here, *meri jaan*."

They hear the report of gunfire from outside the room. Shari clasps her hands over her daughter's ears. "Those were our men, protecting us. It will be all right." Like any parent would, Shari lies. She has no idea if it will be all right. In fact, she doubts it.

Jamal wraps his arms around both of them. His girls. His life. "We're here, sweetie. We're here."

All three start to cry. Because they are scared but also because they are together.

In that moment they are full of love, and they are happy.

"They won't hurt you, *meri jaan*," Shari promises. "I won't let them."

"Nor will I," Jamal says. He squeezes his loves, and also squeezes the grip of the gun. He gives Shari a sad look, and in that instant she wonders: *Will he? Will he do what I cannot?*

Jamal closes his eyes. Kisses each on the head. His arms are hard and strong. His breath is quick.

Shari hugs their daughter tighter, thinks of the small child on the

Chinese bus, the one she and Big Alice helped to bring into this world, this doomed world.

I am a human being.

Tighter.

I am a compassionate human being and I renounce Endgame.

I renounce you.

I say no to the gods.

Because there are none.

Then there is the sound of more gunfire and three slugs slam into the door, *thwap thwap thwap.* She knows what that means. Paru. Her own father. Gone.

Little Alice shudders, and Shari cries quietly.

All of the Harappan line.

Gone.

Jamal stands. "You need to keep her safe, Shari. Hide over there."

Shari nods, overcome with terror. She ushers Little Alice behind a wall cut from the stone. She pulls an empty crate in front of them. Little Alice hunkers between her legs. They can just see the door between the wooden slats of the crate.

"Don't cry," Shari says. "Be quiet."

Shari wraps her arms around Little Alice.

"Aim for the head, my love," Shari says.

"I will."

"Show no mercy."

"I won't."

"For they will show you none."

AISLING KOPP, POP KOPP, GREG JORDAN, GRIFFIN MARRS

सूरय को अन्तमि रेज, *Valley of Eternal Life, Sikkim, India*

Aisling and her team picked their way through Little Bertha's carnage at the entrance to the fortress without incident, being careful where they stepped, trying not to dwell on what they'd done. *So many dead,* Aisling thought, *so many. And no sign of Shari Chopra. She isn't here. She's somewhere else.*
With her daughter.
With Sky Key.
The Celt leads them through the suddenly empty stone fortress. Signs of life put on pause everywhere. Cups of warm tea. The strands of a beaded curtain swaying back and forth. A chair still warm to the touch. A radio crackling with static in a control room on the 2nd sublevel. A small cloth doll in this room too, discarded on the floor, forgotten.
But no one is left.
They've either been killed or they're hiding.
There are no more green dots displayed on their HUDs. The fortress walls are too thick. But there are still clues. From the control room Aisling goes into the hall and finds a scuff mark, and farther down a thread from a brightly colored piece of cloth, and down some stairs a 9-millimeter bullet—not a casing, just a bullet. They keep going down. Aisling finds a feather floating in the air on the 5th sublevel. She pinches it between her fingers. Smells it. Inspects it.
A peacock startles them, running across the hall from one room to another. It disappears.
"Uh, everyone else saw that, right?" Marrs asks.

They nod.

"Good," he says.

"We need to go all the way to the bottom," Aisling says, ignoring the bird. "That's where they're keeping her."

"You sure?" Jordan asks.

"Not completely, but that's where I'd take a little girl if I were terrif—" She's cut off by the telltale rattle of gunfire.

Aisling hoists her sniper rifle and takes off at a trot and they don't say another word.

Down they go.

SARAH ALOPAY, JAGO TLALOC

The Depths, सूर्य को अन्तमि रेज, *Valley of Eternal Life, Sikkim, India*

As soon as Maccabee and Baitsakhan leave the room, Sarah blinks and sits and pushes her back into the wall. She knows these two have just made a terrible, and hopefully mortal, mistake. They should have taken 10 or 20 seconds and put a bullet in her head and in Jago's, but they didn't.

The little sadist, Baitsakhan, he seemed crazy enough for such a lapse. Like he wanted to enjoy his time killing them.

But Maccabee? Sarah's not sure why he spared them. He seemed more concerned with pushing forward, with leading Baitsakhan on.

Whatever. Thanks for the freebie, boys.

She unsheathes her knife and slices a hole in her shirt at the shoulder and tears the cloth free. Using her good hand and her teeth, she works it around her arm just below the elbow and ties it tight, slowing the blood that flows out of her forearm. This will have to do for now.

Sarah crawls to Jago, careful not to put any weight on her wounded arm. As she covers the dozen feet between them, she is overcome by the powerful odor of ammonia. Smelling salts. One of the others must have dropped them.

She snaps up the packet and continues crawling. Jago's on his side, rolling back and forth. His diamond teeth glitter.

She reaches him. She holds the smelling salts to her face and inhales, and the odor goes up and under her eyes and swirls through her sinuses to her temples and her brain lights up like it's run through with electricity. She's suddenly very conscious, and her arm sears with pain, the skin and muscles throbbing at the tourniquet.

She shakes Jago. *"¿Que?"* he utters.

"Wake up, damn it!" she whispers. "We've got to fight!"

He mumbles something unintelligible before Sarah practically jams the salts into his nostrils.

His back goes straight as a board as he pops into a sitting position and swipes frantically at his face. Sarah claps her good hand over his mouth before he can cry out. He pushes the salts away and they fall to the floor. His eyes are wide and bright.

"Shh," Sarah says. "Other Players are here. The Donghu and the Nabataean. Can you move?"

Her arm throbs. She needs him to be able to move, to be whole and able-bodied.

Jago pushes her hand from his lips. *"Sí.* I feel good." And he does. He unholsters his pistol and racks it quietly.

"You're shot," he whispers.

"I'll be fine."

Jago stands. He holds out a hand for Sarah and pulls her up. She is not as steady as he is. "Are you sure?" He realizes that he's standing in a pool of blood. His chest tightens. "You've lost a lot of blood."

Sarah shakes her head and points her chin at Renzo. "I'm sorry, Feo. It's not all mine."

And there's Renzo, sprawled on the ground, eyes open and blank, his mouth full of shimmering blackness.

"He saved my life," Sarah says.

Jago bites his lower lip. His nostrils flare. The muscles in his neck twitch uncontrollably. A vein pops on his temple and his scar darkens. "Who?"

"The boy. The Donghu."

Jago faces Sarah. His expression is one of rage and sorrow. "Where?"

Sarah points to the hallway, just as they hear two gunshots and a woman cry "NO!" and scream and then these sounds are hushed by the thump of a heavy door being closed.

Sky Key, Sarah thinks. *So close. You can end this. Now. Here.*

"We have to destroy Sky Key," she says quietly.

"*Sí,*" Jago says, but he's staring at Renzo's body, and Sarah knows the only thing on his mind is revenge.

Jago steps to Renzo and leans over and closes his eyes. Sarah picks up a pistol and stuffs it in her belt. She relieves one of the dead guards of a curved fighting stick with a heavy ball on the end. "Here." She tosses the stick to Jago. He grabs it out of the air and whirls it in front of him, getting a feel. She steps forward decisively and says, as much to convince herself as to remind Jago, "Let's go save the world."

LITTLE ALICE CHOPRA

The Depths, सूरय को अन्तमि रेज, *Valley of Eternal Life, Sikkim, India*

She watches.

The door makes a loud pop, like the lock has been broken from the outside.

It opens a crack. The door is heavy.

Light floods in from the hall. It wasn't lit like that before, not when her father ran with her into this storeroom. It wasn't so bright.

No one is there.

Her father swings his gun back and forth, back and forth, looking for a target, for a sliver of flesh.

The door inches open a little more. More light. Little Alice has to squint her eyes.

Still, no one is there.

A shadow. A gun barrel. Three shots.

Only one from her father, fired into the hallway, into the searing light.

A miss. Her father falls and the door is open and that is all Little Alice sees or hears.

Now that the light is here, with her, close to her, she senses nothing else.

It is like a sun. Terrible and strong and full of gravity pulling her in.

She can't see her mother's frantic hands or hear her cry out for Jamal as he falls to the ground, dead before he even had a chance. She can't hear her own voice saying "Earth Key Earth Key Earth Key Earth Key Earth Key Earth Key" on and on and on in a dry monotone. She can't see Maccabee, the tall one with the crooked face from her nightmares, come and talk to Shari before pulling Little Alice from her mother.

She can't see Shari try to fight Maccabee off. She can't see Baitsakhan stand over Shari, his face twisted with pleasure. She can't hear him say, "This is for Bat and Bold."

She can't.

All she experiences now is the light. It's attached to Baitsakhan's leg.

The light.

That's all there is.

Her and the light and nothing else.

"Earth Key Earth Key Earth Key Earth Key Earth Key Earth Key."

The light and nothing else.

The blinding light only Sky Key can see.

SHARI CHOPRA

The Depths, सूरय को अन्तमि रेज, *Valley of Eternal Life, Sikkim, India*

The door swings open and before she knows it the Nabataean and the little monster are in the room and Jamal is dead.

Just like that.

No heroics.

No fanfare.

No beating the odds.

Her love gone.

Shari cries "NO!" and screams and she holds her daughter ever tighter, but Little Alice is like a zombie, the shock of everything perhaps too much. For some reason she's saying "Earth Key" over and over in a low voice, not desperate, not afraid, not angry, just blank.

The Nabataean appears in front of them. His expression is intense. He looks at Little Alice, full of desire.

"You won't kill her," Shari says, thinking maybe in this last moment she will have the strength to take her daughter's head and snap her neck.

Maccabee leans over. "Kill her? Why would I do that?"

He pries the entranced girl from her mother's arms, and Shari screams and strikes out expertly with her hands and feet, but Maccabee wards off every attack and with a swift kick to her chest she finds herself knocked to the ground. This is it.

Maccabee tucks his gun in his belt and ushers Little Alice away from her mother and picks the girl up tenderly and whispers something in her ear. He takes her to the other side of the room, away from Shari and away from Jamal's body, and Shari can't be sure because her body is shaking now and her eyes are filling with tears and her heart is breaking, no it's broken, so broken, she can't be sure but it looks like Maccabee Adlai is sorry that it has to happen like this. It looks like he is sorry.

Shari jumps to her knees to go after her daughter, but before she can move, there is the little monster blocking her path. He plants a hand on her forehead and pushes her back. She looks up at the monster and all hope leaves her.

She has failed.

Her line, her family, her ancestors.

Big Alice Ulapala, her child, her husband, herself.

She has failed.

Baitsakhan kneels. Their gazes meet. He holds out his left hand. She sees that it is not flesh but metal. He places it on her shoulder, almost like he's consoling her. It is a strong hand. He slides the hand to her neck. He begins to squeeze.

"This is for Bat and Bold."

She has failed. She turns inward. Looks for love. Tries to push compassion and empathy across the room to her daughter and out of this room and out of this fortress and over the mountains and into the sky and toward the heavens. She is not afraid for herself. Death is easy. But she is afraid for her precious daughter.

Very afraid.

BAITSAKHAN

The Depths, सूर्य को अन्तमि रेज, *Valley of Eternal Life, Sikkim, India*

Happiness wells in his heart as he sees the fear in this waste of a Player. He wonders where her preternatural calm is now. Baitsakhan doesn't have the emotional wisdom to understand that the source of her calm in China was Little Alice, but now that Little Alice is taken, the source is dry.

Now Little Alice is the source of something different.

Fear.

Baitsakhan loves it. He doesn't care where it comes from, just that it's there.

He squeezes a little tighter.

Shari chokes.

A little tighter.

Her leg kicks out and Baitsakhan sits on it.

A little tighter.

He smiles.

"I am going to rip your throat out."

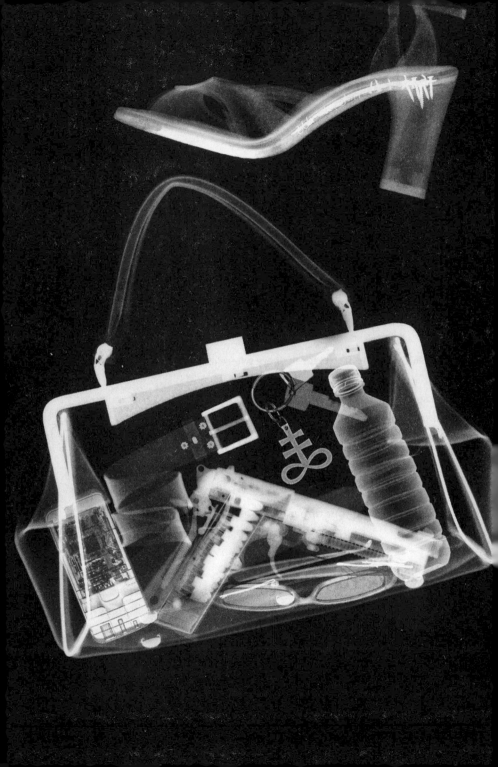

MACCABEE ADLAI

The Depths, सूरज को अन्तमि रेज, *Valley of Eternal Life, Sikkim, India*

Maccabee Adlai puts Little Alice on the floor.

"Don't look, sweetie," he says.

"Earth Key Earth Key Earth Key Earth Key," she drones.

Her eyes are blank. Her mouth moves as if automated.

He waves a hand in front of her face.

Nothing.

"Can't see anyway."

He stands and takes the pistol from his waistband. Baitsakhan's back is to him. Shari's eyes are tear filled. Her face is turning blue. Her hands are clasped on Baitsakhan's wrist. He's going slower than he has to. He's taking his time.

Maccabee aims the gun at Shari. Says, "I'm sorry."

Without looking, Baitsakhan asks, "What for? This is glorious."

It makes Maccabee sick.

He lowers the gun and quickly takes the fob Ekaterina made for him and taps it three times. *Click, click, click.*

And the hand releases Shari. She inhales sharply, color returning to her face almost immediately. Baitsakhan recoils and stares incomprehensibly at his bionic appendage. "Wha—" he blurts, but before he can even finish the word the hand zips toward his own neck and locks around his throat. The hand he was born with grasps his left wrist and tries to pull the mechanical hand from his neck. He pulls and pulls but nothing comes of it. He falls over on his side, away from Shari. She stares at Baitsakhan with a look of grotesque wonder as he presses his elbow into the floor, trying to use it to force his hand away from his neck.

But it's impossible.

Blood wells around the mechanical digits. His face turns purple and his eyes bulge from their sockets and his tongue darts from his lips and his nostrils flare and the hand squeezes squeezes squeezes and then there is a terrible squishing and popping noise as the hand becomes a fist in Baitsakhan's throat and blood splatters over the floor and his body falls to the ground. It shakes and quavers for several seconds, and Shari looks on, transfixed and terrified and—she can hardly believe it—deeply satisfied.

The terror named Baitsakhan is dead.

Maccabee lets the fob fall to the floor.

Shari, still staring at Baitsakhan, says, "How?"

"Does it matter?"

Shari shakes her head. "No. It doesn't." She shifts her eyes to Maccabee. "Thank you," she manages to say.

"Don't." He swings the gun back to Shari. His finger hovers over the trigger. Maccabee hesitates, looks to Little Alice, makes sure she's still in her trance. She is. Maccabee sighs. "Like I said, I'm sorry."

"You don't have to be," Shari whispers, her voice cracking, her throat aching. "The game is bullshit."

Maccabee shakes his head. He will never believe this. Never. "It'll be painless. It won't be like he wanted."

Shari looks at Little Alice. Her daughter is gone. An empty shell now. But she might one day return.

"Take care of her."

"I will. Until the end, I promise." Maccabee squeezes just a little bit more. Shari closes her eyes. She can't see him look from the mother to the daughter and to the mother again. He looks at what's left of the Donghu. Thinks of the Koori, of Ekaterina.

Fuck, Maccabee thinks.

He wants to win—he *will* win—but the Harappan is right that this is bullshit.

He looks from the mother to the daughter to the mother again.

And then he raises the gun and steps forward silently. Shari still waits, her eyes closed, her face serene, her cheeks bright with tears. She's still waiting.

And he brings the butt of the gun down on her head with a crack and she falls over. He spins to Little Alice and holds out his hand. "Come on, sweetie. Time to go."

SARAH ALOPAY, JAGO TLALOC, MACCABEE ADLAI

The Depths, सूरय को अन्तमि रेज, *Valley of Eternal Life, Sikkim, India*

Sarah pulls the door all the way open as Jago bursts into the room. Maccabee dives to the side and fires. A bullet zips past Jago's scarred cheek. Jago fires back, his bullet grazing Maccabee's shoulder.

Jago sprints forward. Maccabee tracks him. Shoots again.

This one hits Jago in the chest.

His bulletproof vest absorbs it.

Jago holds his breath and ignores the crunching pain. The Olmec does the trick where he runs along the wall. He sails over Jamal's body, firing until there isn't a bullet left in his pistol. Maccabee fires too, his rounds biting into the stone at Jago's heels.

All shots miss.

Jago slides to the ground and takes cover behind the wall that Shari and Baitsakhan are slumped near. Both look dead. Baitsakhan certainly does, anyway.

Maccabee advances. He was more frugal with his ammo and has two bullets left.

But before he can get a shot off, Sarah steps into the doorway. Her gun is trained on Maccabee and she's ready to shoot, but then she sees the girl, crawling along the floor toward her mother, and Sarah shifts the gun to her.

End what you started! she yells to herself, and she puts the slightest pressure on the trigger as she takes in this girl, all of two years old, innocent, a victim of Endgame, maybe *the* victim of Endgame, and Sarah zeroes in on her and doesn't notice as Maccabee takes his attention off Jago and turns his gun on Sarah.

Jago lunges out of cover with the fighting stick and cracks it onto Maccabee's arm. The pistol drops to the floor. Jago whips his wrist around and swings the stick back up. Maccabee steps back and catches the stick mid-arc. He and Jago are nose to nose.

Jago smiles, his diamonds catching the light. "It's on."

Meanwhile, Sarah still hasn't pulled the trigger.

End what you started! End what you started!

Save humanity, Sarah Alopay!

SAVE IT!

LITTLE ALICE CHOPRA

The Depths, सूर्य को अन्तमि रेज, *Valley of Eternal Life, Sikkim, India*

There.
The light.
Move toward the light.
There is only the light. The blinding light.
"Earth Key Earth Key Earth Key Earth Key."

AISLING KOPP, POP KOPP, GREG JORDAN, GRIFFIN MARRS

The Depths, सूरय को अन्तमि रेज, *Valley of Eternal Life, Sikkim, India*

Aisling reaches the bottom of the stairs and holds up a fist. None of them speak. She peeks around the corner. A hallway, a doorway on the right with the bodies of three men just inside the room. At the end of the hall is an open door, another corpse nearby. Blocking the open doorway is the back of Sarah Alopay, her right arm holding a pistol, her left arm tucked in front of her like it's injured. Aisling senses a commotion just past Alopay, but she can't tell what's happening.
And then Aisling catches a glimpse. Through Sarah's legs, deeper in the room, a little girl crawls across the floor from left to right.
Sky Key.
Alice Chopra. Not more than a baby.
No wonder Sarah hesitates.
Aisling looks at the others. *Don't make a sound,* she mouths.
They don't.
She readies her sniper rifle and swings around the corner and takes a bead on the girl. Her scope reads due south. She breathes in but the Cahokian steps in her way.
Move, Aisling thinks. *Move so I can end this.*

xix

JAGO TLALOC, MACCABEE ADLAI, SARAH ALOPAY, AISLING KOPP, LITTLE ALICE CHOPRA

The Depths, सूरय को अनतमि रेज, *Valley of Eternal Life, Sikkim, India*

Jago drives the heel of his palm toward Maccabee's cheek. He narrowly misses as Maccabee leans back, pivots, and swings the handle end of the stick at Jago's side. Jago tightens his stomach muscles and takes the hit to the gut. But before Jago can grab the stick and take it back, Maccabee throws the thing away, and it clanks into the far wall.

Jago steps back one pace to gain some room. Maccabee plants a foot behind him. At the same moment he surreptitiously flicks his thumb and opens the lid to his poisoned ring on his left hand.

Oh, it is *on,* Maccabee thinks.

He lashes out with his right hand to distract Jago from the real danger—the ring. Jago backpedals two feet, deflecting blows with his hands. He takes three glancing blows to the chin and realizes he's fighting a southpaw. He ducks under a heavy left backhand, and when he pops up, he switches his feet, putting the right in front.

Righty, lefty, it doesn't matter. He's fought them all.

Maccabee cocks his left hand for another powerful swing.

Two more right jabs, Jago's head bobbing and weaving, and here comes the left again and Jago steps into it and moves his head to his left and drops his right shoulder, his eyes tracking Maccabee's fist as it sails past the flesh of his neck. And there, he sees the ring.

Watch that hand, Jago thinks as he lands five lightning blows to Maccabee's side. Then he jumps back and says, "Boxing's for pussies."

Maccabee changes his stance and squares his shoulders and brings his hands in front of him and says, "Fine."

The huge Nabataean charges. Jago drops and plants his hands on the floor and twirls sideways, his legs flashing in every direction in a showy but deadly display of capoeira. He lands four shots on Maccabee, one on his temple, one on his nape, one to his ribs, and a useless one to his upper arm. He is about to wrap his legs around him and take him down when a meaty fist crashes into Jago's back and smashes his entire body into the floor.

Maccabee stands over him and punches down, but Jago rolls over and kicks his legs and catjumps into a standing position.

Maccabee slices toward Jago's chest with the ring, but Jago sidesteps and grabs the pinkie the ring encircles. With a precise jerk, he snaps Maccabee's finger so it flops against the back of his hand.

Maccabee claps his other hand over the Olmec's shoulder and pulls him in tight.

"You are so fucking ugly," Maccabee says and, even though Maccabee knows that he'll probably break his nose again, he rears back and delivers a vicious head-butt.

Except Jago is too slippery. He goes limp, falls out of Maccabee's arms, and slides to the ground. Maccabee stumbles forward with his own momentum, and as Jago passes through his legs, he thrusts upward, both his fists clenched together, right into the Nabataean's groin.

Maccabee makes a horrible retching sound and doubles over. Jago is on his feet in a flash, walks around his opponent, and takes Maccabee by the chin.

"Adios."

Jago brings a heavy uppercut into Maccabee's jaw, and the huge Nabataean is forced up, his back arching, before he falls on top of Baitsakhan, utterly unconscious.

Jago breathes hard, his fists balled at his sides, his entire body slick with sweat. He looks around and grabs a knife from the floor and stands over Maccabee to finish him off.

"STOP!" Sarah yells, still standing outside the doorway, still blocking Aisling's shot.

Jago whips his head to Sarah. "What?"

"Not you. Her."

And the girl does stop, just shy of the pile of Players. The Harappan, the Donghu, the Nabataean. Her small face to Sarah, her lips moving in the same pattern over and over. Her eyes looking through Sarah, through everything. Blank and dilated.

"Earth Key," Sarah says to the little girl, still pointing the gun at her. "I know. I shouldn't have taken it. I shouldn't have started all this."

Jago looks from Sarah to the spaced-out little girl. He clenches the knife.

"Sarah . . ." He's worried that she's snapped again.

Sarah ignores him.

"Earth Key," Little Alice repeats, losing interest in Sarah, the light no one else can see calling her.

Sarah cocks her head. "What happened to you?" Sarah asks.

"Earth Key," Little Alice says. "Earth Key."

"Do it," Jago says to Sarah.

"I . . ."

"End it."

Come on, Aisling urges silently. *You're one of the good ones, damn it. Do it.*

Sarah thinks, *I have to do it. I have to. It will save billions of people. I have to.*

Memories flash before her—Tate, graduation, her father driving her to a doctor's appointment, kissing Christopher—all mundane memories of her normal life, the one she definitely had but that now feels like a dream. Memories. As if she is about to take her own life and not the life of yet another innocent person who didn't ask to be in the crosshairs of Endgame.

I have to.

And she remembers Christopher's face in his last moment and she knows. He wanted to die because he couldn't live in a world where Sarah Alopay was a psychopathic killer. He just couldn't.

And she realizes that's what has been tearing at her since she shot her best friend.

That she can't live in that world either.

If she truly is going to save humanity, then she must salvage her own first.

She lets the gun drop to her side.

And just like that, her mind settles. Sanity washes over her.

"Sarah!" Jago protests.

Aisling whispers, "Goddamn it." Presses her cheek against the rifle's cold metal. *Move, or I'll blow a hole through both of you.*

"I . . . I can't do it. Not again."

"Earth Key."

"But we have to."

"Christopher saw. He understood."

"Earth Key."

Move! Aisling thinks.

"That *puto* won't die, will he?"

"I wish he hadn't."

"Earth Key."

"Billions, Sarah. Billions of people! We have to do it!"

The gun trembles at Sarah's side. She stares at Jago. "We're killers, Jago. All of us. That's what the Makers taught us thousands of years ago. How to build machines and how to hate and how to fear. And when you put those things together, you end up with death, with violence." She points the gun at Maccabee and Baitsakhan. "I'll kill people like them, people like you, like me, but I can't kill people like her. Not again. I won't. I just won't."

"Then I will." Jago pulls the gun from Sarah. Stares at Little Alice. Raises the pistol. Points it at her.

Aisling watches this exchange. *Do it. Do it.* She doesn't want to be the one to take the shot.

"Earth Key," Little Alice says.

He looks down at her. So sweet, so strange.

The gun drops to Jago's side. And Sarah is relieved. So relieved.

"I ... I can't."

"Right," Sarah says, a sad smile on her lips. "Because you're strong, Jago. You're good, and good people don't shoot two-year-olds in the face. If this is the off switch for Endgame—well, it's their off switch. The Makers'. And it's bullshit. We'll find another way."

Jago wonders if they're watching. If kepler 22b can hear their words. If the alien knows that this is the beginning of another rebellion.

"We aren't like them," Sarah insists, her voice strong, passionate.

She means the Players, the Makers, all their sick and twisted and brutal human ancestors. She means all of them. She falls against Jago, pressing her chest to his, resting her chin on his shoulder.

"You're a human being," she says in a whisper, her eyes full of tears, her mind blessedly quiet. "We're not gods. We're not aliens. We're human beings."

"Earth Key."

Fuck, Aisling thinks as Sarah steps into the room and out of sight. Aisling aims at the girl's head. She's going to do it. She has to. She has to.

The little girl starts to move again. Aisling follows. Puts pressure on the trigger. The little girl passes her mother's body and stops. Her lips move. More pressure on the trigger. The girl reaches out for the leg of one of the fallen Players. Her lips move.

Forgive me, Aisling thinks.

And she closes her eyes and pulls all the way.

The shot rings out, and for the briefest of moments that is all that any of them know or hear or see or understand.

LITTLE ALICE CHOPRA

The Depths, सूरय को अन्तमि रेज, *Valley of Eternal Life, Sikkim, India*

Little Alice slides her hand over Maccabee's shoulder and touches
Earth Key, a small hard ball hidden in Baitsakhan's pocket.
There is only the light.
Sky Key and Earth Key, together. Joined. Inseparable.
There is only the light.
Ever brighter.
Ever brighter.
There is only the light.
And there is no sound of the rifle shot.
There is no sound because Sky Key and Earth Key are joined,
and anyone touching either of them, dead or alive, is with them.
Baitsakhan is with them. And Maccabee is with them, alive but
unaware.
There is no sound because Sky Key and Earth Key are joined.
And they are no longer in the Harappan fortress called सूरय को अन्तमि
रेज, in the Valley of Eternal Life, in Sikkim, India.
They are no longer there.
They are safe. They are joined. The first two keys came together, and
they are saved.
Saved so that one lucky Player may take them and Play on, right
through to the end.
The light is gone and everything is blackness and silence and Little
Alice is suddenly terrified. She can't remember where she is or what's
happened.
"Mama?" she says weakly. "Papa?"

The only thing she hears is the sound of grunting.

"Mama!" she yelps.

A man clears his throat. And then says, "I'm here. I'll take care of you now. No one will hurt you."

He flicks on a lighter, and Little Alice sees her nightmare come true.

Maccabee holds out his hand. "No one will hurt you now, my Sky Key."

These Old Ones were gone now, inside the earth and under the sea; but their dead bodies had told their secrets in dreams to the first men, who formed a cult which had never died. This was that cult, and the prisoners said it had always existed and always would exist, hidden in distant wastes and dark places all over the world until the time when . . . the stars were ready, and the secret cult would always be waiting to *liberate*[xx] him.

HILAL IBN ISA AL-SALT

Suvarnabhumi International Airport, Bangkok, Thailand

Hilal stands at the baggage carousel, anxious to figure out a way to see if any of the other Players have heeded his message.

He does not have to wait for long.

A newscast plays on a screen mounted in a nearby waiting area. He's not watching it, so he doesn't notice when the regular broadcast cuts off and is replaced with the unaltered face of kepler 22b.

He does notice when someone screams and points.

Instead of pushing his way through the crowd to get a better look at the monitor, he pulls his smartphone from his pocket and looks at its screen. There too is the Maker.

He turns up the volume and cups his hands over the speaker.

Esteemed Players of the lines, and all people of Earth, hear me now.

More screams echo through the terminal, followed by gasps and shushes and more than a few tears.

The kepler's voice is as Hilal remembers.

Earth Key and Sky Key are joined. One Player possesses both.

Congratulations to the Nabataean of the 8th Line. May you have continued success in the Great Puzzle.

Hilal reels and struggles to keep on his feet. His heart weighs heavy in his chest. His message did not work. Ea is gone, but he has failed otherwise. Failed.

The Endgame has been better than anticipated, it has been a surprise, and we thank the Players for it.

Hilal swings from deep sorrow to anger and hatred. *They are dispensing with all pretense. They are outing themselves. They are every bit as evil as Ea was. Maybe more.*

And there are more surprises as well. The Event—this Abaddon—will come sooner than your scientists think. It has been moved closer. It is imminent, and its arrival will be sudden. Less than three days remain, my humans.

The airport erupts in chaos. People run everywhere. Hilal hunkers to the floor and pushes the phone to his ear. kepler 22b is not finished.

Now go and find Sun Key, if you will. Live, die, steal, kill, love, betray, avenge. Whatever you please. Endgame is the puzzle of life, the reason for death. Play on. What will be will be.

kepler 22b disappears. That's it.

Hilal sits on the floor and lets the people run and watches the fear grow like a contagion.

And then his phone rings.

He answers. "Master Eben?" he says.

"No. It's Stella."

"Stella. Did you hear?"

"Yeah. Everyone did. Where are you?"

"Bangkok."

"Good. That's good. Can you get to Ayutthaya? It's not far."

"Yes. I think."

"Good. Stay on that side of the world. Abaddon won't hit there. I'm airborne and will meet you in exactly thirteen hours."

"All . . . all right."

"I'm sorry we couldn't stop it, Hilal."

"I am too. More than you know."

The line cracks. "I gotta go. Ayutthaya. Thirteen hours."

"Ayutthaya. Thirteen hours."

"And Hilal?"

"Yes?"

"Don't die. You hear me? I'm going to need you. Do not die. This isn't over yet."

And then the line falters and goes silent.

And Hilal thinks, *No. It isn't.*

Because this is Endgame.

And this is war.

(Endnotes)

[i] http://eg2.co/200

[ii] http://eg2.co/201

[iii] http://eg2.co/202

[iv] http://eg2.co/203

[v] http://eg2.co/204

[vi] http://eg2.co/205

[vii] http://eg2.co/206

[viii] http://eg2.co/207

[ix] http://eg2.co/208

[x] http://eg2.co/209

[xi] http://eg2.co/210

[xii] http://eg2.co/211

[xiii] http://eg2.co/212

[xiv] http://eg2.co/213

[xv] http://eg2.co/214

[xvi] http://eg2.co/215

[xvii] http://eg2.co/216

[xviii] http://eg2.co/217

[xix] http://eg2.co/218

[xx] http://eg2.co/219

They have one goal: stop Endgame. They are the Zero line.
Keep reading for a sneak peek at . . .

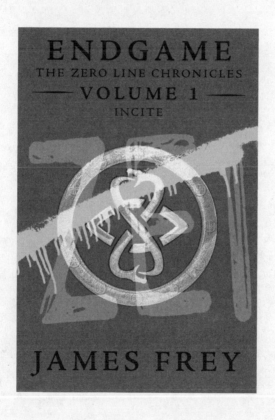

CHAPTER ONE

It was a beautiful May afternoon as the bus drove into Berkeley. I was finally getting out on my own, leaving Pasadena, my job, and my parents behind. My mom had given me a halfhearted hug. We'd never been close. I wondered if my mom had ever been close to anyone. She was small and subservient and never talked.

My dad did the talking for both of them. He barked orders around the house from the minute he got home at night until long after I'd gone to my room.

He'd never wanted me to go to college. Well, to tell the truth, I was never sure what he wanted of me. After high school, I tried working at the family business for a year—Dad ran a furniture store—and I couldn't remember doing anything that he approved of. I could never meet the outrageous quotas that he gave me, and he certainly didn't make an effort to teach me anything. But when I told him I was going to college—that I'd saved up enough for tuition—he sneered at me as though I'd just said I was joining the circus.

But I'd held on to my money—everything I'd ever earned at the furniture store, and everything I'd earned the summers I'd worked for the Forest Service. My friends loved to go out to movies and dinner and spend money on girls and weed, but I knew I needed to be a penny-pinching miser if I ever planned to get out from under Dad's thumb.

After I told him that I was going to Berkeley, of all places, he stopped talking to me. It was the best two months I'd ever had at home.

I wasn't starting school until the fall, but I'd managed to get a janitorial job cleaning the empty dorms over the summer. The school let me move in early, into one of the dorms that held guys year-round, and it gave me a chance to earn a little more money and leave my parents' house.

I couldn't help smiling on the bus. This was everything I wanted. Freedom. A place where I could be in the middle of the action: the protests, the rallies, the parties, the free life and free love. I wanted a place where I could be my own man, voice my own opinions, be part of something important.

I was finally there.

After checking in at the administration building, I found my dorm and headed upstairs to room 117.

"Hey!" a guy said, jumping up when I opened the door. "Are you the new guy? I've been expecting you!"

"I'm the new guy." I had a backpack and an old duffel bag I used to store my football gear in, and dropped them both on the empty bed. "Mike Stavros." I held out my hand to him.

He shook it enthusiastically. He had medium brown skin and black hair that fell to his shoulders. "Tommy. Tommy Selestewa."

"Good to meet you."

"What are you here for? They told me you were coming, but I don't know why anyone would come this time of year. School just got out."

"Job brought me early," I said. "Why are you still here?"

"Just trying to graduate earlier. I'm a sophomore, and I don't have anything else to do—no reason to take summer off. I've loaded up on classes." Tommy sat down at his desk. "Got a major?"

"Not sure yet. I'm thinking city planning, or forestry. Or maybe political science." I sat on my bed. The mattress was thin and hard.

Tommy laughed a little. "No worries, man, you've got time."

I looked at Tommy's desk and bookshelf. He had a typewriter. A book lay open beside it—Plato's *Republic*—and under it was *Nicomachean Ethics* by Aristotle. It made me feel a little small that my roommate was studying such great philosophies. This was why I'd wanted to come to college. To learn about something bigger than myself.

"I used to work for the Forest Service," I said, "during my summers in high school. I was part of a fire crew that saved a neighborhood from a forest fire. It was coming from two sides, and we were able to redirect the flames. I was really proud of that. It makes me want to do something that will make a difference. Become someone important.

Or, well, just *do* something important. Not just be a furniture salesman like my old man."

"Why school, then? Why not join the fire department?"

"I thought about that, but I decided that, on the fire crew, I was just one person with a shovel and a mattock. What if I could do something bigger? Design a subdivision where fires are less likely? What if I could invent something—some kind of emergency sprinkler, or I don't know what. Something."

"I get that," he said. "So you want to fight fires on a big scale."

"Not necessarily fires. Anything, as long as it's something worth fighting for. My old man has never done shit. I just haven't figured out what I'm going to do yet." I smiled. "How about you?"

"I haven't declared yet. I've just been doing my generals. I think I'll end up in engineering. But this summer I'm taking a lot of ancient history classes."

"Whoa. Those are pretty different."

"I read a lot." He motioned to the bookshelf above his desk. It was filled with titles like *Turning Points in Ancient History* and *Inventions of the Gods*. "I'm sure I'll be boring you to death with some of my theories soon."

"Go for it. I have nothing else to do. I don't know anyone north of Santa Barbara, and I was worried it was going to be a long, lonely summer."

Tommy laughed. "You want to go out tonight? Some of my friends and I were talking about having some beers, shooting some pool. Interested?"

I was exhausted, but I didn't care. I was finally on my own, and I couldn't wait to celebrate. "Absolutely. What time?"

Tito's was a local dive, about a 20-minute walk from our dorm. It was busy, and Tommy led me through the crowd of students to a row of pool tables in the back. There was no one in the place who looked over 30, but they were all dressed better than average. Tommy had changed from jeans and a T-shirt into corduroys and a zippered sweater. I was more casual—a pair of beat-up jeans and a Rose Bowl sweatshirt.

A small group in the back called out to Tommy, and we made our way over to them.

"Guys," he said. "This is Mike, my new roomie. Mike, meet Jim, Julia, and Mary."

"Hi," I said, and stretched out my hand. Jim grabbed it. He was black, with silver-rimmed glasses and a newsboy cap.

"Jim Jefferson," he said. "Not James, definitely not JJ."

"Mike Stavros," I said back. "Good to meet you." But my eyes weren't on him. They were glued to the blonde sitting next to him, the one Tommy had called Mary.

I reached out my hand to her.

She took it in a firm grip and stood up. "This isn't a business meeting, you know."

"Is shaking hands too formal?" I asked, letting go and laughing at myself. "I've been living the life of a furniture salesman. Salesmen shake hands with people. It makes them feel at ease."

Mary laughed, a sweet, melodic tone. "I can assure you, I'm feeling very at ease." She picked up her beer and took a quick sip.

"I'm Julia," the next woman said. She was black, with short hair, and dressed in purple paisley. She reached for my hand, and I shook back. "Where you from?"

"Pasadena," I said. "You guys?"

"Northern California," Mary said. "Ever heard of Susanville?"

"Never."

"You're not missing out," she said with a quick laugh. "I grew up north of there on a ranch. Moved to Piedmont when my dad retired."

"I've never heard of Piedmont either," I said, and she laughed again.

"Touché, Mike." I beamed.

"So, how'd you all become friends?"

I noticed a look between Tommy and Mary. Mary shook her head

4

slightly. My stomach dipped—I hoped that didn't mean they were together.

"Julia and I are locals," Jim said. "Grew up in Oakland, known each other since kindergarten. You play pool?"

"A little."

"Eight ball," Jim said. "You and Mary, me and Julia." He handed me a cue.

I was about six feet tall, and Mary had to be a foot shorter than me. But she was gorgeous. Long, blond, curly hair that flowed loose down her shoulders like a waterfall. I didn't want to say no to being on her team, but I turned to Tommy.

"That'll leave you out."

"The night is young," he said. "I'm going to get something to drink. Want anything?"

"Not now," I said.

Julia racked the balls and stood back. Mary looked at me. "You wanna break?"

"You go for it," I said. I hadn't played a lot of pool at home, and I wanted to pull off looking cool in front of this girl for as long as I could.

She broke, and the 14 ball fell into a side pocket.

"Do all of you guys go to Berkeley?" I asked.

"We do," Jim said, gesturing to himself and Julia. "Art program. She paints; I sculpt."

"Not me," Mary said, lining up her new shot. "Stanford. Prelaw."

"Really?"

"It gets better," Julia said. "She's there on scholarship. Smart kid."

"Why are you here if you're at Stanford? That's like an hour away."

"Taking a quarter off," she said. "I'm interning for a firm across the bay. Divorces and bankruptcies." She rolled her eyes and added, "Real exciting stuff." She missed her shot.

Julia took a pull from her beer and bent down, taking aim at the 3 ball.

5

"So, Mike," Jim asked, "why are you showing up in the summer?"

"I'm starting in the fall," I said, "but I got a job over the summer. It's no internship with a law firm, though. You're looking at Berkeley's newest janitorial staff member."

"Nice," Jim said with a laugh. "I hope you're not the poor sap who has to clean up Wurster Hall. My studio is a mess."

Julia missed, and I was up. I searched for a good shot. There was a long one, right along the bumper. I knew I couldn't make it, so I tried a closer, easier shot and missed, of course.

"No worries," I said. "Just cleaning out empty dorms."

Jim was really good. He got three balls in before missing on an awkward, reaching shot.

Tommy came back with a beer.

"So," I said as Mary leaned over to take her shot, "prelaw, huh? What kind of lawyer do you want to be?"

"It's better to ask what kind of lawyer I *wanted* to be. I'm probably going to drop out. The biggest thing I've learned about the law is that I hate it. Taking notes during back-to-back-to-back divorce settlements has made me swear off marriage too."

"John!" Tommy shouted. At once, the whole group turned. Someone was walking toward us, a huge grin on his face. Everyone smiled wide when they saw him.

"Tommy!" The guy waved as he made his way over. John was tall, wearing jeans and the coolest jacket I'd ever seen. It was denim, but embroidered intricately all over the back, shoulders, and arms. Bright splashes of color—flowers, spirals, and a peace symbol.

It was clear everyone in the place knew him. He slapped hands with the people at the bar and hugged one of the waitresses.

"What's up, man?" Jim asked, and gave him a hug, thumping him loudly on the back. John kissed Julia and Mary each on the cheek. When he got to Tommy, they did some kind of secret handshake.

"Everything is up, guys. It is a good day." He turned to the waitress and shouted, "Bring a round of—what are you guys drinking? Looks like three beers and a . . . What's that, Julia?"

"Jack."

"Three beers, a Jack, and I'll take a Scotch and water." He turned, noticing me for the first time. "You want a drink?"

"No thanks, I'm good."

"Suit yourself. I'm John, man. Good to meet you." He stretched out his hand and I took it.

"Mike," I said.

"Cool," he said, clapping me on the shoulder. "So who brought you?"

"Tommy," I said. "I'm his new roommate. Spent the day on a bus ride from Pasadena, and this is my first look at Berkeley nightlife."

"Well, we better make it a good one, then. You're not drinking anything, so we'll need a higher level of discourse."

Tommy laughed. "Higher than beer and pool?"

"Did you guys see the news today?" John asked as he sat down. I looked back at the pool table. It was my turn.

"No," Julia said, her brow crinkling. "I was in the studio all day. What's happening?"

"The bastard just said that he's mining Haiphong Harbor."

"The bastard?" I asked. I took a shot and missed the pocket by an inch.

"We don't say his name," Jim said with a laugh.

Mary laughed. "If you say Nixon three times into a mirror, he'll appear next to you."

"What's Haiphong Harbor?" I asked.

John took off his hat and twirled it in his hands. "Don't know your Vietnam geography?"

"I know Hanoi and I know Saigon," I said. "I know the Ho Chi Minh Trail and the Gulf of Tonkin."

"And what, may I ask, is your position on the war?"

It was Mary's turn, and she drilled the 5 ball into the side pocket. She held out her hand as she walked past me and I slapped it. "Good shot."

"Thank you." She lined up another one.

"My father," I said to John, "would tell you that the Vietnam War

7

is being fought to prevent the vile spread of Red Communism and strengthen our alliance with Australia. I worked with him nine to seven almost every day of the year, selling furniture, and he said that at least four times a week."

John smiled and put his hat back on. "And what do you say?"

"I think we're sending kids over there to die just so the president can say we're doing something about the 'communist threat,' with the false belief that, as a superpower, we have the right to invade any small country we want."

Mary knocked in the 7 ball and then stood up.

John nodded his agreement, and the waitress arrived. She set the drinks on the table beside John. John paid her and, if I was seeing correctly, gave her a huge tip.

"And today," John said, "the bastard has declared that he's going to be placing mines in Haiphong Harbor, the main port of North Vietnam. There are military ships in those waters, but it'll mostly affect imports, like food and medical care. Yeah, it will hurt the army, but it's sure as hell going to hurt the civilians more."

Jim nudged me. "He was over there."

"You're a vet?" I looked at John.

He stared back at me and then pulled up his sleeve. There was a tattoo of a skull wearing a green beret.

Mary walked over next to me. "You coming? I don't want to have to win this all by myself."

"She could too," John said.

I stood up. John looked older than everyone else. He looked weathered. "John, what do you do?" I asked.

John exhaled, a deep, slow breath. "It's a long story."

Mary pulled on my arm. "Come on."

He grinned. "It's called Endgame. Now go play pool."

IN THE ENDGAME SERIES, THE HUMAN PLAYERS
ARE TRYING TO SAVE THE EARTH FROM BEING
DESTROYED BY ALIENS.

AND IN THE I AM NUMBER FOUR SERIES,
DIFFERENT ALIENS ARE ALREADY HERE
ON EARTH, LIVING AMONG US.

CONTINUE READING FOR A PREVIEW OF THE FIRST
BOOK IN THE *NEW YORK TIMES* BESTSELLING
I AM NUMBER FOUR SERIES.

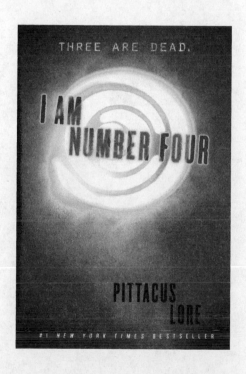

CHAPTER
ONE

IN THE BEGINNING THERE WERE NINE OF US.
We left when we were young, almost too young to remember.
Almost.

I am told the ground shook, that the skies were full of
light and explosions. We were in that two-week period of
the year when both moons hang on opposite sides of the
horizon. It was a time of celebration, and the explosions
were at first mistaken for fireworks. They were not. It was
warm, a soft wind blew in from off the water. I am always
told the weather: it was warm. There was a soft wind. I've
never understood why that matters.

What I remember most vividly is the way my grand-
mother looked that day. She was frantic, and sad. There
were tears in her eyes. My grandfather stood just over her
shoulder. I remember the way his glasses gathered the
light from the sky. There were hugs. There were words
said by each of them. I don't remember what they were.
Nothing haunts me more.

It took a year to get here. I was five when we arrived. We were to assimilate ourselves into the culture before returning to Lorien when it could again sustain life. The nine of us had to scatter, and go our own ways. For how long, nobody knew. We still don't. None of them know where I am, and I don't know where they are, or what they look like now. That is how we protect ourselves because of the charm that was placed upon us when we left, a charm guaranteeing that we can only be killed in the order of our numbers, so long as we stay apart. If we come together, then the charm is broken.

When one of us is found and killed, a circular scar wraps around the right ankle of those still alive. And residing on our left ankle, formed when the Loric charm was first cast, is a small scar identical to the amulet each of us wears. The circular scars are another part of the charm. A warning system so that we know where we stand with each other, and so that we know when they'll be coming for us next. The first scar came when I was nine years old. It woke me from my sleep, burning itself into my flesh. We were living in Arizona, in a small border town near Mexico. I woke screaming in the middle of the night, in agony, terrified as the scar seared itself into my flesh. It was the first sign that the Mogadorians had finally found us on Earth, and the first sign that we were in danger. Until the scar showed up, I had almost convinced myself that my memories were wrong, that what Henri told me was wrong. I wanted to be a normal kid living a normal life, but I knew then, beyond any doubt or discussion, that I wasn't. We moved to Minnesota the next day.

The second scar came when I was twelve. I was in school, in Colorado, participating in a spelling bee. As soon as the pain started I knew what was happening, what had happened to Number Two. The pain was excruciating, but bearable this time. I would have stayed on the stage, but the heat lit my sock on fire. The teacher who was conducting the bee sprayed me with a fire extinguisher and rushed me to the hospital. The doctor in the ER found the first scar and called the police. When Henri showed, they threatened to arrest him for child abuse. But because he hadn't been anywhere near me when the second scar came, they had to let him go. We got in the car and drove away, this time to Maine. We left everything we had except for the Loric Chest that Henri brought along on every move. All twenty-one of them to date.

The third scar appeared an hour ago. I was sitting on a pontoon boat. The boat belonged to the parents of the most popular kid at my school, and unbeknownst to them, he was having a party on it. I had never been invited to any of the parties at my school before. I had always, because I knew we might leave at any minute, kept to myself. But it had been quiet for two years. Henri hadn't seen anything in the news that might lead the Mogadorians to one of us, or might alert us to them. So I made a couple friends. And one of them introduced me to the kid who was having the party. Everyone met at a dock. There were three coolers, some music, girls I had admired from afar but never spoken to, even though I wanted to. We pulled out from the dock and went half a mile into the Gulf of Mexico. I was sitting on the edge of the pontoon with my feet in the water, talking to a cute, dark-haired, blue-eyed girl named Tara, when I felt it coming. The water around my leg started boiling, and my lower leg started glowing where the scar was imbedding itself. The third of the Lorien symbols, the third warning. Tara started screaming and people started crowding around me. I knew there was no way to explain it. And I knew we would have to leave immediately.

The stakes were higher now. They had found Number Three, wherever he or she was, and Number Three was dead. So I calmed Tara down and kissed her on the cheek and told her it was nice to meet her and that I hoped she had a long beautiful life. I dove off the side of the boat and started swimming, underwater the entire time, except for one breath about halfway there, as fast as I could until I reached the shore. I ran along the side of the highway, just inside of the tree line, moving at speeds as fast as any of the cars. When I got home, Henri was at the bank of scanners and monitors that he used to research news around the world, and police activity in our area. He knew without me saying a word, though he did lift my soaking pants to see the scars.

In the beginning we were a group of nine.

Three are gone, dead.

There are six of us left.

They are hunting us, and they won't stop until they've killed us all.

I am Number Four.

I know that I am next.

CHAPTER
TWO

I STAND IN THE MIDDLE OF THE DRIVE AND STARE up at the house. It is light pink, almost like cake frosting, sitting ten feet above the ground on wooden stilts. A palm tree sways in the front. In the back of the house a pier extends twenty yards into the Gulf of Mexico. If the house were a mile to the south, the pier would be in the Atlantic Ocean.

Henri walks out of the house carrying the last of the boxes, some of which were never unpacked from our last move. He locks the door, then leaves the keys in the mail slot beside it. It is two o'clock in the morning. He is wearing khaki shorts and a black polo. He is very tan, with an unshaven face that seems downcast. He is also sad to be leaving. He tosses the final boxes into the back of the truck with the rest of our things.

"That's it," he says.

I nod. We stand and stare up at the house and listen to the wind come through the palm fronds. I am holding a bag of celery in my hand.

"I'll miss this place," I say. "Even more than the others."

"Me too."

"Time for the burn?"

"Yes. You want to do it, or you want me to?"

"I'll do it."

Henri pulls out his wallet and drops it on the ground. I pull out mine and do the same. He walks to our truck and comes back with passports, birth certificates, social security cards, checkbooks, credit cards and bank cards, and drops them on the ground. All of the documents and materials related to our identities here, all of them forged and manufactured. I grab from the truck a small gas can we keep for emergencies. I pour the gas over the small pile. My current name is Daniel Jones. My story is that I grew up in California and moved here because of my dad's job as a computer programmer. Daniel Jones is about to disappear. I light a match and drop it, and the pile ignites. Another one of my lives, gone. As we always do, Henri and I stand and watch the fire. *Bye, Daniel,* I think, *it was nice knowing you.* When the fire burns down, Henri looks over at me.

"We gotta go."

"I know."

"These islands were never safe. They're too hard to leave quickly, too hard to escape from. It was foolish of us to come here."

I nod. He is right, and I know it. But I'm still reluctant to leave. We came here because I wanted to, and for the first time, Henri let me choose where we were going. We've been here nine months, and it's the longest we have stayed in any one place since leaving Lorien. I'll miss the sun and the warmth. I'll miss the gecko that watched from the wall each morning as I ate breakfast. Though there are literally millions of geckos in south Florida, I swear this one follows me to school and seems to be everywhere I am. I'll miss the thunderstorms that seem to come from out of nowhere, the way everything is still and quiet in the early-morning hours before the terns arrive. I'll miss the dolphins that sometimes feed when the sun sets. I'll even miss the smell of sulfur from the rotting seaweed at the base of the shore, the way that it fills the house and penetrates our dreams while we sleep.

"Get rid of the celery and I'll wait in the truck," Henri says. "Then it's time."

I enter a thicket of trees off to the right of the truck. There are three Key deer already waiting. I dump the bag of celery out at their feet and crouch down and pet each of them in turn. They allow me to, having long gotten over their skittishness. One of them raises his head and looks at me. Dark, blank eyes staring back. It almost feels as though he passes something to me. A shudder runs up my spine. He drops his head and continues eating.

"Good luck, little friends," I say, and walk to the truck and climb into the passenger seat.

We watch the house grow smaller in the side mirrors

until Henri pulls onto the main road and the house disappears. It's a Saturday. I wonder what's happening at the party without me. What they're saying about the way that I left and what they'll say on Monday when I'm not at school. I wish I could have said good-bye. I'll never see anyone I knew here ever again. I'll never speak to any of them. And they'll never know what I am or why I left. After a few months, or maybe a few weeks, none of them will probably ever think of me again.

Before we get on the highway, Henri pulls over to gas up the truck. As he works the pump, I start looking through an atlas he keeps on the middle of the seat. We've had the atlas since we arrived on this planet. It has lines drawn to and from every place we've ever lived. At this point, there are lines crisscrossing all of the United States. We know we should get rid of it, but it's really the only piece of our life together that we have. Normal people have photos and videos and journals; we have the atlas. Picking it up and looking through it, I can see Henri has drawn a new line from Florida to Ohio. When I think of Ohio, I think of cows and corn and nice people. I know the license plate says THE HEART OF IT ALL. What "All" is, I don't know, but I guess I'll find out.

Henri gets back into the truck. He has bought a couple of sodas and a bag of chips. He pulls away and starts heading toward U.S. 1, which will take us north. He reaches for the atlas.

"Do you think there are people in Ohio?" I joke.

He chuckles. "I would imagine there are a few. And we might even get lucky and find cars and TV there, too."

I nod. Maybe it won't be as bad as I think.

"What do you think of the name 'John Smith'?" I ask.

"Is that what you've settled on?"

"I think so," I say. I've never been a John before, or a Smith.

"It doesn't get any more common than that. I would say it's a pleasure to meet you, Mr. Smith."

I smile. "Yeah, I think I like 'John Smith.'"

"I'll create your forms when we stop."

A mile later we are off the island and cruising across the bridge. The waters pass below us. They are calm and the moonlight is shimmering on the small waves, creating dapples of white in the crests. On the right is the ocean, on the left is the gulf; it is, in essence, the same water, but with two different names. I have the urge to cry, but I don't. It's not that I'm necessarily sad to leave Florida, but I'm tired of running. I'm tired of dreaming up a new name every six months. Tired of new houses, new schools. I wonder if it'll ever be possible for us to stop.